BORN OF
BOMBS
AND
BULLETS

BORN OF
BOMBS
AND
BULLETS

An Aaron Thornton Thriller

DAVID A. DUMMER

BLADEN CRISFIELD MEDIA

Published by Bladen Crisfield Media LLC
20 S. Charles St. Ste. 403 #1733
Baltimore, MD 21201
www.bladencrisfield.com

To my parents—
the best role models a son could have.

AUTHOR'S NOTE

Queen Elizabeth II died before I finished the novel. Since The Troubles occurred during her reign, I retained all references to her.

GLOSSARY

Loyalists Unionists	Proponents of Crown Rule in Northern Ireland; Generally Protestant
Republicans Nationalists	Proponents of a united and independent Ireland; Generally Catholic
HET	Historical Enquiries Team
IRA	Irish Republican Army; A Republican paramilitary group in Northern Ireland
PSNI	Police Service of Northern Ireland (current)
QUB	Queen's University Belfast
RUC	Royal Ulster Constabulary (preceded the PSNI)
Tout / Grass	Informant, tipster, traitor
UVF	Ulster Volunteer Force; A Loyalist paramilitary group in Northern Ireland
WC / jacks	"Water closet," toilet

USP HAZELTON

THE ALARM AT UNITED STATES PENITENTIARY, Hazelton, interrupted Dr. Aaron Thornton mid-sentence. The eight inmates attending anger management therapy immediately assumed a prone position on the floor with their fingers interlaced behind their heads, as required during emergencies. Thornton retreated behind a gray metal desk, and the only guard in the room readied his baton in case anyone tried to take advantage of the situation. America's most dangerous federal prison was in lockdown.

There were three long blasts of the electric siren, followed by a pause, and then three more bursts. The sound made the walls and floor vibrate. A strobe flashed red above the only door and bathed the dim cinderblock room in an eerie glow. Thornton rubbed his arms as a cold draft pierced the barred second-story window clouded with dirt and streaked with bird shit. He eyed the riflemen standing on a catwalk in the distance, atop the fortified, concrete watchtower.

The alarm signaled immediate danger somewhere in the prison—home to 1,300 violent inmates and nicknamed "Misery Mountain." It would continue blaring until every prisoner was back in his cell.

1

It was never completely safe though. The local chapter of the Federation of Government Employees had long complained about an inadequate number of correctional officers, or COs, at the complex, which had a murder rate far higher than most federal prisons. The staffing shortage was so bad, officials relied on forced overtime and a policy of "augmentation," which drafted the prison's teachers, healthcare staff, plumbers, and cooks to serve double duty and compensate for the lack of guards. But jobs were scarce in the surrounding area of Bruceton Mills, West Virginia, and the area's coal mines were not much safer.

John Grace, the guard in the room, was hired by Thornton two months earlier to administer standardized tests. The young, single dad needed extra money to pay for his twin boys' daycare, so Thornton approved his request to work extra shifts as an augmentee guard.

Thornton, the prison's last remaining psychologist, listened impatiently to the calm female voice with a gravelly Appalachian accent as it crackled over the guard's radio. She methodically directed the orderly return of inmates to their cell blocks. The process took time—inmates outnumbered guards nine to one, and it was unwise to have too many people in the corridors and hallways at once.

The smell of Folgers wafted in from a break room down the hall and mixed with the scent of body odor. The psychologist wished he had stopped for coffee.

"Officer Grace, Control."

The guard on the other side of the room raised his radio and pressed the side button. "Control, Officer Grace."

"Officer Grace, you are clear to return to Section 4."

Thornton was pleasantly surprised to hear the wait would end quickly. Lockdowns tended to agitate inmates, who welcomed any interruption to the monotony of prison life. The eight men in therapy that morning were unapologetic killers serving life sentences. They had nothing to lose and would happily exploit a disturbance if given the chance.

"Control, Officer Grace. Proceeding to Section 4 with eight inmates." The guard holstered his radio, extended a set of keys from his belt, and unlocked the door. He swung it inward and instructed the prisoners to line up in the hallway.

Thornton called to the group. "We'll try again next week. In the meantime, make a mental list of those trigger words and actions I talked about."

Each of the prisoners acknowledged Thornton's reminder. The psychologist had made several improvements to daily life at the prison and was well-liked.

The first six inmates exited the meeting room, but the last two—a white supremacist and a rival gang leader—paused several feet from the door. One of them muttered something to the other, and a scuffle ensued. Officer Grace tried to intervene but was knocked to the floor. A metal chair in his path slid across the room, its legs screeching uncomfortably on the bare tile. Fearing a brawl, the guard winced but managed to kick the self-locking door shut. That left the first six inmates confined in a hallway monitored by CCTV. Next, he pressed the emergency button on his radio to summon backup. Officer Grace tried to rise but could not—the fall aggravated an old knee injury.

The scuffle escalated into an all-out fight. The white supremacist, who had a significant weight advantage, held his opponent in a chokehold and swore to kill him. The rival gang leader made desperate rasping sounds as he punched his assailant's rib cage and kidneys. The red strobe and siren continued their rhythmic warnings. In the hallway outside, the six isolated inmates strained to watch the fight through a small window and banged heavily on the door, shouting encouragement.

"Doc, use this." Officer Grace forcefully slid his baton across the floor.

Thornton reluctantly picked up the metal truncheon and looked across the desk at the inmates ten feet away. The white supremacist maintained a firm grip on his red-faced nemesis, who desperately pummeled his torso with no effect.

"Doc, he's killing him! *Knock him out!*"

Thornton froze. As a child, he left a friend severely disabled after striking him on the head accidentally with a golf club. Even under the current circumstances, he could not bring himself to crack a man's skull *intentionally*.

"Doc, do *something!*"

Another thirty seconds passed. Then the rival gang leader slumped, his eyes bulging grotesquely. His head thumped loudly on the floor as the Emergency Response Team, or ERT, answered Officer Grace's distress call and began to clear the hallway for entry into the room.

The white supremacist—coursing with adrenaline and the rage of a caged animal—turned to the injured guard.

"Doc! *Please! Stop him!*"

The white supremacist picked up the nearby metal chair and raised it over his head. Officer Grace used one arm to maneuver awkwardly on the ground and the other to shield his head. It was no use. The inmate struck again and again until the officer was dead.

Thornton watched panic-stricken from behind the desk.

The ERT burst through the door and tackled the white supremacist just as he turned toward the psychologist.

ALL SAINTS EPISCOPAL CHURCH

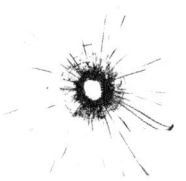

SEVEN DAYS LATER, THORNTON AND HIS WIFE, Claire, began the forty-minute drive to All Saints Episcopal Church for Officer Grace's funeral. The ceremony had been delayed to accommodate the required autopsy, and Thornton gratefully took the week off from work. He initially planned to stay away much longer, but the warden was pressuring his only psychologist to return quickly to the office.

Thornton now thought that might be a good idea. Claire had a busy law practice downtown, and nothing at home could distract him long enough to keep memories of the murder at bay. He suspected the guilt and self-doubt would *never* leave him. The psychologist had nearly decided to return early to work when fate intervened.

Two days before the funeral, Claire received a surprise invitation to become a visiting professor at Queen's University in Belfast, Northern Ireland. It was a prestigious post and a career-making opportunity for Claire, whose interest in social justice was ideally suited to a city scarred by decades of political and sectarian violence. Thornton, though, was reluctant to uproot their lives and move overseas. He also feared his departure would be viewed as running away, or worse—abandonment of his colleagues and patients. Still, it was a once-in-a-lifetime offer that deserved serious consideration.

On their way to the funeral, Thornton and his wife amicably debated the pros and cons of a new life in Belfast. They had not yet reached a decision when they pulled into the church parking lot. Inside, the couple found space in a center pew and looked around the sanctuary. Bouquets of lilies lined the altar and windowsills, and smoke from an incense candle drifted toward the ceiling. It seemed as if the entire town, if not all of Preston County, turned out to honor the slain single father.

The 363rd Military Police Company, an Army Reserve unit in Grafton to which John Grace once belonged, provided an honor guard. The state police arranged for the bagpiper and drummer who accompanied the mourners. The mayor and prison warden offered tributes. But Grace's best man, Shawn Urbas, elicited the most tears when he delivered the eulogy and talked about the slain father's devotion to his three-year-old twins.

When the piper finally led John Grace's coffin down the center aisle and out the back of the church, all eyes fixed on the two bewildered little boys dressed in matching suits. They walked with their "Uncle" Shawn behind their dad for the last time. The twins' mother struggled with heroin and was absent here, as she was for most of their lives. The psychologist's lower lip trembled as he wondered what would become of them.

Thornton clumsily dried his eyes when it was time to exit the pew. He and Claire headed outside and stood alone by a small fountain while the rest of the crowd exited the building. Words failed him, so he stared at the ground and kicked at some pebbles while Claire squeezed his hand. After several minutes, the sound of car doors closing signaled the drive to the cemetery was about to begin. The couple walked solemnly to their car. Thornton gripped the steering wheel and stared straight ahead. "I think we should go to Belfast."

BELFAST

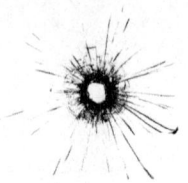

THORNTON AND CLAIRE ARRIVED IN NORTHERN IRELAND two months after John Grace's funeral.

Claire was born and raised in Belfast but left to attend Georgetown University in Washington, DC. She met her future husband there during sophomore year when both resided in Copley Hall. Copley was the "service dorm," and the young couple did volunteer projects together every Saturday. Their shared desire to help others bonded them and shaped their eventual career choices.

One week after graduation, the two idealists married in Dahlgren Chapel, just a stone's throw from the residence hall where they first met. It was an unlikely outcome for a relationship born on a blind date—but classmates correctly assessed the "hottest male athlete" and "woman most likely to succeed" were a great match. Nonetheless, their families and even their friends thought they were moving too quickly, but Claire and Aaron, among other things, shared a stubborn streak.

The couple said their vows and, true to their modern views, kept their respective surnames. They plunged almost immediately into their graduate studies—she at Georgetown Law and he in the clinical psychology program at Johns Hopkins. Three years later, with graduate degrees in hand, they quickly found work. Thornton became a healer for the Bureau of Prisons. Claire started as a public defender and later advocated for immigrants seeking asylum in the United States.

Now they stood an ocean away in the kitchen of a sparsely furnished, one-bedroom flat along a string of stylish row houses on College Green, within walking distance of Claire's new office at QUB. "Welcome to Belfast, Dr. Thornton," she cooed with the Irish accent he found so endearing. He answered her with a long kiss and embrace. It was the first day in their new home, after spending two weeks at the Ibis hotel around the corner.

"Are you sure you're okay with this?" she asked. "It's a far cry from the mountains of West Virginia and the job you loved."

"If it makes you happy, I'm all in," he reassured her. "And honestly, the change is probably good for me after all that happened."

"And you finally get to see where I grew up," Claire added. Thornton was a history buff, and when he first met Claire, he often asked about "The Troubles," a politically and socially violent period in Belfast from the 1960s through the 1990s that killed more than 3,500 people and generated frequent international headlines. She always avoided the topic though, and after a while he abandoned his inquiries for fear of upsetting her.

Thornton's interest in Belfast's history was fueled in part by the discovery, during a middle school genealogy project, that his ancestry included ancient ties to Northern Ireland. The revelation was a surprise to his relatives too, who always believed they descended from exclusively Scottish immigrants. Sadly, no one bothered to record their origins for posterity, and Thornton's efforts to trace the family tree fizzled for lack of information. When Thornton was older, though, films about The Troubles, like *Patriot Games* and *'71*, stoked his imagination. He sometimes wondered how life would have been different if he were born in Northern Ireland.

Now he was free to explore Belfast on his own for several days until he officially opened his new practice. Claire's family connections helped him secure an office suite in the city center and expedited approval of his license to practice psychology. In exchange for the preferential treatment, Thornton agreed to work for a reduced fee with criminal offenders who were entering or exiting the judicial system and required monitoring. The arrangement appealed to him instantly as a perfect match for his skill and experience.

The couple stood in their new kitchen, embracing and relishing the excitement that accompanies the start of a new adventure.

HM PRISON MAGHABERRY

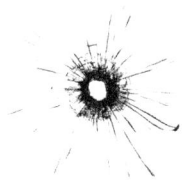

ABOUT A 30-MINUTE DRIVE SOUTHWEST OF Aaron and Claire's new flat, Liam O'Malley sat in his cell on the upper landing of Roe Block in Her Majesty's Prison Maghaberry. As Northern Ireland's only high-security prison, Maghaberry was home to The Troubles' worst offenders. In 2015, a government report labelled it the UK's most dangerous penitentiary, with conditions one inspector dubbed "draconian."

O'Malley was eager to quit the place. Freedom was weeks away, and this time he was determined to keep it. The government released him once before, in 2000, when paramilitaries on both sides of the conflict received amnesty as part of the Good Friday peace agreement that officially ended The Troubles. O'Malley was soon back in prison, though, after a raid by the security services uncovered weapons and explosive materials in the safe house where he sometimes stayed.

O'Malley did not know about the contraband in the home, but the Public Prosecution Service was unmoved—the British saw him, once and forever, as an IRA terrorist. He wondered if the intelligence service watched him all along and planted the evidence while he was at the pub. The prosecutor persuasively argued for a lengthy second prison sentence by characterizing

11

O'Malley as "one of the most prolific and indiscriminate murderers ever to emerge from the Provisional IRA."

O'Malley was proud of his skill as a killer and bomb maker, although he preferred "assassin" to "murderer." But the prosecutor's characterization of O'Malley's work as "indiscriminate" offended him. His killings were hardly indiscriminate.

It was true—O'Malley killed more British soldiers, policemen, politicians, and government workers than any other Provo as part of the IRA's campaign to drive the Brits from Northern Ireland. But the Protestant British government had brutalized O'Malley's fellow Catholics and robbed them of dignity for centuries.

O'Malley viewed the people he assassinated—representatives of the Crown—as legitimate targets in defense of his oppressed Irish brethren. There was just one exception, and it had been a horrible mistake. Even now, after so many years, the guilt associated with that incident tore at his conscience.

O'Malley exited his cell and stood on the landing to consult with Patrick Linden—a fellow Provo who lived in the next cell. Roe House held only Republicans, or "dissidents" as the British screws called them. Every faction of the IRA was represented here and, like most families, they squabbled. Only four prisoners could congregate at one time. Otherwise, the Republicans were free to roam the cell block's two landings. Loyalist paramilitaries—supporters of Crown rule in Northern Ireland—lived separately in Bush House. Prison authorities took great care to ensure the two opposing forces never came in contact.

Linden was the head of the Roe House Council, comprised of representatives from each faction of the IRA housed in the unit. The Council unofficially but convincingly governed interactions among the Republican prisoners, arbitrated disputes, and enforced its own rules as needed. The screws did not interfere with the Council's influence and considerable power, mostly because they kept order in the prison—and partly out of fear. The Council could exert its will, through various IRA splinter groups, far beyond the prison walls.

On the Council's orders, one Maghaberry guard was shot dead outside a local pub last month. A car bomb severely injured another screw at her residence a few years earlier. Republican prisoners accused both of unfair treatment.

Visitors to Roe House served as couriers between the Council and their comrades outside the prison and kept both parties fully informed about developments on either side of the wall. Intelligence reports from the street went directly to Linden. Consequently, Linden knew some Republicans outside the prison were advocating the resumption of sustained violence despite the long-standing peace agreement.

Linden and O'Malley, as legendary figures from the past, were no strangers to violence. They met as young street fighters in the gritty Clonard section of Catholic West Belfast. The British Army occupied Belfast in 1969 and—joined by Loyalist paramilitary gangs—began a decades-long campaign to harass the Catholic community and drive them from their homes. Linden and O'Malley felt it their duty to defend the neighborhood, and the Provisional IRA offered the best means to do it. As their skill and reputation as combatants grew, O'Malley and Linden became cult-like figures.

The pair remained comrades-in-arms until the Good Friday peace agreement of 1998, and over that 30-year period known as The Troubles, they raised hell against the Brits until informers—still unknown to either man—gave them up a few years apart.

They bonded in a way only men who went through combat together understand.

"Look here, Uilliam," Linden called to O'Malley, using the full Irish version of his name. It was a subtle form of protest against the prison overseers, who tried to eradicate Irish culture in Roe House. "Yer a fuckin' cunt to leave me in this shite hole," he said with a laugh.

"I don't like it either, mate. I need someone to watch me back." O'Malley knew his imminent release was the talk of Belfast, a city in which one's past deeds on either side of The Troubles, no matter how old, could still invite retribution without warning.

O'Malley's notoriety would make it impossible to find steady employment. The more militant Catholics—ones who felt the peace agreement was a mistake—would quickly welcome him as a hero and look after him. But they would also pressure him to resume violent resistance and join the New IRA, a modern offshoot of the parent organization that still viewed armed struggle as the only way to reunite the north and south of Ireland.

O'Malley believed fervently in unity, but doubted the Brits would ever leave Northern Ireland except under extreme pressure. Yet thirty years of armed resistance achieved very little, he thought—and O'Malley knew firsthand they gave it their best shot. Many comrades sacrificed their lives for the cause. But fifty years after The Troubles began, the IRA still had not met its objective. *What more could be done?*

O'Malley doubted another half-century of violence would make a difference. In any event, he was determined to stay out of prison this time, and that meant avoiding trouble. So he regarded his old neighborhood warily, unsure how to navigate a web of shifting strategies, allegiances, and alliances.

"Be careful out there, mate. It's not the same now," Linden warned. "Ya don't know who ya can trust anymore."

O'Malley took his best friend's advice seriously. Linden, as head of the Roe House Council, was well informed about life on the outside and privy to many closely guarded secrets—including the one that haunted Liam.

"Ya don't know who ya can trust anymore," Liam repeated to himself.

1972

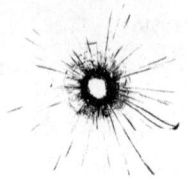

Liam O'Malley turned eighteen in January 1972. His younger sister, Deidre, organized a surprise birthday party for him, and for several hours that Friday night, Liam, his family, and friends forgot all their worries.

Deidre idolized her dashing big brother, whose electric blue eyes and disarming smile were a frequent topic of conversation among Deidre's boy-crazy classmates. Although five years apart in age, Liam and Deidre were as close as two siblings could be. In their father's absence, Liam read her bedtime stories and chased the monsters from under her bed. He walked her to school and fixed her dinner on the many nights when their mother was out. And if a boy showed too much interest in Deidre, or teased her about her ginger hair and freckles, Liam was quick to sort him out.

Each week, for as long as Deidre could remember, Liam treated her to a tube of her favorite sweets—strawberry-banana Toffos. Sometimes he concealed it under her pillow, or in the pocket of a dress, or in one of her mittens. Once he hid it in an empty shampoo bottle. It became a game for them.

As Liam's eighteenth birthday approached, Deidre wanted to do something special for her big brother. She was giddy to see Liam *genuinely surprised by the party and pleased by the large crowd that attended it. He told her it was the most fun he ever had.*

Just five months later, Deidre lay unconscious on Oranmore Street, felled by a British soldier's rubber bullet. She ignored the neighbors' warnings to stay indoors while the men and boys of the Clonard district hurled bricks and glass bottles at British soldiers across the barricade at the junction with Springfield Street. The barricade was manned around the clock in shifts to protect the neighborhood from British troops and Loyalist paramilitaries, who were keen to drive Catholics from their homes. Local residents were proud the barricade had not been breached in the six weeks since a couple of stolen, burned-out lorries were set across the road and fortified with mounds of debris.

On that afternoon in May 1972, the Brits seemed intent on breaking through the barricade and reasserting their authority over the district. The tension on both sides heightened, and Deidre heard murmurs of a looming confrontation. She knew Liam would head straight for ground zero. She went in search of him, partly to keep a watchful eye but mostly because she loved to watch her handsome, strong, courageous big brother stand up to the Brits and fight for the neighborhood—for her. Deidre found him at the barricade and crept closer, unseen by Liam, until she was standing just behind him when he hurled a petrol bomb toward the Army position. A whiff of gasoline stung her nostrils, and she felt her brother's jacket brush against her cheek when he raised his arm to launch the bottle. The smell of spent matches and burning wood from a nearby bonfire lingered in the air alongside the crude taunts of boys and men.

As usual, Liam hit his target. The car used as cover by two British soldiers was bathed in a blue-orange flame that washed over the top and down the sides of the vehicle. Their comrades in a nearby armored vehicle answered with a volley of rubber bullets, and one of the project-

iles—considerably larger than a traditional bullet—struck Deidre on the temple.

At the same time, a whistle pierced the air from the Loyalist side, and a column of armored vehicles lurched forward from a side street. Leading the group was a Muir Hill A5000 bulldozer, nicknamed "Scooby Doo" by British soldiers. It took little effort for the dozer to breach the barricade and allow the armored personnel carriers to rumble through. Following closely on foot were British marksmen, who shot out the streetlights so IRA snipers would have a harder time finding their targets.

Residents scattered into the neighborhood's narrow alleyways and onto the rooftops to escape the immediate onslaught and resume their defense of the district from more protected positions. Soon, brightly colored paint bombs descended on the Army vehicles to make them better targets for projectiles. The trucks' armored plating protected the soldiers while inside, but the Brits had to exit the vehicles to search suspected IRA safe houses for Provos and weapons. Knowing the position of the painted vehicles made it easier for IRA snipers to track the soldiers going in and out.

Deidre lay motionless in the street as a British Saracen—a tank-like armored personnel carrier—rolled past the barricade on its six over-sized wheels. At the sound of the whistle, a seasoned member of the IRA wearing a balaclava labored his way through the fleeing crowd toward Liam. Deidre's brother was caught in a flood of people and carried a hundred feet from where she fell. He tried in vain to go back, against the current, and reach his little sister. He screamed her name as if to wake her.

The lead Saracen continued forward, undeterred by the unconscious girl in its path. The smell of petrol, exhaust, smoke, and sulfur mixed with the rumble of heavy wheels on pavement, the crunch of broken glass, and the loud banging of pots and bin lids—used by Catholic women as a form of protest and to warn of advancing British troops. The anxious shouts of men on both sides of the conflict and the crackle of flames in the street added to the chaos. A flurry of rocks, bricks, and glass bottles now descended from the rooftops as the defenders of Clonard regrouped and tried to slow the Army's advance. If they were lucky, they would maim a soldier or two.

Liam finally broke from the torrent of people and stood to the side of the road, his back pressed against the front wall of a butcher shop. He looked toward the column of Saracens through the holes cut in the cloth bag he wore on his head. The disguise kept British intelligence from photographing and identifying him as a protester. Suddenly his whole body went numb, and he could not move or make a sound. Events shifted into slow motion.

The Saracen rolled closer and closer to his sister, foot by foot, until the right front wheel pinned her head to the pavement and crushed her skull. Her eyes and brain ejected onto the street amid shattered pieces of bone as the driver maintained course and speed. Horrified witnesses later described hearing a loud pop at the moment of impact, followed by screams from onlookers. They all knew the thirteen-year-old redhead by name.

The seasoned IRA man finally reached Liam. It was too dangerous to remain outdoors. He pulled Liam toward the junction with Dunmore Street, where a warren of houses and back alleys would allow them to escape arrest and likely torture. Liam—still screaming Deidre's name—resisted at first, but soon realized the soldiers were getting too close. While the Provo led him away from the British advance, Liam kept turning his head to look toward Deidre. As the IRA man dragged him around the corner toward safety, Liam caught one last glimpse of his sister's lifeless body and the tube of strawberry-banana Toffos lying beside it.

CLONARD MONASTERY

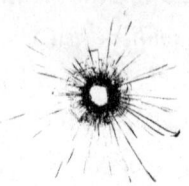

The IRA man pulled O'Malley through the front door of a safe house, stashed his balaclava under a floorboard in the hallway, and led O'Malley quickly to the kitchen. There he grabbed some vinegar, baking soda, a rag, and a bottle of water before leading O'Malley into an alleyway behind the building. He pulled the bag from O'Malley's head and tossed it over a wall. The man extended his hand. "I'm Patrick Linden. That's a fine throwin' arm ya have."

O'Malley introduced himself and looked around anxiously for British soldiers, aware that he smelled of petrol. Still sensing danger, his brain allowed him to focus only on survival, and Linden was the embodiment of it. The IRA man hastily dumped the water, poured the baking soda and vinegar into the empty bottle, and hustled O'Malley away from the safe house. He doused the rag with the mixture and handed it to O'Malley. "Rub that everywhere you smell petrol," he instructed.

O'Malley did as he was told while the two men made their way to another row of flats at the far end of the alley. Linden led his new protege through the rear door of a second safe house, where they discarded the cleaning supplies, continued out the front door, and found themselves facing Bantry Street. The woman of the house placed the cleaning supplies in the cupboard and said nothing as the pair passed through. The clanging pots and bin lids outside signaled the Brits were still advancing behind them, and O'Malley instinctively followed Linden away from the threat.

The two dashed up Bantry Street and turned right onto Kashmir Road, in the heart of Republican territory. The IRA policed this neighborhood, and O'Malley breathed easier as they distanced themselves farther from the Brits. Back on Oranmore Street, the soldiers went house to house looking for any sign of dissidents.

At the junction with Clonard Gardens, Linden and O'Malley hastened right again and crossed the road. There, less than a block away, loomed Clonard Monastery.

Fr. Matthew Clark peered discreetly through a window on the second floor of the monastery, alerted by the banging pots and bin lids. As soon as the alarm went up, he and the other occupants of the massive complex sealed the entrances. They barricaded inner offices and passageways as well, and then dispersed to their designated posts.

Fr. Clark watched intently as the newcomer followed Linden to a side entrance by Waterville Street. He descended from his post when Linden made the prearranged knock and then called out to him in Gaelic. Linden answered in code to reassure the priest he was not under any duress. Fr. Clark released the weighty door and allowed Linden and his companion to enter the vestibule.

O'Malley scanned the unfamiliar surroundings as the trio passed the altar and stopped at another locked door. Fr. Clark pulled a heavy metal key from his pocket, swung the thick wooden door open, and signaled for Linden and O'Malley to descend the stairwell on the other side.

O'Malley followed Linden into the cellar. The air was cold and damp against his face, and he felt his feet slip slightly on the moist stone steps. He gripped the handrail tightly, and the splintered wood dug at the fleshy base of his fingers. O'Malley's sense of safety increased as he descended the stairs with his newfound protector. He did not yet question *why he had never seen Linden in the neighborhood or wonder about the IRA man's sudden interest in him. Nor did O'Malley realize that behind him, Fr. Clark still held a revolver beneath his cassock. O'Malley was simply grateful for a safe place to hide—with fellow Catholics—until the Brits moved on.*

The grief and rage over Deidre's murder would consume O'Malley once the adrenaline subsided and the protective part of his brain relinquished control. It would take far longer to realize what Linden was up to—and to discover Clonard Monastery was the IRA's headquarters in Belfast.

BALLYCASTLE BEACH

AS AARON AND CLAIRE CELEBRATED THEIR ARRIVAL in Northern Ireland, Tommy Magee sat on Ballycastle Beach north of Belfast and stared at the lighthouse across the sound. The surf crashed just a few feet ahead of him. Here, between the pile of black rocks and the wooden pedestrian bridge, he was always happy as a little boy—playing for hours in the sand and, under the watchful eyes of his parents, splashing in the sea. Twenty-five years ago, they spent their final weekend as a family at this very spot. It was the last time Tommy felt happy.

Tommy watched the ocean churn. The grief, the loneliness, the helplessness, and especially the anger washed over him. Memories of the foster homes, the abuse, the schoolyard fights, and that horrible afternoon at Sheehan's furniture store swirled in his mind.

The moon would be full tonight, and Tommy knew the riptides were strong. He twirled the bottle of sleeping pills in his coat pocket. The doctor said they would get him through the night. Tommy just hoped they were powerful enough to kill him. He planned to swallow the entire lot and, once he felt drowsy, wade into the water until sleep and the tide took him.

He doubted anyone would notice his absence, let alone report him missing.

Tommy sat with his knees bent and his arms wrapped around his shins. He rocked back and forth as tears splashed down his face. He could not take it any longer. Ever since that horrible afternoon at Sheehan's store, his life had been a pitiful mess. He tried to move on—he really did—but a cloud of misfortune seemed tethered to him.

The nightmares robbed Tommy of all but a few hours of sleep each night and forced him to relive the worst day of his life over and over. Employers, when he was lucky to find work, did not tolerate his angry outbursts for long, and his coworkers were only slightly more understanding when he arrived at the job drunk. Women did not stick with him either, and a shared interest in getting drunk or high seemed to be the only thing that bonded him to his mates.

So there he sat, a sleepless, jobless, nearly friendless, homeless orphan with no future, as he summed it up. He knew other lads who offed themselves too. *The lucky ones. The smart ones.*

Tommy's life was supposed to be different. His parents doted on their only child. His father was a decorated officer with Her Majesty's Customs in Belfast and had a promising career. His mother was a British Army nurse. Twenty-five years ago, they bought their first home and were at Sheehan's store to pay the final installment on some new furniture while eight-year-old Tommy waited in the car. Then—in a flash—Tommy's world was stolen.

The explosion that killed Tommy's parents struck without the customary warning that accompanied most IRA bombings. Afterward, the eight-year-old sat alone, strafed by shards of glass and gripping his bloodied ears, in the rear seat of the family's Vauxhall Astra outside

Sheehan's furniture store on the Shankill Road in Belfast. Through the car's shattered windscreen he saw the pavement shrouded in dust and strewn with chunks of metal and concrete, splintered timbers, torn clothes, a child's doll, and next to it, his mother's severed arm, still clutching her purse made of multicolored leather pieces stitched together like a quilt. In the distance, a well-dressed man limped toward a ginger-haired girl who stood frozen in place, wailing hysterically and clutching a Paddington Bear next to a pile of smoldering, gray debris. The man scooped up the girl and her bear and carried them away as emergency services arrived. The IRA claimed responsibility for the bombing, but the persons who placed the device were never identified.

The sights and sounds of that afternoon were as vivid now, twenty-five years later, as they were on the day of the blast. Whether they surfaced in his nightmares or unexpectedly by day, they still made his heart race, his breath quicken, and his brow sweat.

The memories and emotions whirled in Tommy's mind until a rogue wave crashed ashore and slapped him with a cold, stinging spray. He scurried backward, and his mood suddenly shifted. *No. Not yet.* He still had one thing left to do. He stood, brushed the sand from his jeans, and hurried back to the bus stop fueled by a quarter-century of accumulated rage and hate.

KIERAN'S FLAT

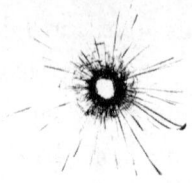

TOMMY REACHED THE MARINE CORNER BUS stop near Ballycastle Beach and realized he did not have the fare back to Belfast. He had not planned to return and now faced a 2.5-hour ride to the city. He scouted for a purse to snatch but did not find an easy target. He abandoned the idea and instead headed for the roundabout to hitch a ride. The first car was headed in the wrong direction, but Tommy caught a break when a lorry emblazoned with the Arms of Ulster pulled to the side. The driver was going to Belfast and agreed to give him a lift.

As he climbed into the cab, Tommy wondered if the man might try to rob or fondle him. He patted the knife in his sock for reassurance and settled in for the ride. The bus, with connections, would have taken three hours, but the direct trip was little more than sixty minutes. The driver, it turned out, had nothing on his mind but the fallout from Brexit. Along the way, Tommy got a crash course on border crossings, transportation permits, customs, and other concerns he did not give a shite about as the lorry driver reacted to news programs on the radio.

The driver left Tommy where the M2 motorway ended near the docks in Belfast. Tommy used the spare change he stole from the center console to board the 11a bus, and twenty minutes later arrived home in the Protestant Shankill ward.

The flat he shared there with Kieran Oliver was spartan. Two thin mattresses lay on the floor of the only bedroom. A round table with four metal chairs sat alongside the galley-style kitchen, and a 1980s-era telly stood on a broken crate in the corner of the living room. On the wall above the telly were a Union Jack and a portrait of Her Majesty Queen Elizabeth II. The prized piece in the room, though, was a disintegrating lounger that belched dust and stuffing with every use. Kieran jokingly referred to the ensemble as "The Curbside Collection," since every item—except, of course, the flag and the Queen's picture—had been rescued from the street on trash day.

Torn, yellowed curtains hung over the windows, and a single floor lamp provided the only additional light. The cooktop was already broken when Tommy moved in a few months earlier, and the refrigerator worked when it wanted to. As a consequence, take-away cartons littered the kitchen floor.

Kieran's job as a deliveryman covered most of the household expenses, and Tommy did odd jobs for his flatmate in exchange for the questionable privilege of crashing there. Tommy had always been good at nicking things, and he relied on that skill to supplement his income when needed. The two lads shared the same foster family for a time as teens, and Tommy, as the bigger of the two, had always had his brother's back during Kieran's many scuffles. Tommy therefore obliged Kieran to take him in when, after his latest breakup, he appeared drunk at the door in the middle of the night seeking a place to sleep.

As the 11a bus pulled away, Tommy approached the flat and spotted the white panel van with a barely perceptible dent on the left side. It was the one Kieran used for work. Stored between the seats were various magnetic signs for display on the doors, depending on the day of the week and whose goods were out for delivery. Despite a recommendation from Kieran, the delivery company refused to hire Tommy as a driver since he went to the interview smelling of beer. Instead, Kieran tossed Tommy a few gigs from the private courier service he ran on the side, which Tommy did on foot or with a "borrowed" bicycle.

Tommy passed through the door to the flat and spotted Kieran on the lounger, eating fish and chips from the shop on the corner and watching the news. Several empty beer cans lay at his feet. Kieran shouted obscenities at the presenter as she reported another car bomb left by the New IRA in Londonderry and a warning from the Police Service of Northern Ireland, or PSNI, about a resurgence of dissident activity fueled in part by the fallout from Brexit.

"Those Catholic cunts will take any excuse," Kieran growled at the television. "Every last one of them is a terrorist or a terrorist sympathizer. They should just get the fuck out if they're so fuckin' miserable here and leave the rest of us in peace." Mere mention of the IRA, without fail, sent Kieran into a rage. Old IRA. Official IRA. Provisional IRA. Continuity IRA. Real IRA. New IRA. "It don't matter what they call themselves *this* month— they're all terrorist cunts."

Kieran's father—a clerk for the Royal Ulster Constabulary, or RUC—was shot dead by an IRA sniper in the late 1980s as he walked home from work on the evening of Kieran's seventh birthday. A photo in the next morning's newspaper showed Kieran's father lying dead on the sidewalk, eyes open, with Kieran's birthday present beside him. The Provisional IRA claimed responsibility, but the gunman was never caught.

Kieran's mum died of cancer less than a year later. Without any family willing to take him in, Kieran became a public ward and went from one care family to another until he turned eighteen. Tommy and Kieran were foster brothers for two of those years and bonded over their shared tragedy and loathing for the IRA.

Tommy's anger about the explosion that ruined his life subsided somewhat on the way home from Ballycastle Beach, but now it surged again as Kieran listed all the indications the New IRA had renewed its campaign of violence. A couple car bombs, the murder of a journalist, and threats against pro-British politicians were the latest signs of agitation. There were even a couple recent kneecappings and other signs of conflict within the Catholic community. In the Clonard district, graffiti appeared on one of the "peace walls," threatening violence to anyone who participated in the ongoing Reconciliation talks—designed to overcome the animosity and distrust that still existed between Catholics and Protestants more than twenty years after the official end of The Troubles.

Tommy listened as Kieran revisited one of his favorite themes—the indignity of knowing that those responsible for the unsolved murders of hundreds of innocent Protestant civilians would never be brought to justice because of the amnesty granted them by the Good Friday agreement. "The police aren't even lookin' for 'em," he screeched. "They're bloody *murderers*. Cold-blooded fuckin' murderers, gunmen, bomb-makers. And proud of it, as sure as I'm sittin' here eating fish and chips. *Allowed* to get away with it, and now gettin' started again."

"Bloody hell," Kieran shouted. "I'm not gonna stand by and watch these Fenians have another go," using a derogatory term for Catholics. He jumped up from the lounger, sprang somewhat unsteadily toward the television, and reached for the Queen's portrait. He snatched it from the wall and pulled at a coin-sized hole in the plaster. To Tommy's surprise, a small panel came loose to reveal a shelf from which Kieran removed two pistols.

"Let's go. It's time to stand up to these bastards."

Tommy accepted one of the pistols, tucked it in his waist-band as Kieran did, and followed his foster brother out the door without a clue what he was doing.

MATTHEW 7:15

FR. MATTHEW CLARK EXITED CLONARD MONASTERY via the doorway closest to the community room, bid good night to the other meeting participants, and walked alone toward the Falls Road. Ed Sheeran's "Cross Me" played loudly from a passing car.

There was a large turnout for that evening's Reconciliation meeting. Business owners, educators, youth leaders, clerics, and concerned citizens from the Catholic and Protestant communities in Belfast gathered regularly in hopes of setting aside lingering animosity. After a tepid initial reception, the concept of Reconciliation was gaining support, and people seemed less afraid of retribution for their participation. By offering the monastery as a safe space for meetings, Fr. Clark wanted to bury the past—Belfast's and his own—for good.

Fr. Clark was an optimist, but even he knew Reconciliation remained a lofty goal. Unsolved murders on either side, amnesty for convicted paramilitaries, government complicity in vigilante killings, double agents, and general distrust—not to mention centuries of animosity—had driven a deep wedge between Protestants and Catholics. Now agitators on both sides, young and old, urged renewed violence to further their political agendas. Rhetoric in Parliament grew more heated, in part because of

Britain's exit from the European Union, and news programs showed discord spilling into the streets again at night. There was even talk of abandoning the Good Friday agreement. Every week, it seemed, brought new revelations about the past that inflamed passions on either side. *Will it ever end?*

The priest stopped short as a football bounced in front of him. With a wistful grin, he joined a group of young Catholic boys who were kicking it around in a nearby alley. Fr. Clark was surprisingly nimble for a man who resembled Father Christmas, and the boys were impressed. The priest complimented each of the lads as they took turns demonstrating their skill with the ball, recalling fondly his own childhood dream of becoming a famous footballer. There was not much else to look forward to as a young man in this neighborhood. Fr. Clark took note of the time and reluctantly excused himself to continue down Clonard Street. He wondered when—if—he would return.

A short distance later, he paused to help a pensioner carry her groceries indoors. She invited him for tea and biscuits, but he demurred. Farther down the street, Fr. Clark stopped at the entrance to the bookmaker's and tried in vain to dissuade the pensioner's husband from wagering that month's income on the outcome of tonight's match.

As the priest turned left onto the Falls Road and walked past the Sisters of Adoration house, he removed his clerical collar and placed the white band into his coat pocket. Fr. Clark was still early for his 19:30 rendezvous at the Bobby Sands mural and momentarily considered popping into the convenience store on the corner for a soda. The proprietor was a parishioner who just became a grandfather, but he had a gift for the gab. Fr. Clark could not risk being late, so he continued toward the mural instead. He politely greeted a delivery man pushing a dolly in the opposite direction and reached for the mobile in his pocket to send a text to the church secretary.

A single bullet to the back of his skull sent the priest sprawling face down on the sidewalk before his hand reached the phone. The gunman casually returned the pistol to the small of his back and hoisted the dolly into a white panel van with a barely perceptible dent on the left side. The shooter climbed into the passenger seat as a pool of blood flowed over the curb and toward the convenience store. "Beware of false prophets, Father," the gunman muttered before the vehicle pulled away. In the distance, a church bell tolled 19:15.

THE WHITE PANEL VAN

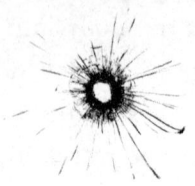

TOMMY JUMPED WHEN HE HEARD THE GUNSHOT just a few feet from where he parked. The rear door swung open, and Kieran hoisted the dolly into the van. "What the fuck was that?" Tommy shouted before Kieran slammed the rear door shut. A moment later, Kieran climbed into the passenger seat. In the sideview mirror, Tommy saw a body face down on the ground. Kieran muttered something out the window and then calmly commanded Tommy to drive at normal speed toward the city center.

Tommy complied but bombarded his foster brother with questions. "Who the fuck was that? Did anybody see ya? What if ya get caught?"

"Hold on, mate," Kieran scolded sternly. "Yer the getaway driver. Ya should be worried 'bout *both* of us gettin' nicked."

Tommy opened his mouth to protest but decided not to antagonize Kieran. Tommy was shaking badly, and his mind raced. *Bloody hell. I am a fucking getaway driver, and I'm carrying a gun.*

Tommy did his share of brawling, had a knack for stealing, and even committed arson with the proper motivation. But he never touched a gun until tonight, nor took part in any murder. "What the bloody hell happened back there?"

Kieran sat quietly for a minute. "I did what needed to be done. That fuckin' cunt of a priest supplied guns for the IRA, and for twenty years nobody's done a fuckin' thing about it. Maybe now those Fenian terrorists will think twice about havin' another go at us. Let *them* feel what it's like to be hunted down in the street."

Tommy swallowed hard. He knew the anguish and rage Kieran felt and often fantasized about avenging his *own* parents' deaths.

"Hang on," Tommy blurted. "How do ya know he ran guns for the IRA? And how did ya know where to find him tonight?"

"Mind yer business, Tommy Magee. Ya know better than to be askin' questions like that in *this* neighborhood."

LEESON STREET

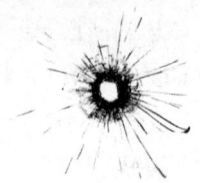

FROM THEIR SURVEILLANCE VAN NEAR THE JUNCTION of Falls Road and Leeson Street, two security agents from MI5 monitored activity around Sinn Fein headquarters. The main office of the Republicans' political party—the former voice of the Provisional IRA—sat directly across from the Bobby Sands mural. Sands was a Provo himself and died in 1981 while on a hunger strike in HM Prison Maze.

At 19:14, the intelligence officers heard a gunshot but were unable to see where it originated. They were on special assignment with strict orders to remain on post and keep an uninterrupted watch over the assigned area. The men scanned their cameras for any commotion or obvious getaways, either on foot or by vehicle, but saw nothing out of the ordinary. They entered the gunshot in their log and left any follow-up to their colleagues at Palace Barracks and the PSNI.

The observers knew a prominent IRA man and valuable MI5 informer was en route to the Bobby Sands mural for an emergency meeting at 19:30 with one of their colleagues. Their job was to provide backup in the event the meeting itself was threatened or disrupted. By 20:15, though, it was apparent the IRA man was a no-show. The area remained deserted.

The senior member of the surveillance team picked up an encrypted phone and called the colleague eating at a chippy not far away. "Mission aborted, Mongoose. Yer man's a ghost."

The MI5 official known to the team only as Mongoose ended the call without a response, pocketed the phone, and exited the shop.

GETAWAY

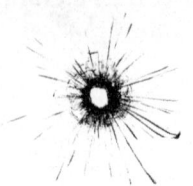

TOMMY STEERED THE VAN TOWARD THE CITY CENTER, checking the mirrors for any sign of the police. Next to him, Kieran removed two identical magnetic signs from a wooden box between the seats. They bore the name of a pizza shop and the smiling caricature of a portly chef. Kieran rolled down his window and placed one of the signs on the passenger door. He passed the other to Tommy and ordered him to place it on the driver's side door.

"I'm tryin' to drive here, mate," Tommy said with irritation. Still, he rolled down the window to avoid angering Kieran. Tommy knew Kieran had a short fuse. Although small in stature, Kieran unflinchingly attacked anyone twice his size at the slightest provocation. Other boys and men in the neighborhood feared him, and "Crazy Kieran" learned to capitalize, then and now, on intimidation and fear to exert his will.

As Tommy placed the sign on his own door, he recalled the time Luke Edwards, a local thug several years older and much bigger than Kieran, snatched a takeaway bag from Kieran while the foster brothers headed home after school.

As the bully walked away laughing with his companions, Tommy watched Kieran enter an alley where discarded lumber from a broken fence was left for collection. Kieran picked up a plank with several nails protruding from one end, casually approached Edwards from behind, and without a word sank the nails into the side of the bully's right knee.

The stunned boy dropped to the ground writhing. His startled mates wheeled around, saw Kieran with the bloodied plank, and backed away. Kieran swung again at the stricken boy and this time landed a blow to the side of his head. Edwards lay unconscious and bleeding heavily while his friends took off running. Kieran retrieved the takeaway bag and resumed the journey home, cockily swinging the plank as he walked. Tommy stood frozen, looking from the injured boy to Kieran and back to the injured boy. Kieran told him to hurry along before the constables arrived.

No one reported the incident to the police though. Kieran already had a reputation for violent outbursts, and Luke Edwards' maiming solidified the neighborhood's belief it was best to stay in Kieran's good graces. No one said a word. Edwards himself claimed to have no memory of the incident, which Tommy thought might actually be true.

THE BODY ON FALLS ROAD

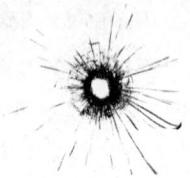

AT 19:23, EMERGENCY SERVICES OPERATOR Lauren Roberts answered an anonymous 999 call from a bookmaker on Clonard Street. The male caller reported a man lying injured near the junction with Falls Road and quickly hung up. Roberts dispatched an ambulance and, given the victim's location, several PSNI patrols.

The paramedics arrived before the PSNI and knew immediately the injured man was already dead from a gunshot to the back of the head. They left a coroner's certificate with the arriving constables and cleared the scene.

Detectives appeared as officers established a cordon of yellow tape. In this neighborhood, a gunshot victim called to mind the IRA—the true police in this ward. A network of drug dealers and organized crime operated in the area under a strict code of conduct. Anyone who violated the rules or committed an unsanctioned offense against a fellow Catholic could expect a swift response. Executions were less common than kidnappings and kneecappings, but still not unusual.

Detective Inspector Will Nichols knelt to search the victim's pockets and found only a mobile phone and a clerical collar. "Hang on," he called to one of the constables. "Do we know who this is?"

"No, sir," PC Harry Hutchinson replied. "There was nothin' alongside the body when we arrived, and we waited for you to search his clothes. The call came from a bookmaker up the street, and there was no one here but the victim when we arrived."

Nichols pulled the dead man's wallet from the pocket of his trousers and read the name on his driving license. He dropped the wallet into a plastic evidence bag and glanced around. He was certain someone saw or heard something, but he knew the residents of the neighborhood would stay silent. They learned from an early age here never to talk to the police.

Recent conflicts between rival IRA gangs had spurred an uptick in local violence and brought increased police attention to the area. Yet nobody cooperated with detectives to reduce the violence in their own back yards. Nichols stared past Hutchinson at a signpost that warned passersby to shun the PSNI. He sighed in frustration.

Just then, the dead man's mobile rang. DI Nichols noted the caller's name and number, pressed the green button, and said, "Hello?"

"Fr. Clark, it's Ruth. I'm so glad I caught ya. The Miller baby has a fever, and the parents wondered if ya could do the baptism at the weekend instead?"

"Mrs. McGowan," the detective answered gently. "My name is Detective Inspector William Nichols. I'm afraid I have some unfortunate news about Fr. Clark." He heard a slight gasp but nothing else. The detective continued. "Fr. Clark was shot on the Falls Road this evening. I'm sorry to tell ya he passed away before the paramedics arrived." The call ended abruptly.

At Clonard Monastery, Ruth McGowan waited only a moment before placing a second call.

THE OTHER END OF THE LINE

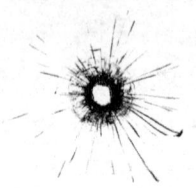

MICKEY SHANAHAN'S FACE betrayed his apprehension as the church secretary described the conversation she had moments earlier with a PSNI inspector. Fr. Clark's violent death on a Belfast street was at once shocking and expected, Mickey thought as he hung up. The man was a priest, after all, and a well-known one at that.

But Clark was also a long-serving IRA man whose exploits over several decades, though cloaked in secrecy, surely put a target on his back. His loss was a blow to Republicanism, but Shanahan had no time for mourning. The PSNI had the priest's mobile and would certainly be analyzing it soon for clues.

Shanahan assessed the situation. Mrs. McGowan was right—they had a problem. Shanahan tallied more than a dozen operations in the last 18 months that used guns and munitions from Clark's ongoing supply network. Officially, the Provisional IRA called a ceasefire in 1997 and signed the Good Friday agreement a year later. In reality, they were as influential as ever, working behind the scenes as a clandestine puppeteer of various IRA splinter groups.

At the height of The Troubles, Clark and his fellow Provos were adept at concealing their activities and connections from the Brits. But advances in technology now made it far easier for the government to track people's movements and intercept their communications. The Provos and their fellow paramilitaries had done their best to keep pace and adjust their tactics, but it was a tricky process.

Just last week, Shanahan warned Clark and other operatives about new software that finally allowed the PSNI and MI5 to unlock any mobile phone and pierce even the military-grade encryption relied on by the modern IRA. Shanahan instructed his crew of Belfast Provos to wipe all data from their phones and then do a hard reset to ensure no trace of their activity was left behind. But he realized now he had made a mistake by not collecting the phones and supervising the process himself. What if Fr. Clark had not yet sanitized his phone, or had not done it correctly?

Now Clark's mobile was in police custody, and would soon be on its way to MI5 if the PSNI caught any whiff of Clark's alleged involvement with the IRA.

Just as his nerves began to fray, Mickey recalled a story his nephew told him about a drug-dealing schoolmate who erased his stolen mobile remotely. Mickey rang the church secretary back. "Meet me in the basement in half an hour," he instructed before hanging up again and heading for the door.

THWARTED

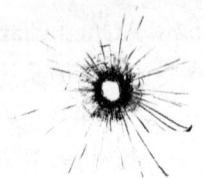

SHANAHAN APPROACHED A RARELY USED side entrance to Clonard Monastery. There was no exterior lighting. He oriented his index finger to the numbers on the cipher lock and entered an eight-digit code to release the bolt and open the door. Shanahan glanced quickly over both shoulders to be sure he was unseen and stepped inside. Once the door shut behind him, he felt for the light switch and illuminated the anteroom. A security camera overhead clicked to adjust to the brightness.

Shanahan hurried to the other side of the chamber and removed a heavy metal key from his pocket. He inserted it in the keyhole of a thick wooden door and turned it 180 degrees to the left. The room was damp, and the door swelled. Shanahan tugged forcefully at the rectangular handle until it finally gave way. He took a step forward, pulled on a string for the overhead lightbulb, and descended a steep, narrow stairwell. The stairs led two stories below ground to the cellar of the church.

The thick stone walls here rendered cellular service, eavesdropping devices, and infrared sensors inoperable. The only connection to the world above was a single loose Ethernet port attached to a long blue cable that dangled from the ceiling. The cable ran back to a junction box that managed seventeen additional cables in a classroom upstairs used for adult education.

Shanahan sat at the large round table in the middle of the cellar. Twelve military cots were stacked in a corner. Adjacent to the cots stood a dozen drums of drinking water and several boxes filled with non-perishable food. A heavy-duty gray metal locker stood against the opposite wall. Its handles were bound by a thick chain secured with an industrial padlock. The cellar was otherwise empty apart from a well-used laptop placed on one of the water drums.

From another corner of the room, Shanahan heard a faint thud and then the distant sound of footsteps as the church secretary, Ruth McGowan, descended a second stairwell from the church vestibule into the cellar. It was the same stairwell Patrick Linden and Liam O'Malley used to hide from the Brits on the day Deidre died all those years ago.

Ruth reached the basement, greeted Shanahan, and retrieved the laptop from the water drum. She placed it in front of Shanahan and used a gray cable she brought with her to connect it to the Ethernet port. "The laptop is nicked and can't be traced to us," she reassured him. "The Ethernet connection is shared by everybody at the church, and we use a multi-layered VPN anyway. It would be impossible to trace the connection to a specific user, especially without the actual device."

Shanahan watched Ruth power on the laptop and navigate to the login page for Fr. Clark's mobile account. She entered the priest's username from memory and slid the computer to Mickey so he could enter the password. When the mobile accounts were created, Mickey insisted no single member of the unit know both the username and password for any account but their own, as a safeguard against informers. He also insisted the tracking feature be activated for all mobiles, in the event any member of the unit went missing for an extended period or came under suspicion.

The login was successful, and Shanahan navigated to the tracking page as his nephew had taught him. He sighed with relief when he saw Fr. Clark's mobile was still online. His relief turned to dismay when the phone's location appeared in an unmapped area north of Belfast. "Shite. Fuckin' shite," he exclaimed. "We might be too late." Shanahan hurriedly followed the prompts to remotely erase the device. "Quick," he commanded Ruth. "Re-enter his username."

Ruth typed it a second time and stepped back to let Shanahan enter the password again. A pop-up window read *Deletion in Progress*, and the pair watched intently as a gray bar slowly advanced from left to right until it reached 100%. Shanahan then deleted all the data backups for the account. "That's it," Shanahan said as he leaned back in the chair. He had rehearsed the steps several times with his nephew and was confident he deleted everything of concern. "Let's hope we did it in time. When exactly did ya speak to the inspector?"

Ruth checked the call log in her mobile. The Millers incorrectly assumed she had already left work for the day and dialed her personal number to postpone the baptism. "I called Fr. Clark just past eight o'clock. The inspector answered and told me what happened."

Shanahan glanced at his watch. Only an hour passed since Ruth spoke to the PSNI. He could not be sure how long Fr. Clark was dead by the time of Ruth's call, but it seemed unlikely anyone processed the evidence that quickly. Even if they had, he doubted there had been enough time to unlock and analyze the phone. *Unless they know who Fr. Clark really was.*

Ruth disconnected the laptop from the Ethernet port and looked at Shanahan.

"You take care of it," he said. "Make sure there's no chance it can be recovered."

Ruth nodded. It was not the first time she destroyed a computer to protect the crew, and she knew exactly what to do. She wished Shanahan good night, and the colleagues exited via their respective stairwells. The church did not know about the secretary's extracurricular activities, and she took care to ensure she and Shanahan were not spotted together.

In his haste to erase Fr. Clark's mobile phone and data backups, Shanahan overlooked a series of outgoing calls in the log, made earlier that day in quick succession to a single number—suggesting the calls were urgent and either went unanswered or to voicemail. It was the emergency number given to Fr. Clark by Mongoose, and Shanahan had just erased the unit's only clue that Fr. Clark had betrayed them.

WIPED

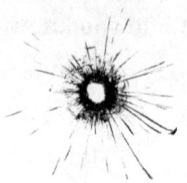

TECHNICIAN BRENDA NIEVES ARRIVED SHORTLY BEFORE 23:00 for the overnight shift at MI5's digital forensics lab in an unmapped area north of Belfast. She was there to relieve Michael Berger, who just finished his first week at the facility. Berger alerted Nieves to a priority assignment that came in half an hour earlier. Because it was close to the change of shift, he did not have time to finish the analysis before heading home, so he let it wait thirty minutes for his replacement.

Nieves said goodnight to Berger and turned her attention to the priority ticket. It was a straightforward request to unlock a mobile phone, extract the encrypted contents, and then package the data in a user-friendly format for examination by intelligence analysts.

Nieves went to the evidence cage, entered her user code, and located the locker with the specified device. She unplugged the phone from the lab's power supply, exited the evidence cage, and connected the phone to a machine that copied its contents to a backup drive. Backups were necessary in case the mobile was configured to detect tampering and then erase itself.

Nieves immediately saw reason for alarm. The crime scene technician who took the phone into evidence—lacking a Faraday bag in which to shield it—forgot to disable cellular and Wi-Fi access. Berger did not catch the mistake when he accepted the transfer. As a result, the phone and its contents remained accessible to any remote user with the appropriate login credentials.

You must be joking. There were two cardinal rules for handling mobile phones taken into evidence—disable their external communications to preserve the contents, and maintain their existing power state, whether on or off.

As expected, the mobile was locked. Nieves connected it to a computer equipped with software that could bypass the security features of any mobile phone currently in existence. It took about ninety minutes to unlock the device.

Because a remote party already could have altered the contents of the phone, its evidentiary value for criminal prosecution was now minimal. But Nieves continued the data extraction in search of anything useful from an intelligence perspective. An hour later, her fears were confirmed—nothing but system files remained on the phone.

Nieves logged into the PSNI records system and pulled up DI Nichols' report of the crime scene. It referenced a call received on the victim's mobile from Ruth McGowan at 20:04. The mobile had been in evidence since then, so data pertaining to the call should have been found on the phone. But it was missing, and Nieves knew someone wiped the contents of the phone from right under their noses. *Bloody hell. What a cock-up.*

Nieves requested a log of all IP addresses used to access the victim's mobile account in the past twelve hours, but knew it was unlikely to reveal anything useful. Anyone sophisticated enough to wipe a dead man's phone that quickly was likely to have covered his or her tracks. The IP address probably traced to a busy Internet cafe, and the culprit likely disguised himself or avoided security cameras altogether. Nieves drafted an expedited summary of the situation, held her breath, and clicked *Submit*.

MI5's watch commander passed the interim forensic report to senior leadership at 01:52. At 02:15, and despite the late hour, the director of the digital forensics lab was contacted at his residence and instructed to terminate Mr. Berger's employment and collect his MI5 credentials, digital key, and mobile phone by 06:00. A second call was placed to the PSNI superintendent in charge of the crime scene technicians, who received a verbal drubbing and afterward needed a double shot of gin to get back to sleep.

WEST BELFAST

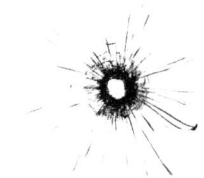

THE NEXT MORNING, A BLACK CAB pulled to the curb by the string of row houses on College Green. Claire was lecturing at the university all day. Thornton still had two days until his practice opened, so he booked a "political history tour" that received high ratings online for its unbiased approach. Thornton hopped into the taxi and introduced himself to the driver as they headed for West Belfast—site of the worst violence during The Troubles. Thornton felt a twinge of excitement. Like many Americans, he held a romanticized view of the IRA as an underdog fighting for independence.

Gerald, the taxi driver-turned-tour-guide, was accustomed to educating Americans whose knowledge of the IRA and The Troubles came mostly from movies and television. Northern Ireland was an emerging hot spot for tourism, due in large part to its popularity as a film location for *Game of Thrones*. Belfast capitalized on its notorious past and the influx of tourists by promoting the black cab tours. Drivers kept the political and historical explanations simple though—most visitors just wanted to see where famous events happened.

"We can stop anywhere for a photo," Gerald declared, "but

I'll stay in the cab with the engine running. If I honk, run straight back, and we'll make a fast exit."

"Isn't it safe?!"

"Mostly," Gerald answered. "At this time of day, the trouble-makers won't be up. But don't return on your own after three o'clock."

The warning surprised Thornton, but he did not press for details.

At the next traffic light, Gerald began his abbreviated history of The Troubles. The Irish and the British, he explained, had feuded for centuries, and from 1919 to 1921 the Irish waged a war of independence from Britain. It resulted in partition of the island—a large Irish Free State, with self-rule, was created in the south, but several counties in the northeast remained part of the United Kingdom and became known as Northern Ireland. The Irish Free State later became known as Ireland and, eventually, the Republic of Ireland.

Gerald noted two-thirds of the population in Northern Ireland were Protestant and identified strongly as British. The remaining third were Catholic and considered themselves Irish. Generally, the Protestants *wanted* to be part of the United Kingdom, while most Catholics opposed the partition and wanted self-rule for *all* of Ireland.

"Now this is where it gets tricky for you Yanks," Gerald said. "The names can be confusing. The people who want to be part of the United Kingdom are called Unionists. They are mostly Protestant, and because they are loyal to the British monarch they're also called Loyalists. Most Catholics, however, want Northern Ireland to rejoin what's now the Republic of Ireland in the south, so they're called Republicans. They were previously known as Nationalists. So to oversimplify it, you have

Protestants/Unionists/Loyalists in one camp, and Catholics/
Nationalists/Republicans in the other."

"I'm with you so far," Thornton reassured him.

"Despite their differences, everyone managed to co-exist in
Northern Ireland without much violence for several decades
after the partition. That's not to say everything was coming up
roses," Gerald acknowledged. "Catholics in the north experienced widespread discrimination in employment and housing.
And many voting wards were redrawn to ensure continued
Unionist victories. Even so, the situation was comparatively
non-violent until the 1960s."

Gerald turned right onto Falls Road. "There's some debate
about the precise event that started The Troubles. But in the
1960s, Catholics began to protest the discrimination they experienced. There were peaceful marches and 'civil disobedience,'
but also riots and bombings and killings. The overwhelmingly
Protestant police force responded brutally at times.

"Armed vigilante groups, or paramilitaries, sprung up on the
Loyalist side to aid the police. They weren't officially sanctioned,
but they weren't discouraged either. Catholics consequently suspected the government, the police, and the paramilitaries were
colluding to rid Northern Ireland of Catholics altogether."

Gerald explained that Loyalists, meanwhile, believed the
Catholic civil rights movement was merely a front for disaffected
Nationalists—bitter about the partition of the island and still
eager to oust the Brits from all of Ireland with violence.

"Now, among those fighters for Irish independence in the
1920s was a faction that vehemently opposed the partition and
refused to recognize either Northern Ireland or the new Republic. They called themselves the Irish Republican Army, or IRA.
For them, it was all or nothing. So they continued sporadic

attacks against symbols of British rule right up to the 1960s, when another disagreement emerged."

Thornton was surprised the IRA preceded The Troubles by several decades. "What was the new disagreement about?"

"Some IRA members felt a peaceful, political solution was the best way to reunite Ireland. The rest believed only violence would defeat the Brits. Both sides dug in their heels, and in 1969 the movement split into the Official IRA and the new Provisional IRA. From that point until the Good Friday peace agreement in 1998, the Provos, as they're called, generated most of the Republican violence. They launched attacks not just here, but in London, Brighton, and Gibraltar too, and they imported weapons from Africa and America. It was a big operation, and the British Army mounted an aggressive counterinsurgency campaign. Ultimately, over 3,500 people died and 30,000 were wounded."

Thornton pondered the loss of life as the taxi passed countless murals memorializing heroes and events on both sides of the conflict.

A few minutes later, Gerald pulled to the side of the road. He pointed to a crosswalk signal and urged Thornton to focus on a large sticker affixed to the pole. On it were references to MI5, Britain's domestic intelligence service, and the PSNI, or Police Service of Northern Ireland. In bright red, blue, and white lettering, the initials PSNI were translated as *People Should Not Inform*.

"That's an IRA warning not to talk to the police," Gerald noted. "They'll shoot you if you do."

Thornton was dumbfounded. He thought the IRA was a relic of the past.

Soon the taxi stopped at the base of an eighteen-foot wall that extended for several blocks. A vertical metal screen heightened it by fifteen feet. Ahead, an open gate allowed cars to pass through. "That's one of several dozen peace walls," Gerald explained, "installed between Loyalist and Republican neighborhoods. At night, the gates close at these 'interface areas' to stop trouble-makers from provoking the other side. The metal screens keep projectiles from crossing the wall. You see, Catholics and Prot-estants mostly live in their own neighborhoods, attend separate schools, marry their own kind, and even have their own taxis."

Thornton was perplexed. "If the Good Friday peace agree-ment ended The Troubles in 1998, why does it seem like Belfast is still in the midst of conflict?"

"The constant violence ended, and the Army mostly left, but memories linger. It's not safe in some quarters to acknowledge service in the Army or past IRA sympathies—it can get you killed in broad daylight. Many people haven't let go of the past. Don't ask too many questions of people you don't know."

THE ANNIVERSARY

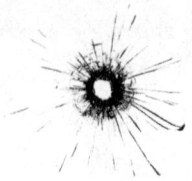

CLAIRE LIED WHEN SHE TOLD HER HUSBAND she was lecturing at the university all day. Once the black cab whisked Thornton toward West Belfast, Claire left their flat and headed north for a rendezvous at the elegant Crown Bar. She walked with her head down, dressed in black and a scarf that obscured her face. As she approached her destination on Great Victoria Street, she pulled her coat tighter and quickened her pace. There, across the road, stood the Europa—the most bombed hotel in the world. The high-visibility landmark hosted a multitude of establishment figures, celebrities, and international correspondents over the years, and thus became a favorite target of the IRA. It suffered more than thirty explosions during The Troubles. Claire held her breath and darted into the Crown Bar.

The familiarity and warmth of the place instantly soothed her. She loved the saloon's carved wood ceiling and pillars, the tile mosaics that adorned the walls and floor, and the ornately decorated bar that seemed a block long. Every inch of the place had been lovingly restored to its Victorian glory. Despite some fierce competition, it remained her favorite pub in all of Belfast. Above all, Claire relished the ten intimate snugs, or booths, that allowed patrons to meet privately and undisturbed, wrapped in a cocoon of mahogany and etched glass. She went straight to their usual enclosure and opened the door.

Robert Inglesby looked up and greeted her with a mix of happiness and solemnity appropriate to the occasion. He was a dapper dresser, if a bit old fashioned, and wore his somber three-piece suit well. The streaks of silver in his otherwise black hair gave him a dignified air. He stood as much as the booth allowed and kissed Claire as she reached out and gave him a lingering embrace. She sat across from him and placed her purse on the plush black cushion.

Inglesby pressed the button on the table to summon a waiter. Claire asked for a cheese and chutney toastie, while her companion ordered a toad in the hole and two Old Peculiers. After the waiter delivered their order and the door to the snug closed, Inglesby produced a single white lily and placed it gently on the table between them in observance of The Anniversary. They bowed their heads for a time and then began to eat. As usual, they maintained a reverent silence until the food was gone. Then Inglesby asked, "What did you tell Aaron?"

"I told him I was lecturing all day." The expression on Claire's face betrayed her guilty conscience. "I hate lying to him."

"It's for the best, sweetheart. The less he knows, the better. We don't want to invite attention," Inglesby cautioned.

Claire nodded. The couple raised their glasses and toasted. "To Courtney!"

They sipped their drinks, returned them to the table, and looked directly at one another. Tears formed at the corners of Claire's eyes. "I couldn't bear to lose you too, Daddy."

A FATHER'S TEARS

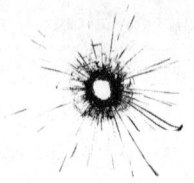

THE GRIEF WEIGHED HEAVILY ON INGLESBY, even after all these years, so he barely spoke to Claire. For the most part, he avoided *all* talk about Courtney. Still, on this one day—The Anniversary—father and daughter felt obliged to acknowledge her death, if only with a quick, silent lunch.

Inglesby paid the bill, and the pair departed the snug. They hugged once more by the door and exited the Crown Bar. Claire turned left and headed to her office on foot while Inglesby walked north toward the car park. The pain in his knee signaled an imminent rainstorm, and Inglesby quickened the pace as he passed the Tesco Express. At Grosvenor Road he turned left and soon arrived where he left the car. A keen observer would have noted the greenish tint of the bulletproof windows and the way the armored passenger compartment sat heavily on specialty tires.

Inglesby unlocked the vehicle and sat behind the wheel. He glanced at the iridescent butterfly pendant hanging from the rearview mirror and touched it gently. With a lump in his throat, Inglesby pulled a wallet from the inner pocket of his suit coat. He removed an aged newspaper article from behind a stack of credit cards and gingerly unfolded the worn, faded clipping. It was a ritual he followed just once a year.

The headline for Tuesday, January 4, 1994, read TERROR IN MIDDLE SHANKILL. Several photographs showed the aftermath of a large explosion. The text explained a suspected IRA bomb detonated without warning just before one o'clock in the afternoon, when the area was busy with pedestrians. The explosion destroyed four parked cars and a couple businesses near a pub frequented by members of the Ulster Volunteer Force, or UVF—but it was not yet clear who or what was the intended target. Eleven people, including a young girl, died in the blast. A spokesman for the RUC said the death toll was likely to rise given the number of gravely injured persons taken to hospital.

Inglesby's lower lip quivered slightly as he re-read the article and recalled that horrible day—the flash of light followed by a concussive blast and then a deafening clap that spewed debris in every direction. It would have been just another explosion in a city numbed by bombings if not for the presence of the little girl mentioned in the article. It still bothered him that her name, like the identities of the other victims, was omitted from the description. "Courtney," he moaned. *"Courtney.* My beautiful little girl…"

Inglesby choked on the words as his head bowed toward the steering wheel. To this day, there was no claim of responsibility for the blast, and the individuals who killed his daughter and the other victims were never held to account. Inglesby vowed on that January day twenty-five years ago to find justice for his daughter. As he gripped the steering wheel, he realized it was a vow he might not be able to keep.

QUEEN'S UNIVERSITY

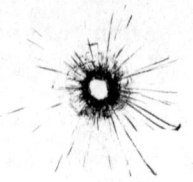

CLAIRE SAT IN HER SECOND-FLOOR OFFICE at the law school with the door closed. The manicured lawn of University Square was visible through the window. She gazed outside and reflected proudly on her career choices. Many of her Georgetown classmates sought the prestige and wealth that came with eighty-hour work weeks at the nation's top law firms. Claire preferred to toil at "ground level," as her husband liked to say, and advocate for the mistreated and disadvantaged.

Claire was always drawn to cases that were too controversial or unpopular for most lawyers to touch. She endured searing public scorn early in her career for representing a young Black man who appealed his conviction for killing a decorated police officer. Claire filed papers asserting key DNA evidence was mishandled and therefore should have been excluded by the court. Throughout the appeal, police unions, elected leaders, and significant swaths of the public decried Claire's attempts to free her client on a perceived "technicality."

Claire persevered and won her client's release. He was killed six weeks later when a vigilante mob recognized him on the street and beat him to death. Shortly afterward, an investigative reporter exposed multiple cases of mishandled evidence and contaminated DNA samples at the same crime lab responsible for convicting Claire's client. The lab lost its accreditation, and dozens of pending criminal cases were thrown into limbo. A judicial panel then ordered the review of more than one hundred convictions that relied on evidence processed at the lab. None of Claire's critics apologized.

Now, as a visiting law professor at QUB, Claire taught a seminar on social justice and ran the school's legal clinic. Her credentials attracted the attention of an independent commission in Belfast that hired legal scholars to review the convictions of paramilitaries—Republican and Loyalist—who appeared to be unjustly accused and convicted of serious offenses. The Commission on Northern Ireland's Court System, or CNICS, hoped, despite its unfortunate acronym, to restore faith in Northern Ireland's criminal justice system. Although the effort was privately funded and unaffiliated with the university, its mission and high profile appealed to the school's administration, who authorized Claire several hours each week to work on Commission matters from her office on campus.

Fueled by her lunch at the Crown Bar, Claire now focused intently on a stack of files in front of her. *CONFIDENTIAL* was emblazoned in bold red letters across the topmost folder. Beneath the banner were a government seal and the letters *HET*.

The HET, or Historical Enquiries Team, was disbanded in 2014, but its work was preserved in a restricted area at PSNI headquarters. The secrets buried in the HET archive were as explosive as any IRA device, and access to them was granted only by special permission. CNICS successfully petitioned the government for approval to examine the HET files for a period of twenty-four months, and Claire was appointed co-chair of the review.

The HET tried, with only limited success, to find justice for victims on both sides of The Troubles whose murderers were never identified. The team's work fueled sensational headlines when it exposed previously withheld intelligence reports, the secret testimony of confidential informers, and evidence buried to protect rogue government officials and military officers—all of which undermined the legitimacy of many high-profile criminal convictions. It also revealed the existence of double agents within IRA and Loyalist paramilitary units.

Claire wished the HET had been more successful. It pained her to think of all the victims whose killers escaped justice. She found it equally disturbing that here in Northern Ireland, as in the States, people were unjustly imprisoned by incompetent or corrupt public officials who perverted the course of justice. She knew her work could change that.

Despite her own family's Loyalist leanings, Claire was deeply offended to learn of the UK government and the Army's misconduct. In their zeal to stop the IRA, some officials used unsanctioned or illegal means to arrest and convict Republican paramilitaries, while others ignored the misconduct or actively covered it up. It also appeared Loyalist paramilitaries were used as both proxies and scapegoats to shield guilty government officials from prosecution. Justice, Claire knew, must be blind and balanced. *Wrong is wrong. Now let's do something about this.*

Claire glanced at the top-most file in the stack. Her colleagues at CNICS flagged it as the next case to receive a vote by the Commission. She opened the folder and read the inmate's name—Patrick Linden of HM Prison Maghaberry.

MILL BARRACKS

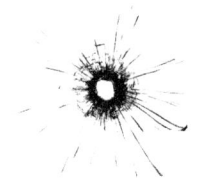

ROBERT INGLESBY STEELED HIMSELF and exited the car park after his lunch with Claire. He initially headed north toward his office, but an impulse overcame him. Instead, he headed west on the Shankill Road. An unusual desire to reconnect with Courtney at the place of her death lured him to the scene of the explosion. Ordinarily, Inglesby avoided it.

The storefronts had changed since that horrible afternoon, but the street names were still familiar. Dover, Carlow, Craven, Northumberland. Suddenly vivid images from decades earlier hijacked Inglesby's brain, and fear gripped his body. His chest tightened, and he struggled to breathe. His hands went numb, and he feared he might vomit in the car. Inglesby pulled to the left and stopped the vehicle just before he reached it—not the scene of the explosion, but North Howard Street.

The Mill Barracks once stood here, so named because the British army converted an old linen factory into a base of operations at this spot during The Troubles. Inglesby was stationed here for three years during the 1980s and regularly passed along North Howard Street with his friends and colleagues.

Just a few feet away from where the car now idled was the green gate through which Army foot patrols once entered and exited the barracks. Next to the gate stood a red brick wall that had begun to crumble and buckle. Still visible amidst the bricks were an observation port—partially filled in with cement and covered with an oversized gray metal plate—and the rusty, fortified door to the sentry box.

The pace of Inglesby's breathing approached hyperventilation, and he became lightheaded. His mind played tricks with his memory and returned to the early evening in 1987 when he and two other members of the security services passed through that very gate and paused near the sentry box.

Karl Llewelyn, just 23, dropped first, to Inglesby's immediate left. The IRA sniper fired again and felled 29-year-old Keith Baxter, who was standing so close to Inglesby's right that their shoulders nearly touched and a piece of Baxter's brain landed on Inglesby's cheek.

At the sound of the second shot, British soldiers in the area began to return fire. Inglesby fell to his knees to tend to his comrades but realized nothing could save them. He knelt transfixed, staring at the lifeless, bleeding bodies of the two friends with whom, just seconds earlier, he was talking excitedly about the birth of Baxter's first child. Someone grabbed Inglesby under the shoulders and dragged him to safety inside the sentry box. Despite an extensive search, the sniper escaped. The spot where Inglesby's friends died became known as Sniper Alley.

Inglesby's memories rippled forward to November 1988, when an IRA bomb littered North Howard Street with debris and the remains of nine British Army personnel. Inglesby had just turned a corner at the far end of the street and heard the blast a split second before the ground shook and he stumbled to the pavement. There were other similar close calls during his military service, but these incidents on North Howard Street— the *first* two—affected him the most.

Inglesby escaped The Troubles without physical injury, but he carried the emotional scars. Sometimes he wished his wounds were visible and someone would ask how he was doing. Instead, the trauma stayed hidden, and when Inglesby's mind decided to toy with his emotions, he did what most of his Army buddies did and reached for a bottle.

Inglesby waited in the car fifteen minutes for the flashback to subside, although he did not know to call it that. To him it was just a bad memory, suddenly intruding and taking him back to events he tried in vain to leave behind.

When his heart rate slowed and his breathing returned to normal, Inglesby picked up his mobile. He dialed a fellow veteran of The Troubles who lived just a few blocks away. Courtney would have to wait for another time.

"Hallo," answered a familiar voice. "What are ya gettin' me into this time?"

Inglesby chuckled. "It's personal. No business, I promise. Can ya meet me for a pint, mate? I need to get me head sorted."

"Of course. I was expectin' yer call, seein' as it's The Anniversary and all."

"So it is. I'm just down the street. Are ya at the pub already?"

"Already? I've been here all day, so I have. I'll send the crew away so we can talk alone. C'mon in when yer ready."

"I'll only be a minute."

THE LONG ARM OF THE TROUBLES

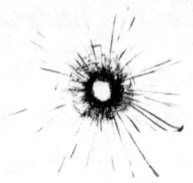

ROBERT INGLESBY ENDED THE CALL and drove a short distance farther west. He parked along the Shankill Road near the junction with Tennent Street in a spot visible from the pub. Inglesby checked the pistol strapped to his ankle and exited the car. Although he was in Loyalist territory, a man in his position could not be too careful. He knew Republican paramilitaries operated everywhere.

Inglesby nodded curtly to the stout, surly man smoking a cigar on the patio outside the Cocky Rooster. The man knew to watch the car without being asked. Inglesby entered the pub and headed for the usual table at the rear corner of the building, under the telly. Garth Peters waited there with two Old Peculiers at the ready.

"Cheers," Peters said. "And here's to Courtney. May she rest in peace."

Inglesby joined the toast, and the two men sipped their ales. Inglesby looked at Peters and said, "I think I'm losin' me mind again, Petey." It was a nickname only Inglesby used, from their shared time in military intelligence. "It felt like I was havin' a heart attack just before I called ya, only I knew it wasn't. And the images started playin' in me mind again, as if I was right back there re-livin' everything. It all went away, just like before, but it felt so *real*, Petey. It scared the fuckin' shite out of me, and I'm worried it's gonna happen again when someone else is around to see it."

Inglesby trusted Peters more than anyone. As a pensioner from the Royal Ulster Constabulary, or RUC—the predecessor to Northern Ireland's modern police force—and a veteran of the Army, Peters understood the emotional baggage carried by former policemen and soldiers. They shared their trauma only with a few, close confidants from their service days. For some, the flashbacks came unexpectedly. Others saw a pattern to their distress and learned to avoid certain triggers. Often, they turned to alcohol to quiet their minds.

Inglesby and Peters knew one poor fellow for whom the drink was not enough. He had worked as a bomb disposal technician during The Troubles, survived many close calls, and persevered for a quarter-century, only to kill himself a month ago. There were other suicides over the years.

"Isn't yer son-in-law a psychologist? Maybe he can make it go away, or at least explain it."

"For fuck's sake, Petey, I don't want Aaron to know. He'll tell Claire, and then I'll have both of 'em worryin' about me and lookin' at me like I'm daft. And if the boss hears about this, I'll be sacked for sure."

"Ya know I won't breathe a word of this to anyone. But yer not alone in feelin' that way. Other fellas have the same concerns. I wish I had a solution fer youse. What I don't get is how some of us are still affected by what happened, and others seem to have forgotten all about it."

Inglesby had wondered the same. They *all* knew incalculable tragedy—grisly bombings, tortured and dismembered bodies, young widows, orphans, betrayal, and the outright loathing of a Catholic population they were sent, at least initially, to help. All that suffering was inflicted by a ruthless, cunning, soulless band of terrorists without a conscience or any regard for human life. For some service members the terror never stopped, Inglesby concluded. It just took a different form.

Inglesby focused his attention elsewhere. "Listen, I need your help gatherin' info on a priest that was shot."

"And I need to fill ya in on the fuckin' cunts selling drugs for the New IRA."

UNJUST IMPRISONMENT

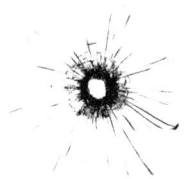

CLAIRE INTENTLY READ THE HET'S FILE on Patrick Linden. He was a shadowy figure about whom few confirmed details were known. Linden appeared to have joined the IRA in the early 1970s, when he was photographed by the security services attending the funerals of IRA men and women. On two occasions, they spotted him near known IRA safe houses in the Clonard neighborhood. One informer claimed Linden started as an agitator who incited Catholic mobs to attack Army patrols and later became a recruiter of young Provos. Intelligence reports asserted, without attribution, that Linden became an IRA enforcer who facilitated the "disappearance" of at least six Republicans suspected of being touts in the early 1980s.

Less than a decade later, he was rumored to be on the Army Council, whose seven members directed the activities of the entire Provisional IRA. Separate entries in the file suggested Linden was actually the OC, or Officer Commanding, of an elite bomb-making unit. Either way, Claire thought, he would have been responsible for some of the IRA's worst atrocities. Yet, as a lawyer she was keenly aware the dossier on Linden was mostly hearsay and speculation, neither of which justified putting a man in jail for twenty-five years.

The HET file revealed Linden was under surveillance for extended periods of time but never caught in the act of committing a crime. Officials suspected an insider tipped him off, but could never prove it.

Shortly after the Good Friday agreement was announced in 1998, an anonymous informer claimed Linden and his colleagues planned to bomb high-profile targets in London to derail the peace process. Forensic tests at the time of his arrest indicated Linden recently handled explosives. Officers who interrogated Linden over a period of several days claimed he confessed to planning a series of attacks during the Queen's official birthday parade. During the trial, Linden denied handling explosives and accused the police of torture and forging his signature on the confession. The constables' testimony and the forensic evidence nonetheless yielded Linden twenty-five years at Maghaberry.

Because he was convicted after April 10, 1998, Linden was not eligible for the amnesty. However, the HET uncovered evidence that the two officials who testified against Linden gave false testimony in several other cases involving suspected IRA men. Consequently, an HET investigator wrote, "they cannot be considered credible, and their testimony in all trials must be discounted in the absence of other evidence." The HET also noted inconsistencies in the forensic records "suggesting the evidence against Mr. Linden was planted."

So why is he still in prison? Claire surmised no one shared the HET's findings with Mr. Linden or his legal team. She wondered how many other inmates were jailed on false testimony and fabricated evidence.

Claire pondered the situation. Any new revelations that the police and the Public Prosecution Service were complicit in the false imprisonment of Republican dissidents would inflame passions in the Catholic community, rankle Loyalists, and further strain the already fragile truce between the two communities. "But wrong is wrong," she reminded herself. One of her husband's favorite expressions also came to mind. "Put the discomfort where it belongs." And in this instance, it belonged with the people who framed Linden.

Claire grabbed a sticky note, placed it on the cover of Linden's HET file, and wrote a short list of observations: *Hearsay. Unsourced intelligence. Inconclusive surveillance. Anonymous tip. Torture. False testimony/evidence.* It was a solid basis on which to seek Linden's release. Claire exited her office, left the file on her assistant's desk, and returned to the window. She wondered what sort of man Patrick Linden truly was, and who within the government or the Army had it in for him.

PALACE BARRACKS

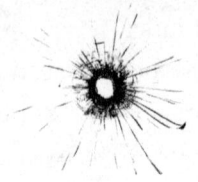

AS AARON THORNTON TOURED WEST BELFAST and his wife read the HET file, an elite team of analysts worked frantically through lunch in an unmapped area north of the city to assemble the few available details about Fr. Matthew Clark's murder. They labored in a suite of offices atop a blast-proof, five-story brick building with bulletproof windows and no signage in the northeastern quadrant of Palace Barracks. A sophisticated array of communications antennae sat on the roof, disguised as a cellular telephone tower.

Palace Barracks, a sizable military installation about twenty minutes north of Belfast, once served as the hub of British Army activity during The Troubles. Now it housed, among other things, the Northern Ireland headquarters of the United Kingdom's Security Service, better known as MI5.

So far, the team of analysts knew little. At 19:23 the prior evening, a male 999 caller reported a man lying injured alongside the Falls Road near the junction with Clonard Street. The man died of a bullet to the head before police arrived. There were no known witnesses. The detective inspector on scene reported the victim's mobile received a single call from a secretary at Clonard Monastery, who declined to speak with police. MI5 interrogators

72

were now en route to change her mind. A digital forensics analysis completed overnight concluded the victim's mobile phone was remotely erased while in police custody.

An MI5 surveillance team was a block away and heard a shot at the approximate time of the murder but saw nothing. CCTV cameras captured moderate vehicular traffic in the area but nothing unusual, and analysts were compiling a list of the observed number plates for review. The surveillance log showed a call placed at 20:16 to "Mongoose," a deep cover MI5 operative who gathered intelligence within the dissident community. Mongoose, whose identity was known only to the director and deputy director, was scheduled to meet Fr. Clark just fifteen minutes after the priest was gunned down. MI5 years earlier had dropped arms smuggling charges against the cleric in exchange for his cooperation as an informer.

Since then, the priest helped foil several IRA attacks, facilitated MI5's infiltration of IRA factions, and helped identify persons responsible for half a dozen unsolved crimes from The Troubles. Last night, Mongoose planned to extract Fr. Clark to an MI5 safe house after the priest signaled his cover was blown.

The extraction of such a high-value informer warranted extra caution, so a surveillance team was dispatched to watch for anything unusual in the area before or during the encounter. At the time of the murder, Mongoose was ensconced in a fish and chips shop several blocks away waiting for the surveillance team to declare the area safe. Instead, they reported Fr. Clark was a no-show.

Now, MI5 leadership was panicked. The murder of a high-level IRA informer just minutes before his extraction to an MI5 safe house was an unlikely coincidence, and evidence had been compromised almost immediately after it was seized. *Was there a leak in the security service? Had the IRA infiltrated MI5? Was Mongoose exposed? How was Clark's cooperation discovered?* The team of analysts raced to find the answers.

THE CHURCH OFFICE

THE TWO INTERROGATORS FROM MI5 HEADED NORTH on Clonard Gardens and turned right onto a gravel drive just south of the monastery. The drive curved behind the church and ended at a car park. The male operative pulled into an open space as his female colleague surveyed their surroundings. They were at the heart of IRA territory.

The couple exited the sedan and walked toward the main entrance to the building. They posed as PSNI inspectors to conceal MI5's interest in Fr. Clark's death and had an appointment to speak with Ruth McGowan about her call to the cleric on the night of his murder. The real inspectors were directed to stay away.

Ruth McGowan met them at the bottom of the church steps. The interrogators introduced themselves as DI Timothy James and DI Lisa Redmon. They offered their condolences and asked to go inside and have a private chat. They were mostly concerned about their own privacy and avoiding any IRA lookouts with cameras.

"Where's the other fella?" Mrs. McGowan asked as she led the couple up the stairs and into the sanctuary. She was on the waiting list for a knee replacement and moved gingerly.

"Who would that be?" James replied.

"You know, the inspector I spoke to on the phone. What was his name?"

James was caught off guard, but Redmon had a photographic memory and saved him. "DI Nichols," she answered.

"That's it. He had a kind voice. I was hopin' to thank him for his understanding."

Neither James nor Redmon fell for the sweet old lady routine, but they played along in hopes McGowan would let her guard down. Once inside the church office, they closed the door and got to the point. "We know this is a difficult time for you, but we need to ask you some very direct questions," Redmon began. "Who had a motive to kill Fr. Clark?"

"I can hardly believe he's gone. He was a gentle soul. But we did have a wee bit of trouble over the Reconciliation meetings. A few fellas were unhappy with Father for hostin' them here at the church. I wish I could remember their names for you, but at my age…" She shrugged with a grin.

Redmon sensed she was toying with them and had no intention of cooperating, but she continued the questioning.

"Why did you call Fr. Clark on the night he was killed?" Redmon asked.

"He was scheduled to baptize the Miller baby the next morning, but the wee 'un fell ill and the parents wanted to postpone it."

"And after you spoke with DI Nichols, what did you do?"

"Well, I called the Monsignor to tell him the awful news, and also the Millers."

"Who else, Mrs. McGowan?" Redmon's tone changed slightly.

McGowan hesitated. She could not remember if she called to warn Mickey Shanahan on her personal mobile, which the police could check, or the church phone, which anyone could have used. She gambled and said, "No one that I recall, Inspector."

Redmon pounced. "How do you know Mickey Shanahan?"

The church lady silently cursed herself for being careless on her mobile phone and struggled to think of a safe response. "Mickey Shanahan? The name sounds familiar but I can't quite place it," she said, stalling. "Is he a parishioner here? We have hundreds, you know." She remembered her training. Admit nothing.

Redmon recognized her discomfort and pressed ahead. "You called him immediately after you spoke to DI Nichols, and talked for just over five minutes, so don't tell me it was a wrong number."

McGowan had to think quickly. If they knew about her call to Shanahan, they might also know he came to the church later that evening. She needed to link the two events in a plausible way. Otherwise, increased scrutiny could endanger the whole crew. "Oh, would he be the fella that lives by Divis Tower?"

"He is," Redmon confirmed.

"Then he must be the fella whose wallet I found outside the church. It had his business card with a mobile number on it. In all the commotion about Fr. Clark's death, it must have slipped my mind." The grin returned to her face.

"You want us to believe the moment you learned of Fr. Clark's death, your first thought was the fella whose wallet you found outside the church?"

That's precisely what I want you to believe, you fuckin' Tan. Aloud, she said, "I knew immediately life around here would be turnin' hectic over Father's death, and I didn't want that poor fella to be forgotten and without his wallet. Like I told you, I called the Millers, too, about the wee 'un's baptism."

Redmon knew it was a lost cause. The woman had no intention of telling them anything useful. Redmon stood and extended her hand. "Thank you for your time. We'll let you get back to work."

McGowan accepted the handshake and said, "Thank you, dear. Good luck with your investigation. I hope you catch whoever did this." It was her first sincere comment to the pair.

"Good day, ma'am," James said curtly as he followed his partner out the door without offering his hand.

THE PRISON PSYCHOLOGIST

THREE DAYS AFTER HIS TOUR OF WEST BELFAST, Thornton sat in a cold, damp, poorly lit office at HM Prison Maghaberry waiting for the prisoner to arrive. A single exposed fluorescent tube hummed irritatingly overhead. There were no windows apart from a small observation port in the door. The furniture consisted of a metal table bolted to the floor and two metal chairs tethered to the wall by chains to prevent their use as weapons. It was his first time in a prison since the white supremacist murdered Officer Grace. Thornton involuntarily rubbed his arms and fought to keep the memories of West Virginia at bay.

The psychologist was here as a consultant for the Northern Ireland Prison Service and the Parole Commissioners of Northern Ireland. His father-in-law, Robert Inglesby, was influential in law enforcement and correctional circles and persuaded the necessary officials to grant Thornton the position on a temporary basis at a discounted rate of pay.

The Parole Commission had a backlog of pending cases and was under political pressure to reduce the number of Republican and Loyalist paramilitaries still incarcerated, to elicit goodwill from both sides and help "preserve the peace." The amnesty already set a precedent for releasing violent offenders, but senior officials remained wary of putting known murderers back on the streets lest they kill again and embarrass the government. An American psychologist with correctional experience was qualified to serve as an evaluator and would make a convenient scapegoat, if needed.

Thornton understood the risk, but his curiosity overcame all hesitation. *How many American psychologists get the opportunity to work closely with inmates from Northern Ireland's most notorious prison?* In any event, he needed to log a respectable number of clinical hours in Northern Ireland to build credibility as a newly established private practitioner. In the back of his mind, he suspected the university would offer Claire a permanent position. He needed a long-term plan of his own and was eager to ingratiate himself with the penal system.

Footsteps approached and the door opened. Two guards escorted a distinguished-looking, athletic, white-haired man with unusually blue eyes into the room and sat him on the only available chair. Thornton nodded to the guards as a sign they could leave the room. When the door locked shut, he sat alone with Liam O'Malley, the IRA's most notorious killer.

THE AMERICAN

THORNTON INTRODUCED HIMSELF.

O'Malley was startled by the American accent. "Are they plannin' to ship me to America then?"

Thornton smiled. "No, Mr. O'Malley. Not yet anyway."

"A darn shame," O'Malley replied. "I've never been." He liked being called Mr. O'Malley.

Thornton explained his role as a consultant who advised prison officials on an inmate's suitability for parole. "From what I've read in your file, you've led a very violent life."

Anger flashed across O'Malley's face. "You've only heard one side of the story."

"Tell me your side then."

"What's the point? You've already made up yer mind."

Thornton studied O'Malley for a moment. "To be fair, I did say, 'from what I've read in your file.' Is the file wrong?"

O'Malley was unnerved, not by the question but by the American asking it. Ordinarily, O'Malley had nothing but contempt for the usual British interrogators and government lackeys, but he saw the psychologist in a different light. True, he was working for the government, but O'Malley somehow sensed Thornton might not be entirely on the government's side. "How long have ya been in Northern Ireland, Doc?"

Thornton hesitated. "I moved here a month ago."

O'Malley burst out laughing. "Ya don't say? A month ago? Shite! You don't understand how *anythin'* works then, do ya?"

Thornton bristled but said, "No, I don't, Mr. O'Malley. So tell me what I need to know."

O'Malley stopped laughing and leaned forward. "How much time have ya got?"

THE DEAL

THORNTON STAYED WITH O'MALLEY FOR NINETY MINUTES before the COs returned him to his cell. By necessity, Thornton at the outset tackled the standard list of questions for a first meeting. O'Malley remained cautious during that initial phase and declined to say anything about his childhood or family. The only symptom he acknowledged was difficulty sleeping. However, he seemed uncomfortable when asked about significant losses, feelings of guilt, or repetitive or intrusive thoughts. Thornton made a note to return to those themes during a subsequent session.

Once he dispensed with the clinical questions, Thornton opened the floor to O'Malley. "I appreciate you helping me with the required paperwork. Now, for the rest of our time together, tell me what you want me to know."

O'Malley looked at the floor and remained still. When he finally looked up, it was like someone flipped a switch. "I'm not a bad man," he said softly.

It was a common theme among inmates. Thornton nodded and encouraged O'Malley to elaborate.

"I probably did most of the things they accuse me of in that file. The shootings and the killings and the bombings. To be honest, I don't know how many people I've hurt, although it had to be done. The Brits weren't goin' to leave us alone or get out of Ireland if we didn't stand up for ourselves. And they're hypocrites. The Brits are responsible for just as many people being murdered or maimed. But they had a police force and an army and the government on their side, and we had only ourselves. All I did was stand up for me people, who were being mistreated."

Thornton wanted to keep the focus on O'Malley and asked, "Is there anything about your life you *do* regret?"

O'Malley shook his head and forcefully exhaled. "Yer askin' a lot, Doc."

"We can come back to it another time. There *is* a question I have to ask now, and I think you'll agree it's a fair one. Given the shootings and the killings and the bombings you've already acknowledged, how do I know you won't commit more of them after you're released?"

"I didn't shoot anyone or make any bombs the *last* time I was released. I just needed a place to stay the night. I honestly didn't know the stuff was in the house. And besides, what's to be gained now from more shootings and bombings? The Brits are still here. Ireland is still divided. It didn't work the first time, and at this point in me life I just want to enjoy me remaining years outside of a prison."

It sounded reasonable, and Thornton wanted to believe him. But inmates are extremely manipulative, and this was only his first interaction with the IRA man. "What are you willing to do to prove you've abandoned the violence and won't return to it?"

O'Malley considered his answer carefully. "What if I meet with ya every week after I'm released? If I don't show up or ya think there's something wrong, ya can send me back here."

The idea appealed to Thornton, but he suspected O'Malley knew all the right things to say. "It's a good start. Is there anything else you can think of that would be a more visible demonstration of your commitment?"

O'Malley struggled to come up with something. He knew his release depended on it. Then it hit him. "Have ya heard about the Reconciliation meetings, Doc?"

THE DEBRIEFING

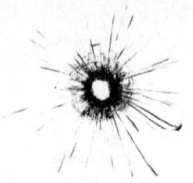

THE GUARDS ESCORTED O'MALLEY BACK TO ROE HOUSE after his meeting with Thornton. Patrick Linden, ever suspicious of outsiders, waited there to debrief him.

"So they've not sent ya to the loony bin," Linden said wryly.

"He said I'm already in it." O'Malley winked. "He seemed alright, Paddy. I don't think he's a bad fella. American, so he is."

"American? What the fuck is an American doin' here askin' ya questions? Tell me everything he wanted to know." Linden was even more suspicious now.

"He seemed mostly concerned about me goin' back to buildin' bombs when I get out. He wanted to talk about me childhood and me family, but I didn't give him anything."

"What else?" Linden pressed.

"He asked a lot of strange stuff. Like if I sleep well, or have nightmares, or mood swings, or trouble eatin'. I didn't see the point of it."

Linden sat quietly for a minute, trying to figure out what the psychologist was up to. "How much did he already know about ya?"

"He had a whole file on me, Paddy. A big, thick one. He said that's where he read about the people I killed and the bombings.

But he wasn't like those British bastards. He actually wanted to know *why* I did it and didn't seem to hate me fer it."

"And the killings? The bombings? What did he want to know about them?"

"That's just it, Paddy. Nothin'. He said he already knew what was in the file and wanted to hear *me* side of the story. Like I said, he seemed alright."

Linden was unimpressed. "Yer being naïve, mate. How did an American end up lookin' at yer file and askin' ya questions just as yer about to leave here?"

"He said he's advisin' the Parole Commission on whether it's okay to release people like me. He's only been in Belfast a month, Paddy. How much of a threat can he be?" A shadow of doubt flitted across O'Malley's face.

"It seems too convenient. Think on it. A newly arrived American shows up just as one of the IRA's most celebrated paramilitaries is up for parole. He magically gets assigned to the Parole Commission and then tries to befriend ya while posin' as a psychologist. If ya ask me, he's workin' undercover for the Brits and plannin' to trick ya into revealing secrets." Linden let the words sink in before asking, "So what happens next?"

O'Malley told Linden about his pledge to meet Thornton once a week and attend monthly Reconciliation meetings as conditions of his parole.

Linden grew agitated. What if this was all a scheme to get O'Malley to give up information on *Linden*? The Brits would love nothing more than to keep the head of Roe House Council locked up for life. "Christ, Uilliam. He's settin' ya up to look weak to the movement with those Reconciliation meetings. And he'll be spyin' on us with the office visits."

"Paddy, it's me yer talkin' to. I'm not a fool, and I'm no tout. The doc won't learn shite from me. And the Reconciliation meetings will help to convince the Brits I'm not a danger. Anyway, I don't have a choice, do I, if I want out of here?"

Linden understood Thornton and the Brits held all the strings, but he still did not like the conditions of O'Malley's release. O'Malley knew too much, and Linden worried the psychologist might find other ways to pressure him. He wanted to know more about the American and decided to have him watched. "Yer right, mate. Yer more valuable to me on the outside. Stick to the conditions of yer release, but do not trust the American fella. Understood?"

"Aye, Paddy. Ya have nothin' to worry about from me."

LINDEN'S MOTIVATION

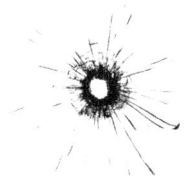

PATRICK LINDEN RETREATED TO HIS CELL in a foul mood after the debrief. He wanted to believe it was apprehension about the psychologist's intentions, but deep down he knew he was envious of O'Malley too.

Maghaberry was an awful place. Linden wore a brave face to inspire his men and deny the Brits the satisfaction of knowing he hated it there. As head of the Roe House Council, Linden enjoyed more privileges than his fellow inmates. Still, if given the chance, he would leave in an instant. Relinquishing his role on the Council would be easy—he could wield even more influence from the outside, where most of the action remained.

Linden was a strategist and a combatant at heart. Being sidelined in prison all these years robbed him of his purpose in life—to avenge his younger brother's death and drive the Brits from Ireland forever. He learned as a youth never to trust the government or the military, and he was not about to fall for the American's ruse.

Patrick's brother, Sean, was only fourteen when British soldiers broke into the house in Derry where Sean was watching the telly with friends while truant from school. The soldiers meant to raid the home next door, where a known IRA man lived, but confused the addresses.

89

One of Sean's friends cursed at the Brits and yelled for them to get out. He was struck on the head with the butt of a rifle and suffered a seizure.

When Sean went to aid his friend, a sergeant tried to restrain him. Sean jerked his arm from the sergeant's grasp and accidentally struck a third soldier on the cheek with his elbow. The army men descended on Sean in a pack, beat him to the ground, and kicked him in the torso and head with their boots until he lay motionless.

An hour passed before they called an ambulance for either boy. By then, it was too late for Sean, who bled to death from a ruptured spleen.

The official report filed by the officer in charge covered up the Army's mistake. It falsely claimed the soldiers responded to an anonymous tip about guns and explosives in the house where Sean died. None were found, of course. The boys' truancy and "aggression" were cited as evidence of IRA sympathies though, and that was sufficient to exonerate the soldiers. They were back on patrol less than forty-eight hours after the raid.

The entire Catholic community of Derry turned up for Sean's funeral. Exactly one month later, the British Army officer who submitted the false account turned the ignition of his car and detonated a blast that killed him, his wife, and his two daughters in a massive fireball. The next afternoon, Patrick Linden found a blank clasp envelope in the post. Inside were before and after photographs of the Army officer's vehicle. Scrawled across the latter photo were the words, For Sean. Patrick volunteered for the IRA the very next day. His mother gave no objection.

Sean became a martyr to Derry's Catholic community, and Patrick consequently was too well known there to be of any use to the Provos. They assigned him instead to the Belfast brigade, where his intellect, charisma, and zeal impressed the leadership. They tasked him with recruiting other young talent in the Catholic neighborhoods around IRA headquarters in Clonard.

For six weeks after his arrival in the district, Patrick observed local residents and sized them up for recruitment. He was careful to exclude braggarts who might boast of their connections and jeopardize the movement. He was also wary of touts recruited by the British to infiltrate the IRA and inform on its operations.

Infiltrators were typically brought in from other cities and towns where they ran afoul of the law but agreed to inform on the IRA in exchange for leniency. They were of no use in their hometowns, where their arrests would cast doubt on their loyalty. So they were often sent to Belfast, where it was easier to maintain a cover story despite their non-local accents. As a result, Patrick recruited only local residents with deep roots in the neighborhood.

Patrick liked to observe potential recruits in action. Whenever banging pots and bin lids signaled a British advance, Patrick took to the streets in search of conflict. He watched from the sidelines to see who knew his way around the neighborhood, moved stealthily, and reacted quickly. He looked for young men and women who were charming, persuasive, and calm under pressure. Most of all, he assessed each candidate's animosity toward the Brits and the reasons for it. A personal motivation to fight ranked highly on the list of desirable qualities.

That's why Patrick Linden was studying Liam O'Malley on that chaotic afternoon when a British Saracen crushed Liam's sister in the middle of Oranmore Street. The two boys bonded quickly over the shared loss of a younger sibling at the hands of the British Army. Each of them lost his father too—Liam's to alcohol, and Patrick's to a car crash.

They became both surrogate sibling and protector to one another. And like siblings, they developed a rivalry that fueled competition and a craving for approval from their adoptive fathers in the IRA. Liam and Patrick looked so much alike and spent so much time together that *everyone came to believe they were blood brothers. It was a kinship born of bombs and bullets, and it had lasted nearly forty years so far.*

Linden sat brooding in his cell and recalled their exploits together. It seemed unfair that O'Malley alone was eligible for early release. O'Malley himself could not explain it, even after talking to the psychologist. Linden's envy again edged toward anxiety. O'Malley had been at Linden's side his entire adult life and literally knew where the bodies were buried. *What if...?*

Linden caught himself. *Not a chance. He'd never turn.* Linden felt guilty for entertaining the possibility. But Linden was nothing if not cautious, and he decided to have his men outside the prison watch the American *and* O'Malley, just to be safe.

THE COCKY ROOSTER

KIERAN OLIVER STRODE UP TO THE COCKY ROOSTER on the corner of Shankill Road and Tennent Street as if the place were named for him. A Union Jack fluttered over the entrance alongside the flag of Ulster, and a memorial to deceased Loyalist fighters stood several feet from the door in an open-air patio filled with wooden picnic tables. Several strings of miniature British flags snapped noisily in the wind above the tables.

At one end of the patio stood a decorative arch with a large purple banner that proclaimed *UVF 1912* in large orange letters alongside an oval crest with a red hand at the center, encircled with the words *For God and Ulster*. The stout, surly man sat at his usual table, smoking a cigar. He stared hard at a Chinese tourist who snapped photographs from a passing black taxi tour.

Kieran greeted the guard and entered the pub eager to find his UVF mates. The Cocky Rooster had been a popular Loyalist hangout since before The Troubles began. For a brief time in the 1970s, it even served as headquarters for the UVF, one of several Loyalist paramilitary groups in Belfast. The modern UVF was formed in 1966 as a sworn enemy of the IRA and to ensure Northern Ireland remained part of the UK. Its founder,

Gusty Spence, was a former military police sergeant in the British army. A framed photo of Spence, wearing aviator sunglasses and a black cap, still hung on the wall behind the bar.

The air inside smelled of whiskey, stale beer, and men. At a corner table in the back, beneath a television, sat Kieran's crew. The sound from the telly helped to deter eavesdroppers. Kieran headed in their direction, eager to boast about the priest's murder, when he realized Garth Peters, the crew boss, had started the meeting already. Kieran slid into an open chair just as Peters shared news from Maghaberry Prison.

"Ya won't believe the shite I heard from our man McAllister," Peters began. Garrett McAllister was a guard at Maghaberry Prison and a longtime supporter of the UVF and Loyalist causes. "The government's plannin' to release that cunt Liam O'Malley, can ya believe it? He'll be out 'fore the weekend. McAllister escorted the prick to an appointment with the prison psychologist and overheard them talkin'."

Kieran did not recognize the name, but it was clear from the older men's reactions they had a strong dislike for O'Malley. Peters noticed Kieran's confusion and explained, "O'Malley was probably the IRA's best bomb maker. The security services say he used the most sophisticated detonators and timing devices ever seen during The Troubles. There's no tellin' how many innocents he murdered. He blew up a couple pubs on this very street, so he did."

As the rest of the men nodded, Kieran felt his anger rising. "Then why the fuck are they lettin' the cunt out?!"

"The government's gone soft on terrorism," answered Peters' second-in-command. "They're all 'bout 'maintainin' the peace' and 'Reconciliation' and all that shite. And sure as I'm talkin' to ya right now, they'll fuck us all with this Brexit shite."

"Yer not wrong," said a third man at the table, who bore a striking resemblance to Prince Philip. "There's talk they may be releasin' some of *our* men too, Garth. What do them prison boys know about that?"

"I've heard the same rumors, Ian. That's why Loyalist leaders aren't protestin' the dissident releases too loudly. We want our men back as well. I don't mind tellin' ya I think *we* can deal with those IRA bastards more effectively once they're back on the streets."

There was a loud chorus of approval from the group that momentarily drew the attention of other patrons in the bar. They quickly averted their eyes when they saw who made the commotion.

Peters lowered his voice and leaned forward to signal he had something sensitive to pass along. "Listen 'ere. I want youse to keep yer ears open for any loose talk. There was an unsanctioned hit a couple nights ago. A Catholic priest on the Falls Road. Turns out the security services were tailin' him in connection with something big, and now their whole operation is fucked. An old friend of mine had a hand in it and asked me to find out what I can. Let me know if youse hear who's responsible."

Prince Philip's twin looked at Kieran and said, "Are ya alright, wee 'un? Ya don't look well."

"I got pissed last night, is all," Kieran said weakly.

CARRICK-A-REDE

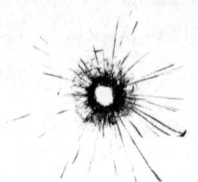

IT WAS A BUSY MONTH, and Claire nearly forgot her husband's birthday. Guiltily, she marked the occasion with a surprise getaway for the couple. Thornton was a huge fan of *Game of Thrones*, which frequently shot on location in Northern Ireland. Claire booked a full-day tour of the show's film sites, knowing it would also be a great opportunity to use the new camera she gifted him.

The fantasy genre did not appeal to Claire, and she disliked the violent aspects of the series. Still, she knew Thornton would be thrilled to walk in the footsteps of the Starks and Lannisters. Her husband had indulged the couple's move to Belfast, and Claire was keen to reciprocate. Thornton burst into a grin and hugged his wife when she showed him the tickets.

The next morning, they boarded a coach filled with mostly foreign tourists. To Claire's relief, the group declined the driver's invitation to don costumes from the show. Claire suspected her husband would have joined the silliness, and frankly she was glad to be spared any photos of her dressed as the Mother of Dragons or Brienne of Tarth. But she kept those thoughts to herself.

It was a perfect day to be outside. The bus made several stops along the Antrim coast that, while beautiful, were unrecognizable to Claire as scenes from the television program. Thornton, on the other hand, knew every location without any help from the driver. Claire dutifully posed with her husband for the obligatory photos at each stop and simply enjoyed that the love of her life was having so much fun.

After a 45-minute stay at the Giant's Causeway—Northern Ireland's most popular tourist destination—the driver announced Carrick-a-Rede as the next stop. Thornton sensed something and asked if Claire was alright.

"Carrick-a-Rede is a rope bridge, hon, that stretches over the sea between two cliffs."

Thornton nodded knowingly. Claire had a paralyzing fear of heights.

The coach coasted into an open slot at the car park. Claire took Thornton's hand, and they filed off the bus behind a French-speaking family. After a few minutes' walk, the group reached a tall, metal stairwell that descended to the crossing. The rope bridge was single-file and looked barely two feet wide. It stood ten stories above the water and stretched seventy-five feet to the other side.

"Claire, I don't want your day ruined. We don't have to do this."

"No, no. I knew it was part of the tour when I signed up. If those little boys can do it, so can I." She laughed as she pointed to the French twins who charged ahead of them.

The rules allowed only eight people on the bridge at one time, and wardens at either end of it controlled the flow of traffic. As the couple neared the edge of the cliff, Claire saw the nets that formed the sides of the bridge had openings large enough for limbs to pass through. The floor was nothing more than two parallel wood planks, on either side of which extended a few more inches of netting. One slip, she thought, would easily thrust someone into a terrifying entanglement.

Claire caught her husband's sideways glance. "I'll be fine," she said. "Just stay right behind me and give me a shove if you need to."

"Keep your eyes fixed on the horizon as you cross, and don't look down. I'll be two steps behind you."

When her turn came, Claire hesitated. Then she grabbed the rope handrails, looked straight ahead, and began to cross. The couple were a third of the way over when the French twins, about twenty-five feet ahead, gleefully jumped up and down a couple times before their parents sternly admonished them. The movement, in combination with a sudden wind, made the bridge bounce and sway. Claire stopped, but only long enough for the boys to reach the other side. She made it the rest of the way without incident.

Thornton gave Claire a congratulatory hug before the couple found a scenic spot to watch the parade of people. The pair often made a game of guessing an individual's occupation or the state of a couple's relationship. This time, though, Claire noticed Thornton focused on the antics of the French youngsters and the unique way twins communicate. She knew they reminded him of Officer Grace's boys. Thornton wanted children of his own—and Claire hoped to avoid any more conversation on the topic.

As if on cue, Thornton asked, "When do you suppose *we'll* get around to having kids?"

"One change at a time, love. We've only just moved here and started new jobs." Motherhood was an uncomfortable topic for Claire, and she knew at some point she would have to explain her reluctance to have children. But that would mean revealing the only secret she ever kept from Thornton, and it would hurt him deeply.

Thornton bowed his head slightly and said, "You're right. There's a lot to think about before we start our own clan."

Claire squeezed his hand and swallowed her guilt. "Speaking of new jobs, tell me how things are shaping up. We've barely had time to speak the past few weeks."

Thornton described the taxi tour and his visit to the prison, without divulging any details. He told her about his plans for the grand opening and the government jobs that would provide income while he grew the practice. He also mentioned how excited he was to resume meaningful work.

Claire saw that he was happy, and her conscience eased a bit.

The couple jumped up when they realized their group had crossed the bridge to return to the bus. On the way back, Thornton checked the brochure and discovered that Hedge Row was the final stop. "That's the Kingsroad," he exclaimed. "Can you believe it? We're going to walk the actual Kingsroad from *Game of Thrones!*"

Claire laughed at her goofy husband and leaned into his shoulder. She held his hand and prayed he would never leave her.

A SISTER'S TORMENT

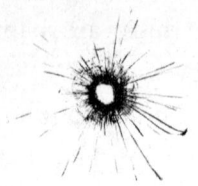

THE TOUR BUS ARRIVED IN BELFAST shortly after seven o'clock. Despite the long day, Claire convinced Thornton to walk home and grab some takeaway en route. There was a chippy around the corner from their flat. Claire ordered the fish, and Thornton opted for chicken tenders with a large portion of the thick, chewy French fries he liked. Claire rolled her eyes playfully when her husband refused to call them "chips."

It took them fifteen minutes to devour the meal at the kitchen table. Neither had the energy to go out for a drink, so they opted to watch television. From the outset, Claire good-naturedly vetoed *Game of Thrones* and voted instead for *Fleabag*. Thornton pitched *Line of Duty*. In the end, they watched both programs and a news broadcast before going to bed and falling promptly asleep.

Two hours later, Claire awoke trembling and terrified. The nightmare returned out of nowhere. Her eyes darted toward Thornton, but thankfully he remained asleep.

Claire stared at the ceiling, fighting back tears. *No, no, no! I can't do this again.* It was a dream she last had in grammar school. It was more a memory than a dream, about her sister's death. Claire wondered if it was triggered by the evening's news about a New IRA bomb the police defused near a youth club. Or possibly the talk with Thornton about having kids.

The sisters, aged 4 and 7, were on their way home from nursery with their father when he got an urgent message on his pager. He stopped the car to run inside a pub and make a call. Before exiting the vehicle, he turned and spoke sternly to Claire. "Stay in the car and mind yer sister. I'll be back straight away. Do not get out of the car."

Courtney played with her new Paddington Bear while Claire glanced through the car window at the busy street. The elder girl spotted a sweet shop nearby and, forgetting her promise to her father, decided to have a look at the display. She stood wide-eyed on the sidewalk, staring at the candies for sale, when she heard the car door shut. Claire turned to see Courtney and Paddington Bear headed in the opposite direction, past Sheehan's furniture store, in pursuit of an old lady with a puppy. Claire opened her mouth to call out to her sister, but a deafening explosion silenced her.

Courtney disappeared under a mound of rubble. Claire stood immobile on the sidewalk, hands clasped to her ears, trembling and howling in fright. She heard adults yelling and screaming in the distance, and dogs barking. From her perspective, the smoke and dust looked like fog, and she thought it was snowing when ash and other fine particles floated to the ground around her. A clerk from the sweet shop tried to pick Claire up and bring her inside, but Claire screamed and twisted out of her grasp. She ran in the direction her sister went but then hesitated alongside the smoldering mess until she saw Paddington Bear ahead to the right, leaning against a bin. She ran to him, held him in a hug, and froze again when she spotted bodies lying in the roadway. She clutched the bear tighter, bent over, and wailed.

Suddenly Claire felt her father scoop her and Paddington Bear into the air. He carried them across the road and around the corner of a nearby building. She was relieved to get away from the commotion.

Claire looked at her father while he stroked her hair and tried to comfort her. Once her sobbing eased, he asked her gently, "Did you see where Courtney went, luv?"

Claire looked down and remained silent.

"It's alright, luv. Just tell me what ya saw," her father said encouragingly.

Claire avoided her father's eyes but pointed toward the scene of the bombing. "The building fell on top of her."

Claire and her father hugged tightly as they leaned against the side of the building. "Can we go look for her, Daddy?"

Inglesby's voice faltered. "I'd like to, luv, but we have to go. Do you remember daddy got a call on his pager? That was daddy's office tellin' us we need to leave cuz it's not safe to be here."

"But what about Courtney?"

Claire's father bowed his head for a moment. Then he looked up and said, "The policemen are goin' to look for her while I take you home, luv."

Claire's fists gripped her father's coat as he hustled her farther away from the carnage and any remaining danger. She studied his face and saw beads of sweat leave wet trails as they descended to his jawline. His breathing sounded loud to her, and his aftershave smelled stronger up close. When Claire hugged her father tighter, she felt his whiskers brush her face. She did not understand why they could not go back for Courtney.

Claire never had to answer questions from the authorities about the bombing. Her father also suppressed in the media any mention or photographs of her at the scene. A deadly attack on the family of a security services official would put a spotlight on them and embolden Republican paramilitaries. So as far as the world knew, Claire and her father were somewhere else when the IRA bombed Sheehan's furniture store. Courtney was listed as a casualty under her mother's maiden name; Inglesby had insisted the girls not take his surname for safety reasons.

MI5 was unable to confirm the intended target of the bomb, but Claire later realized her father's undercover work and frequent meetings at the local UVF headquarters were obvious considerations.

Claire never had a chance to process the trauma of that day. Her father taught her to avoid all mention of the event, her family, or her father's work for the government. Belfast was a small town, and Inglesby already had a target on his back. Fear for her father's safety, and her own, forced Claire into emotional isolation. To her, it was normal and natural. She never knew anything different. Over and over throughout her life, her father reminded her—no one else could ever know. Not even now— not even Thornton.

Her father was Claire's only possible confidant. Wracked with guilt, she tried once to talk with him about what happened but immediately saw how the conversation pained him. Reluctant to upset him any further, she never brought it up again. From that point forward, Inglesby incorrectly interpreted Claire's silence, almost gratefully, as a sign she had "moved on." In fact, she was walled off, isolated in guilt, with no outlet for her grief.

On rare occasions, when the pent-up emotion threatened to break free, Claire longed for her mother. Not *her* mother so much as *a* mother. Claire thought it was strange to miss someone she barely remembered—the woman who abandoned her husband and two small children, never to be heard from again. Her mother's abandonment was even more painful than Courtney's murder, so Claire blocked it, too, from her consciousness.

For the most part, she succeeded. Claire's graduation from high school and college were the first milestone events to breach her defenses and expose her mother's absence. Claire's marriage triggered the next emotional assault and forced her through a gauntlet of questions about the "mother of the bride." Claire swatted them away with the same terse response: "She won't be coming to the wedding." But sure enough, memory of her mother showed up anyway as an unwelcome guest on Claire's big day.

Now Claire lay in bed, staring at the ceiling with the bed sheet clenched in her fists. Years of pent-up emotions suddenly fought for attention. Guilt, grief, and abandonment collided with fear, anger, and resentment. She wanted to lash out at her mother *and* her father, and Thornton too. She couldn't make sense of the turmoil in her head. A lifetime of carefully cultivated and perfected defense mechanisms now seemed likely to fail her. *I'm not fit to be a mother. I'm losing control and probably Aaron too. My work and reputation will be ruined. Everything I've worked so hard for in life will be gone.* Claire's thoughts spiraled toward catastrophe. "Oh, God, what is *wrong* with me?"

Claire spoke the last sentence aloud and was startled to hear her husband reply, "Absolutely nothing is wrong with you, love. It was just a bad dream." He reached across to pull her tight to his side and kissed her gently on the forehead. "I'm here, hun. Go back to sleep. Everything's okay."

For the first time in Claire's life, she doubted him.

THE NUMBER PLATES

EARLY MONDAY MORNING, Robert Inglesby strode into the office suite at Palace Barracks with a box of warm pastries from the bakery near his home. He barely had time to set them on the table in the reception area. Inglesby's administrative assistant alerted him straight away the director was already asking for another update on the Clark murder. Inglesby thanked her and exited the suite.

Two floors down, Section 6 ran a control center with links to every government-installed CCTV camera in Northern Ireland. If needed, and with proper authorization, the center also could tap into any privately installed security camera connected to Wi-Fi. More impressive, from Inglesby's perspective, was the Section's ability to identify faces from the footage and trace individuals' movements. They could also track number plates.

Inglesby wanted to know what the Section learned over the weekend about the people and vehicles in the area before and after the priest's murder. Ordinarily, such narrowly focused intelligence was produced within a couple hours, but a bug in the newly installed software delayed the results.

The Section chief hurriedly exited her private office when

she saw Inglesby enter the cubicle bay where analysts worked. "Good morning, sir. How can I help?"

"I'd like to see the preliminary list of number plates for the Clark case, as well as the facial recognition results."

"We can do even better, sir, and give you the final analysis," the chief said proudly. "The staff came in early today to finish it once the server rebooted after the patch."

"The results are preliminary until I say otherwise, isn't that right?" Inglesby asked.

"Of course, sir." The Section chief looked chagrined. "I only meant to say the *Section's* analysis was finished."

A tired-looking but smartly dressed young man at a nearby cubicle handed the Section chief a folder. She, in turn, passed it to Inglesby. He opened the file and flipped through the pages. Facial matches for known and suspected criminals were always placed on top. There were only three. Inglesby recognized one of them immediately but concealed his apprehension. He turned to the single page of number plates and saw it lacked the usual vehicle descriptions. "I expect to see the number plates with the make, model, color, and owner of each vehicle included, please."

The smartly dressed analyst stammered an apology and handed back the correct version. He only recently transferred from another section and was still learning the correct protocols. Inglesby scanned the list of vehicles and spotted the white panel delivery van.

"Chief, delete this man and this vehicle from your lists, and then send final copies to me and the director. I'll forward them to the PSNI."

The newly transferred analyst objected. "But, sir, that compromises the integrity of—" The Section chief cut him off as other staff members tried to silence him with their eyes.

"That will be all, Hendrickson. Do as Mr. Inglesby instructed."

Inglesby locked eyes with the Section chief to register his displeasure at the junior staff member's challenge and left the suite without further comment.

Once Inglesby was safely out of earshot, the Section chief intentionally admonished Hendrickson in front of his peers. "Mr. Hendrickson, that was Robert Inglesby. He is MI5's director of undercover operations in Northern Ireland, and if he tells you to delete a number plate, or a facial match, or anything else from your report, you will do it. Immediately. Without question. Is that understood?"

"Yes, ma'am. I ap-ap-apologize."

Two floors up, Inglesby bit into an apple turnover and hoped the Section chief was not too hard on the poor analyst. But his thoughts quickly returned to Section 6's now-deleted identification of Kieran Oliver and the white panel van. He hoped to God "Crazy Kieran" wasn't responsible for the murder of MI5's most valuable informer.

PROXY

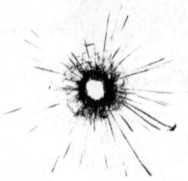

INGLESBY SAT IN HIS OFFICE BROODING over the discovery of Kieran Oliver near the scene of Fr. Clark's murder. Ever since Kieran turned eighteen, Inglesby had been running him as an MI5 "proxy"—someone involved, under the direction of an official handler, in matters with which the government could not legally or even politically be associated.

MI5's secret use of proxies was, Inglesby reluctantly acknowledged, in a "gray area." As a practical matter, though, undercover investigations and counterintelligence operations often benefited from the support of unsavory characters who could infiltrate criminal and terrorist organizations more easily and credibly than government agents. Inglesby and his colleagues sometimes found it expedient, in the interest of national security, to allow otherwise legal informers to become extrajudicial actors—encouraged to do things the government could not endorse but happily turned a blind eye to.

One of Inglesby's contacts inside the PSNI first told him about Kieran—a fearless serial offender with violent, antisocial traits and a rabid dislike for Republican paramilitaries. Inglesby reviewed Kieran's record and noted he was more than just a brute—he could actually be quite clever and resourceful, and he worked well alone. Kieran's emotions, though, sometimes got the best of him, and he was prone to boasting—two characteristics that were usually disqualifying in Inglesby's line of work. Still, Inglesby took a chance on Kieran, in part because he sensed there were no limits to what Kieran would do for the Loyalist cause.

So the next time Kieran was arrested—for a violent assault—Inglesby got a call from the PSNI and met privately with his pending recruit in a special interrogation room with no cameras or recording devices. There, Kieran agreed to do Inglesby's bidding in exchange for "unofficial immunity," as Inglesby called it, for all crimes except rape and murder. There were no written terms and no witnesses. Kieran would receive a generous monthly cash stipend and communicate only with Inglesby, using disposable mobiles delivered to a drop site every two weeks. Inglesby *claimed* to represent the PSNI's Organised Crime Branch, or OCB. If Kieran ever suspected the truth, he never let on.

Over the next ten years, Kieran stole cars for use in special operations, purchased weapons on the black market, broke into homes to search for contraband, tailed persons of interest, and otherwise spied on his friends and neighbors—all at Inglesby's behest, and all in support of the government's clandestine pursuits. Inglesby knew anyone who discovered Kieran's activities would simply assume he acted as an operative for Garth Peters' UVF crew at the Cocky Rooster.

In reality, Peters knew nothing of the arrangement between Kieran and Inglesby. Kieran understood the OCB would terminate the cash stipend, the unofficial immunity, and possibly Kieran himself if Peters—or anybody else, for that matter—ever learned of the arrangement.

Now Kieran and the van registered to him had been spotted on camera near the place where the government's most valuable informer was shot just minutes before his extraction to an MI5 safe house. Inglesby focused MI5's attention elsewhere by having Section 6 remove Kieran's name and vehicle from the intelligence report. But it would be harder to redirect the PSNI. Inglesby's contacts there generally informed him of developments *after* they occurred. If he tried to insert himself into an active PSNI investigation—especially one as sensitive and highly scrutinized as this one—he risked suspicion of his motives and more unwanted attention.

Dammit. If the PSNI's investigation led to Kieran, the lad might boast about his unofficial immunity and all the undercover assignments he completed for the OCB to worm his way out of trouble. If backed into a corner, Kieran would resort to self-preservation by any means. Inglesby was certain of it.

Kieran knew enough secrets to get Inglesby, MI5, and the British government into a *lot* of trouble. They were secrets Inglesby could not afford to have in the PSNI or the media's hands. He knew he had to keep Kieran quiet. The question was how best to do it.

THE TAIL

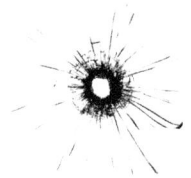

PATRICK LINDEN FOLDED A NEWSPAPER and placed it under the mattress in his cell. The article about Matthew Clark's murder weighed on him. The priest secretly remained a valuable member of the IRA while publicly appearing to support Reconciliation. His death would temporarily disrupt access to small arms and munitions from sources outside the UK—supplies used by the Provisional IRA to maintain order and legitimacy in Republican circles. But Linden knew the disruption would be short-lived. One of Clark's deputies would soon fill his shoes.

Of more lasting concern was the New IRA's increasing defiance of the Provisional IRA's leadership. The New IRA in Belfast was headed by Devin Dingle, a half-Irish and half-Chinese thug who the Provos derisively nicknamed "Dingleberry" after hearing the term used in an American movie. Dingleberry was flexing the New IRA's muscle with a growing network of criminal activities.

To protect their turf in West Belfast and maintain order in their neighborhoods, the New IRA were dispatching "enforcement units" to discipline anyone who disobeyed or challenged them. Consequently, there was a perception in some circles that the Provisional IRA was losing influence. Linden already took steps to reign in the upstarts, but now he worried the priest's murder might have been Dingleberry's handiwork and a more direct challenge to the Provos' supremacy. If true, Linden would have to take more drastic action.

Linden looked at his watch and saw it was 13:40. He had a visitor scheduled in twenty minutes. He changed into a dress shirt, put on a tie, and headed onto the landing. One of the screws blew a whistle to signal there were more than four inmates present, and the youngest of them quickly stepped back into his cell.

"I see ya still need four of youse to watch four of us," Linden said to the screw. "How's that wee 'un of yours, Officer Loftis? He's the spittin' image of ya."

Officer Noah Loftis locked eyes with the senior Provo to show he was not intimidated. The experienced guards knew that the DRs, or dissident Republicans, used various forms of psychological warfare to test for weakness. A favorite tactic was to let an officer know someone went to his house to observe his family.

Officer Loftis taunted Patrick with a smirk. "My, my, inmate. Don't ya look fancy in yer shirt and tie? Seein' a special fella at two o'clock, are ya?"

Linden winced. His contempt for the Brits was limitless, and it stung to be under their yoke. "Aye," he answered. "Been looking forward to it all week. We're gonna have a lovely chat about ya and yer mates at the King's Arms."

Officer Loftis' smirk became a sneer at the mention of his favorite pub. "Take this piece of shite to the visiting ward," he instructed a junior officer. "I need to toss his cell for contraband."

Linden maintained his composure as the junior officer escorted him downstairs. He knew there was nothing of concern in his cell, but it would take an hour to clean up the mess.

The junior officer stopped at the entrance to the visitor ward, swiped an electronic key card, and pressed his right hand up to a glass panel on the wall. The door clicked open, and Linden walked inside. At the opposite wall stood one empty chair and a table, where Mickey Shanahan sat waiting for him.

Visits were permitted to last an hour, but Linden launched straight into business. "Mickey, yer top priority this week is to find out who killed Matthew Clark. If it's Dingleberry's crew, I want ya on alert."

"On alert" meant to call an Active Service Unit to duty, in preparation for an armed operation. In this case, the ASU would come from outside Belfast so as not to be recognized by anyone loyal to the New IRA. Without proof of a Provo assault, the New IRA would hesitate to retaliate and escalate tensions further.

Linden continued his instructions. "In the meantime, send a bouquet of flowers to Dingleberry's mum"—code for a shotgun blast through the front door of a residence. A drive-by shooting at a residence or business in the Catholic community served as a final warning. Some of the old-timers preferred a kneecapping, but a gunshot to the knee required close proximity to the target and put the enforcer at greater risk.

Mickey took only mental notes and waited for the boss to continue.

"Now this next assignment stays between you, me, and whoever ya choose to carry it out. I want to know everything about the new prison psychologist assigned to Liam O'Malley. Everything. His work history, his family, who he meets with, *everything*. I want eyes on him as often as possible until I say otherwise. But Liam is not to know about it, understood?"

"Aye, boss. Consider it done. Anything else?"

"Aye, keep eyes on Liam, too, for his own protection."

Mickey nodded, and Linden stood to exit the room without shaking hands. Physical contact between a visitor and inmate was forbidden.

The junior officer waiting outside answered Linden's knock on the door. The pair headed back to Roe House, where Linden cleaned up his cell.

THE TRICOLOR PUB

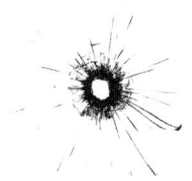

ON THE DAY OF HIS RELEASE, Liam O'Malley emerged unceremoniously through a side gate at HM Prison Maghaberry with trepidation. He had no idea what to expect. One of Linden's men waited across the road to give him a ride, and the pair chatted awkwardly as they drove toward West Belfast.

A group of current and former IRA paramilitaries and Republican sympathizers awaited them at the Tricolor Pub. O'Malley and his mates, like their families before them, had gathered there for decades. The throng of well-wishers, some wearing green, white, and orange face paint, erupted in song when O'Malley breached the doorway. Chants broke out, quoting lines from popular Republican anthems—"Ooh, ahh, up the 'RA" and "Every man will stand behind, the men behind the wire." Applause erupted as the crowd continued, "For eight hundred years, we've fought you without fear, and we'll fight you for eight hundred more."

O'Malley held his hands up to quiet the crowd, but it was futile. They were here for a party, and not even O'Malley could silence them. He broke into a wide grin, waved his arms in defeat, and the crowd carried on.

It was a hero's welcome, and despite the early hour, O'Malley drank round after free round. As word spread throughout Republican wards, the pub filled with well-wishers and those curious to lay eyes on the newly liberated IRA legend. The younger lads pressed O'Malley for stories of his exploits against the Brits, while his contemporaries vied to catch him up on the neighborhood news and politics.

It became a day-long affair and a target-rich environment for government spies. So a Republican security perimeter manned by IRA personnel extended two blocks in every direction to ensure only known locals passed through. Patrons had to clear a second checkpoint to enter the pub.

The adulation was at once flattering and off-putting to O'Malley. His social interactions had been limited to three people at a time for years, and he felt claustrophobic. He was equally uncomfortable with any talk of past adventures. Despite the countermeasures in place, the Brits were sure to have eyes and ears on the place to gather as much intelligence as possible about the people in attendance. At the same time, several New IRA members lurked in the corner, hoping for a private word with the legendary fighter—a conversation O'Malley was keen to avoid. As he warily surveyed the room, it dawned on him that The Troubles ended before half the clientele was born. "Cease-fire babies," his mates called them.

At one point, a broad-shouldered tough with white hair whispered something in O'Malley's ear. Soon the newly freed Republican headed for the jacks, where he retrieved a handgun, sealed in plastic, from the water tank of the toilet farthest from the door. O'Malley hid the gun in the waistband at the small of his back in case a Loyalist hit squad tried to mar the celebration.

As O'Malley exited the loo, an athletic man in his twenties locked eyes with the legend and headed earnestly toward him. O'Malley watched as the lad drew closer and reached for something in his coat pocket. Before Liam could react, a husky man appeared from nowhere and tackled the aggressor. It was the minder Patrick Linden ordered to keep watch over O'Malley. The lad now lay face down, spread eagled and sputtering under the suffocating weight of O'Malley's protector.

"Get the fuck off me, ya fuckin' bastard!"

The minder ignored the man's whining and searched his pockets as a drunken crowd gathered around, ready to tear the assailant apart. The only item in the unfortunate man's possession was a mobile phone.

"I'm just a fuckin' messenger, ya dumb shite. I was supposed to hand the mobile to O'Malley and have him answer a call. Devin Dingle sent me."

O'Malley recalled Patrick's disdain for Dingleberry, the upstart New IRA leader who was challenging the old guard and aggressively expanding his territory. "I don't make a habit of talking to people I haven't met," O'Malley told the lad. "Now piss off before ya get hurt." O'Malley walked past the New IRA messenger and rejoined the crowd as the husky man escorted the poor boy out the back door and told the security men he was not welcome to return.

Several minutes later, the sheepish youngster called his boss to report what happened.

OLD MAN KELLY'S STORE

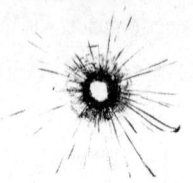

SEVERAL DAYS PASSED SINCE THE DEATH of Fr. Clark, and Tommy felt no better about the incident. His already frequent nightmares were now even more common. He still had flashbacks to his mother's severed arm clutching the multi-colored leather handbag. Only now, the images were intermingled with the body of the priest laying prone in the street. At first the flashbacks seemed unpredictable, but Tommy noticed they popped into his head whenever he passed through Middle Shankill or anywhere near a church. *Maybe that fuckin' priest really is hauntin' me.*

Tommy wondered if the priest's family hated Tommy the same way Tommy hated the IRA bastards who killed his parents. He kept reminding himself he did not pull the trigger and had not *planned* to be a getaway driver. Besides, Kieran said the dead priest was an IRA man. Tommy thought that was bollocks, but Kieran said he heard it from someone in the security services. Tommy thought that was bollocks too.

Kieran must have truly believed the priest was a terrorist though, because he showed no remorse. *He shot a man dead in the street but hours later slept like a wee baby!* Sometimes Tommy wished he were more like Kieran. People respected Kieran—

or at least feared him. And he didn't take shite from anyone, including Tommy.

Tommy had not looked for a job since the killing, and Kieran was pressing him to contribute more toward household expenses. Tommy wanted to tell him, "There's no point submitting an application when they're just gonna check me references and give it a pass." Yet he saw Kieran was losing patience with him, and it was never good to have Kieran Oliver cross with you. In any event, Tommy had nowhere else to go. He knew he needed to find some money quickly.

Tommy's first thought was to nick a few purses. He was never good at lifting wallets, but lady pensioners liked to carry cash and could not chase after him. But just in case that priest's ghost really *was* haunting him, Tommy decided to play it safe and break into Old Man Kelly's convenience store after closing. Old Man Kelly could spare the cash.

But Tommy did not know about the new hidden security camera and the silent alarm at Old Man Kelly's store, and now he found himself at the PSNI station on Tennent Street.

Tommy sat chained to a table in a side room with the door slightly ajar. Out by the main desk, Old Man Kelly argued with the sergeant. Tommy could not make out their words.

The arguing stopped, and Tommy heard footsteps approach. The sergeant threw open the door and stood with his hands on his hips, staring disdainfully at Tommy. "Stand up," he commanded. Tommy complied, and the sergeant removed the chain from Tommy's wrist. "Old Man Kelly is a fool but a friend," he muttered. Tommy eyed the man with a confused look.

"Go on. The old fool doesn't want ya remanded in custody. He says he remembers your mum and feels ya deserve another chance. I told him you'd had a dozen chances already, but his mind's made up. So yer going into the new diversion program."

"What's that?"

"It's meant fer people far younger than yerself who aren't yet career criminals. Ya go on probation, meet with a social worker, stay out of trouble fer a year, and the crime magically disappears. It's a waste of time if ya ask me, but if it makes ya somebody else's problem, then I guess I won't whinge about it. See the clerk on yer way out. He'll give ya a date, time, and a place to show up. Be there, or I'll be haulin' ya back in here again, and even Old Man Kelly won't be able to save ya then."

A bewildered Tommy picked up the diversion summons on his way out. Old Man Kelly had already departed, so Tommy was spared the embarrassment of thanking him. He looked at the summons and saw that he was to report in a week to an address in the city center. *What a load of shite this is gonna be.*

THE DEBATE

CLAIRE HURRIED INTO THE GLASS-WALLED CONFERENCE room at Goodwin & Haley and slid into her usual seat just as the meeting started. The law firm in Belfast city center hosted the CNICS meetings every Wednesday evening since the Commission launched its work earlier that year. Claire sensed the tension in the room and knew the discussion would be heated.

The Commission's chairperson, Christopher Hoffman, called the group to order. He thanked his fellow legal scholars for their continued participation and reminded the group the sole purpose of the meeting was to approve or reject Patrick Linden's nomination as their next client.

Kim Kline, a barrister from Ballyclare, spoke first. "I can't imagine a worse miscarriage of justice than the one presented here," she said, stabbing emphatically at her copy of Patrick Linden's HET folder. "This is precisely the sort of misconduct that undermines confidence in our criminal justice system. Torture, coerced confessions, false testimony by the police, and falsified evidence have no place in our courts, and this Commission was created for the very purpose of invalidating that type of behavior. I vote to accept Mr. Linden as our next client."

There were several murmurs of assent. They fell silent when William Ward, a somewhat pompous but highly regarded barrister from Lisburn, lifted his right index finger. "I, too, am troubled by any hint of misconduct by the police or the Public Prosecution Service. But how many times has the government been falsely accused by a paramilitary for propaganda purposes? Such accusations cannot be accepted at face value and are best investigated and—if credible—prosecuted through established channels. This Commission's reputation and the credibility of the justice system will suffer if a man with obvious ties to a terrorist organization—who was duly convicted, with proper legal representation, of serious offenses—is released. There must be a more suitable candidate for our services."

Kim Kline was about to rebut the elder barrister's argument but yielded to Claire, whose cheeks were flush with passion.

"Mr. Ward," Claire began, "how can we acknowledge misgivings about the conduct of the police and the actions of the public prosecutor and simultaneously recommend those misgivings be addressed through 'established channels'? The police and the PPS *are* the established channels! The public no longer shares your confidence in those institutions, as the news media makes clear with daily stories of Republicans and Loyalists alike seeking to right the wrongs of the past. Until corrective steps are taken, people on either side of the conflict are simply unable and unwilling to move forward. I would also challenge the suitability of the evidence used to convict Mr. Linden, but I think my colleague across the table intends to make that point." Claire nodded toward David Murrin, a fellow law professor at QUB.

"Mr. Ward," Murrin began, "I'm a great admirer of your legal texts and hold you in the highest regard. With all respect, how can we ignore the conclusion of the PSNI's own detective who, while assigned to the HET, concluded the two constables who testified against Linden were not credible, and the evidence used to convict him was likely planted? Surely those circumstances alone warrant review."

"He confessed, dammit. Innocent people don't confess," interjected a portly, red-faced man near the door. Damian Bradley, a retired RUC constable, spit the words out with no effort to conceal his disdain. Although all voting members of the Commission were legal scholars, the group invited other key constituencies to send non-voting representatives.

"Constable, a confession obtained through torture is not worth the paper it's written on," Kim Kline shot back.

"*Alleged* torture, without a scintilla of proof presented by Mr. Linden," answered William Ward. "A very convenient tactic to undermine the prosecution when one has no legitimate defense."

"Hear, hear," the retired constable agreed.

Christopher Hoffman raised both hands to quiet the group and keep emotions from escalating. "I appreciate the passion and candor we all bring to our work. The debate is necessary and healthy. I'm mindful of the time though, and want to be sure everyone who wishes to share an opinion can do so. We haven't heard yet from a few of our members, and I offer the floor to them now if they wish to express an opinion."

Patrick Kilcarr took the opportunity to address his colleagues. "You've all raised valid points. Before you vote, I ask you to consider the entirety of the record. It is worth remembering that Mr. Linden stands convicted of possessing bomb-making materials and plotting multiple explosions during the Trouping of the Color. A planned attack against the Sovereign, although thwarted, is still treason. Even if Her Majesty were not the intended target, the only purpose of a bomb is to destroy property and lives."

"And we cannot ignore Mr. Linden's prior conduct either," Kilcarr continued. "This is a man who was photographed at IRA funerals and at IRA safe houses, who allegedly recruited paramilitaries to attack government officials, and who reportedly served as a senior commander of the IRA. Dissident organizations are clandestine by design and difficult to infiltrate and monitor, but where there is smoke, there is fire. I cannot in good conscience vote to pursue the release of a man who, in all likelihood, is responsible for innumerable deaths and injuries. Imagine the firestorm that will erupt in the Loyalist community if this man's conviction is overturned. Better to let sleeping dogs lie. I stand with William—there must be a less controversial figure we can support."

Christopher Hoffman looked around the room to see if anyone else wished to speak. Finding no one, he offered some observations of his own. "We were given, as a result of the HET's work, a list of Republicans and Loyalists imprisoned under questionable circumstances. We don't have the resources to challenge *all* their convictions and must choose the ones most likely to advance the cause of justice. Passions are strong on both sides of the conflict. There will never be an easy choice for us. Our work is *inescapably* controversial and sure to face disapproval from one side or the other. It seems to me we must offer our best legal representation to an equal number of Republican and Loyalist inmates and let the law be the overarching principle that guides and, in the end, unites us. As messy and painful as the path may be, we must pursue the truth."

Hoffman announced a ten-minute break to allow people to gather their thoughts and reflect on the choice before them.

Then the group cast secret ballots. Hoffman and a law clerk who kept notes for the Commission tabulated the results in a corner of the room. The chairman returned to his seat at the head of the table, and the group looked at the clerk expectantly. "By a vote of six to three, the Commission agrees to petition the Court for a review of Mr. Linden's conviction."

The committee chose Claire Davis to inform Mr. Linden of his good fortune.

MR. MAGEE

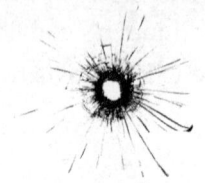

TOMMY MAGEE HESITATED OUTSIDE the modest brick building with a torn green awning on Ormeau Road, a short distance from the Probation Board. The diversion summons directed him to report to Suite 2A here at 14:00. He expected a government edifice or some sort of medical complex. The structure in front of him bore no external signage and resembled a private residence.

Tommy opened the gate, walked across a small courtyard to climb a half-flight of steps to the front door, and stepped inside a vestibule. He consulted a directory on the wall and learned there were six offices in the building, two on each floor. He thought it odd the suites had numbers but no names. He made his way up another flight of stairs to a dark wooden door marked 2A and stepped inside.

Tommy sat in one of the four chairs squeezed into the otherwise empty waiting area. A second door, with *Dr. Aaron Thornton* stenciled on it, stood across from the entrance. The police sergeant told Tommy there was no receptionist and to take a seat until called. He glanced around uncomfortably, but there was nothing on the walls to distract him. The only sound was a fluorescent light humming overhead.

Tommy did not recall ever talking to a psychologist and was unsure what to expect. Kieran that morning warned him not to divulge *anything* to the shrink, and *especially* nothing about the priest's murder. Tommy wondered if the psychologist would know he was hiding something or somehow read his mind. His knee began to bounce, and he chewed his upper lip as the anxiety increased. He was tired of Kieran always telling him what to do. But in this instance, he agreed silence was the best strategy.

The inner door opened at precisely two o'clock. A man who looked like a young David Beckham greeted Tommy by name and waved him in.

He's a fuckin' Yank! Tommy stood and remained as stoic as possible. He wondered how much the shrink could learn just from his body language. Tommy weakly shook the psychologist's outstretched hand without making eye contact and followed him into a study. Tommy sat stiffly in an overstuffed chair that was ten times better than the lounger at Kieran's place. He stared at the posh carpet on the floor and waited.

Thornton sat in a matching chair directly across from Tommy and smiled. He introduced himself, explained his role as a consultant for the Public Prosecution Service, and said it was his job to help Tommy stay out of jail after the break-in at Old Man Kelly's store. "How does that sound to you, Mr. Magee?"

Tommy grinned involuntarily. No one ever called him Mr. Magee. "Ya'd do better to call me Tommy, Doc. And I'm good with the idea of skippin' prison. But what do I gotta do to make that happen?" he asked warily.

Thornton explained that Belfast recently launched an experimental program to divert non-violent offenders from the criminal justice system toward alternative ways of addressing crime. Advocates believed most non-violent offenses resulted from joblessness, drug use, untreated behavioral health conditions, and the like. By pairing offenders with helping professionals, proponents of the program hoped to steer participants down productive paths and spare them the stigma of a prison sentence. Thornton was assigned to help Tommy with those goals. "So the question, Tommy, is what would you rather do *instead* of going to jail?"

"Can I just stay home and drink?" Tommy asked seriously.

"Of course you can. Let me ask it a different way," Thornton countered. "If you had the power to do anything, what would you *change* about your life?"

Tommy's eyes narrowed, and his head tilted slightly to one side. A flood of ideas rushed through his mind. He would bring his parents back. Or find a job that lasted and paid well, and maybe a girlfriend. He would get his own place, with good furniture and appliances that worked. But then his brain flipped a switch and brought him back to reality. "There's no point playin' this game, Doc. People like me don't choose what happens to us."

"People like you," Thornton echoed. "Tell me what that means."

Tommy started to answer but caught himself. *Is this a trick? Why would someone I just met care about someone like me? The doc is just pretendin' to be interested—that's what he's paid to do.* Instead of explaining himself, Tommy looked back at the floor, bit his lip again, and waited for Thornton to say something else. But the psychologist kept quiet. Tommy fidgeted as the silence grew longer and more awkward. Finally, he looked at the psychologist. "Why do you care?" he blurted to break the tension.

"That's a fair question. When I read your police report, two things stood out. First, the man you robbed did not want you to go to jail. That's pretty unusual. And secondly, you broke into the shop after hours—so I'm guessing you didn't want to confront the clerk or any customers while the store was open. In other words, you're not a violent or threatening person, or someone who takes risks. So it seems to me, and to the store owner, that you're not a lost cause. I know from my previous job that prison is a brutal place. I'm not convinced you belong there. I'd like to help you keep your freedom, if you'll let me."

Tommy locked eyes with Thornton, determined not to lower his guard but curious to know what would happen if he did.

Thornton tried again. "So what do I need to understand about 'people like you'?"

"Why don't you just read the file?" Tommy asked defensively. He instantly regretted his tone and quickly followed with, "What do you want to know?"

"Well, I did read the file, but that only had what the police chose to put in it. I'm interested in hearing your side of the story. The court system is willing to overlook the break-in, but only if you and I can agree to a plan that keeps you out of more trouble. Since we've only known each other for ten minutes, I thought maybe you'd like to tell me something about yourself first."

Tommy decided to feed the shrink a few scraps of information to make him think he was cooperating, without giving up anything important. He mentioned sharing a flat and needing money to pay his share of the costs, but said it was impossible to find legitimate work with his past record. Tommy explained he liked Old Man Kelly and did not choose him out of malice. Rather, he figured the shopkeeper already had lots of money and would not suffer the loss. "Look, Doc, I know yer tryin' to help, but I don't trust the peelers, and I really don't think the government gives a shite what happens to Tommy Magee."

"Why do you say that?"

Tommy suspected a trap and went silent. Kieran's warning to keep quiet echoed in his head, and Tommy worried he'd said too much already. His gaze returned to the floor, and he ignored Thornton's question.

"Tommy, I know it can be awkward to talk about personal things with someone you've just met. My only goal here is to support you in whatever ways *you* decide are most helpful. Everything we discuss stays between us. I won't tell the prosecution service anything you don't approve first. I think you're a good guy who found himself in a rough patch and tried to get through it without hurting anyone. A guy like that deserves a break. As we talk more, I bet you'll think of some other things you'd like help with. And if you're willing to share them with me, I will gladly work with you to make those situations better too. All you have to do is ask. I'm not going to force anything on you."

Tommy fidgeted in the overstuffed chair as he wrestled with his thoughts. Life long ago taught him to expect the worst from every situation. People he knew better—and a lot longer—than Thornton betrayed him. And now he was involved in a murder for which Kieran, if threatened, could implicate him. *So why am I so fuckin' keen to talk to this bloke?* Tommy finally answered, "I'll have a think, Doc, and let ya know next time what I decide."

Thornton beamed.

"Why are ya lookin' at me all happy like that?"

"Because you're planning to come back."

"Maybe so, but I haven't decided to *say* anythin' yet." Tommy wanted to keep the upper hand.

"Fair enough, Mr. Magee. Fair enough."

Now Tommy, too, was smiling at the way Thornton used his proper name again. The two men used the rest of the session to complete a standard questionnaire and some paperwork for the court. When they finished, the pair shook hands and said goodbye.

Tommy walked through the inner door of the office into the waiting area and started a mental list of things he wanted to ask Thornton at their next session. He continued downstairs and out the front door with a bounce in his step. As Tommy passed through the gate and turned right, he donned a bright red *Peaky Blinders* cap he nicked from a coat rack in the first-floor corridor.

MONGOOSE AND
THE GUNRUNNER

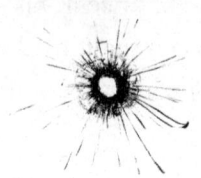

MONGOOSE SAT ALONE IN A READING ROOM next to the MI5 archive at Palace Barracks and reviewed the top-secret file on Fr. Matthew Clark. The director was apoplectic about the loss of the agency's most valuable informer and the investigation's lack of progress. Mongoose knew Clark better than anyone, but pulled his file anyway in search of an overlooked clue that might point to his killer. The folder read like a movie script.

In the 1980s, Clark was a handsome and charming young priest with a disarming smile and a cracker sense of humor. His concern for the poor and affinity for other cultures led him to the Church's international aid program, where he capitalized on his likability to excel as a fundraiser and goodwill ambassador. The Vatican appointed the Belfast native to a senior post overseeing multiple international charities, all of which flourished under Clark's leadership. He regularly appeared in photos alongside rich and powerful people.

Fr. Clark understandably spent a lot of time in Africa and the Americas, where the Church was especially active and had extensive networks. The prelate split his time between affluent and destitute communities—taking from the rich and giving to the poor. *The Lord's work. Except for that bit about the guns.*

MI5 never determined precisely when Fr. Clark joined the IRA. Mongoose surmised the Provos recruited him once they realized his international work provided a perfect cover for their overseas activities. And a brilliant and fruitful cover it was, while it lasted.

Under the cloak of humanitarian fundraising, Clark funneled hundreds of thousands of pounds to the IRA's Swiss bank accounts from sympathizers in multiple countries. Irish-American organizations in the States were particularly generous contributors. The Provos used the donations to purchase increasingly sophisticated weaponry, including assault rifles, machine guns, anti-tank mines, rocket-propelled grenade launchers, flame throwers, high explosives, modern detonators, frequency switches to thwart British jamming of IRA bomb signals, and even a pair of portable surface-to-air missile systems, or SAMs, acquired from illicit traders in Africa. The list of shipments linked to Clark showed most of the IRA's armaments came from Libya and the United States.

Clark and his fellow Provos went to great lengths to conceal these purchases from the authorities, including the Church. They kept Clark's activities hidden until the early 1990s when the Libyan regime—seeking permission to import British oil-producing machinery—tried to curry favor by alerting MI5 to an arms shipment destined for Belfast. The security services intercepted the weapons and ammunition at sea under the ruse of looking for illegal immigrants. MI5 traced the funding for the arms to Clark and quietly picked him up during a visit to South Africa.

Operatives there presented Clark with an easy choice—either continue business as usual and become an MI5 informer or be arrested publicly and falsely made to *look* like an informer. Clark gambled on MI5's protection, and for more than two decades fed Mongoose a steady stream of intelligence about the IRA's activities.

Mongoose combed through the file for any forgotten tidbits that might now prove useful. The biographical section, psychological profile, and summary of illicit activities were all familiar. The recent insert with details of Clark's murder was still fresh, but Mongoose reviewed it anyway. The only unresolved matter in the file involved an intelligence memorandum filed five years earlier, after the Historical Enquiries Team shut down.

The memo explained that when the IRA declared a permanent ceasefire in 2005, it pledged to decommission all arms "under its control." The Irish and UK governments and an independent international commission verified the decommissioning of vast amounts of weaponry and explosives. They claimed publicly the IRA had nothing left. But an MI5 analyst who served as liaison to the HET cast doubt on that assertion, citing repeated references in HET files to rumored IRA weapons stockpiles in Northern Ireland and the Republic as recently as 2014.

The analyst quoted multiple witnesses who alleged IRA sympathizers maintained massive caches of weapons and explosives for use in the event of renewed conflict. Estimates suggested the dissidents had enough supplies to sustain a two-year campaign against the British. Of particular concern was an unverified claim that Republican paramilitaries controlled two portable SAM systems and a dozen missiles stored just south of the border.

According to the confidential source of that intelligence, the missile systems were inoperable when received from the Libyans in the 1980s, and the IRA at the time lacked the expertise to place them in service. Instead, the components were transported to the Republic and hidden for later disposition. The source told HET investigators that the New IRA had since taken possession of the SAMs, repaired them, and would soon be able to operate the devices. Nothing more was known about the members of that team or the present location of the SAMs. If the reports were accurate, the analyst noted, it meant dissidents were for the first time capable of downing military and commercial aircraft.

Mongoose remained skeptical of the information summarized in the analyst's memorandum. The New IRA lacked the sophistication and discipline to conceal, repair, and operate a SAM. Every intelligence service on the planet actively monitored the black market for spare missile parts, and the New IRA had a poor reputation for covering its tracks. Neither the UK nor any allied government had detected anything suspicious. Mongoose viewed the rumors as fairy tales concocted to give the New IRA an air of undeserved legitimacy. On the other hand, the security services had long assumed Republicans kept a secret stockpile of more conventional arms and explosives.

Mongoose continued flipping through the pages, but nothing else in the file stood out. The director would have to wait for answers.

IN THE SHADOWS

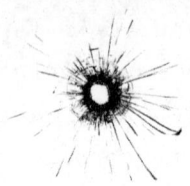

THE DAY AFTER HIS RELEASE FROM MAGHABERRY, Liam O'Malley approached the modest brick building on Ormeau Road. A chap wearing a red *Peaky Blinders* cap passed him on the sidewalk without making eye contact. O'Malley stopped at the entryway, inhaled deeply, and pondered the steps for a moment. Thornton wanted to begin their meetings at once to ensure O'Malley's reintegration to society began smoothly. O'Malley was skeptical about his chances.

O'Malley summoned the courage to climb to the second floor and entered the empty waiting room for Suite 2A. Ten minutes later, the inner door opened, and Thornton beckoned him inside. "Welcome, Liam. It's good to see you again. Come on in and tell me how it feels to be a free man." The doc looked bigger and stronger than O'Malley remembered. O'Malley always sized up potential threats.

O'Malley sat in the overstuffed chair reserved for clients and felt surprisingly at ease. The office seemed more like a cozy lounge. Apart from the humming fluorescent light in the waiting area, it was a far cry from the cold, sterile meeting room where he met Thornton at Maghaberry.

"So tell me about your first day," Thornton exhorted.

O'Malley described how the prison released him unceremoniously at ten o'clock the previous morning with a plastic bag for his meager belongings and a twenty-pound note. For some reason he withheld the detail about his waiting ride, and instead mentioned that he spent most of the day and night at the Tricolor Pub.

"What was that like?"

O'Malley described the crowd, the warm welcome, the singing and cheering, and all the free rounds. He then paused and weighed whether to mention the youngsters' interest in his past or the scuffle with Dingleberry's messenger.

Thornton noted, "You don't have to mention anything you don't want to. I'm curious, though, if you have any concerns that might keep you from telling me something important."

"Well, I'm sure not gonna tell ya anythin' that would send me back to prison." O'Malley remembered their discussion about the limits of confidentiality. Past terrorism offenses were not protected from disclosure.

"Without going into detail, did something happen at the pub that might not be covered by confidentiality?" Thornton sounded concerned.

"No, no—I'm done with all that. I just meant in general. I've done a lot of things that aren't in yer wee file there, and ya can be sure I won't be sharin' those details with ya," Liam said with a wink.

Thornton relaxed.

"Look, I get it, Doc. If they even think I've returned to a paramilitary unit, they'll lock me up again, and I'll have no hope of another release. No worries. I'm done."

"And yet something made you hesitate a moment ago, when talking about the pub."

O'Malley studied Thornton's face. There was no sign of malice or deceit. He seemed genuinely interested in understanding what made O'Malley uncomfortable. O'Malley was flattered but said, "Look, Doc, all this attention from you and the crowd at the pub makes me uncomfortable. I prefer to be unseen, in the shadows."

"Do you feel safer in the shadows?"

O'Malley considered the question. "Aye, I do. All me life I feel like someone's been watchin' me, waitin' for me to slip up so they can pounce. And I'm not just talkin' about the Brits. The IRA is paranoid too, always on the lookout for touts. If an operation went wrong, everyone involved became a suspect. And the IRA's internal security team are a ruthless set of bastards, let me tell ya." O'Malley stopped short, replaying the words in his head, wondering if he said too much.

"It makes perfect sense that you'd want to avoid all that attention. At the same time, any barriers to communication will limit our progress in therapy. What can I do to help you feel safer and more comfortable, so we can talk about what's on your mind and address anything that needs work?"

O'Malley looked quizzically at Thornton, puzzled by the doc's seemingly sincere motivation to help him. He felt an inexplicable urge to reciprocate. "Look, the reason I hesitated is because a lot of people at the pub yesterday—especially the youngins—were pressin' me for stories about the past. And there were folks there that I know want me to join them in a new string of attacks against the Brits. But I didn't want ya to think that any of that was because of somethin' I did. It's nothing I want to be part of. Like I said, I'm steerin' clear of any future trouble and, as fer the past, it's probably best to let sleepin' dogs lie. No good can come of it."

"That sounds like a solid plan, and I appreciate your trust and candor. It's a good sign that you were able to talk honestly about what's on your mind. I promise I'll never press you to share anything you're not comfortable telling me."

"Just don't expect any excitin' tales about me glory days." O'Malley laughed.

"Fair enough. Let's review the deal we made at the prison. We'll continue these meetings at the same time every week, and you'll participate in the Reconciliation meetings. I looked into those, and there's a group that meets near the address you registered with the police, at Clonard Monastery on Thursdays. How does that one sound?"

"No problem, Doc. I think I know the place," O'Malley said with a sense of irony that was lost on Thornton.

For the rest of the session, they revisited unanswered questions from their first encounter at Maghaberry. O'Malley was still uncomfortable talking about his childhood and family, but did acknowledge occasional nightmares for the first time. The pair agreed to set those topics aside until the following week, since time was short.

In the last five minutes, O'Malley asked how Thornton ended up in Northern Ireland doing work for the prison system and parole commission. Thornton noted psychologists are supposed to stay focused on their clients, but acknowledged the unusual circumstances. The American shared that he and his wife moved to Belfast for her new job, and he wanted to be productive himself. Since he worked in a prison previously, it made sense to continue in the same field. O'Malley decided that was good enough for now.

As the pair stood and headed for the door, Thornton congratulated O'Malley for showing up and engaging in what could be an uncomfortable process. "I promise you, it gets easier. And remember, it's designed entirely to benefit *you*. Let's discuss next week what you want to accomplish with our talks, and if you need to meet sooner than planned, just call the number I gave you last week."

O'Malley was intrigued by the invitation to set his own agenda. "I'll definitely give it a think, Doc. Thanks."

O'Malley descended the stairs and stepped into the sunshine. He scanned left and right, as he always did when leaving a building. He pretended not to notice the bloke in the car across the street who was watching him.

CURIOSITY

THORNTON CLOSED HIS LAPTOP and looked about the kitchen. He felt restless and bored. Claire had to work late again and would not be home for hours. After spending all day stuck in the office, he refused to stay home alone and sit some more.

Starting a new life in Belfast had been tougher than Thornton expected. It was hard to meet people, especially with Claire working evenings. Although he understood her desire to make a good impression at the university, he resented her frequent absence at home. Without their old social network for support, Thornton had no one else to turn to. A week earlier he had tried to tell her how much he struggled—especially alone at night—with the recurring image of Officer Grace dying just a few feet away from him. But Claire remained stoic, suggested he give it more time, and changed the subject.

Thornton sensed his distress about the murder might burden Claire during a busy time, so he decided not to share his feelings of isolation with her. He had supported her decision to accept the job and didn't want her to feel guilty about it now. At the time, Thornton assumed the change of venue would make it easier for him to move on after Grace's death. In truth, memories of that violent episode were never far away. Thornton, despite his professional training, did his best to distract himself from the emotional pain whenever it resurfaced—as it often did when he was idle. And right now, he needed a distraction.

Thornton recalled Liam O'Malley's description earlier in the week of the raucous welcome he received at the Tricolor Pub. It reminded him of the boisterous gatherings he and his George-town buddies enjoyed at The Irish Times, Tiber Creek Pub, The Four Provinces, and other Irish bars in Washington. None was close enough to walk to from campus, so he and his friends always piled into a couple cabs. Live music, singing crowds, and loads of drunken foolishness occupied them until closing most Saturday nights. *I miss those days.*

Thornton knew O'Malley was helping a friend move that evening, so he impulsively decided to visit the Tricolor Pub while there was no risk of seeing each other. He ignored the taxi tour guide's warning to avoid West Belfast at night and hailed a cab.

Thornton had a history of flirting with danger. He joined his high school teammates and chased down a mugger during a spring break trip to New York City. While in college, he accepted a dare and ran with the bulls in Pamplona. And at a bachelor party in Ogden, Utah, he was the only guest willing to bungee jump from a bridge three hundred feet above the Crooked River. So it was no surprise when he chose to work with dangerous criminals. The stories of their exploits captivated him, although here in Northern Ireland they were less forthcoming. Still, being with and learning about killers and terrorists brought him as close to actual violence as he was willing to get. And as an out-sider in Northern Ireland, he assumed his nationality shielded him from serious trouble.

Thornton paid the driver and stepped onto the curb at the Tricolor Pub. He heard music inside and the loud, drunken banter of a sizable crowd. The heavy-set man at the door eyed him closely but allowed him to pass. Inside, Thornton sensed people in every corner studying him. Most of the clientele sat at tables or booths with family and mates. Thornton chose a seat at the bar next to a solitary older man and started a conversation.

The pensioner heard Thornton's accent and said wryly, "Ya must be lost, son."

"My wife had other plans tonight, so I decided to see what a genuine Irish bar is like."

"We're genuine alright, but we don't see many tourists 'ere. Or anywhere else in this part of town."

The barkeep nodded.

"I'd much rather hang out with locals anyway. How long have you lived here?"

The old man sipped his beer and stared straight ahead. "All me life. Most families in these parts 'ave been 'ere for generations. And we 'ave no plans to leave."

"So you lived through The Troubles then?" Thornton concentrated on the old man and missed the flicker of apprehension on the barkeep's face. The American knew O'Malley and other prisoners could not tell him stories of the past, but he assumed no one here would feel threatened by a *foreigner's* curiosity.

"So I did. A terrible time. Why do ya ask, lad?" The pensioner turned to study Thornton.

"I watched news stories about it in the States and always wanted to understand things better. You know, see things for myself and talk to people who experienced it firsthand. I'm a psychologist." *I can't believe I'm sitting in a real IRA hangout in the heart of West Belfast! I wonder what stories this man can tell.*

"What did ya expect to find in this pub, son?"

"Well, from the flags outside, I figured it must be a Republican bar. Maybe I'd meet someone who could tell me what it was like during The Troubles. Maybe even talk to someone who was close to the action." Thornton ignored the tour guide's second warning too. *"Don't ask too many questions of people you don't know."*

The barkeep and the pensioner exchanged glances. The old man leaned toward Thornton. "Close to the action, ya say?" Then in a whisper, "Ya mean *the IRA?*"

Thornton nodded enthusiastically.

The old man looked at the barkeep. "Seamus, are there any IRA 'ere?"

The barkeep shook his head.

The old man looked back at Thornton with a severe expression. "Who are ya really, son, and why did ya come?"

Thornton repeated his earlier explanation.

"Of all the Republican pubs in West Belfast, why'd ya pick *this* one?"

The question caught Thornton off guard. He could not name O'Malley as the source of his interest but struggled to think of something else. The failure to produce a quick answer fueled suspicion.

"Stand up."

Thornton looked quizzically at the pensioner but slowly did as instructed.

At the old man's signal, the bouncer approached Thornton and told him to stand like a scarecrow. He frisked the psychologist for weapons and a wire but found neither.

The pensioner nodded toward the back of the pub, and the bouncer shoved Thornton in that direction. Two more men joined them from opposite sides of the room. Behind them, a woman locked the main entrance.

Thornton grew anxious and regretted not telling Claire his plans for the night. He glanced around the pub for an unobstructed way out but saw none. "Look, I'm sorry. I didn't mean to make anyone uncomfortable. Let's just forget the whole thing, and I'll leave."

The bouncer merely grunted as the group reached a private room.

Thornton spotted a rear exit from the building, but his path was blocked by one of the guards.

The exit door suddenly opened, and Liam O'Malley crossed the threshold. "Doc? What are *you* doing 'ere?" O'Malley glanced at the security surrounding the American and saw where they were taking him.

The bouncer turned toward O'Malley. "You know this bloke? He was asking too many questions at the bar and the boss got nervous."

"It's alright. I know him. I'll get him outta 'ere."

The bouncer shrugged. O'Malley's recent release generated a lot of publicity in the city, and there had been other busybodies hoping to catch a glimpse of the famous Republican. If O'Malley vouched for the lad, there was nothing more to do. The bouncer and his crew returned to their posts.

O'Malley led Thornton out the back. When they cleared the rear lot, he asked, "What the 'ell were ya thinkin', Doc? Ya don't belong in there. Shite, ya shouldn't be in this neighborhood a'tall."

"Liam, I'm sorry. I know this looks bad. When you told me about your homecoming celebration, I got curious about the place and just wanted to see it in person. My wife is out, I got bored, and I knew you were at your friend's place. I didn't expect to bump into you, but I'm sure glad I did."

"Aye, we finished early. They were about to rough ya up, Doc."

"Thank God you were here. I'm so sorry. I never should have come. I just wanted to see the neighborhood and get a better idea of what life is like here. But I crossed a boundary. You shouldn't have to worry about me showing up unexpectedly. The truth is, I've always been kind of fascinated by people like you and the world you're a part of. My curiosity got the best of me. It won't happen again."

"To be honest, Doc, I'm a bit flattered. A lot of outsiders don't understand me world and judge me fer what I've done. And yer not the first thrill-seeker whose curiosity got the best of 'im. At least ya kept an open mind and decided to see things fer yerself. But ya can't be doing that anymore. Now let's get ya outta 'ere before ya get yerself hurt."

PRIVATE TOUR

THE NEXT DAY, O'MALLEY SAT IN FRONT OF THE TELLY and wondered if he was naïve to dismiss Thornton's visit to the pub as innocent curiosity. *But if the doc really was working for the Brits, they'd never let him be so clumsy about it.*

O'Malley switched off the midday news program. The closing segment reported the overnight murder of an ex-IRA man in Derry. O'Malley wondered how much time *he* had left. His thoughts returned to the Tricolor Pub and the psychologist's near-suicidal interest in O'Malley's world. The American appeared sincere in his desire to understand The Troubles better and their effect on O'Malley. *You'd have to be, to take a risk like that.* And O'Malley never met anyone less judgmental.

O'Malley always felt misunderstood and rejected—first as a Catholic *before* Deidre's murder, and afterward as a "terrorist." Now, an outsider seemed genuinely interested in knowing and understanding him, free of any labels. O'Malley felt an urge to connect with the bloke on a human level. *Who better than an American shrink to confide in?*

Still, he hesitated. The psychologist held all the power, and it left O'Malley feeling controlled and vulnerable. For every session, O'Malley had to leave the safety of West Belfast and submit to uncomfortable questions on Thornton's turf. And one phone call from the American could send him back to prison without warning. The imbalance chaffed at O'Malley. He decided to turn the tables.

O'Malley dialed Thornton's number. "Doc, it's Liam. I've been thinkin' about yer visit to the Tricolor Pub."

"Liam, I am so sorry about that."

"Naw, Doc, don't worry yerself. I'm actually callin' to invite ya on a wee tour. What are ya doin' this afternoon?"

"A tour? It's a bit unorthodox to meet a client outside the office." He paused. "But I suppose we've already crossed that line. I'm done at one-thirty. What exactly do you have in mind?"

"Ya said ya wanted to understand me world better. So I'm goin' to show it to ya. Meet me in front of the Tricolor Pub at two. I'll be waitin' fer ya, so there's no trouble."

"That's an invitation I can't refuse."

———

Thornton arrived ten minutes early.

"This may sound strange, Doc. But I think it'll be easier to work together if I show ya some things first."

"Fair enough, Liam. If you think it will help, I'm in."

They began with a pint in the Tricolor Pub, where the barkeep apologized to Thornton for the prior misunderstanding. Then O'Malley led Thornton on what became a three-hour walking tour of Republican West Belfast.

They visited the Solidarity Wall, where O'Malley explained the significance of the political murals and answered Thornton's questions about historical events and figures—from the Republican perspective. At one point, O'Malley opened a news app on his mobile and showed the American one of the headlines.

Loyalist Displeasure with Brexit Prompts Calls to Abandon Peace Agreement. "That's not the IRA callin' for war—that's the Prods."

Several blocks up the road, O'Malley stopped at the Bobby Sands mural and shared memories of his good friend, another Provo legend who died in 1981 on a hunger strike at HM Prison Maze. "Bobby was twenty-seven, just three months younger than me. We had a surge in volunteers when he passed. But he was just one of *thousands* of Catholics mistreated by the Brits. Now, people are talkin' and evidence is comin' to light about crimes committed by British soldiers in the '70s and '80s. So what's the Loyalist response? They want a general amnesty for *all* offenses durin' The Troubles! Now why why would they need *that* if they're so innocent?"

Thornton shook his head.

The pair headed next to one of the peace walls separating Republican and Loyalist districts, and from there to Clonard Monastery—site of the Reconciliation meetings. Along the way, O'Malley pointed out Catholic homes that were torched by Loyalist mobs, shops that were vandalized, and places where fathers and mothers were beaten in front of their children by British agents. He knew them all by name. Then O'Malley traced the route he took to escape the Brits on the day Deidre died in 1972. At the spot where she died, he stopped but said nothing.

Thornton silently studied O'Malley.

"Sorry, Doc. I guess *this* story will have to wait for another day. But how do you feel about a thirty-minute walk to one more place that's on me mind a lot?"

"Lead the way." Thornton recognized this was a tour only O'Malley could give. And without an escort, he now knew, he would have been *persona non grata.*

The pair continued southwest on the Falls Road until they

reached a large, gated arch. It marked the entrance to Milltown Cemetery, where the IRA for more than a century had buried its dead. O'Malley led Thornton through each section—past monuments of every size and shape—and stopped frequently to share the exploits of his dead friends. Interspersed with tales of their cunning and courage were mundane descriptions of them as sons and daughters, siblings, and parents. Some fallen IRA volunteers were teenagers. Others were grandparents. O'Malley had known them all.

At the end of the tour, the men stood somberly at the grave of Bobby Sands. All the IRA dead here were colleagues *and* friends, many of whom shared in O'Malley's success. O'Malley still felt the kinship, if not the same fervor. "Ya know, Doc. More than 3,200 *more* people—includin' children and pensioners— have died in sectarian attacks *since the peace agreement was signed*. And ninety percent of children still attend segregated schools. I heard one bloke call it a 'self-imposed apartheid.' They made incredible sacrifices, but there's nothin' to show fer it now. We're at a stalemate."

"So where does that leave you, Liam?"

O'Malley wrestled with the question. "I honestly dunno, Doc. But I want me life to *mean* somethin'—I need to do some- thin' *good*. Otherwise, I'm just another pretty face on a mural."

Thornton nodded sympathetically, and the two men headed back to the pub in silence.

When they reached the entrance, O'Malley said, "I hope I didn't overwhelm ya, Doc."

"Not at all. Thanks for sharing that with me. It couldn't have been easy, but you've given me a much better understanding of what you and other Catholics have been through."

"I figured it might help bridge the gap a bit. Now when we talk, ya won't seem like such an outsider."

EVERYTHING

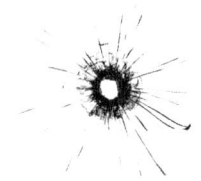

PATRICK LINDEN'S WORDS ECHOED in Mickey Shanahan's head. "I want to know everything about the new prison psychologist assigned to Liam. Everything. His work history, his family, who he meets with, *everything.*"

With contacts at the Royal Mail, the Driver and Vehicle Agency, Northern Ireland Water, Northern Ireland Electricity, Northern Ireland Gas, Stormont, the Ministry of Defense, the PSNI, and most other places, Shanahan was the man for the job. He handled the IRA's intelligence and security matters for Linden in the Belfast district. Shanahan was great at gathering intelligence *about* people, but he was even better at *extracting* information from individuals less willing to divulge it.

Shanahan's online sleuthing turned up surprisingly little social media activity for Thornton. The few accounts he had were private and in any event contained scant personal details or photos. Thornton appeared a few times in the American press, in connection with a couple murders at a U.S. prison and in an article about understaffing at penitentiaries. An online directory of medical providers listed his name, education, insurance provider number, and an old work address in West Virginia, which labeled him "inactive."

Shanahan took these details and ran them through an online data aggregator, using login credentials he hacked from a local business. A long list of Thornton's likely relatives emerged, but only one—Claire Davis—shared with him both a former residential address and an address at Georgetown University. Shanahan deduced the couple had dated and lived together, or possibly married, and he confirmed his hunch by finding their old wedding registry stored in an internet cache. But Shanahan found no property owned in either name in Northern Ireland.

Instead, Shanahan struck gold with an international shipping declaration filed with Her Majesty's Customs in Belfast. Aaron Thornton and Claire Davis were the recipients of a delivery several weeks earlier at a flat on College Green. Claire Davis, he learned, was a guest lecturer at QUB's School of Law, and she looked quite fetching in the photo posted online with her faculty profile.

Next, Shanahan checked for utility bills at the College Green address and learned the building was owned by Singh Properties Limited, a real estate conglomerate with multiple addresses in the capital. The couple obviously were renters. Shanahan drilled down further but found neither vehicle registrations nor drivers permits.

Shanahan then pursued Thornton's business activities and discovered his registration with the Health and Care Professions Council, or HCPC, as a practicing psychologist. The IRA man saw the registration resulted from an expedited petition sponsored by Ms. Rebecca Tucker of Colby & Prince, Solicitors. He made a note to look into it.

Ms. Tucker and the law firm appeared again on the paperwork filed with the Northern Ireland Parole Commission in support of Thornton's application to become a psychological examiner at HM Prison Maghaberry. *Definitely worth checking out*, Shanahan thought, when he realized the application to the Parole Commission was submitted shortly before Thornton's meeting with Liam O'Malley. *It looks like everything fell into place quickly for the good doctor.*

Shanahan's curiosity was piqued. He wondered who the watchers at Thornton's office would see entering and leaving the place. In the meantime, he wanted to know more about Thornton's wife, Claire Davis, who seemed to have stronger ties to Northern Ireland. He would pass along everything he learned during his next visit with Linden in two days.

JEALOUSY

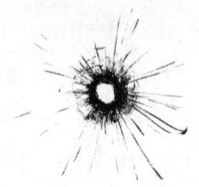

KIERAN WAS WATCHING THE TELLY when Tommy returned from Thornton's office. Tommy knew he wanted details.

"So, how was it?"

"It didn't add up to much," Tommy replied. "The doc seemed alright. He's a Yank, so he is."

"An American?! What the *fuck* is an American shrink doin' in Belfast askin' *you* questions?"

"I dunno really. He said somethin' about workin' on a special project with the prosecution service to keep people like me out of jail. It wasn't that bad really."

"Christ, Tommy, *'people like you'*? You're so fuckin' *gullible*. He's not on yer side. Remember who sent ya to him. He works for the *police*. What did ya tell him?"

"Nothin' really. He only asked what I wanted to change about me life."

Kieran burst out laughing. "You? Fuckin' *everythin'*, I imagine. He's not a *social* worker then, he's a *miracle* worker!"

Tommy flushed with anger, which he quickly suppressed. He would not give Kieran the satisfaction of seeing his reaction. And what if the doc really *could* help change his life? *It's not like I have anythin' left to lose.*

"I think he's just a good guy who's tryin' to help. It's weird, cuz he doesn't tell me what to do or *make* me tell him stuff, like I expected. It's like *I'm* supposed to decide what I want."

"*Jayzus*, Tommy. Keep your guard up. He's just tryin' to get ya to trust him enough to reveal somethin' he can tell the peelers."

"I'm no tout. You should know that by now. I only told him stuff about breakin' into Old Man Kelly's store, which he already knew from the file he had."

"Make sure that's *all* you tell him. So he didn't ask ya *anythin'* about the priest?"

"Naw, and if he had, I woulda played dumb. I'm not fuckin' stupid. And the only way he'd know to ask anythin' about the priest is if the peelers told him, and if the peelers thought we had somethin' to do with the priest, don't ya think they woulda come around here first?" Tommy felt smug about his reasoning.

"Aye, probably so. But I don't like it. Keep that fuckin' Yank out of our business. He could mess things up for both of us, so be done with him quick as ya can."

Tommy resented Kieran telling him what to do, but sensed he was driven by more than self-preservation. He wondered if Kieran might actually be jealous that someone took an interest in him.

Tommy cracked half a smile as he headed to the jacks.

CASTLECOURT CAR PARK

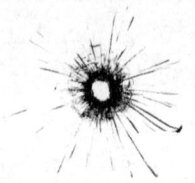

KIERAN OLIVER FELT UNSETTLED after his conversation with Tommy about the shrink. He left the house to clear his head. It was the fifteenth of the month, so he decided to retrieve the new disposable mobile left for him at a rented commercial mailbox on the Shankill Road. Every two weeks, a colleague of Robert Inglesby at the Organised Crime Branch, who also had a key to the box, left a new phone for Kieran.

Kieran arrived at the storefront, surveyed his surroundings, and entered the building. The mailboxes were obscured from public view, and the place was empty of patrons. Behind the counter, a clerk continued texting on her smart phone without looking up. Kieran made the swap and exited the store. After a couple of minutes, the new phone rang, and Kieran realized he was being watched, perhaps by the clerk with the smart phone.

"Hallo, guvnah," Kieran answered.

Inglesby's response was unusually stern. "Meet me on the fourth level of the CastleCourt car park in thirty minutes."

It was a straight shot, and Kieran covered the distance on foot with time to spare. He smoked a cigarette on the corner and glanced about for anything suspicious before taking the stairs to the fourth level. Inglesby taught him to avoid elevators.

When Kieran exited the stairwell, he paused as if trying to remember where he parked. The beep of a wireless car lock drew his attention to the left, and the sound repeated. He spotted the car's flashing lights the second time and sauntered toward the vehicle. It was alongside a work van that blocked the view of a nearby security camera. Inglesby stood at the rear of the car and raised the boot as Kieran approached. Kieran joined him behind the upright lid.

"What the fuck were ya doin' on Falls Road last Thursday night?" he asked abruptly.

"Nothin' big. Why?" Kieran was unfazed.

"Why? Because a fuckin' priest was executed on the street, and yer face and number plate showed up on CCTV around the same time! That's why!"

"Aye, I heard about that at the pub. Can't say I'm broken up about it. And yeah, I was in the area lookin' for some Fenian who ruffed up my UVF brothers the night before. But I can't tell ya any more about that priest."

"Can't or won't? Our deal doesn't cover murder, Kieran. Whoever killed that priest really cocked things up, for reasons I won't go into. If I find out yer lyin' to me, our deal is off. No more cash. No more immunity. Are ya hearin' me, Kieran?"

"Aye, I'm hearin' ya. But ya have nothin' to worry about from *me*." Kieran eyed Inglesby's facial expressions to see if the ruse was working. It seemed to be, but Inglesby was hard to read.

"Ya best remember who takes care of ya, Kieran Oliver. If you fuck with me, there'll be no one to save ya." Inglesby slammed the boot lid shut and rubbed his hands together as if clearing them of dirt.

"Aye, govnah. I hear ya. Don't worry yerself." Kieran headed back the way he came as Inglesby unlocked the car, got behind the wheel, and drove off.

Kieran departed the carpark and weighed his options. Armed with knowledge of the CCTV footage and convinced that Inglesby would do nothing to protect him from the consequences of *this* transgression, he needed to create a diversion.

Kieran veered inside the CastleCourt Centre and strolled past the shops until he spotted one crowded with students. He eyed a carelessly placed mobile on one of the counters. He nicked it while the owner tried on some jewelry and headed to a secluded area outside. There he called CrimeStoppers and, with a disguised voice, reported the priest killed on the Falls Road was executed for crimes committed as a member of the IRA.

Kieran tossed the stolen phone into a bin and congratulated himself for handing the PSNI at least a hundred new suspects in the killing of the priest. Now the peelers would have to consider every Loyalist paramilitary and rival IRA faction as the culprit.

I bet some of them were also captured on CCTV that night.

CROSS-GENERATIONAL IMPACT

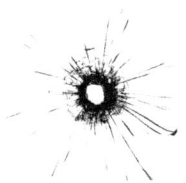

THROUGHOUT HIGH SCHOOL AND COLLEGE, Thornton was a varsity swimmer. He still maintained the classic swimmer's physique, with broad shoulders and a well-defined chest. Although his six-pack abs were a thing of the past, you could still count four—but "only on a good day," as Claire liked to tease.

Claire's position on the faculty at QUB afforded the couple free use of the university's athletic facilities, of which Thornton happily availed himself. The aquatic center had an Olympic-sized pool that he visited three or four times a week for at least an hour. His good looks and schedule were noted by other patrons, which accounted for an increase in attendance during the four o'clock hour. Thornton feigned ignorance of the attention and relied on his wedding band to keep the admirers at bay.

As Thornton hoisted himself out of the pool and reached for the towel he left on a bench by lane six, he saw an attractive brunette in her early twenties walk toward him. He found himself staring at her impossibly blue eyes. When she flashed him a bright smile, he blushed, smiled shyly in return, and quickly looked away.

"Excuse me," she called out. "May I borrow yer goggles if yer done? I left mine in the car and don't want to go back for them now that I've changed."

My God, she's beautiful. Thornton shifted the towel to cover his form-fitting swim trunks and answered, "Of course." With one hand, he stripped the eyewear from his forehead and extended it toward her. Her hand brushed against his as she took the goggles.

"Yer American?"

"Guilty as charged," he answered with a laugh. "What gave it away?"

"The baseball cap I've seen you wear was a clue, but that adorable accent confirmed it."

"My wife thinks it's ugly," he said, almost apologetically. "The hat, I mean."

The attractive brunette laughed and was undeterred. "I'm Siobhan."

"Aaron," he said as he shook her hand. "Are you a student here?"

"I'm in my final year of graduate studies in psychology."

"Outstanding! I'm a psychologist myself." He wished he had not sounded so enthusiastic.

"Are ya?! My graduate research involves the cross-generational impact of trauma. Are you familiar with The Troubles?"

Thornton was intrigued and wanted to know more but was suddenly very conscious of standing nearly naked in front of a very beautiful younger woman. "I've read up on it and took a history tour not long ago. I've tried in the past to ask my wife about The Troubles, but she avoids the topic."

"Is she Irish then? She may have been impacted herself."

Thornton doubted Claire was suffering the effects of

Troubles-related trauma but did not want to sound dismissive. "I hadn't thought of that."

"It's worth readin' about. Northern Ireland has unusually high rates of post-traumatic stress, suicide, self-harm, and alcoholism. Leave your email address with the towel girl on the way out, and I'll send some articles and a web link for you to read. I'll give the goggles to the attendant when I pick up yer email address, and ya can retrieve them tomorrow."

Thornton agreed and thanked her. Siobhan placed the goggles on her face and dove into the pool. Thornton headed for the locker room, unaware that his conversation with Siobhan was closely observed by a man on the balcony overlooking the pool.

———

That evening, Thornton received a message from Siobhan Dooley's email account at QUB. It included a link to a comprehensive study on transgenerational trauma and several attachments pertaining to behavioral health trends in Northern Ireland.

The data was striking. NI's suicide rate was more than twice that of the Republic of Ireland and nearly double the rate in England. It had the highest recorded rate of post-traumatic stress disorder, or PTSD, *in the world*. The studies also noted alarming trends in alcohol usage and alcohol-related deaths in both genders, and particularly among persons aged 45-64. In other words, Thornton calculated, people born between 1955 and 1974 were especially at risk—people who were adolescents during The Troubles.

It was fairly common to encounter these themes in the American prison population, but their prevalence among a broad spectrum of the Northern Irish population alarmed him. Thornton dozed off wondering to what extent these themes affected his new clients from the judicial services.

Thornton awoke to the sound of Claire returning home late from a faculty meeting. They retreated to the bedroom and made loud, passionate love. He noted guiltily that he was especially ravenous that evening. Claire offered no objection.

A WORLD BLOWN APART

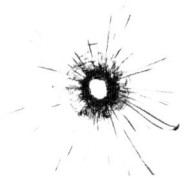

THORNTON WAS WORKING ON BILLING FORMS at the office
the next morning when a courier arrived with Tommy Magee's
file from the Health and Social Care Trusts (HSC). It consisted
of two thick volumes that consumed the psychologist's attention for the next two hours.

The file was a chronological record of Tommy's life from the
age of eight, when he was orphaned by a presumed IRA bomb
in Belfast, until he turned eighteen and aged out of foster care.
Thornton counted eleven fostering homes over that decade.
One foster carer lasted two years, and only a handful made it
past eight months.

It was a rocky road for Tommy and the foster carers. Immediately after the blast, Tommy refused to go outdoors and
rarely spoke. He wet the bed most nights for the first year. He
screamed in his sleep and had to be awakened from nightmares,
which he refused to discuss. Many well-intentioned foster carers
tried to connect with him, but Tommy was reluctant to bond
with adults, likely for fear of abandonment. When the bed wetting and sleep disruptions proved too much for a couple of the
families, they withdrew as foster carers and reinforced Tommy's

163

lack of trust in adults. The social workers struggled to reach him emotionally.

After a couple years, Tommy outgrew the bed wetting and resumed limited outdoor activities, but only in the immediate vicinity of his foster homes. Tutors helped him manage the school he missed, but his social skills suffered. He lagged intellectually behind his peers despite high intelligence and aptitude scores. The nightmares continued but became less disruptive.

An astute social worker recognized concurrent symptoms of depression and PTSD, but there were no programs available for the treatment of trauma in children. Instead, Tommy's carers focused on fully reintegrating him into a normal school routine in hopes that socialization with other kids would mitigate the depressive symptoms.

But Tommy struggled academically and socially, and his classmates teased him. He lashed out and frequently got into fights. He was suspended from school dozens of times, which put additional strains on the foster carers who were required to pick him up after each incident. Tommy consequently bounced from one foster home to another.

Teenagers are hard to place in foster care, but one home with two other fostered teen boys agreed to take him in. Tommy ran away from the home after just a month and was found forty-eight hours later living in an abandoned car. He told the police that one of the other boys and the foster father had sexually abused him in separate incidents, but Thornton could not find any documented resolution to the allegations.

As Tommy grew older, he progressed to petty theft to support himself financially. There was one recorded incidence of arson, which Tommy claimed was a fire-for-hire scheme instigated by a businessman seeking insurance benefits. Thornton guessed it was true, because the charge against Tommy was dropped, presumably in exchange for cooperating with the Public Prosecution Service.

At first Thornton thought Tommy's transgressions stopped when he reached late adolescence, but then he realized the HSC file ended at age eighteen. He would have to reach out to the PSNI for Tommy's complete record as an adult. The folder he received from them previously mentioned only the break-in at Old Man Kelly's store and made just vague references to serial thefts and a pattern of public drunkenness.

After two hours of intense review, Thornton made three key observations. First, Tommy was never formally diagnosed or given meaningful, effective therapy. Secondly, of the eleven foster carers who took Tommy in, ten lasted less than two years. And thirdly, the entire chain of unfortunate events ensued from that one afternoon that claimed his parents' lives. *No wonder he's acting out. That bomb blew his entire world apart.*

COLBY & PRINCE

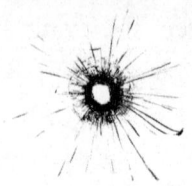

MICKEY SHANAHAN USED AN UNTRACEABLE MOBILE to contact clerks at various government offices and continue his research on Aaron Thornton and Claire Davis. Most of his contacts cooperated because they had family ties to the IRA. Two were simply greedy and well compensated. One had a predilection for young girls and was the target of Republican blackmail.

The clerks' reports indicated Colby & Prince, Solicitors, appeared on paperwork filed with government offices throughout Belfast in support of seemingly unrelated activities. Of course, there were the expedited HCPC petition and Parole Commission application signed by Rebecca Tucker on behalf of Thornton. But the firm also participated in the purchase of residential and commercial properties, a few vehicle sales, some international shipping, and applications for a wide assortment of government permits.

One particular transaction, reported by a clerk at Belfast City Hall, caught Shanahan's attention. It involved a permit for electrical work done at an address near Clonard Monastery a decade ago. The referenced row house might have escaped his notice if not for the fact that it was Fr. Matthew Clark's home for two years while renovations were underway at Clonard Monastery. Curious, he thought, but not necessarily alarming.

Armed with new details, Shanahan scoured the internet for more connections to Colby & Prince but came up empty. The phone number posted on the firm's website was answered by a pleasant woman with a Belfast accent who confirmed the office would be open until 16:00. Shanahan sent one of his men there posing as a lost motorcycle courier.

The scout reported a plain single storefront in good repair, with a lone receptionist posted in the waiting room. A security camera monitored the only visible entrance. He could not see what was beyond the door behind the receptionist, but heard no sound apart from music playing on a radio. Shanahan's man watched the one-story building from the end of the street for forty-five minutes before and after his contact with the receptionist. Nobody entered or left the premises, and a Ford B-Max was the only vehicle in the car park.

Shanahan pondered everything he knew about Colby & Prince and wondered if he was onto something or just paranoid. A call from one of his contacts at the central records bureau settled the question. After finding no electronic records for Rebecca Tucker, the industrious Christine Murray—motivated by Shanahan's "no info, no money" policy—searched the microfilm archives and discovered that Ms. Tucker, former legal secretary, died in a car crash thirty-four years ago and could not have signed Thornton's documents. To eliminate the possibility of two Rebecca Tuckers, Murray compared the deceased woman's signature to the paperwork for Thornton and found them similar but not identical. Shanahan doubled Murray's pay despite the bad news.

At Palace Barracks north of Belfast, a clerk reported in the daily log that a lost motorcycle courier visited Colby & Prince, Solicitors—one of MI5's covert storefronts—that afternoon and asked for directions to a local business. The entry noted the courier's envelope was intended for a business several blocks away, but the street number was smeared and illegible. A photograph of the courier was taken, but the reflection off his smoked, raised visor made facial recognition impossible.

THE CHINESE RESTAURANT

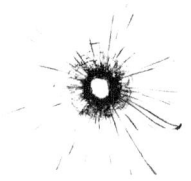

ACROSS TOWN, DEVIN DINGLE SAT AT A TABLE in the Chinese restaurant owned by his parents near one of the peace walls in Belfast. Unbeknownst to the elder Dingles, their son used one of the private dining rooms as the New IRA's headquarters. Now, an anxious Billy Hoyt—the messenger tackled while trying to deliver a mobile to Liam O'Malley at the Tricolor Pub—sat across from his equally agitated boss.

"What the fuck happened, Billy?"

"They saw me reachin' into me pocket when I approached O'Malley and thought I had a gun. One of his mates took me straight to the floor."

"Why didn't ya tell them I sent ya?"

"I did, I tell ya. But security was extra tight. O'Malley didn't seem the type to communicate by mobile though. He's old school. I'm not even sure he'd know how to use one," Billy said, trying to lighten the mood.

"Mind yerself, Billy. He's a legend, and we need him with *us* instead of the Provos."

Billy stopped smiling and looked away.

"*Fuck!*" Dingle slammed his hand on the table. "The optics would have been perfect. A Provo legend talkin' to the leader of the New IRA on his first day out of prison. Instead, he refuses to even say hello, and they toss ya out. Now we look weak. They need to show some respect."

Respect was a sensitive subject for Dingle. As a biracial youth, he never felt fully accepted as Caucasian or Chinese. Persons of Chinese descent were less than one percent of Northern Ireland's population, so there were not many Chinese to accept him in the first place. With the added sectarian divisions, Devin grew up constantly on the defensive—until he joined the New IRA, learned to play offensively, and maneuvered himself into a leadership role.

Older generations of the IRA saw Dingle—a ceasefire baby—as young, inexperienced, and lacking both perspective and credibility. But Dingle was exceptionally savvy when it came to social media—something the older generations did not grasp—and he effectively used that skill to craft a brand that mobilized his peers.

Dingle started the rumor about the New IRA's possession of the SAMs and ability to deploy them. He then manipulated social media until mainstream news picked up the story. It was a major public relations coup for the New IRA and an excellent recruiting tool. In reality, Dingle had no idea where the SAMs were, if there really *were* any missiles.

Dingle knew an overt alliance with the newly released O'Malley, or at least the appearance of an endorsement from him, would catapult the New IRA to a position of superiority over the IRA's old guard—without a protracted power struggle. And if the talented Mr. O'Malley were willing to design explosive devices for the New IRA, then even better.

"Billy, we need to figure out what flips O'Malley to our side. The rest of the Provos lost their will to fight and never finished the job. The whole point of the ceasefire was to give the political process a chance to succeed. Look where *that* got us—we're as divided as ever. If we don't resume armed struggle, then Republicanism is dead. Get close to the people who know O'Malley well and find me some bait. We need to hook him while he's still the center of attention so we can capitalize on the publicity."

"I'm on it, boss."

"Make it quick. We need to act in the next couple days. You can fill me in when we go over this week's receipts." Under Dingle's leadership, the New IRA was starting to monopolize drug sales and fencing operations in the Catholic wards to fund its larger ambitions. Initially, the income helped to outgun local rivals. Then it helped to buy support—often in the form of information—throughout Catholic neighborhoods. Dingle rationalized that *someone* was going to sell drugs and sell stolen property anyway, so it might as well be his crew that got the money. "Oh, one more thing. Any word on who shot me parents' door?"

"Not yet, boss, but I'm looking into the possibility it was that crew from the Cocky Rooster. Apparently one of our guys sold some crank to a Prod while his usual dealer was locked up, and we're thinking the UVF fired the shot as a turf warning."

Devin knew a turf war with Loyalist paramilitaries would divert resources he needed to outmaneuver the Provos. "Punish the idiot who sold to the Prod and make sure the UVF hears about it. And tell our crew that anyone else who does business with Loyalists will answer to me."

TRAWLER

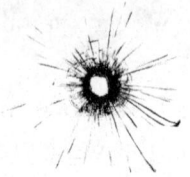

ANALYST PHILLIP JOHANNSEN was reviewing his team's daily reports on a computer at Palace Barracks when a red pop-up window alerted him to an urgent Trawler message. MI5 installed the Trawler software to monitor the digital records of incoming calls to 999 and CrimeStoppers.

While police operators typed descriptions of every call into their computers, Trawler scanned the entries—in real time—for keywords pre-programmed by the security services. The system alerted MI5 to any matches. As a result, MI5 knew about critical reports as quickly as the police and, if necessary, intervened in the interest of national security.

In this instance, Trawler matched multiple keywords and triggered the highest alert level. Johannsen's eyes grew wide when he saw the keywords: *IRA*, *killed*, *priest*, and *Falls Road* were all highlighted in yellow in the transcript. According to the male who telephoned CrimeStoppers, "the priest killed on the Falls Road" had been a "member of the IRA" and "executed for his crimes."

Solving the murder of Fr. Matthew Clark was the director's highest priority. Johannsen immediately routed the Trawler alert to his superiors.

As head of MI5's undercover operations, Robert Inglesby received Johannsen's alert on his secure mobile within seconds. He had just exited the CastleCourt car park. He pulled to the curb and read the message with considerable suspicion.

Although multiple theories about Clark's murder were under consideration, MI5 thought it most likely the IRA discovered his betrayal and killed him. If true, they were unlikely to report him to CrimeStoppers as an IRA criminal. Instead, they would publicize Clark's exposure as a tout to embarrass MI5 and discourage other potential informers. Also, the caller omitted the customary code words used by the IRA to authenticate their communications and distinguish them from pranksters.

Inglesby concluded that the IRA did not make the call. The tipster did not even use Clark's name. Moreover, he characterized the killing as an "execution" for the priest's "crimes" as a "member of the IRA." He sounded more like a Loyalist. But if the Loyalists wanted Clark dead, why did they wait so long?

Inglesby was fond of noting to MI5 trainees that "all behavior is purposeful." As he puzzled over the Trawler alert, he asked himself who benefited most from it. He glanced in the direction Kieran Oliver walked minutes earlier and reluctantly accepted that their relationship was about to end.

THE OFFER

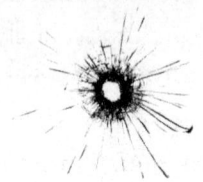

A GUARD ESCORTED CLAIRE DAVIS into the same room at HM Prison Maghaberry where her husband met with Liam O'Malley several weeks earlier. She knew nothing about that meeting, and Thornton knew nothing about this one. Waiting for Claire at the lone metal table was Francis McCarthy, attorney for Patrick Linden. The two lawyers talked previously on the phone but were meeting in person for the first time.

McCarthy stood and extended his hand. "It's good to meet you, Ms. Davis. Thank you for coming. I'm still a bit stunned by the Commission's interest in Patrick's case."

"I'm sure it was quite a surprise. But like I said on the phone, a majority of the CNICS committee, including me, was uncomfortable with the way Patrick's case was handled by the police and the prosecution service. We feel his conviction deserves review. I'll explain that to him today, and then all I need is his formal acceptance of our offer to represent him on appeal."

The door to the meeting room clicked and a guard swung it open. The escort waited outside as Linden approached the table and eyed Claire warily.

"It's alright," McCarthy told him. "She's here to get you out."

Claire introduced herself as an attorney and representative of the Commission on Northern Ireland's Court System. She explained CNICS' role in reviewing the cases of paramilitaries convicted of serious offenses under questionable circumstances and disclosed that the Committee selected Linden's case for judicial review.

She noted the group's concerns about the PSNI and the prosecution service's heavy reliance on hearsay and unsourced intelligence reports, the absence of any witnesses or hard evidence, and the anonymous tip that placed Linden under investigation in the first place. "Do you stand by your previous claim that you were tortured while in police custody?"

"Absolutely."

"And do you still allege the police forged your signature on the confession?"

"Aye. It's the truth."

"Mr. Linden, are you familiar with the Historical Enquiries Team?"

"Just a bit, I suppose. I've heard those boys did some pokin' around and found some shady shite that made the government uncomfortable, but not much more."

"Did anyone from the HET ever discuss your case with you?"

"No. I didn't even know they looked at me case. Did they find somethin'?" Linden's voice ticked up in volume.

"The HET discovered the two police officers who testified against you gave false testimony in other cases and were therefore not credible witnesses. The HET also found indications that the evidence against you may have been planted. Was any of that communicated to you?"

"It sure as shite was *not*." Linden whistled softly. "That's it then. Am I bein' released?"

"It's not quite that easy, but that *is* our goal—to overturn your conviction and have you released as quickly as possible. Does CNICS have your permission to work with Mr. McCarthy and appeal your case?"

"Is the Pope Catholic?! Yeah, yeah, let's get after 'em. So when did they figure all this out?"

Claire hesitated, and McCarthy interjected. "Patrick, the HET was disbanded about five years ago after a decade or so of investigations, but CNICS only got the files a few months ago."

"They've known about this for at least five years?! And nobody said a fuckin' thing to me about it?!" Linden's face reddened as he leapt to his feet. The guard dashed into the room with a baton ready. Linden quickly raised his hands above his head and sat down, seething. The guard lingered behind Linden until both attorneys assured him it was okay to withdraw.

McCarthy knew how to channel his client's anger and took over for Claire. "This is our chance to get you out and prove to the world what we've been saying all along. It's a PR nightmare for the government, the PSNI, and the Army, and they'll have *no choice* but to release you. The HET was part of the PSNI, so they've already *admitted* in *writing* they bolloxed the whole thing. Now CNICS will be the independent, *neutral* body that makes the case for us in court and finally gets justice. This won't be the IRA's standard string of objections. It will be the HET and CNICS crying foul. You couldn't have scripted it better yourself, Patrick."

Linden knew his lawyer was right. The review would be disastrous for the government and generate a lot of attention in the media. Despite his anger about the delay, he realized from a strategic perspective that the revelations came at a good time.

Once released, he would be in a stronger position to deal with Dingleberry, find Clark's killer, and keep watch over Liam.

Then Linden's face clouded. It seemed too convenient and too good to be true. First Liam and now him. Both men set free so close together and so randomly, or so it seemed. *What am I missing? There must be some angle here. What could the Brits be up to?*

If Linden had known Claire was married to Liam's psychologist, he would have walked away without another word. Linden studied Claire and asked, "Who else is on yer list to set free?"

"We focus on one client at a time, and you're the first. After evaluating several options, we concluded your case is the strongest. We want our initial appearance in court to be a successful one."

"I see." Linden locked eyes with McCarthy.

McCarthy turned to Claire and said, "Ms. Davis, would you excuse us for a moment while I confer with Patrick in private? The guards allow an attorney to wait in the hall for a few minutes."

Somewhat startled, Claire replied, "Oh, of course."

"Just knock sharply on the door, and the guard will know you'd like to exit. Tell him we just need a couple minutes."

Claire did as instructed. As she stepped into the hall and the door closed behind her, she wondered what was wrong.

LEGAL PERIL

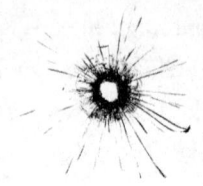

WITH CLAIRE OUT OF THE ROOM, Linden leaned forward and spoke to his lawyer. "Are ya sure this isn't some kind of set-up?"

McCarthy was taken aback. "In what way? I don't see how this could be anything but helpful."

"It seems too easy. Too coincidental. About a month ago, this American psychologist appears out of nowhere and meets with Liam as a last-minute condition of his release. Says he works for the Parole Commission and wants to make sure Liam won't resume his paramilitary activities. Then the shrink convinces Liam to meet with him once a week on the outside to make sure everythin's going okay. Now this lady shows up and wants to spring me too? As a representative of some other Commission? It's all too strange."

"It's apples and oranges, Paddy. They identified Liam for release over a year ago because of political pressure to reduce the number of jailed paramilitaries. It's normal for so-called violent offenders to have a psychological screening and ongoing super-vision on the outside. It *is* unusual to have an American involved, but would it make any difference if he was Irish? You don't trust *anyone*. And Liam *did* get released. He has as much to lose as anyone if he reveals too much to the psychologist. Besides, he knows what happens to touts."

Linden felt somewhat reassured.

"Now, your situation is different, Paddy. This is not a scheduled release. It's an appeal to be filed by a neutral third party seeking to have your conviction overturned because of the corrupt way your case was handled. CNICS is a legitimate commission seeking reforms of our legal process. I checked them out before agreeing to this meeting. And the appeal is based primarily on the investigation by the HET—also a legitimate organization that was around for about a decade. If the appeal is successful, you get out. If not, everything is status quo. I don't see any risk. Plus, Claire Davis is from Belfast."

"What if the appeal exposes other stuff I was involved in?"

"It won't. The review is strictly limited to the procedural failures by the police and the prosecution service that led to your current incarceration. They have to stick with what's already on the record."

Linden remained apprehensive. "If I agree to this now, and later decide it's all a set-up, can I tell this lady to fuck off?"

"Absolutely. It's the same as for you and me. If you no longer want CNICS to represent you for the appeal, they're done and have to walk away."

"Alright then. Let's do it. I've been in this shite hole long enough."

McCarthy signaled to the guard to let Claire back in, and the trio formally agreed that CNICS would handle Linden's appeal.

THE DOG WALKER

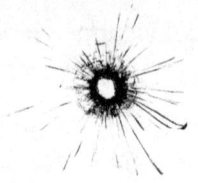

PAULA HALL STROLLED PAST the modest brick building on Ormeau Road. She pretended to text someone. She was actually snapping photos of Thornton's office building and taking notes about activity in the area. It was not easy with a Pomeranian, a Shih Tzu, and a corgi in tow, but Paula's instructions were clear—pass by the office as often as possible and report everything.

Paula had the gift of *craic*—the Irish word for a fun time or friendly conversation. Her friends joked that she could make friends with a corpse and get him talking again in five minutes. She never forgot a face or a name. Once she engaged you in conversation, it was only a matter of time until you lowered your guard and began to overshare. In short, she was the perfect spy.

Like all good spies, Paula maintained legitimate employment that gave cover to her clandestine activities. She was a professional dog walker with an unofficial license to roam anywhere in Belfast without arousing suspicion. She became a familiar face in every ward and never looked out of place. Whether Paula lingered or hurried along, it always seemed natural—and she had the keys to homes in every part of the city. The keys alone legitimized her presence anywhere she went and provided an abundance of observation posts wherever she needed them.

Paula's clients included politicians, psychiatrists, police inspectors, journalists, hairdressers, teachers, flight attendants, and even employees of the security services. Her personality and reliability boosted demand for her help, and what began as a recurring favor for a cute neighbor who flew long haul flights for British Airways grew into a profitable business for which Paula hired two assistants.

The handsome pilot with a healthy libido sadly relocated to London with his labradoodle. During a subsequent girls' night out in Belfast city center, Paula spotted an equally muscular though younger man staring at her from across the pub. Never the shy one, Paula bid the girls good night, seized her opportunity, and took Mickey Shanahan back to her flat for a raucous night of sex. Mickey later boasted it was the funnest recruitment he ever undertook.

Mickey and Paula's encounter was no accident. The Provos needed a new cover for their surveillance operations after the exposure of an IRA-controlled delivery service, and Mickey's team several times spotted Paula and her two dog-walking assistants in both Loyalist and Republican-controlled areas. Mickey did his homework and knew that Paula was the only child of a mixed marriage—one between a Catholic and a Protestant. Both parents were born in Britain and now dead. At first glance, she might have been perceived as non-sectarian or slightly Loyalist in her views, but Mickey's sources reported otherwise.

As a teenager, the ostensibly Protestant Paula had been badly bullied for dating a Catholic boy. The boy, too, was harassed and, to prove his Republican loyalties, took to throwing petrol bombs at the police and participating in low-level mischief with other Catholic teens in his neighborhood. Love is love though, and he continued to court Paula in secret.

One evening, as the Catholic boy walked Paula home in a Protestant neighborhood, a gang of Loyalist youths pounced on the pair. The group repeatedly punched the boy, knocked him to the ground, and told him he did not belong in that part of town. When the gang laid hands on Paula and called her a slut and a traitor, the Catholic boy tried to leap to her defense. The Loyalist boys kicked him back to the pavement, where one of them stabbed him twice before the group fled. Paula saw her first love bleed to death while the neighbors watched from the windows, unwilling to help. Paula's family relocated to the Republic, but after her parents' deaths she returned to her birthplace.

And so it was that after a night of incredible sex, Mickey confidently pitched a partnership between Paula and the Provos. Paula accepted the offer on one semi-serious condition—Mickey's sexual services would have to be part of the deal. "Anything for the cause," he answered jovially. Though unmarried and often living apart, they were an unofficial couple ever since, and over a period of many years Paula became the Provos' best "watcher" in Belfast.

The job of watching Thornton would prove to be her most consequential assignment yet.

THE CROWN JEWELS

AS PATRICK LINDEN'S RIGHT-HAND MAN and the head of security and intelligence for the Provos, it was Mickey Shanahan's job to anticipate and prevent problems. While most Provos viewed Devin Dingle and the New IRA dismissively, Shanahan knew better than to discount an ambitious, media-savvy upstart with a team of restless young thrill seekers at his disposal. He also recognized Dingle's attempt to court Liam O'Malley as a genius power play and public relations move. He decided to have a chat with one of the Provos' old guard, Maxwell Mayhew, to see if there was anything about O'Malley's past—apart from the obvious—that might have attracted Dingle's interest.

Mayhew retired completely from the IRA and moved to the Republic when the Good Friday Agreement was signed in 1998. Until then he was the only person apart from Linden to work closely with O'Malley. Since a candid discussion with Linden in Maghaberry was out of the question, Shanahan arranged the next best thing. Mayhew was extremely reluctant to reconnect with anyone still active in the IRA, but curiosity got the best of him and he agreed to meet Shanahan in the basement of Clonard Monastery.

It was cold and rainy, so few pedestrians were on the street as the bell struck 19:00. Shanahan spotted Mayhew through a window as he ascended a short flight of stairs at a side entrance to the building. Shanahan swung open the heavy wooden door and welcomed him warmly. The two men strode across the vestibule. As Shanahan paused to unlock the stairwell door, Mayhew wistfully observed it had been more than a quarter-century since he last visited the cellar. "It's still the safest place in Belfast," Shanahan said.

Once the two men were cocooned in the electronic dead zone, Shanahan revealed the purpose of their meeting. Mayhew leaned back and took a deep breath.

"O'Malley was easily the best explosives handler and assassination planner we ever had. He was unbelievably clever and studious. He could combine ordinary household chemicals, fertilizers, and random ingredients into powerful bombs using recipes stored and refined only in his head. He could identify a bomb's components just from the smell of it. Early on, we were plagued with problems related to the size and instability of many explosives, so O'Malley devised ways to make the bombs smaller and safer to handle.

"For a while he worked to improve our timers, which sometimes triggered prematurely or not at all. Then he introduced us to some truly revolutionary detonators. Remotely controlled devices became the norm thanks to O'Malley. We loved them because we could stay at a safe distance and still explode them at precisely the right moment. When the Brits got good at jamming our signals, O'Malley designed bombs we could trigger with infrared beams. He even discovered a way to use flash attachments for cameras to remotely detonate explosives. The guy was a genius, I tell ya. Even a bit diabolical.

"Car bombs were our signature device for such a long time, but they weren't always effective. The ones that relied on timers sometimes malfunctioned and missed their targets. They could also be spotted and disarmed. So O'Malley produced motion-detecting detonators that activated only when a vehicle moved and was surely occupied, or when touched by a bomb disposal technician. We considered either outcome a win. And do you remember those light bulb bombs that detonated when the wall switch was turned on? They were O'Malley's invention. He could disguise a bomb to look like *anything*. There was just no limit to his creativity, and he had a solution for every problem. As a result, we grew more effective with time and really seemed to be gaining the upper hand.

"That's why the Brits started recruiting informers—they made a lot of judicial deals and spent a small fortune to infiltrate and undermine us. And while we couldn't match their numbers in terms of people and pounds, we did infiltrate them at least as well as they infiltrated us. That's how we discovered they could jam us and were monitoring our purchase of agricultural supplies, for example. We even had an insider who told us the Army's step-by-step procedures for disarming devices, so we could alter our wiring. It was a constant game of cat and mouse. I think you may have had a hand in that yourself, if what I hear is true."

Shanahan just smiled. "I grossly underestimated O'Malley's value. This has all been incredibly helpful, Max. What else should I know?"

"There's one more thing, mate. After you contacted me to arrange this meeting, I had an old friend visit Linden in Maghaberry. The boss sent back permission to tell you anything, so now you get access to the Crown Jewels." It was never a good idea to talk out of turn, even if you had been away from the IRA for twenty-five years.

Mayhew continued, "This last bit of information may be the *real* reason your boy Dingle is interested in O'Malley. Those rumors about the SAM missiles? They're true. We got our hands on two launching systems and ten missiles. The Libyans fucked us, though, and removed a couple key components required for detonation. It was around that time we started to compartmentalize internal operations to guard against informers—as long as no one person knew too much, he or she couldn't hurt us too badly if they grassed. So I don't know where the missiles ended up. But last I heard, O'Malley was working on a solution to fix the detonation problem. And I wouldn't bet against Liam O'Malley."

Shanahan frowned. "Bloody hell," he said before pulling a pistol from beneath the gray metal table and shooting Mayhew between the eyes. "That information is too valuable to be shared with anyone else."

SECRETS

LIAM O'MALLEY WALKED into the Reconciliation meeting in the community room at Clonard Monastery a few minutes early. It was his first appearance, since the gatherings were temporarily suspended after Matthew Clark's murder. The size and age of the group surprised him. About forty people, mostly under the age of forty-five, were seated theater-style in the space. Only a handful from his generation were present.

At precisely 18:00, a Protestant minister clad in a gray shirt and black pants walked to the front of the room and introduced himself as the facilitator. He acknowledged the absence of his previous co-leader, Fr. Matthew Clark, whose murder on the Falls Road a couple months earlier remained unsolved. The minister asked for a moment of silence.

O'Malley choked at the sound of Clark's name, which the group mistook for grief. Although Fr. Clark's murder was common knowledge in the area, Clark's leadership of the Reconciliation effort was news to O'Malley. O'Malley knew better than most people the role Fr. Clark played in keeping the IRA well-armed. O'Malley wondered how sincere Clark's efforts at Reconciliation had been. He also thought it ironic—almost

perverse—that the IRA once used this very building as its headquarters. He assumed no one else in the group knew.

The minister broke the silence by welcoming new faces in
the crowd. He explained the group's objective, in the simplest
of terms, was to promote a sustainable peace for Northern Ireland. To date, he noted, the group funded interfaith summer
camps and overnight trips for youth, brokered negotiations for
the non-violent implementation of the bonfires and parades
that annually sparked tension between Protestants and Catholics, published articles in the local press, promoted collaboration
among local merchants, and coached local politicians on ways
to avoid inflammatory remarks and actions. "I know these are
sensitive topics, and I appreciate yer willingness to tackle them
with us."

The minister then called one of the younger participants to
come forward and review the group's rules. An enthusiastic and
cheerful lass bounced to the front of the room with such energy
that her ponytail flew into the air. "Please remember to avoid
identifying people by their faith and focus on the present and
future as much as possible. We do our best to avoid mention of
specific past wrongs, apart from acknowledging in non-sectarian
terms the emotional reactions they caused. Remember that we
all share and understand the same emotions. Yeah, so that's it
really."

The minister returned to the front of the room and thanked
the young lady. He announced the group's focus that evening
was the increasing unrest among teenagers at the interface areas,
where Protestant and Catholic residential areas border one
another.

The ensuing discussion yielded a consensus that teenage boys
and young men in their early 20s were the main participants in

the unrest, which generally consisted of petrol bombs, stolen and burned vehicles, thrown bricks and bottles, and graffiti and other vandalism. Although pistols were occasionally brandished or seen tucked in waistbands, no one had been shot in the past year or so. Still, the number of unruly nights was increasing along with the number of participants, and tensions seemed near a breaking point. Many people attributed the unrest to fiery political speeches on both sides that included talk of ditching the peace agreement and resuming violence to achieve political goals.

A social worker at the meeting wondered if Protestant and Catholic youth were competing to be the dominant group. Some residents thought the hooliganism was just a rite of passage and a way to prove your bravery or to be part of something bigger and more powerful than yourself. One mother of preteen boys thought it was merely "something fun and thrilling" to pass the time.

An older man felt the young mother's view was naive, since he knew middle-aged men and women were teaching young people how to cause trouble without getting caught. Several others in the crowd echoed his sentiment and thought these "mentors" aligned with the political firebrands who wanted to stoke violence for political purposes.

In response to a question from the minister, the group agreed that most residents, of either faith, would be unwilling to speak too strongly against the unrest or those promoting it—for fear they would become targets themselves. Both Catholic and Protestant neighborhoods, it was clear, still had a code of conduct that local gangs unofficially but effectively enforced. It was best not to look "soft" against the "other side."

As the meeting neared its end, a teen boy who had remained quiet all night raised his hand. The minister invited him to share his thoughts.

"I know we're not talkin' about a plan to fix all this right now, and I don't want to sound pessimistic or anything. But I feel like no one my age is going to listen to our parents or teachers or clergy or politicians anymore. We've already heard it all, and let's face it, the adults haven't done a very good job of fixin' things. To be honest, yer the ones who messed it all up to begin with. My generation is more likely to listen to an influencer or a celebrity, so maybe we can be thinkin' about that between now and next time."

O'Malley made a mental note to learn what an influencer was and shifted in his seat. He did not consider himself a celebrity, but knew his words carried weight in Republican circles. He worried the group, if they ever realized who he was, might try to enlist him for some sort of public campaign. He certainly did not want to be thrust into the spotlight. His past life already put a target on his back, and there was no sense making that target easier to see. And he still had too many secrets to keep.

It occurred to O'Malley that a *lot* of people kept secrets. Fr. Clark certainly had. And apparently the IRA kept its use of Clonard a secret. For that matter, he thought, the Catholic Church itself had been keeping all sorts of sordid secrets for decades. He wondered who else in the room was keeping secrets.

Outside, the IRA man Mickey Shanahan assigned to keep watch over O'Malley leaned against his car and smoked a cigarette. He decided against following O'Malley inside the monastery for fear of exposure. *How much trouble can you get into at church?*

GUILT

WHEN O'MALLEY EXITED THE RECONCILIATION MEETING and stepped into the cool night air, the teen boy who mentioned influencers walked up and welcomed O'Malley as a newcomer to the group.

O'Malley eyed the youth warily, wondering if the boy recognized him. "Where are ya from, lad?" He was surprised to hear the boy lived in the Protestant Shankill ward. "Who came here with ya?"

"Came on me own," the boy answered indignantly. "I'm seventeen, so ya know."

O'Malley's instincts told him it was unwise for a Protestant lad to be walking through these parts at night by himself, but he held his tongue. *Maybe there's been a wee bit of progress after all.* "So what prompted ya to join a Reconciliation group?"

"I grew up hearin' stories from me pa and granddad about family members who were killed or injured by the IRA. Their photos are on the wall at me house and all me relatives' homes, so we won't ever forget 'em. I never met 'em, but one was a government clerk and pregnant. Another was a newlywed killed on his way out of the church, and my granddad's brother was killed when a bomb went off at a train station. But those photos and stories just keep makin' everyone mad, over and over. The anti-Catholic sentiment in me family runs deep, and it's pretty intense.

"But *I* don't feel that way. I have Catholic friends, and I know Loyalists killed people too. Still do. Honestly, it feels like the adults on both sides just try to goad each other with parades and threats and inflammatory speeches. But they're bein' hypocritical for denouncin' the other side for the same things they themselves are guilty of.

"So I see me parents, uncles, and granddad drinkin' and hatin' and stirrin' up trouble and tryin' to get me to join in. I don't like it. I don't want to be like them, and I don't want me kids to be like that."

O'Malley was struck by the impact of The Troubles on the boy. He guessed there were others like him. They were born after the peace agreement and had no personal memory of The Troubles, yet they were haunted by what happened. He knew Catholic families kept shrines to their dead and passed down hatred too. And the walls and buildings of Belfast were blanketed with murals paying homage to martyrs and heroes of the past, on both sides of the conflict.

Suddenly O'Malley felt a lump in his throat and a churning in his stomach. *Am I to blame for this kid's family being so fucked up?* At the time, it never occurred to him that a legitimate assassination might curse future generations. It was never his intention to hurt the innocent. O'Malley grew uncomfortable as he contemplated the unintended consequences of his actions. For a split second he wanted to apologize to the boy for the pain he suffered—if not because of O'Malley, then certainly because of O'Malley's comrades. But he caught himself and kept his own counsel. *Let sleeping dogs lie.*

"I'm sorry, sir. I don't mean to bore ya."

"Yer not borin' me, son. Ya just got me thinkin' is all. Maybe we'll talk again at the next meetin'."

O'Malley and the boy said good night before heading in opposite directions. Across the road, the IRA man Mickey Shanahan assigned to keep watch over O'Malley stared at the teen, trying to remember where he had seen him before. Then it hit him—he was the grandson of Garth Peters, the UVF boss at the Cocky Rooster. The watcher had taken his photo when the crew was gathering information about Peters' family a year ago.

MS. TUCKER

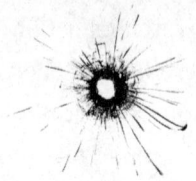

INTELLIGENCE ANALYST VERONICA SPELL sat in a technical suite at Palace Barracks and monitored activity across several computer systems. She had just read about an unidentified motorcyclist's visit to Colby & Prince, Solicitors, a fake law firm used by MI5 as a cover for some of the service's clandestine activities. Since Colby & Prince did not serve the public, it was unusual for anyone to show up there.

A receptionist staffed the front desk merely to create the illusion of a real business. A couple MI5 clerks worked in the back room and could pose as employees of the law firm in the unlikely event such a charade became necessary. Every so often, undercover operatives would visit the location to create the appearance of activity, but in reality the building was there merely for show.

Spell noted the motorcyclist kept his face concealed from the security camera at the entrance to the building. She also noticed he claimed to be a courier in need of directions to a nearby business whose address was smeared on the package he sought to deliver. Spell saw the courier had a mobile and wondered why he had not simply looked up the business' address online. She suspected the storefront was being probed.

Spell generated a list of names used by MI5 in connection with Colby & Prince and ran them against a collection of other databases for any recent inquiries. She was about to chalk her suspicions up to routine paranoia when the computer returned a single match. The name *Rebecca Tucker* was entered as an archive search at the central records depository—two days before the courier's visit to the storefront. The real Rebecca Tucker had died in 1985, before personal computers, the internet, and the digital age. Someone went out of their way to find her.

Spell then checked the name of the researcher who queried the archive. It was Elizabeth Regina. Spell sighed. It was highly unlikely Her Majesty the Queen had any interest in the late Ms. Tucker, and Spell was perturbed by the archive clerk's inattention to the researcher's identity.

Spell completed one last search of the computers, to see whether anyone living used the name Rebecca Tucker—and if not, whether anyone at MI5 had bothered to create bogus digitized records that would create the *appearance* of a living person with that name. Clearly, if Rebecca Tucker were currently employed by Colby & Prince, there would be a digital footprint for her. Spell was chagrined to find no such electronic trail, and she knew the jig was up.

Spell switched to a secure messaging system and issued a terse alert to all personnel who used Colby & Prince or Rebecca Tucker as covers for their activity. "Colby & Prince, Solicitors, probed by unknown individual. Rebecca Tucker exposed. Take appropriate measures."

CLEANUP

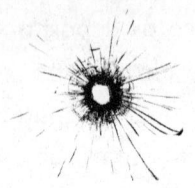

ROBERT INGLESBY HAD JUST SAT DOWN for a bite to eat when the alert about Rebecca Tucker's exposure flashed on his secure mobile. *Bloody hell. I don't have time for this.* He quickly finished his lunch and went to his car to call the office securely.

"Patch me through to analyst Veronica Spell, please."

"Please stand by, sir."

Inglesby adjusted the temperature in his car while he waited for the analyst to connect.

"This is Spell."

"Ms. Spell, this is Robert Inglesby, Director of Undercover Operations. Verification 85253."

The analyst confirmed the code in the staff directory and asked, "How can I help, sir?"

"I've just seen your alert on my mobile. What prompted it?"

Spell explained her concerns about the courier who appeared to probe the Colby & Prince storefront and the search for Rebecca Tucker's name in the records archive. She emphasized that there was no current digital footprint for anyone with Tucker's name.

"Can't we still create one? I'm confident the storefront will survive scrutiny, but it was definitely a mistake not to create a fake digital trail for Tucker."

"We absolutely can, sir. Might it already be too late though? If they were thorough enough to check the microfilm archive, surely they've already done an online search."

Inglesby knew she was right. "I have an idea. Let's capitalize on the searcher's attention to detail and hope he or she keeps diggin'. Create all the usual digital records we would establish for our undercover identities but then block them from the search engines and government indexes. Create a few bogus stalkin' complaints with the police in Tucker's name, going back a few years. Then post a fake protective order in the judicial records system. When our inquisitive friend continues pokin' around, they'll find the protective order, see the reports of a stalker, and hopefully assume Tucker's digital records were masked for her protection. At the very least it gives a plausible explanation for her digital absence."

Spell was impressed with the director's ability to come up with a solution so quickly. "Should I create fake social media accounts as well, sir?"

"No. Anyone with a stalker would have deleted that sort of thing. Stick to the usual driver's license, healthcare, and other government records. Have the artificial intelligence team generate a photo for you, and use one of our undercover postal boxes as Tucker's address."

MI5 was well practiced in creating artificial records and false identities, so Spell confidently assured Inglesby everything would be handled by the end of the day.

"It should've been handled a long time ago, but you did well to catch it and send the alert. Thank you for your help." Inglesby ended the call and started the car. As he eased into traffic, he wondered who was investigating Tucker and whether he erred by using her name on the applications for Thornton's healthcare license and position with the parole board. He assumed wrongly that no one would pay much notice to a psychologist recently arrived from America. But at least there was no link between him and his son-in-law.

MARZIPAN

PATRICK LINDEN TOOK HIS SEAT across from Mickey Shanahan at the bare metal table in the visitor ward at HM Prison Maghaberry. They said a brief hello and launched straight into business once the guard exited the room.

Shanahan confirmed he met with "that fella from the Republic," taking care not to mention Maxwell Mayhew by name. "He's on holiday in Spain now," Shanahan added, using code to let Linden know Mayhew's body had been disappeared. "But you should know Dingleberry is actively tryin' to meet with O'Malley."

"That can't happen," Linden said. "That little shite is tryin' to use O'Malley to make a name for himself and thumbin' his nose at the rest of us in the process. Did you deliver the flowers to Dingleberry's mum?"

"Yeah, boss, but he and his crew are actin' like nothin' happened."

"Then let's up the ante. Leave some marzipan at his parents' restaurant." Marzipan was code for a bomb, since the candy in log form resembles a brick of raw C-4 explosive.

Shanahan was apprehensive about the escalation in tactics but nodded. He knew the Provos had to keep Dingleberry from gaining more influence—and O'Malley's apparent ability to fix the detonators on the SAM missiles would give the New IRA an insurmountable boost. "By the way, I made sure O'Malley got the package you sent him," referring to the pistol left for O'Malley's self-defense in the bathroom at the Tricolor Pub on the day of his release from prison.

"Good, Mickey, good. I know ya have someone mindin' him, but we can't be too careful. The man is valuable to us, and we need to keep him alive."

"No worries, boss. So far no one but Dingleberry has shown any interest in him. We have eyes on him 'round the clock."

"What about those Reconciliation meetings and the appointments with the shrink?"

"Aye, boss, he goes to both, but nothin' looks unusual. Did you know the Reconciliation meetings are held in Clonard Monastery? There's a wee bit of irony for ya."

"What else?" Linden was not in a joking mood.

"I have different eyes watchin' the American. He meets at his office with a few low-level offenders referred to him by the courts. No one notable. He eats lunch and exercises alone. So far nothin' strange about his personal contacts or history. His background in America checks out. He moved here with his wife last summer—she's now a professor at QUB. But there *is* somethin' strange goin' on..."

Linden motioned impatiently for him to continue.

Shanahan lowered his voice. There was no code for what he was about to tell Linden. "It's about the American's applications for a healthcare license and a position with the Parole Commission. They were both submitted by Colby & Prince, Solicitors, of Belfast, and signed by someone named Rebecca Tucker. Only problem is, Tucker died 34 years ago. And we can't find anyone by that name alive today."

Linden made a deliberate effort to remain calm and think through the implications. "How reliable is your source?"

"She's worked with us for years. A real digger, and her intel has always been correct."

"So why would Thornton want to forge his applications with a dead woman's signature?"

"And why use a law firm to file the applications instead of just doing it himself?"

"Yer right, it doesn't make sense. Clearly Thornton isn't who he claims to be, or he's workin' with someone who doesn't want to be identified. Either way, O'Malley could be in jeopardy."

Shanahan was inclined to agree, but then his thoughts turned to the murder of Fr. Clark, the priest's seized mobile, and the interrogators' visit to the church secretary. *Was it all somehow related to this new prison psychologist and O'Malley's release from prison? Was O'Malley being set up? Or worse, had he turned?* Shanahan did not dare voice his doubts about the boss' best mate. He didn't have to—the same thoughts already crossed Linden's mind.

Linden spoke sharply to Shanahan. "Maintain full-time watches on the American and O'Malley. I want to know about *everything* they do, and *everyone* they communicate with. Eventually someone will make a mistake and we'll know fer sure what we're dealin' with. Put the ISU on standby." The Internal Security Unit, colloquially known as the Nutting Squad, was the team responsible for the Provos' counterintelligence and interrogation activities. They were ruthless, effective, and universally feared. No one was beyond their reach.

"Anything else, boss?"

Linden paused but said nothing about the lady lawyer and the plan to spring him from prison. "Isn't that enough?"

"Aye, I've got me hands full." The boss' worried look unnerved Shanahan. "It'll be alright, boss. I've got it all under control."

Linden had the utmost faith in his right-hand man. Still, he sensed that things were about to become very much *out* of control.

CLAIRE'S TAIL

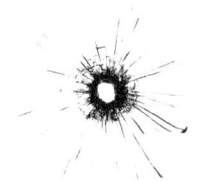

MICKEY SHANAHAN LEFT HIS MEETING WITH LINDEN grateful the boss did not ask more questions about the American psychologist. He needed more time to research Claire Davis and figure out that business with Rebecca Tucker.

Shanahan got into his car and headed for Clonard. He dialed Paula Hall while sitting in traffic.

"Hallo, lover," she said with a sultry voice.

"What I wouldn't give to be naked in bed with ya right now. Or naked with ya *anywhere*, for that matter."

Paula laughed and said, "Did ya call me just to have phone sex, or do we have pressin' matters to attend to?"

"Pressin' matters, regretfully. I need yer help with a job."

"Name it."

"Ya know that American psychologist, Thornton, whose office yer watchin' on Ormeau Road? He's linked online to a woman named Claire Davis from Belfast. Apparently she's a professor at QUB. I need to know more about her, who she meets with, and what her connection to Thornton is. All the usual stuff."

"No problem, hun. What kind of timeline are we workin' with?"

"As soon as possible, like everything else. I know ya can only be in one place at a time, and I already asked ya to keep an eye on Thornton's office. Ya can pick one of the lads to help ya out, but stay on top of this. The boss is gettin' really agitated about keepin' O'Malley safe, and he doesn't trust this American fella."

"Got it. I'll see what I can do."

"Oh, I *know* what ya can do," he said playfully. "I'll see ya tonight."

"Lookin' forward to it, ya horny bastard."

CATHARSIS

TOMMY MAGEE SMILED AND MET THORNTON'S GAZE directly as he entered the psychologist's office and dropped into the overstuffed chair. The pair had met eight times, and Tommy was more comfortable now with the process. Thornton was coaching Tommy on how to recognize his "automatic negative thoughts" and replace them with healthier interpretations of events to boost his self-esteem.

"Well *you* seem to be in a good mood this afternoon! What's on the agenda for today?"

"Before I get to that, can you go over the rules again about keepin' stuff secret?"

"Sure. Generally speaking, I am not permitted to disclose anything we talk about without your permission. There are a couple exceptions to that rule though. For example, if you reveal anything about terror offenses or the funding of terrorism, I have to report it to the authorities. And if I feel you are an immediate danger to yourself or someone else, I'm required to intervene and protect anyone at risk."

Tommy considered Thornton's explanation. "Okay. So, if I'm not blowin' shite up, payin' someone to blow shite up, and not gonna kill meself or some other bloke when I walk out the door, it stays just between us?"

"That sums it up. And if you're ever unsure whether something's confidential, just ask me hypothetically what would happen if you brought it up. I'll tell you honestly what the rules are, and then you can decide whether you want to mention it or not. Did you know I used to work in a maximum-security prison in America?" Thornton shifted slightly in his seat.

"No." Tommy was intrigued.

"It was a rough place with extremely violent criminals who kept very dark secrets. Several inmates required to meet with me didn't believe things would stay confidential, even though the rules are stricter in the States. So whenever they wanted to talk about something sensitive, but didn't want to worry about me reporting it, they just introduced the topic by saying, 'If someone came to see you who did X, Y, and Z, and he's having nightmares about it, how would you help him?'"

Thornton paused as the faces of inmates at Hazelton Prison briefly surfaced in his mind. "And then we'd talk about 'the friend.' I knew we were probably talking about the inmates themselves, and they knew I knew that, but it gave them a way to get things off their chests without me having to report them. It was better than not being able to talk about it at all."

Tommy grinned. "That's clever, Doc. I like it."

"I'm glad you asked me that question, because it's an important one. We can't fix what we don't talk about. So, what do you feel comfortable talking about today?"

"I was thinkin' about yer question the first time we met, about things I'd like to change. It would be good to find a new place to live and get a different roommate. Mine can be…" Tommy remembered Kieran's warning not to say anything to Thornton and abruptly stopped talking.

Thornton tilted his head to one side but waited silently for Tommy to continue.

"That probably won't happen though, 'cuz I'd need money to do that but can't get a job. The only money I make now is from odd jobs Kieran gets me."

"Let's reframe that, like you've been practicing."

"Sorry, Doc. That probably won't happen cuz I need money to do that but *haven't found a job yet.*"

Thornton nodded encouragingly. "Better. Or, 'When I find a job, my income will help pay for a new place.'"

Tommy savored the thought. "And my new roommate can help pay for it."

"Exactly!" The two laughed. "You've known Kieran for a long time, haven't you?" Thornton wondered why Tommy avoided talking about his roommate.

"Aye, we were foster brothers for a couple years, and he's probably the closest thing I have to family, even though he can be a real bother sometimes." Mention of his foster care suddenly flooded Tommy's mind with intrusive memories of the bullying, the fights, and the abuse. He felt the anger return. He thought about his trouble holding a job, his financial problems, the drinking, the nightmares, Kieran's volatility, the priest's murder, and the prospect of jail as one negative thought cascaded toward another in a downward spiral of despair.

The anger surged into rage, and the rage took aim at the faceless culprit responsible for all of it—the killer who orphaned Tommy and sent him down a path of hopelessness and helplessness.

Tommy's face flushed bright red. Even his ears went crimson. His fists clenched, his jaw tightened, and his knee bounced incessantly. Then his eyes moistened.

Thornton watched patiently as the process unfolded on its own.

Tommy finally snarled through gritted teeth. *"I want to kill the fuckin' bastard!"*

Thornton stayed calm. "Can you tell me why?"

Unexpectedly for both of them, the dam burst and twenty-five years of accumulated emotion flowed unrestrained. Tommy sobbed loudly as his body rocked in the chair. Snot formed at his nostrils, and he labored to catch his breath. Guttural, almost inhuman sounds rumbled from his chest. The catharsis continued for several minutes, uninterrupted and unimpeded by Thornton, until Tommy was able to spit out four tortured words. *"He killed me parents!"*

Thornton managed to conceal his surprise. After a moment's hesitation, he said, "Tommy, I am so sorry. That's awful. It must be incredibly hard for you to share a flat with him. No wonder you want to move out."

Tommy looked at Thornton quizzically and then realized what happened. "No, no, Doc," Tommy said, sniffling. He cleared his throat and clarified, *"Kieran* didn't kill my parents. The fuckin' *IRA* did."

Thornton's eyes widened, and he leaned farther forward. Tommy's file made only brief mention of a bombing, and Tommy had not mentioned it until now. "Tommy, I am so sorry."

"Naw, *I'm* sorry, Doc. I don't know where all that came from. Didn't mean to dump that on ya," he said with embarrassment.

"Don't apologize. You've obviously been holding onto a lot of emotion for quite some time and needed to let it out. What better or safer place than here? And of *course* you need to talk about your parents' deaths. I'm sure that had a profound impact on you."

Tears still flowed down Tommy's cheeks, though less steadily now. "All that stuff in my file, and all those boxes I ticked on that questionnaire ya gave me…" Tommy's words trailed off while he blew his nose. "That's all because of the bastard who killed me parents. He killed them and fucked me life. *That's* the guy I want to kill."

Tommy's earlier question about confidentiality hung in the air alongside his comment about wanting to kill the man who murdered his parents. Thornton asked apprehensively, "Do you know his name?"

"Naw," Tommy sniffled. "They never caught 'im. Or her. For all I know, there could have been more than one."

Thornton looked relieved. There was no need to breach confidentiality without an identifiable person at risk. But then he asked, "Tommy, have you ever thought about killing yourself?"

Tommy looked stunned. "How did ya know?"

"I didn't, but homicidal thoughts and suicidal thoughts often occur together. Tell me more about wanting to kill yourself."

Tommy described his visit to Ballycastle beach with the sleeping pills a few months earlier and the reasons he wanted to end his life.

"What kept you from doing it?"

"I sat there thinkin' about all the fucked-up things that happened to me after me parents died, and I got so fuckin' mad, I tell ya. I wanted revenge. I guess I just decided to take the bastard out with me. But when I got back to the flat, Kieran was riled up about somethin' else and I forgot all about me own revenge. Anyway, I didn't know *who* I wanted to kill. And since then, I haven't thought any more about killin' *meself*, but if I ever do find out who killed me parents, you can be sure the bastard won't be long for this world."

"What did you do with the sleeping pills?"

"I sold 'em to pay what I owed Kieran that month."

"Do you have access to any other way of killing yourself?"

Tommy hesitated. Kieran disposed of the gun used to kill the priest, but they returned the second pistol to its hiding place behind the Queen's portrait. "Naw, Doc, those are the only pills I had," Tommy said.

"How about any guns or knives or rope?"

"Jayzus, Doc. I don't have the stomach to do meself in *those* ways."

"So no access to any of those things?"

"No," Tommy lied. He didn't like to deceive Thornton, but knew it was too risky to acknowledge the gun.

Thornton spent several minutes coaching Tommy on what to do if the suicidal thoughts returned. "But I think we can keep those thoughts at bay if we work on all those things you said were weighing on your mind at the beach. Are the job and new place to live still the things you'd like to address first?"

"Honestly, revenge is number one on the list—I owe that to me parents. But until I find out who killed them, then gettin' away from Kieran is the next most important thing. And to do that, I'm gonna need a job."

"Alright then. We'll start work on that next week. I know we took a couple detours today, but they were important ones. And they proved we can talk about difficult things in here. When you feel ready, it could be very helpful to talk more about your parents. In the meantime, we'll focus on the immediate issue of getting you that job and a new place to live."

The two men shook hands, and Tommy headed out the door.

Outside, a woman with several dogs in tow secretly snapped a photo of Tommy as she passed him on the sidewalk.

A JOB

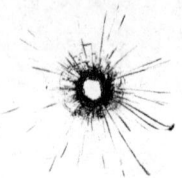

AFTER TOMMY DEPARTED, Thornton paced the room. The situation was a difficult one. In his file and during their sessions, there were indications Tommy was dependent on alcohol. In the past, an addiction took precedence over other treatment goals because of its propensity to get in the way of everything. The current standard of care called for simultaneous treatment of multiple diagnoses in hopes of achieving incremental progress on several fronts at once.

Tommy's desire to kill the person or persons responsible for his parents' deaths seemed to be more than just a revenge fantasy, but Thornton was still unsure. Tommy's thoughts of suicide, on the other hand, clearly resulted in overt steps to end his life, even if he did abandon the plan at the last minute. Both situations required close clinical monitoring, especially because Tommy was more likely to act on his homicidal and suicidal thoughts while drunk.

At the same time, Thornton realized Tommy did not come to him voluntarily. To remain engaged over the long term, Tommy had to perceive a personal benefit from their meetings. Staying out of jail certainly qualified, but even more motivating for Tommy right now was the desire to get his life back on track—

he already identified a job and a new place to live as the first steps toward that goal. Thornton knew he needed to focus on what Tommy wanted. If Thornton could help with the job and a new home, then Tommy was more likely to stick around and work on the other concerns too.

It was a delicate balance. Tommy's drinking could easily and without warning provoke new challenges. It could also heighten the risk of suicidal and homicidal behavior—and that would demand clinical attention at the expense of Tommy's goals. If that happened, Tommy might abandon therapy and miss the chance to turn his life around.

Thornton decided he had to move quickly. He sat at the large wooden desk in the corner of his office and flipped through a stack of papers to find the names and telephone numbers of his contacts at the Health and Social Care Trusts, the Public Prosecution Service, and the Parole Commission. Over the course of two hours, he spoke with all of them, but none was able to suggest viable job opportunities for Tommy. His criminal record and checkered work history were too much to overcome.

Intent on proving Tommy could surmount his past, Thornton left a voicemail for his father-in-law, Robert Inglesby. He did not know much about Inglesby's work for the government, but he knew he was well-connected and able to pull strings, just as he did to get Thornton this job and office. It was unorthodox to involve a family member—even remotely—in a client's therapy, but Thornton didn't want to let Tommy down. He just needed the name and number of someone who could overlook a disadvantaged past and give someone a second chance—Tommy would never have to know about Inglesby's involvement. *And it will prove I can adapt and get things done on someone else's turf.*

Thornton packed up his things and locked the office. On the way home, his father-in-law called back. Thornton outlined the problem and answered Inglesby's questions without identifying Tommy specifically. Inglesby sympathized with the circumstances and offered to call a friend in the Shankill ward.

Fifteen minutes later, Inglesby called Thornton again. His friend knew an auto mechanic in the Shankill who accepted apprentices with "difficult histories," as Inglesby put it. The mechanic owed a favor and would surely agree to help. Thornton was eager for Tommy to find a job quickly and saw no other way to assist his client. He accepted the suggestion, and Inglesby agreed to text him the mechanic's name and number along with the date and time of an interview for Tommy.

Several minutes later, Thornton reached the one-bedroom flat along the string of stylish row houses on College Green and stepped inside. The man who followed him home stopped across the street and checked in with the boss.

THE MECHANIC

A WEEK PASSED BEFORE THORNTON'S NEXT MEETING with Tommy. The psychologist excitedly shared the good news. "Tommy, I think you're going to like this. I spoke to a colleague of mine, and he knew someone in the Shankill area with good connections in the community. The man asked around and found an auto mechanic who needs a shop assistant. He set up an interview for you on Monday, if you're interested. How does that sound?" Thornton did not disclose that his "colleague" was actually his father-in-law, and of course he had no idea his father-in-law enlisted Garth Peters, the local head of the UVF, to arrange the interview.

Tommy was ecstatic. *Finally—a chance to work a real job and earn some decent money!* Thoughts of a new place to live, nice furniture, working appliances, and a girlfriend flowed through his mind again. This time, he stifled the instinct to assume everything would turn to shite—the sessions with Thornton were paying off. Tommy was determined to make it work. "That sounds great, Doc. Thanks! There's just…" Tommy looked embarrassed. "It's just that I'm not really sure what to say during the interview."

Thornton realized Tommy lacked any formal job skills training, so they used the rest of the session to rehearse questions and answers for the interview. Thornton also coached Tommy on how to interact with people in a professional setting.

As the session drew to a close, Thornton handed Tommy a piece of paper. "Hang on tight to this. It has the name and address of the shop, plus the owner's name. And I circled in red the date and time of the interview. Remember to arrive early."

Tommy studied Thornton's handwriting, did not have any questions, and tucked the slip in his wallet. He looked Thornton in the eye, and his voice cracked as he said, "Cheers, Doc."

Thornton looked proudly at Tommy. "I can't wait to hear all about it next week." The psychologist decided to delay questions about Tommy's homicidal thoughts until a later session. Tommy was in a good place right now, and Thornton didn't want to sour the mood.

THE BRICK WALL

LIAM O'MALLEY WALKED TWENTY MINUTES FROM the Reconciliation meeting to the Tricolor Pub. The doorman greeted him warmly as O'Malley crossed the threshold into his second home. The place was unusually crowded. At the center of the room, a boisterous hen party drank from inappropriately shaped mugs. A trio of factory workers by the window argued about the greatest footballer of all time. O'Malley glanced about the place to take stock of the clientele. Several of his former comrades were among the group. They gave each other quick nods of acknowledgement but kept to themselves.

O'Malley went to the back of the room, where a ring of patrons gathered around a pub session. The musicians—regulars here—were a bawdy bunch who mixed dirty jokes with traditional songs and some lively storytelling. The fiddler had just finished a racy tale about the *Sidhe*—Ireland's "wee folk," or fairies—when O'Malley pulled up a chair. The group launched into a raucous rendition of "The Wild Rover" that soon had everyone in the bar clapping in unison.

When the performers took a break, O'Malley struck up a conversation with a pensioner who resembled a bearded Brendan Gleeson. In the distance, over the old man's shoulder, O'Malley caught an attractive blonde no more than half his age staring at him. She smiled when their eyes met, and O'Malley winked playfully at her. He was about to excuse himself from the conversation with Gleeson's doppelgänger and join the young lady when he felt a tap on his shoulder. He turned to find Mickey Shanahan.

"Join me in the snug."

O'Malley bid goodnight to the doppelgänger, shrugged at the pretty girl, and followed Shanahan to the tiny room at the end of the bar. Shanahan closed the door as the music resumed. The two men sat down with their drinks.

"I need yer help with an order from the boss," Shanahan said. "He wants to send a message to Dingleberry by blowin' up that Chinese restaurant he uses as a base of operations."

O'Malley eyed Shanahan cautiously. "He wants *you* to send a message. I have nothin' to do with that."

"Aye, but this one is a wee bit of a challenge. I need ideas from ya. The boss is real serious about it."

"My active days are over, Mickey, and I hear ya been managin' things just fine without me. I've been away 17 years and am out of practice anyway. Have one of the other fellas give it a think."

"Those Reconciliation meetings aren't makin' ya soft now, are they?"

O'Malley was surprised Shanahan knew about the meetings but quickly deduced it was Shanahan's man following him around town—and Shanahan took orders straight from the boss. O'Malley realized Linden was uneasy about something and wanted to keep a watchful eye on things. O'Malley was annoyed, but decided not to fan any suspicions. "Don't be a twat, Mickey. I was waist-deep in this shite before ya were born. I guess I can give ya some ideas, but I won't be engineering' anythin' for ya or helpin' ya to place any devices."

"Fair enough." Shanahan began to diagram the restaurant and surrounding area on a napkin. "Dingleberry uses this room in the back corner of the place as his headquarters. It will be tough to get a man inside the buildin' since tensions between us are so high, but a car bomb would have to be pretty powerful to take out the back of the buildin' from the street. And that's the problem. We're talking about a Catholic neighborhood, with Republican-friendly businesses on either side of the restaurant and Catholic homes behind it. A bomb that big would cause collateral damage. We can't risk alienating any of our support at a time when Dingleberry is already trying to steal it from us."

"What exactly did Patrick tell ya to do?"

"He said to send a message by bombin' the place."

"Alright, so he's just tryin' to scare the kid, not kill him. And he didn't say 'destroy the place.' So that leaves ya lots of options. What are ya workin' with these days?"

Shanahan explained that in 2002, right after O'Malley went to prison the second time, the Provos obtained a cache of C-4 explosive from the ETA, a Basque separatist group in Spain. The ETA delivered the explosive in exchange for IRA training on the use of GPS and remote-controlled technology in bomb-making. Shanahan noted the timing was perfect, since the IRA had just relinquished, as part of the Good Friday decommissioning, the large leftover cache of Semtex it got from Libya in the 1980s and 1990s.

O'Malley chuckled. Semtex had a shelf life of ten years. His comrades gave the Brits a couple tons of expired explosive to demonstrate their commitment to the peace agreement. Then they replaced it with fresh C-4 that, if stored correctly, would last indefinitely—and it was virtually odorless, so only specially trained sniffer dogs could detect it. "Ya pulled the wool *right* over their eyes."

"Aye, it was well played."

O'Malley was unaware of, but not surprised by, the Provos' bartering agreement with the ETA. In his day, the IRA also trained the Palestine Liberation Organization, Black September—the group responsible for the assault on Israeli athletes at the 1972 Olympic Games in Munich—and the FARC, a guerrilla movement in Colombia.

The training was mostly about bomb-making techniques and the improvised use of explosives, and it generated significant income for the Provos. The FARC used the IRA's approach to mortar attacks, in particular, with great effect and even experimented with shells modified to carry unsophisticated chemical weapons.

That was a step too far, even for the Provos. *The Green Book*—the IRA's training manual—limited volunteers to the use of conventional munitions and specifically prohibited the use of chemical weapons. The Provos' ingenuity with explosives was otherwise unlimited.

O'Malley asked, "How much damage do ya want to do? And what about casualties?"

"Enough damage to be noticeable to the neighborhood, but we'll hit the place when it's closed to the public so we don't harm any patrons. I'm not losin' sleep if we take out Dingleberry or any of his crew though."

"Too easy, mate. Is yer diagram drawn to scale?"

"Aye, pretty close."

"And what about this alley behind the restaurant?"

"It's the width of two cars. They have a couple industrial bins along the back wall for the rubbish."

"And what's the wall made of?"

"Brick. It's an older buildin'."

"There ya go, mate. Ya don't even need to get inside. Disguise a pound of C-4 to look like a brick and place it into the back wall of the office as close to the midway point as ya can, about four to five feet above the ground. Remove a loose brick to make way if there aren't any gaps already. Just be sure one of the metal bins is behind the C-4 to shield the far side of the alley. That much explosive will rip right through the wall and destroy everythin' in the room. But it won't be enough to bring down the restaurant or do much damage to the place next door."

Shanahan looked triumphant. He knew O'Malley would have the answer. "Leave it to me, mate."

"Yer fucking right I'm leavin' it with ya. This has nothin' to do with me, Shanahan."

Shanahan nodded quickly as the two men stood and opened the door to the snug. In the main bar, the crowd roared at the punchline to another one of the fiddler's dirty jokes.

THE NIGHTMARE

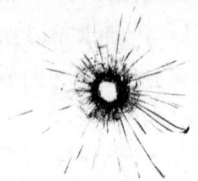

LIAM O'MALLEY LEFT THE TRICOLOR PUB disgruntled. He was annoyed with Mickey Shanahan for involving him in current activities and mad at himself for participating. He knew he was playing with fire, and he was disappointed by how quickly and easily he abandoned his commitment to stay clear of trouble. *When did I become so weak?*

Patrick Linden's decision to target fellow Republicans also troubled O'Malley. The movement always had its share of infighting and feuds, but bombing a Republican restaurant still offended O'Malley's sense of honor. The Troubles were about standing up to oppression and seeking freedom. There was no honor in attacking or killing one of your own except in self-defense. O'Malley supposed Linden saw it precisely that way— as self-defense.

For the first time in his life, O'Malley wondered if there was honor in killing *anyone*. He recalled the boy he met at the Reconciliation meeting and all the suffering his family, and so many others, experienced as the result of The Troubles. Had all that killing been worth it? Had it gained them *anything*?

At that moment, O'Malley saw Dingleberry's man, Billy Hoyt, and another youth approaching from across the road.

Before the two could initiate a conversation, O'Malley vented his frustration by charging at the pair. "Don't ya fuckin' *think* about sayin' one word to me." He snarled and stabbed the air with his finger. "I'm not interested in anythin' youse or yer boss has to say, so fuck off, ya stupid cunts."

Hoyt and his companion, caught off guard by O'Malley's outburst, stopped dead in their tracks. Hoyt knew the boss was keen to recruit O'Malley, so he held his tongue. But his companion took a step forward and pointed an angry finger back at O'Malley. Billy interrupted him by pushing the youth's hand back down to his side and said firmly, "Don't."

Hoyt stood beside his companion and stared at O'Malley without saying a word. O'Malley clearly had no interest in the boss' second attempt at a sit-down. Hoyt decided not to antagonize O'Malley and drive him further away—if that were even possible. So he simply raised both hands in defeat, turned around, and led his companion back in the opposite direction. They disappeared into the darkness.

A block behind O'Malley, the watcher stood in the shadows ready to intervene if necessary. But Dingleberry's messengers were gone. The remainder of the evening was uneventful, at least for the watcher.

Overnight, O'Malley had another nightmare. It featured an explosion and a ring of fire through which a parade of disembodied and unknown screaming faces passed. There were pensioners, pregnant women, and children, and they all locked eyes with O'Malley. Then the flames and nameless faces dissolved into a scene he *did* recognize. It was the aftermath of a bomb O'Malley and Linden detonated prematurely on the Shankill Road twenty-five years earlier.

Through a window across the street from Sheehan's furniture store, O'Malley saw the pavement shrouded in dust and blanketed with chunks of metal and concrete, splintered timbers, torn clothes, a child's doll, and next to it, a severed arm, still clutching a purse made of multi-colored leather pieces stitched together like a quilt. In the distance, a well-dressed man limped toward a ginger-haired girl who stood frozen in place, wailing hysterically and clutching a Paddington Bear next to a pile of smoldering gray debris. The man scooped the girl and her bear under his arm and carried them away as emergency services arrived.

FAMILY STRIFE

THE TEEN BOY WHO TALKED TO O'MALLEY after the Reconciliation meeting passed through the open gate of the peace wall along Cupar Way into Loyalist territory and headed home. It took fifteen minutes to make his way to the two-story brick house at 304 Matchett Street. He opened the gate, crossed the courtyard, and was about to reach for the knob when the front door flew open and his granddad, Garth Peters, appeared silhouetted in the entryway.

"Where the fuck have *you* been?" Granddad growled.

"It's none yer business, Granddad. I can go where I please." The boy refused to make eye contact and tried to slide past the old man.

Granddad blocked his way. "Answer me. And show some respect. This is me house yer livin' in." The familiar smell of alcohol floated about him.

"Yeah, I know, ya remind me every day."

"Mind yerself, lad. One of the boys at the pub just called and said he saw ya at the interface area comin' from Clonard. What the hell were ya doin' on *that* side of town?"

"Again, none yer business, Granddad. Wind yer neck in. Now can I please go inside?"

"Were ya at one of those fuckin' peace meetings yer always talkin' about?"

"They're called Reconciliation meetings, and what if I was?"

Granddad raised his hand to strike the boy's head but was not quick enough. The teenager, accustomed to his grandfather's discipline, anticipated the move and ducked the blow.

Granddad managed to grab the youth's shirt instead and pinned him against the wall with his full body weight. The old man was still strong. "You listen to me, lad. I spent most of me life fightin' those fuckin' terrorists. They killed me brother, yer *pregnant auntie*, and yer cousin *on his weddin' day*."

"I *know*, Granddad. I've heard it a million times. But that's all in the past. What's done is done, and ya have to let it go. That's *yer* life, not mine."

The old man's eyes widened, his nostrils flared, and his face went from crimson to purple. "Let it *go*, ya say?! All in the *past*?! Not fer me it isn't, and not fer any of us who *lived* it."

The boy tried to withdraw into the wall but made no move to escape. He knew from experience that "the rage," as his family called it, could turn violent at the slightest provocation. It was best to wait motionless, wordless, until it subsided.

"You and yer mates understand *nothin'*," Granddad snarled. "I saw it with me own eyes, every day fer more than twenty years. People blown to pieces right in front of me. Severed arms in trees. Crawlin' on me hands and knees at a crime scene lookin' for pieces of flesh and bone. Bodies with their heads shot off. *Have ya ever smelled a burnin' body, lad? Have ya?*"

The boy shook his head.

"Well, I 'ave. Every day I left fer work at a different time and took a different route to avoid bein' shot. At the station, we were under constant threat of mortar attacks and car bombs. Half the calls we got were hoaxes, tryin' to lure us out in the open where we could be shot or blown up by bombs along the road. And after each explosion, we wondered about secondary devices designed to kill anyone who came to help.

I constantly worried they'd follow me home and shoot me in front of yer grandmother or yer ma or uncle. We kept the curtains closed at night so they couldn't see us. I became a policeman to *help* people, but there was nobody helpin' *us*. We'd come back to the station from one horrible scene after another and be expected to go right back out fer the next one. I couldn't trust anyone but me mates, and I lost dozens of 'em—all good men, with families—to those Fenian bastards. And they mostly got away with it. *So you tell me, lad…*"

The boy looked at his grandfather.

"*How am I supposed to forget all that?*"

THE MECHANIC'S SHOP

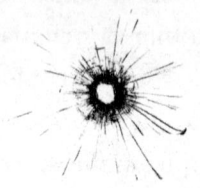

TOMMY MAGEE WALKED INTO THE AUTO MECHANIC'S SHOP in the Lower Shankill shortly before 09:00 on Monday morning and asked for Gerry.

A gruff, weathered-looking woman behind a gray metal desk yelled over her shoulder for the owner. A beer-bellied man with a bad hip lumbered into the office. In the background, several men shouted to each other over the noise of power tools.

Gerry wiped grime from his hands and asked, "What can I do fer ya?"

Tommy extended his hand as Thornton taught him to do, locked eyes with the owner, and introduced himself.

The owner looked puzzled until the woman said, "He's the fella Garth Peters sent over." There was a hint of disapproval in her tone.

The owner brightened immediately. "Yeah, yeah, of course, sorry, mate. It's still early." He laughed and motioned for Tommy to follow him into the garage.

It was bigger than Tommy expected, with eight car lifts and workers busy at each one. Pneumatic tools hung from the ceiling, and through the bay doors at the left Tommy saw a car park with at least a dozen vehicles of various ages and conditions.

"You'll be a mechanic's assistant, which means ya do whatever the boys or I ask ya to. Shift is from 07:00 to 16:00 with an hour fer lunch startin' at 11:00. We're closed at the weekend. If yer not here, ya don't get paid. Simple as that. Wage is ten pounds an hour, paid from the office every Friday afternoon."

Tommy stifled a smile. He never earned that much money in his life. "Thank you, sir. Ya can count on me. I used to work on—"

The owner held up his hand. "I don't need to know anythin' about yer past. If Garth Peters vouches fer ya, that's all I need to know. Let me introduce ya to the boys." Gerry whistled loudly and the garage fell silent. "This here's Tommy. He's one of Garth Peters' boys. He's here to do whatever we need. Keep 'im busy."

The mechanics nodded silently. They were all around Tommy's age, apart from a man in his sixties. They resumed their work when the boss turned his back.

Tommy followed Gerry to the office. The woman was on the phone arguing with someone about a missed deadline.

"That's Dorene. Stay on her good side or she'll bite ya."

Tommy studied Gerry's face, but it didn't seem like he was joking. "When can I fill out an application, sir?"

Gerry laughed. "There's not much paperwork here, mate. And call me Gerry or boss."

"When can I start, boss?"

"Ya just did. Go out back and see what the boys need from ya. Lunch is at 11:00, and ya finish at 16:00."

Tommy had not expected to start immediately and was wearing his best clothes. He did not object, though, and walked into the garage to meet his co-workers.

Tommy's first week at the new job went smoothly. He got on well with the mechanics his own age, but he felt uncomfortable alone with the older man.

The work was easy. Tommy floated from one bay to the next, offering an extra pair of hands where needed. Occasionally, they sent him on a motorbike to pick up parts. Otherwise, he cleaned, hauled trash, and did odd jobs. After Tommy shared that he once helped his foster father restore an old car, a couple of the more experienced mechanics began teaching him new skills.

Tommy noticed a lot of people coming and going in the front office and at the side gate. He thought it odd that many of them did not drop off or pick up cars, although a few of them retrieved or left small packages. It was strange, too, that some of the cars on the lifts changed overnight—he never saw them driven on or off the lot during business hours. But he was making four hundred pounds a week for the first time in his life, and he was not about to put his nose where it did not belong.

DISCOVERED

TOMMY ENJOYED A STELLAR WEEKEND. The auto shop paid him cash for the first week at work. It was a small fortune, and he was giddy. Tommy bought himself a big meal at the local chippy—the good one—and picked up a couple new shirts and another pair of pants for work. Then he went to the pub and drank as much as he wanted while watching the match on the telly. He still had almost three hundred pounds in his pocket.

The only downside to all that cash was how to handle Kieran. Tommy owed him two hundred and fifty pounds for expenses at the flat, and he was tempted to pay it off all at once. But Tommy had not told Kieran about his new job, and he would surely question the sudden wealth. Tommy decided it was better to pay his foster brother in small installments while he searched for another place to live. Then, when he found a new flat, he would pay Kieran the remainder and walk away debt-free.

In the meantime, Tommy needed a place to stash the surplus cash. He decided against hiding it in the flat, but didn't trust banks either. He heard stories about revenue agents using people's deposits to collect unpaid taxes, and he was sure he had a few of those. Instead, he decided to bring the money to his next appointment with Thornton and see if the psychologist would hold onto it for him. Until then, he would carry it in his wallet and keep it out of Kieran's sight.

Tommy arrived early for work on Monday, excited to see his new mates and earn more money. In just seven days, his life changed drastically, and he knew he owed it to Thornton. Tommy chastised himself for not trusting the psychologist in the beginning—he saw now the doc was sincere about helping him. For the first time since his parents died, Tommy felt connected to someone.

Tommy spent Monday helping the mechanics and running errands. There seemed to be more "visitors," as he called them—the mostly young men who frequented the shop but did not have a car to drop off or pick up. They met only with Gerry, either in the office if Dorene was away, or in a private side room used only by Gerry. Tommy wondered what they talked about.

Tuesday started as usual. Then, around 11:00, something wholly unexpected happened. Kieran arrived at the shop to drop off a package. He spotted Tommy standing beneath a Ford sedan, helping to drain the oil. "Oy, what the fuck are *you* doin' here?!"

Tommy recognized his foster brother's voice and spun around. "I w-w-work here." Tommy had not stuttered since he was a child.

"Since when?! And why the fuck didn't *I* know about it?" Kieran shouted above the noise of the power tools. Some of the mechanics stopped work to hear what the commotion was about.

"I d-d don't need yer p-p-permission," Tommy said, looking down at the oil-stained floor.

"That's brilliant. Ya think keepin' yer job a secret will stop me from collectin' what ya owe?" Kieran's voice grew louder and angrier as he realized Tommy deceived him.

Gerry heard the yelling and stepped out from the office. "Oy, Kieran. I'm payin' the man to work. Sort this on yer *own* time. Now fuck off."

Kieran glared at Tommy. "We'll finish this conversation at home." Then he slithered out the side gate.

Tommy trembled as he watched "Crazy Kieran" depart.

THE BOMB

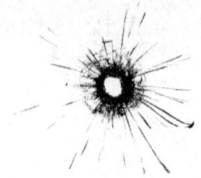

NO ONE PAID ATTENTION TO THE STOLEN WORK VAN parked in the alley behind the Chinese restaurant. If they had, they would have seen a mason repair the brick wall at the rear of the building and drive off ten minutes later. The heavily armed duo inside the vehicle remained unnoticed the entire time. Barely more than a week had passed since Liam O'Malley coached Mickey Shanahan about how to set the device.

Later that morning, Billy Hoyt showed up as scheduled to review the week's receipts with Devin Dingle in the restaurant's back room. Drug sales were trending upward, and income from the fencing operation remained steady. Dingle was pleased with the reliable cash flow. Billy decided to capitalize on the boss' good mood.

"We tried to make contact with O'Malley again a couple nights ago, but he's not havin' it. This time we approached him on the street near his home. We thought maybe he'd be more willin' to talk there since his mates at the pub wouldn't see us. But it didn't make any difference. I couldn't get a word out."

Dingle never had a chance to respond. The explosive brick positioned in the wall about four feet behind him detonated in a thunderous blast that obliterated everyone and everything in the room. The explosion sent thousands of pieces of debris slicing through the air for about twenty-five feet in all directions. The kitchen and its gas-powered appliances were well within that range. A shard of metal severed one of the fuel lines before striking a metal oven. It caused a spark that ignited a secondary explosion. The result was a fireball that collapsed the two-story building.

In a stolen car parked across the street a couple blocks away, Andy Michaels stared in disbelief. "Jayzus, Mary, and Joseph," he exclaimed to his companion, who had just detonated the explosive brick remotely. "How much fuckin' C-4 did ya use?!"

"I did exactly what Mickey told me to. It was just a pound, I tell ya, placed right where he showed me on the drawing. *Bloody hell!*"

Michaels hit the accelerator and headed south toward Newry. Along the way they would ditch the car and set it alight at a pre-arranged location. There, a comrade waited to give them a ride back across the border into the Republic of Ireland.

THE APPEAL

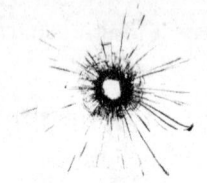

AROUND TEN O'CLOCK THE NEXT MORNING, the tip lines at the *Belfast Telegraph*, *The Irish News*, and the *Belfast Newsletter* rang in quick succession. Each publication had a clerk at Her Majesty's Court of Appeal in Belfast on its unofficial payroll to alert editors whenever something newsworthy transpired.

That morning, staff throughout the Royal Courts of Justice were buzzing about an appeal filed by the Commission on Northern Ireland's Court System, or CNICS. It sought judicial review of Patrick Linden's incarceration for terrorism offenses, with the goal of overturning his conviction and releasing him from HM Prison Maghaberry. Linden was widely believed to be one of the highest-ranking IRA members ever jailed, and even the *possibility* of his release—let alone a complete reversal of his conviction—sent shockwaves through Loyalist *and* Republican communities.

Claire Davis wrote most of the brief filed on Linden's behalf, but the document named CNICS as the petitioner. The decision to list only the Commission was intended to shield its members from the inevitable backlash. It also allowed multiple barristers to represent Linden on a potentially rotating basis. If one barrister had a family emergency or needed to recuse him or herself, a fellow member of the Commission could stand in with minimal delay to the proceedings. CNICS was eager to present itself as an effective and efficient advocate for justice and reform.

Once the news media were aware of the appeal, reporters began reaching out to community leaders for comment. One of them got hold of Garth Peters on his mobile while the UVF boss sat at the usual table under the telly at the Cocky Rooster.

Kieran Oliver sat with him and watched the blood drain from Peters' face. A torrent of expletives burst from the boss' mouth.

Peters ended the call and hurled the mobile against the wall. *"Bloody fuckin' hell.* It's not bad enough our spineless politicians released Liam O'Malley. Now there's a move to get that cunt Patrick Linden out of Maghaberry too. Turnin' those two Fenians loose is an insult to Loyalists and all we've fought and bled for. I won't have it, I tell ya. It's time to take matters into our own hands, lad."

Kieran smelled blood and leaned forward. "Tell me what to do, boss."

FEMME FATALE

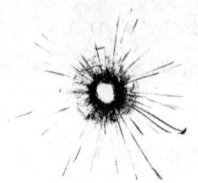

ROBERT INGLESBY SANK INTO THE PLUSH LEATHER CHAIR in the study of his flat in the distinctive Boat Building overlooking River Lagan and Belfast Harbor. Lights shimmered on the water far below as night set in. In the distance, streams of red and white flowed across a traffic bridge. Farther out stood Samson and Goliath—the twin yellow cranes of Harland & Wolff, builder of the *RMS Titanic*. Inglesby could just make out the illuminated Titanic Museum on the horizon.

He scrolled through the news headlines on his phone. One particular story in the BelTel app caught his eye. It described an effort to release the notorious IRA boss Patrick Linden from HM Prison Maghaberry on grounds that he was convicted on false testimony and planted evidence. The article delved into revelations from the closed HET files and mentioned the release of Linden's protégé, Liam O'Malley, a few months earlier. There was predictable outrage from communities on both sides. Republicans crowed about institutionalized bias toward Catholics and the miscarriage of justice, while Loyalists voiced outrage that yet another terrorist murderer might be returned to the streets of Belfast.

Inglesby grew anxious. The media gorged itself on conflict and profited from salacious headlines. There was a lot here to feed on. Inglesby knew better than most people the sort of secrets buried in the HET files. He was intimately familiar, too, with dozens of old crimes that remained unsolved and largely forgotten by the public. He wanted them to remain that way.

Patrick Linden's appeal would generate a media firestorm. Every reporter and editor in the city—and media outlets overseas—would be digging for scraps of information about the IRA in hopes of challenging foregone conclusions or making sensational new revelations. The competition among them would be fierce and relentless. Any number of dangling threads, if pulled, could unravel a carefully woven shroud of secrecy and plunge Inglesby's life and career into chaos. In particular, he feared more scrutiny of Matthew Clark's murder.

Inglesby surveyed the loose threads. There was that smartly dressed young analyst from Section 6—the one who initially objected to Inglesby's instructions to delete Kieran Oliver's name and vehicle from the number plate analysis. And there was Kieran himself—the very definition of a wild card. Inglesby also recalled the anonymous tip to CrimeStoppers about Clark being executed for IRA crimes. Any one of those threads could be trouble.

Inglesby already concluded Kieran, for reasons not yet known, went rogue and killed the priest without realizing the cleric was a valuable MI5 informer. Inglesby was nearly certain it was Kieran, too, who placed the call to CrimeStoppers and tried to make the killing sound like a Loyalist hit to divert attention from himself.

The absence of any reference to Clark's murder in the BelTel article gave Inglesby some comfort. And an internal security

review—including polygraph examinations of key staff at MI5—
failed to detect any leaks or betrayals. Inglesby reasoned that if
MI5 had not yet figured out who killed Clark, then the press was
unlikely to do so.

Still, with a media frenzy looming, the situation was simply
too fraught with risk. Inglesby knew a preemptive strike was
needed. It was not the first time one of Inglesby's proxies out-
lived his usefulness and became a liability. The senior MI5 official
switched to his secure mobile and sent a coded text. About twenty
minutes later, an MI5 undercover operative deeply embedded
inside the New IRA called Inglesby to check in.

"Hello, Mum," the operative began, to signal he could talk
freely.

"Right, I won't keep ya long. What are the New IRA sayin'
about the bomb at the Chinese restaurant?"

"They're not sure who did it. Some think it was the Provos
assertin' their dominance. Others suspect the UVF because of
recent tensions with Loyalist drug gangs. Either way, we're in a
power vacuum. Dingle and Hoyt were the top dogs. There's no
plan of succession, and no single person is strong enough to run
things right now. It's a serious blow to the crew."

Ironically, it was not what Inglesby wanted to hear. He needed
the New IRA to remain strong as a foil to the Provos, especially
if Patrick Linden were to be released from prison and resume
full control. If the two factions were feuding, then they would
weaken each other and have less time and energy to attack
Loyalist interests. Linden was a charismatic figure, able to inspire
and command all of the IRA's various splinter groups apart from
Dingle's followers. With Dingle out of the picture and no one
ready to assume control of his crew, Linden would be the sole

and undisputed leader of Republican paramilitary activity—and that was a dangerous proposition.

"We need to keep Dingle's crew viable—the information you've been providin' about their activities and funding is too valuable," Inglesby noted. "I'm goin' to share with ya some top-secret intelligence, and I want ya to pass it along discreetly to the person you think most capable of runnin' the New IRA in Dingle's place. Someone with the same drive and social media savvy who can rally support among the younger generations."

"Understood."

Inglesby then lied without hesitation or remorse. "We have reliable reports that the person responsible for the bombing at the Chinese restaurant is a rogue UVF enforcer named Kieran Oliver. He's a loose cannon who could undermine several on-going and highly sensitive operations. He frequents the Cocky Rooster, but we have assets there that I don't want harmed. I'll text you his home address instead. Pass this information on to the best candidate to take Dingle's place. Avengin' Dingle's death will give him the credibility he needs to take over the New IRA. But ya must emphasize Kieran acted alone—blame *cannot* spill over to the rest of the UVF."

"Understood, sir. But it will give *her* the credibility *she* needs to take over for Dingle."

"Interestin'. Carry on then." Inglesby ended the call bemused by the prospect of Kieran meeting his demise at the hands of a Republican *femme fatale*.

REMORSE

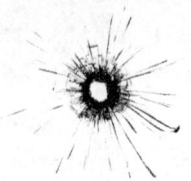

AN UNUSUALLY WARM AFTERNOON made Thornton's office uncomfortable, and the American stood at the wall adjusting the thermostat. Liam O'Malley eyed the psychologist and silently debated whether to mention the nightmare. O'Malley rhythmically rubbed the thumb of his right hand around the tips of his index and middle fingers. It was a self-soothing habit he subconsciously developed as a child.

Thornton returned to his seat. "Where would you like to start this week?"

O'Malley took the plunge. "Do ya have any tricks for makin' nightmares go away?"

"Sure. There are different types of nightmares, though, and a few ways to tackle them. It would help to know more about what you're experiencing."

O'Malley bit his lip. Thornton was his only potential source of help—and a neutral, objective one at that. O'Malley figured he was the only person in Belfast who leaned neither Loyalist nor Republican. But O'Malley found it hard to trust *anyone*, including Thornton. He had to be careful.

As much as he wanted to make the nightmares and the guilt go away, O'Malley knew Thornton would have to report any talk about terrorism offenses. And Patrick Linden's misgivings about Thornton echoed in his mind. So O'Malley proceeded cautiously. "I've been havin' 'em for a few months now. Ever since I learned about me release. They wake me up most nights. People tell me I get to shoutin' sometimes."

"I noticed you checked the box about nightmares on your intake questionnaire. I'm glad you felt comfortable bringing them up now. Is it always the same nightmare, or does it change?"

"There's a couple different ones. They change a wee bit from night to night but stay mostly the same. I usually have one or the other, but last week they blended together into the worst one yet." O'Malley swallowed hard, and his eyes glistened a bit.

"You seem to have a strong reaction even talking about them now. Can you help me understand why?"

O'Malley fought in vain to keep a tear from running down his cheek. He waited until he was confident his voice was steady. "They're not scary, like the nightmares about monsters hidin' in the closet when I was a kid. It's that the images are horrible, and after seein' them I feel so…" O'Malley looked at the carpet.

Thornton waited.

Finally, O'Malley continued. "I'm sure you've figured out, from that wee file they gave ya, that I've done some not-so-nice things in me life. I hurt a lot of people. I did it with good intentions, and at the time I felt justified. Now I'm not so sure, and I think me mind is gettin' a bit fucked up about it. Like, maybe I didn't deserve to be released, ya know?"

"Where do you think that doubt is coming from?"

O'Malley smiled ruefully. "A fuckin' teenage boy, can ya believe it?! I was already in prison when he was born!"

"Who's the boy?"

"I met him at a Reconciliation meeting. He's from the Shankill—that's a Protestant neighborhood. And he talked about how the adults fucked everythin' up fer his generation and were basically holdin' grudges and teachin' them to hate. But this kid didn't feel that way. He talked to me like I was any other bloke. I doubt he knew who I was, but he knew I'm Catholic. And he didn't care. Said he even has Catholic friends. And he talked about all his relatives who died during The Troubles and how fucked up his family is, but he doesn't want to be spiteful like them. It just made we wonder."

"Wonder about what, Liam?"

This time O'Malley's voice cracked and the tears flowed. "I was already doubtin' meself back in prison. Like, was it all worth it? What did we achieve? All the people dead, on both sides. And fer what?" O'Malley sniffled. "Then they go and tell me I'm bein' released, and I can't believe it. Me of all people! Why? I mean, I did those things—*hypothetically speakin'!*" O'Malley remembered the rule against disclosures that might trigger a call to the authorities.

Thornton nodded reassuringly.

"So I was already questionin' meself in prison. Now I'm out and there's the Reconciliation meetings. I see how hard people are tryin' to mend things and come to terms with what's happened. And it's all stuff from twenty-five to fifty years ago! I can't believe how fucked up everythin' still is. And then I meet this kid who was born after the peace agreement. And he's in a fucked-up situation. And as I'm hearin' him talk about his family, I can't help but wonder, 'Did I do this to him? Did *I* fuck up this kid's family and put him in this situation?' Listenin' to him just turned me doubt straight into guilt cuz even if I didn't fuck up

his family, I know I fucked up *other* families. I can see that now."
The tears flowed freely down O'Malley's face.

Thornton continued to lean forward and maintain eye contact but did not interrupt.

"So, the night I talked to that kid, I had my worst nightmare yet—sort of a combination of all the other ones. There's an explosion, and then constant flames, like in hell. And screamin' faces of people I don't know. No bodies, just the heads. And there's one after another. They just keep flyin' at me in an endless stream. And they're all starin' at me hard, like they're angry. Or maybe disappointed. But there's dozens of them, and they just keep comin' at me. Then the scene changes, and I'm lookin' at the Shankill Road after a bomb has gone off."

Thornton kept a neutral expression and nodded for O'Malley to continue.

"And I think that's what gets to me the most. It's just an awful scene to look at. But there's three things that catch me attention. One is a child's doll, lyin' in the rubble. Near it is an arm—no body, just the arm—and it's still holdin' onto a lady's purse. One of those bags made from different colored pieces all stitched together, like one of those blankets. And the arm with the purse is just lyin' there on top of all the debris from the explosion. And on the other side of the street from where I'm standin' is this wee red-haired girl. She's cryin' hysterically and holdin' onto a Paddington Bear. And she reminds me of me sister, Deidre." It was the first time O'Malley mentioned his sister.

Thornton started to speak but stopped when O'Malley took a deep breath.

"So that combination nightmare is the one that really fucked with me mind, Doc. And I need to make it stop. Even more fucked up is the way people keep seein' me as the old Liam, the

Liam I was before I went to prison. I'm not that person anymore, and circumstances are different now. But people seem stuck in the past. They want me to think and talk and act like I used to, but I don't want that. I guess I kinda identify with that kid from the Reconciliation meeting."

"Liam, you are doing a great job of explaining things. And I'm impressed by your candor and self-reflection. What else do you want me to know?"

O'Malley continued. "There's just one more thing, Doc. It looks like my best mate is about to be released from prison too. We were neighbors in Maghaberry. I guess I don't need to explain to ya how he ended up there. But if he gets out, then I could *really* be feelin' the pressure to be Old Liam. It's all just weighin' on me right now." O'Malley made no mention of Patrick Linden's name, or the controversy surrounding his pending release.

"Liam, you've done a fantastic job educating me about the things that are on your mind, and how they're reflected in your nightmares. There's a lot there for us to pursue. As much as we'd both like to start tackling some of it right now, we're out of time and I have back-to-back appointments this afternoon. But there *is* a way you can start combating those nightmares on your own until we meet again next week. How would you feel about keeping a detailed journal of the nightmares for the next seven days and, just as importantly, what you're thinking and feeling as soon as you wake up from them? We can use the journal as our starting point next week, if you'd like."

O'Malley hesitated. He was not keen on writing. But he asked a few questions about what to put in the journal and agreed to give it a try, especially once Thornton said he could burn it after they talked about it. As he exited the building moments later, O'Malley again pretended not to notice the bloke in the car across the street who was watching him.

DALLIANCE

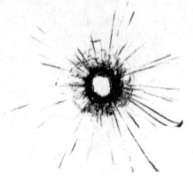

THORNTON FINISHED HIS CLINICAL NOTES for the day and closed the laptop. Claire had a meeting that night and would not be home until late. Back in the States, that would have meant a night out with the guys, but in Belfast, Thornton found it difficult to make friends independently of Claire. He reluctantly resigned himself to another night alone at home.

Thornton packed up and headed for the hallway. Liam O'Malley's comments about The Troubles' lingering effects echoed in his mind. *It's just like that graduate student at the pool suggested—transgenerational trauma.*

On impulse, he searched his phone for Siobhan Dooley's email about her research. He scrolled to the bottom of the message, found her number, and made the call.

"Hallo?"

"Siobhan, it's Dr. Thornton. Aaron Thornton, from the pool at QUB."

"Dr. Thornton, what a nice surprise. How ya goin?"

"Please, call me Aaron. And I'm fine, thanks. I was just headed home and thinking about some things a client shared with me about transgenerational trauma. Since that's your area of expertise, I thought maybe we could meet somewhere. I'd love to pick your brain. I know it's short notice, so if you're busy, I completely understand."

"Actually, it's perfect timing. I'm in between projects. Meet ya at Maggie Mays Cafe in an hour? Do ya know it?"

"I do. See you there!"

————

An hour later, Thornton and Siobhan sat at a corner table sipping pints and talking animatedly about their work. The young graduate student was well versed in primary and vicarious trauma. To Thornton's surprise, she even knew the latest research on epigenetics and the transmission of trauma to subsequent generations. *She's gorgeous AND smart.*

"Enough about psychology," Siobhan suddenly exclaimed. "I want to know more about *you*. How did an American therapist end up in Belfast?"

"In a nutshell, I followed my wife here." He quickly added, "But I was happy to do it, and always wanted to see Northern Ireland."

"How did ya manage to open a practice so quickly? It takes us *ages* to sort all the paperwork."

"Connections," Thornton said playfully.

"*Really?* You must be *important*." Siobhan gave him a mischievous wink.

Thornton enjoyed the feminine attention. "Well, I'm lucky to know a well-placed person or two in the government."

"*Very* well placed, I'd say. What *other* strings can you pull, Dr. Thornton?" She rested her chin on her fist and tilted her head to one side.

"Well, if you know anyone who's been unjustly imprisoned, I could put in a good word and maybe get him—or her—out."

He spotted a flicker of curiosity on Siobhan's face and decided to capitalize on her interest in The Troubles. "I could even get you files from the secret HET archive."

Siobhan reached out and placed her hand on Thornton's bare forearm. "Aaron, you are a man of many surprises. We *have* to stay in touch."

UNDERCOVER

MI5'S UNDERCOVER OPERATIVE, JAMES DWYER, ended the call with Inglesby. Before his recruitment, Dwyer was a freelance hacker who evaded arrest for six years despite several high-profile network intrusions—all conducted on behalf of wealthy anonymous clients who contacted and paid him on the dark web. He worked exclusively from his basement apartment in Belfast, using equipment he assembled himself.

But then Dwyer hacked Scotland Yard and delivered to his buyer a trove of sensitive files about prominent politicians. The buyer published the material online, and the ensuing scandals were a supreme embarrassment to the police—not to mention the politicians. Under intense public pressure, investigators launched a massive manhunt for the culprit. Dwyer was en route to Spain for a cooling-off period when the police nabbed him at the airport. He was sentenced to ten years. Neither Dwyer nor the police could identify the buyer.

MI5 approached Dwyer in prison and offered to shorten his sentence if he agreed to work exclusively for the UK government. They dangled a substantial, tax-free salary as inducement. Dwyer agreed, under threat of an even longer prison sentence if he ever reneged on the deal.

Dwyer's cellmate at the time was Danny Donovan, whose sister, Brianna, was a rising star in the New IRA. Dwyer's assignment was to get close to Danny, meet Brianna, and infiltrate the crew.

The platinum beauty did not look like an IRA operative. She did not even look Irish. Although Brianna's family had deep roots in Belfast, most strangers assumed she was Scandinavian—perhaps Swedish or Danish. Brianna's tall, athletic figure and long blonde hair attracted first notice, but her azure-blue eyes and turned-up button nose left admirers smitten. She had more than 100,000 Instagram followers, who voraciously consumed the beauty and fitness content she posted as one of the UK's top influencers. Her sponsors would have been stunned to know the truth.

Brianna originally joined the New IRA out of love. Not love for the movement, but for her boyfriend at the time, who inspired her with romantic idealism. When her beau moved to Australia with his family a couple years later, Brianna remained with the crew out of loyalty and kinship. She enjoyed the camaraderie and shared sense of purpose, but she *really* liked being a "bad girl," as her brother teased.

To underscore the point, Danny gave his sister a solid jade ring, beautifully etched on top with complex geometric designs. But hidden from view on the bottom half of the band were a skull and crossbones. Brianna wore the ring proudly, delighted that every time she waved, she flashed a hint of her dangerous side. People said the ring was nearly as gorgeous as Brianna.

Brianna had always been clever, with a mischievous—even manipulative—streak. As a teenager, she learned her looks gave her power over men, and she took every opportunity to test the limits of her wiles. There seemed to be none. The crew saw her as a woman who could get anyone to do anything.

But then Brianna met the handsome, athletic, smooth-talking James Dwyer drinking with her brother at the pub several weeks after his release from prison. Dwyer knew the power of *his* good looks too, and he was just as crafty. The chemistry between them was instantaneous. It was raw sexual attraction enhanced by the realization they were intellectually matched and equally, delightfully cunning. For the first time with a man, Brianna felt a lack of control. And to her surprise, she loved it.

The pair began dating. Four months later, Dwyer convinced Brianna he was struggling to find a job because of his prison record. She suggested he sell his services to the crew. Devin Dingle and Billy Hoyt trusted Brianna and liked the suggestion. They also liked Dwyer, and after confirming his breach of the Scotland Yard database, recognized the value of his unique skill set.

The crew welcomed Dwyer as its new technology guru. His primary job was to shield the New IRA's communications and financial transactions from official scrutiny. Occasionally, they asked him to gather online intelligence for them too. As far as they could tell, he did an exceptional job—the New IRA remained mostly unmolested by the security services. They seemed to have no inkling MI5 was privy to every communication and the movement of every pound sterling.

Dwyer also established himself, alongside Brianna, as a sound strategist. Despite Dingle's encouragement to lead several small operations, the couple eschewed all leadership roles and instead cultivated their reputation as loyal soldiers.

But now Dingle and Hoyt were dead, and the crew desperately needed capable new leadership. Dwyer knew Brianna was better suited to the role than anyone else. He also knew he would score major points with MI5 if he maneuvered her into the position. But there had never been a female commander in the New or Provisional IRA, and both organizations prided themselves on tradition. It would take something extraordinary to catapult Brianna to the top role. And Robert Inglesby had just delivered it.

WHEELS IN MOTION

JAMES DWYER MET BRIANNA outside their favorite pub. The couple kissed, walked inside, and sat at a secluded table beyond anyone's earshot.

Brianna looked at James expectantly. "What's got ya so excited?"

"It's about the bombing."

Brianna's eyes swept the room. "What about it?"

"I know who did it."

Brianna leaned forward conspiratorially. "Was it Linden's boys?"

"No. It was a UVF thug they call Crazy Kieran."

Brianna silently mouthed "wow" and leaned back in her chair. "That fuckin' UVF crew has some balls."

"That's just it. It wasn't the UVF. Kieran acted on his own."

"Then Kieran has some *serious* balls. How did you find out?"

"I'm still in touch with a guy I knew in prison. He reached out to see if I was okay after the bombing. Said he overheard this Kieran fella boastin' to his mates about takin' out Devin when he thought no one else was around. Apparently he felt the UVF wasn't doin' enough to stop the IRA."

It made sense. Brianna had her own sources and knew there was frustration among some Loyalists about the UVF being too soft. "Do we know where Crazy Kieran hangs out?"

"Aye, he has a flat in the Shankill. Shouldn't be too hard to get to him."

Brianna distractedly tapped her jade ring against the edge of the tabletop. Suddenly she looked up and asked, "Who knows about this?"

"Just the two of us, and the guy who told me obviously. Should we tell the rest of the crew?"

"No. They'll want to hit back right away. We need to be smart about this, and we're not ready. There's no one in charge to call the shots."

"Soooo, we do nothin' then?" James goaded her.

Brianna knew he was teasing but shot him an annoyed look anyway. "Noooo, we get *even*. I just need a few days to come up with a plan. Until then, don't tell anyone else about Crazy Kieran."

PARANOIA

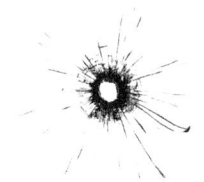

KIERAN OLIVER SAT ON THE DISINTEGRATING lounger that belched dust and stuffing, stewing in anger. Although he would never admit it, Tommy's deception hurt him. It also scared him. Kieran ordinarily knew everything that happened in Tommy's life, but his foster brother's decision to work for the UVF's local quartermaster came as a shock. In Kieran's world, surprises were usually bad news.

As quartermaster for Garth Peters' UVF crew, Gerry the auto mechanic provided a variety of services. He delivered untraceable vehicles, often outfitted with secret compartments to smuggle goods. Weapons and mobile phones were ordered and discarded through the shop, disguised to look like auto part deliveries. Whatever the crew needed—or needed to get rid of—flowed through Gerry's garage.

Jobs at the shop ordinarily were given to proven, loyal members of the crew who could be relied upon to keep their mouths shut. *So how did Tommy earn the privilege? Was he secretly workin' for the crew all along? Maybe keepin' tabs on me for Peters? Did Tommy tell the boss I whacked that priest? And what was that American psychologist really doin', workin' with the police and meetin' with Tommy?*

Could they be usin' Tommy to get to me? Kieran grew increasingly agitated as he downed his sixth beer in less than thirty minutes.

———

Tommy spent several hours at the pub after work with his mates, hoping Kieran would pass out before Tommy arrived home. Now Tommy approached the flat reluctantly, unsure what to expect. He knew how volatile—how dangerous—Kieran could be, but until now he never felt his foster brother might actually harm him. Tommy regretted keeping the job a secret and not giving Kieran all his money at once.

Tommy opened the door to the flat just enough to peer inside. The lounger was empty. Tommy breathed easier. Kieran must already be in bed. Tommy eased the door open just enough to step inside without making any noise. That is when Kieran, using the door to conceal his position, raised the pistol to Tommy's right temple and hissed at his foster brother to raise his hands.

THE DISCUSSION

KIERAN INSTRUCTED TOMMY TO TAKE A SEAT on the lounger. He kept the pistol aimed at his foster brother's head while he dragged one of the metal chairs from the kitchen. Kieran sat a couple feet across from Tommy.

"Kieran, what the fuck are ya doin', mate?" Tommy's voice was surprisingly steady.

"Oh, I'm yer *mate*, am I? *Mates* don't keep secrets from each other, Tommy. *Mates* pay what they owe each other. I don't know what ya are anymore, but yer not me *mate*." Kieran stabbed the air with the pistol to emphasize the word "mate" each time he said it.

"Just let me explain, will ya? We've been brothers fer I don't know how long. Give me a chance to tell me side of the story."

"Crack on then." Kieran cocked his head and narrowed his eyes to study Tommy.

"I've only had the job a week. I was goin' to tell ya—"

Kieran didn't let him finish. "How'd ya get a job with *yer* history? And how'd ya get one *there*?"

"The American psychologist got it for me. He called someone he knows, who arranged the whole thing. I went for an

interview with Gerry, the boss, last week, and started workin'
that day."

"I know who the fuck Gerry is. But *yer* not in the UVF. Why
would he take ya on?"

"I don't know what yer talkin' about. UVF?! I'm just a mechanic's assistant and an errand boy."

"*Everyone* workin' there is UVF, Tommy. Ya expect me to
believe yer *not*? Why would ya keep *that* a secret from me, of
all things? And how the fuck does an American shrink get ya
hooked up with a UVF job?"

"All I did was tell him I wanted a job so I could make some
money. The next week, he hands me a slip of paper with Gerry's
name and the address of the shop on it. I showed up when he
told me to, and that was it. He hired me straight away." Even
Tommy thought that sounded suspicious.

"For fuck's sake, Tommy." Kieran's tone softened a bit. "I
warned ya about that fella. So he waved a magic wand and suddenly yer workin' for the UVF quartermaster? Shite, Tommy,
the American works for the *police*. They must have *wanted* ya
there. He's gonna pump ya for information now, just ya wait."

Tommy hesitated. It had not *seemed* that way to Tommy.
But hearing Kieran describe it now made sense. Still, he trusted
Thornton. The psychologist had only reacted to what Tommy
told him. And he always let Tommy choose what to talk about
and to skip any questions that made him uncomfortable. Tommy
was confused.

"What did ya tell the American about the priest?"

"*Nothin'*, Kieran. I swear. It never even came up. I haven't
mentioned it to *anyone*. Do ya really think either one of us would
be sittin' here right now if I *had*?"

"Does he know about me? Does he know me name?"

"Kieran," Tommy said plaintively. He broke eye contact with his foster brother.

"Awww Jayzus, Tommy. You told him me *name*? No wonder he got ya that job. They're workin' *you* to get to *me*." Kieran stood up and circled the chair anxiously.

"It's not like that, Kieran. All he knows is I have a roommate named Kieran. That's it. Nothin' more. I swear to ya." Tommy kept mum about his plan to move out. It would only fuel Kieran's paranoia and anger.

Kieran walked up to Tommy and leaned down to speak directly at his face. "So if this is all so innocent, *why didn't ya tell me about the fuckin' job?*"

It was the question Tommy feared most. He couldn't let Kieran know about his plans to move out—not when he was already this agitated. "I was bein' selfish," he finally said as he looked sheepishly at the floor. "It was the first time in years I had any real money in me hands. It felt good, Kieran, and I wanted to enjoy it. So I went to the pub with the fellas, and I bought some new clothes. I bought meself dinner at the posh chippy. I was livin' like a royal, I tell ya."

"And why's all that gotta be a secret?"

"Cuz I knew if ya found out I had money, you'd take it from me. I *knew* I owed ya a lot, Kieran. I just wanted to enjoy some of it before ya took it all." Tommy hoped Kieran had no idea what Gerry was paying him. "Let me give ya fifty pounds now. I'll give ya the rest on Friday, I promise."

"Make it seventy-five, and the rest on Friday. No excuses."

Tommy breathed a sigh of relief. Kieran appeared mollified, at least for the moment.

Kieran read his mind. "But don't think yer off the hook just cuz ya paid me what ya owed. I'm still mad about ya keepin' secrets. Don't think I won't bury ya in a bog if I find out ya lied to me or have any *other* secrets. Foster brother or not, a tout is a tout, and ya know what happens to touts. Now off with ya." Kieran eyed his foster brother as Tommy headed to the jacks. He decided it was time to learn more about the American psychologist.

THE HEARING

ONCE PATRICK LINDEN GAVE CLAIRE DAVIS permission to proceed with the appeal, the Commission on Northern Ireland's Court System prepared and filed the necessary paperwork with blazing speed. If a man was wrongly convicted, they reasoned, then the injustice must be swiftly corrected.

Some of the country's top legal scholars comprised CNICS, and they wielded their skill to great effect. By citing an obscure, centuries-old legal precedent, they secured a hearing for Linden in less than twenty-nine days, and the proceeding was scheduled to begin in just two hours. Linden was already en route by armored transport, under heavy guard, to the court room. His presence was not required, but he craved the inevitable publicity and wanted to make a spectacle of the event.

The government, however, felt differently about the publicity, and unbeknownst to Linden successfully petitioned the Lord Justices to close the hearing—"for reasons of security"—to both the press and the public. A large crowd nonetheless gathered outside the Royal Courts of Justice, with equally vocal representation from the Loyalist and Republican communities. The police, in full riot gear, worked hard to keep them behind metal barricades on opposite sides of the building. A massive assortment of media surrounded the complex, ready to broadcast developments around the world in a split second.

Again for security reasons, the barristers scheduled to appear in court—Claire Davis among them—were told to enter via a secure driveway off May Street, park in an underground car park, and use a subterranean entrance to the building. Their identities were withheld from the public to thwart harassment. All of them chose to accept rides in armored vehicles offered by the PSNI, with smoked windows to conceal the occupants.

Court came to order at precisely 10:00 with only the Lord Justices, courtroom staff, prosecution service, CNICS team, and Patrick Linden in attendance. Linden fumed when he saw the empty gallery.

The appellants presented their case first, with Claire Davis doing most of the oratory. It was her first appearance in a Northern Irish courtroom, and she excelled. The prosecution team apprehensively admired her skill, and even a couple of the Lord Justices appeared impressed.

When the appellants yielded, the prosecution made a surprise move. They agreed to withdraw the government's opposition to Linden's release on the condition he remain behind bars for thirty more days to determine whether any new charges were pending against him. The appellants turned to one another with stunned expressions.

The chief prosecutor explained the Crown's position. "Although we concede the police did not follow proper procedure at the time of his arrest, we remain convinced of the inmate's guilt. But there is no merit in debating the point—the crimes are now more than twenty years old. The passage of time has degraded the physical evidence and impaired the witnesses' memory. Our case, on review, would be insurmountably weak."

Patrick Linden smiled at the acknowledgement. His legal team grew more confident of his release.

The chief prosecutor continued, "There is one small matter though. The appellants accelerated the date of this hearing. Consequently, the government has not had sufficient time to assess if the inmate is presently the subject of any undercover police investigations or intelligence operations. Activities of the sort are, by their very nature, shielded from easy identification and review and may involve complex protocols for the handling of classified material.

"Imagine releasing the inmate now and then discovering, in a month's time, he is to be charged with additional terrorism offenses. It would make all of us look foolish, endanger the public welfare, and risk the inmate's escape to another jurisdiction. If, as CNICS asserts, the inmate is innocent, then he has nothing to fear from the government's review and can look forward to his release in just thirty days."

One of Claire's colleagues rose to make an objection. "This is merely a stall tactic to give the security services time to manufacture some other reason to keep Mr. Linden in prison. What new evidence or crimes could they possibly present against a man who has been at Maghaberry, under the government's watchful eye, for the past two decades?"

The chief prosecutor countered, "The Crown contends the inmate remains a leading figure in dissident Republican circles and wields considerable influence among terrorist factions, even from prison. It is entirely reasonable to think he is a co-conspirator in terror offenses as yet uncharged."

Claire Davis stood to rebut the government's argument. "It is precisely that type of thinking that brought us here in the first place. 'I believe it, so it must be so' is *not* a recognized legal principle in this country. What the chief prosecutor *thinks* and what he can *prove* are two distinct matters. And it's entirely *unreasonable* to think the Crown would actually disclose the existence of these highly secretive investigations, were they to find any. This is nothing more than a thinly disguised attempt to buy more time and come up with a new offense—based on nothing more than *conjecture*."

After a twenty-minute break in the proceeding, the Lord Justices sided, at least temporarily, with the Crown. Linden would remain incarcerated for thirty more days. If by 10:00 on the thirtieth day the government did not charge him with new terror offenses, he would be released from custody on the spot.

A FATHER'S DISAPPROVAL

CLAIRE DAVIS AND THE TEAM FROM CNICS were just entering the underground car park after Patrick Linden's hearing when her mobile rang. "Hallo, Daddy."

"Meet me upstairs at Fox in fifteen minutes." Robert Inglesby ended the call without waiting for a response.

Claire inhaled deeply. She turned to her colleagues and said, "I have to make a quick stop nearby. Go on without me. I'll get myself back to campus in time for the debrief this afternoon."

After assuring the team she would be fine on her own, Claire headed back into the Royal Courts of Justice and exited the complex through a little-used side door at the northeast corner. She walked up Oxford Street a couple blocks until she reached the restaurant. At the entryway, Claire braced herself. From his tone and manner on the phone, she knew her father was upset. She already deduced the reason.

Claire entered the establishment and glanced up at the mezzanine, where the private tables were. She spotted her father and went to join him. *Listen but don't engage.*

Inglesby stood to greet his daughter as she arrived at the table. "Hallo, sweetheart," he said tersely. "Thank you for meetin' me."

"Hallo, Daddy." She went to give him a hug but he sat before she had the chance. "It didn't sound like I had much choice. Is everything alright?"

Inglesby answered slowly. "No. Everythin' is *not* alright." Then he lowered his voice and hissed, "Are ya *mad*, Claire, representin' Patrick Linden on appeal?"

She was right—he found out about the appeal and her role in it. *Listen but don't engage.* "I see you disapprove."

He leaned toward her. "Of *course* I disapprove. He's a ruthless, cold-blooded killer. Maghaberry is where he *belongs*, Claire. I've worked hard me entire life to protect us from those monsters. Now ya want to set him *free?*"

Claire calmly pointed out, "There's good reason to question how he ended up in Maghaberry, Daddy. And the government chose not to argue the point."

Inglesby looked surprised. "The government's not fightin' the appeal?!"

"No. They admitted there were procedural errors, and they didn't believe they could sustain the conviction."

"Bollocks! Who's the prosecutor?"

"The chief prosecutor himself spoke for the Crown."

Inglesby looked deflated. "But Linden's back at Maghaberry?"

"Yes. He's being held another thirty days while the government confirms there are no new charges pending against him. It's just a spiteful delay. The prosecution would surely know already if they were less than thirty days from charging him with new offenses."

Inglesby looked pensive, then agitated. "So in thirty days the bastard could be out! Claire, how are ya comfortable with that? Killin' and maimin' are all he knows. You'll have blood on yer hands."

Claire's cheeks and ears darkened. Someone said the same thing to her back in the States when she represented the man wrongly accused of killing the police officer. She was right then, and she believed she was right now. Her blood boiled. "Daddy, you know how the system works. Or at least how it's *supposed* to work." Claire felt her voice grow louder, and she checked herself. "We can't send innocent people to jail and leave them there. It's not right."

"But that's just it, Claire. He's not *innocent*, is he?"

"If he's guilty, the government has to *prove* it. And in this case, the police lied and planted evidence. If they had any *real* evidence they would have *used* it. Is that how you want the police to behave? Is that the sort of thing prosecutors should overlook? *Everybody's* just one false accusation away from prison if we turn a blind eye to the abuse of power. I'm not going to let that happen without any objection."

"Claire, we're at *war* with these people. *They* don't play by the rules. Why should *we*? You forget what they did to yer mother and sister."

Claire recoiled. "How can you say something like that? All I'm doing is defending the rule of law and asking that everyone be treated equally and fairly. We should easily be able to agree on that, Daddy. But instead you suggest I'm somehow *dishonoring Mum and Courtney?*" Tears welled in her eyes, and she did not want her father to see them. "I think they'd be *proud* of me for standing up for what's right. And I hoped you would be too. I'm sorry to be such a disappointment, Daddy." She stood up, gathered her things, and headed for the stairs, still fighting back tears.

"Claire, stay. Of course I'm proud of ya. I'm just tryin' to stop ya from makin' a huge mistake." But she was already descending the stairs.

In the heat of their conversation, neither father nor daughter saw a young man take their picture from a table by the window and text it to Mickey Shanahan.

THE JOURNAL – PART 1

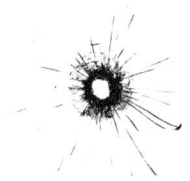

LIAM O'MALLEY STOPPED OUTSIDE THE MODEST brick building on Ormeau Road. The IRA's mightiest assassin and bomb maker was scared—afraid to talk about his emotions with the American shrink in the second-story office. As agreed, O'Malley kept a nightly journal of his nightmares and brought it with him. But he did not need a psychologist's help to decipher their meaning. O'Malley held his breath and ascended the stairs anyway. He knew he needed to do this. He *wanted* to do this.

Thornton greeted O'Malley with the usual hearty welcome. O'Malley wondered if the doc was ever in a bad mood. The two men took their seats, and Thornton opened the conversation as he always did—by asking what O'Malley wanted to talk about.

"What do I *want* to talk about?" O'Malley chuckled softly. "Or what *should* we talk about?"

Thornton raised his eyebrows knowingly but waited for O'Malley to continue.

"Ya know when yer nauseous, and ya know yer goin' to vomit? But ya try so hard not to? Ya keep absolutely still. Ya breathe only through yer nose. Ya do anythin' in yer power to avoid it. But then it comes up anyway, and in that moment ya feel miserable, but then right afterwards ya feel *so* much better?"

Thornton looked at O'Malley quizzically.

"That's what it's like talkin' to ya most weeks," O'Malley finished with a wry smile.

Thornton laughed out loud. "I *think* that's a compliment?"

O'Malley nodded. "Aye, a strange one, but a compliment."

The doc said, "I gather you're about to vomit then?"

"Feels like it," O'Malley said as his mood changed. "It might get ugly today." He paused, took a couple deep breaths, and produced the journal. He placed it on the small table to his left and said, "There's my homework. We burn it at the end of the session."

"Deal."

"But I don't think we need to do any dream analysis. I know what's botherin' me now. That teenage boy I told ya about last time—the one at the Reconciliation meeting. He confirmed what I already feared. I did a lot of damage to so *many* families. As soon as they told me I was to be released, the nightmares started. I knew I didn't *deserve* to be released. I did a lot of horrible things—hypothetically speakin'.

"Those floatin' faces I don't recognize? They must be me victims, or at least who I imagine me victims to be. That's why they stare at me and scream. Most of the time, I didn't stick around to witness the aftermath of the—of my hypothetical actions. But one time..." O'Malley's voice trailed off, and he seemed lost in thought.

"Take your time."

Nearly a minute passed in absolute silence. Then the tears came, and O'Malley described what was etched on his mind. "The air's just filled with dust, with ash. And it's fallin' like snow, onto rubble in the street. There are chunks of concrete, twisted pieces of metal, lots of broken wood. So many jagged edges and sharp points. It's too dangerous fer a child to be there. But there's a wee ginger girl holdin' a bear. And it looks like she wants to climb onto the rubble. She's cryin', wailin'. She keeps repeatin' somethin', but I can't make it out cuz she's cryin' so hard. And then a middle-aged man with a limp comes and carries her away to someplace safe."

Thornton was about to inquire about a couple details when O'Malley continued, as if in a trance.

"She's not the only one there. There's a wee boy, in the back seat of a car. He's cryin' too, and his face is bloodied from broken glass. The windows in the car are blown out. And he's just sittin' there, all alone, cryin' and cuppin' his hands over his ears. There are people wanderin' about, but nobody comes to save the wee boy."

Thornton saw the anguish on O'Malley's face but resisted the urge to comfort him. He sensed there was more.

O'Malley continued sobbing and now struggled to get the words out. It was difficult to understand him. "And then the wee boy crawled out the rear windscreen of the car, cuz he couldn't get the doors open. He slid down the back of the car—it was a Vauxhall Astra with no boot—and dropped to the ground and ran toward the pile of rubble, still cryin'. I wanted to stop him, but I was too far away, and Patrick held me back. Then…"

Thornton mirrored O'Malley's emotions and felt his eyes tear up.

O'Malley made a gurgling sound but stayed transfixed on the images in his head. "And then he scrambled onto that pile of rubble, still cryin', and made his way higher, toward somethin' I couldn't see. Finally, he reached it and stopped, with his back to me. I could tell he was fumblin' with somethin'. Then he turned and started his way back down the pile of rubble, draggin' a woman's forearm and handbag behind him. It was an awful thing to see. But this wee boy was determined to bring that arm and that handbag with him. He made it safely down the pile…"

Thornton struggled to remain inscrutable. He listened as O'Malley continued.

"…but the arm was too heavy fer him. So first he took the handbag back to the car and placed it through the broken window onto the seat where he had been sittin'. And then he returned to the arm. Using both hands, he dragged it to the car too, and somehow managed to lift it through the window and onto the seat as well. Then he climbed back through the rear windscreen and crawled to where he'd started."

Thornton's eyes widened as O'Malley finally looked up at him.

"And then he hugged the arm tight to his chest and began rockin' forward and backward as he cried. That's when I knew it was his mother's arm, and the wee boy had recognized her handbag."

For the first time in his career, Thornton was speechless. Professionally, he was obligated to push his emotions aside. He needed a minute to compose himself. So he simply reached out and silently placed one hand on O'Malley's shoulder while O'Malley purged himself of the remaining tears. The two men cried together.

Several minutes passed before O'Malley looked expectantly at Thornton. There was a lot to process here, and Thornton struggled to suggest a path forward. There was not enough time left in the session to address everything O'Malley just introduced, but he could not send him home in this state. So he broke the rules and extended the session another fifty minutes. "Liam, I think it's a good idea to talk through this before you leave. But we need more than just a few minutes to do it. Are you willing to stay for a second session?"

O'Malley nodded. "If we don't do it now, I don't think I could ever bring it up again."

THE JOURNAL – PART 2

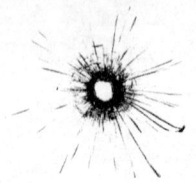

O'MALLEY RETURNED FROM THE WC in the hallway outside Thornton's office, and the two men took their seats. O'Malley jumped back into the conversation.

"I want ya to know something, Doc. The explosion wasn't supposed to happen that way. It was an accident. We never meant—I'm still talkin' hypothetically."

Thornton nodded. "By 'we,' do you mean you and Patrick? The one you said held you back?"

"He's my best mate, but never mind him," O'Malley said tersely. "He's off limits."

Thornton nodded.

O'Malley continued, "All I can say is, things were supposed to go differently that day. I've always felt badly about it. *Guilty* is a better word. I personally don't believe in hurtin' children."

"I believe that, Liam. You said the ginger girl with the teddy bear reminded you of your sister. I didn't know you had a sister."

O'Malley's face turned somber. "I did. Deidre was her name. She was a ginger too. And the sweetest girl. The Brits ran over her with a tank." He said it matter-of-factly.

"My God, Liam. That's awful."

"Crushed her head in the street, so they did. When she was thirteen years old. Can ya believe it? In plain view of the whole neighborhood. She was out there tryin' to look after *me*, and I left her there in the street." Now the tears flowed again. "I *was* on me way back to save her. See, the soldiers shot her with a rubber bullet, and she was lyin' in the street unconscious. The tank started toward her, and I was gonna pull her out of the way. But the crowd was pushin' against me, tryin' to get away. I watched the Brits drive right over her. The bastards didn't even slow down. Hypothetically speakin', that's the day I started doin' all those things they accused me of—to get back at them fer what they did to my sister, and to other Catholic families."

Thornton's mind reeled.

"So that explains me motivation. I didn't set out to do those things. The Brits sucked me into it. But I admit I went willingly. I was so enraged and had nowhere to direct me anger or the blame. I have no idea who the driver was. Trust me, if I'd known, he would have been dead within a week. So *any* British soldier became fair game, and eventually, anyone on the Brits' *side* became fair game.

"But now, I have regrets. Not about standin' up fer Deidre, or fer all the other innocent victims of the Brits. That was the right thing to do. But we were in a war, and in war there are combatants and non-combatants. And after a while, we didn't distinguish between them. And I know—hypothetically speakin'—that my actions hurt a lot of non-combatants and their families. And fer that I am truly sorry. Fer that, I feel guilty."

O'Malley appeared to have finished, so Thornton offered an observation. "I understand why the nightmares coincide with the announcement of your release. Tell me more about the effect of your conversation with the boy from the Reconciliation meeting. You said you had your worst nightmare that night."

"Right, so I was already feelin' guilty about what I'd done and thinkin' I didn't deserve to be released. And then this kid at the meetin' describes how fucked up his family is, decades later, because of The Troubles. And I know I played a role in that. So it reinforces what I'm already feelin'. Now, he doesn't know who I am, but he knows I'm Catholic, and he can see how old I am, so he probably knows I did some things. *And he doesn't hate me.* He has Catholic *friends*. He wants all the hate and vengeance to stop. And it makes me think, if *he* can move past it, maybe *others* can. I mean, there's a lot of people at those meetings, right? If *he* can forgive, maybe others can."

Thornton honed in on the words. "Are you seeking forgiveness, Liam?"

O'Malley exhaled slowly and then looked resolutely at Thornton. "Aye, Doc. I am. I don't think I'll find peace any other way. We Catholics believe in absolution from God, so I think I'm good there. But I need to know I'm forgiven by at least some of the people I hurt here on earth. There's just one problem. I don't know who they are. I didn't stick around long at the scene of me…activities. Maybe that makes me a coward, but I just didn't want to fall into British hands. So I don't know *who* I want forgiveness from. I just know I want it."

Thornton thought for a moment. Then he pointed out, "You *do* know two of your victims—hypothetical victims. That little girl and the little boy. Not by name, but by time and location. Maybe there's a way to identify them from newspaper articles or police reports. I might know someone who can help, if you want to give it a try."

The two men talked about the pros and cons of identifying the two children, and the risks associated with making contact, even anonymously through an intermediary. The potential risks were serious—including the possibility of rejection and legal action, if the explosion was not covered by the amnesty. Thornton explained it was his obligation to explore all options with O'Malley, to weigh the advantages and disadvantages of each one, and then let O'Malley choose a path forward. He was careful to point out that O'Malley could take as much time as needed to make a decision.

"I know in my heart, Doc, I won't find peace and the nightmares won't end unless someone I hurt can forgive me. So I at least gotta try. First let's see if we can identify one of the kids. If we can, we'll talk about what comes next."

"Fair enough. Do I have your permission to contact someone who may be able to help, as long as I don't identify you?"

"Aye, Doc. Go ahead." O'Malley was emotional now at the thought of asking one of his victims directly for forgiveness.

As O'Malley wiped the tears from both eyes with the heel of one hand, Thornton retrieved a small box of matches from a drawer in the side table. He threw open a window and positioned a fan near his client. Then he slid a metal waste bin in front of O'Malley and pointed to the journal. "You've one more thing to do before you go."

Both men watched silently as O'Malley's journal slowly caught fire, flared into a ball of flame, and then extinguished itself—leaving nothing but ash and a few scorched pieces behind.

PILLOW TALK

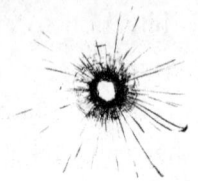

THORNTON WAS ALREADY HOME when Claire arrived after work. She set her keys on the narrow table in the entryway and called to him. Several hours after the lunch with her father, she was still fuming and ready to vent to her favorite psychologist. But Thornton did not answer.

"Hon?" She called louder this time. Claire passed through the kitchen and then to the bedroom. She stopped short when she arrived at the study. Thornton sat forlornly in the plush wing chair. He wore a strange expression. "Aaron, what's wrong?"

Thornton looked up and gave his wife a weak smile. "Just a rough day at the office," he said. The pair usually avoided details about their work to preserve their clients' confidentiality.

"I haven't seen you look like this in a long time." Memories of West Virginia crossed her mind, and she felt a sense of foreboding. She hated to see her husband in more distress, but could not bring herself to deal with added emotion. *There's just too much going on at work right now and a lot at stake. And he always finds a way to bounce back.*

"It was awful, hon. A client described a horrible attack he saw during The Troubles. It brought me to tears."

"My God. It's really bothering you. What did he say?" Claire steeled herself.

Thornton hesitated. He wanted to talk about the session but had to avoid details that might identify O'Malley. "He witnessed a bombing here in Belfast. It was a long time ago, in the '90s, but it was still vivid for him. It must have been quite a blast, because buildings and cars were destroyed. And bodies everywhere. I think what got me most were the kids he mentioned."

Claire recalled her own experience, and her throat tightened. She never told her husband about the bomb that killed her sister. Claire masked her anxiety by reaching for his hand. "Hon, I'm so sorry. The Troubles were a terrible time."

Thornton continued. "There were *children* there, babe. He saw a young red-haired girl clutching a teddy bear who reminded him of his sister. And a little boy who lost his mother. He watched the boy retrieve his mother's severed arm, which still held her purse. Can you *imagine* seeing that, or going through that as a child?"

Only Claire saw the irony in his question. A strange sense of *deja vu* overcame her, but just as suddenly it was gone. She ignored the feeling and refocused on her husband.

"I mean, how can human beings do that to each other? To children? It made me think of that grad student I met at the pool a while back—the one who sent me the studies on transgenerational trauma and The Troubles. The psychological impact, even on people born *after* The Troubles, is astonishing. But it wasn't until today, hearing about the little boy and girl, that it seemed real to me. I can't imagine what it did to those poor kids. There must be so many children like that, all grown up now, who carry the emotional scars."

Claire swallowed hard. *I can't deal with this right now.* "When you were first getting started as a psychologist, you had a clinical mentor that you used as a sounding board. Can the prison system or parole commission provide someone like that for you here? It might help."

"Maybe. I hadn't thought to ask about that." Thornton wanted to tell Claire about O'Malley's remorsefulness and desire to make amends with the little boy and girl, but he thought it best not to reveal his client's association with the bombing. Instead he simply said, "I just feel so badly for all of them."

Claire admired her husband's compassion and empathy and did her best to let him unburden himself further. *The poor guy takes on everyone else's problems.*

Thornton continued, "On a more positive note, I'm making good progress with a guy who was orphaned during The Troubles. He's had a really rough life but finally seems to be turning things around. He's a good guy and deserves better than he got. So at least I feel needed—like I'm doing something good here."

Claire was relieved to hear her husband's shift in tone and gave him a long hug. "I love you, sweetness. Don't ever change. The world needs more people like you, even if it does beat you up from time to time."

Thornton laughed and quickly shifted attention to Claire. "I'm so sorry, babe. Here I am going on and on about *my* day. How did the hearing go?!"

Claire described the government's surprise move and the Justices' interim decision to keep Linden in prison. "So I'm cautiously optimistic—I just hope the prosecution doesn't use the next thirty days to find another bullshit reason to keep Linden in jail."

"Not a chance, with you on the case. They have no idea who they're dealing with!"

Claire looked pleased. She needed the encouragement after her father's earlier remarks.

Thornton continued, "I keep reading the news to make sure your name isn't mentioned anywhere. Do we need to take any precautions if he's released? It sounds like some people are really fired up about the appeal. I don't want anyone directing their frustration at you. Maybe we should talk to your dad."

"That's another thing. I'm not speaking to my father right now. He said some insulting things to me at lunch today about the appeal. He's opposed to Linden's release and my support of it. *Strongly* opposed. I actually walked out on him. I'm *still* furious."

Now Thornton gave Claire a long hug. "I'm sorry, babe. Ignore him. I still support you one thousand percent. You've taken on the establishment before and won. I know you'll do it again."

THE IDEALIST

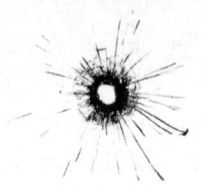

MONTHS AFTER HIS ENCOUNTER with Robert Inglesby, Arthur Hendrickson—the smartly dressed analyst in Section 6 at Palace Barracks—was still angry. He didn't care if Inglesby was MI5's head of undercover operations or the Prince of Wales. Hendrickson wrote a detailed, well-supported intelligence report about Fr. Clark's murder, and he resented the boss' instructions to delete from it a number tag and facial match—for any reason.

Everyone knew Clark's murder was the director's top priority. Inhibiting the free flow of information was insubordinate and compromised the integrity of the section's work. Hendrickson wanted no part of that.

In the short term, though, Hendrickson did as he was told and submitted a revised report. But for weeks he seethed. He expected better of management. And he strongly disliked being admonished in front of his peers—especially as a new arrival in Section 6. It undermined his reputation as a credible analyst.

Hendrickson's colleagues tried to reassure him there must be good reason to withhold the number plate and facial match. It was important to be a team player, they said. Outwardly, Hendrickson played the good soldier, but inwardly he neither forgave nor forgot. He pondered how to make things right and simultaneously protect himself, should the director discover the report was redacted. He knew if that happened, it would be *his* head on the chopping block—not Inglesby's.

After weeks of intellectual wrangling, Hendrickson reached a decision. He bought a disposable mobile phone with cash, taking care to conceal his facial features from any nearby surveillance cameras. Then he placed an anonymous 999 call from a congested area several miles from his home. He reported seeing a suspicious white van on the Falls Road on the night of "that priest's" murder about a month earlier. He provided the number plate but gave only a physical description of the man seen standing next to the vehicle. And he asked the dispatcher to include a code word in the report by which he could later identify himself, if need be.

As the dispatcher typed the details of the caller's report, MI5's Trawler software recognized the keywords *Falls Road, murder,* and *priest,* and sent a high-priority alert to Robert Inglesby's secure mobile—and the mobiles of other senior MI5 officials.

Inglesby's lunch companions saw him blanch when he checked the message on his phone. He excused himself and sought refuge in a stall in the WC. He checked the message again and could not believe his eyes. CrimeStoppers had just linked Kieran Oliver's delivery van and a man matching Kieran's description to the murder of Fr. Clark. *Shite!* If MI5 had not yet sent a team to pick him up, the PSNI soon would. And Inglesby was now powerless to stop either one.

Inglesby dialed James Dwyer, his undercover operative inside the New IRA, in hopes of expediting the retaliatory strike against Kieran. No answer. *Bloody hell.*

Across town, DI Will Nichols was debating whether to accept a double shift at the Grosvenor Road police station when the desk officer called to share the tip about Fr. Clark's murder. Nichols listened carefully and checked the number plate. The vehicle was linked to Kieran Oliver, who was already well-known to Nichols and his colleagues. Nichols was perplexed by the sudden mention of the van after so much time, but he lacked any other leads and decided to check it out. He rallied his colleagues. "We've got ourselves a manhunt, boys."

As the PSNI officers donned their protective gear and heavy weapons and prepared to go in search of Kieran Oliver, a police clerk on the UVF's payroll made a discreet call from a pay phone in the prisoner holding area. Garth Peters did not recognize the number but answered anyway, from his usual spot at the Cocky Rooster. "Hallo?"

"It's me at Grosvenor Road station. They're rollin' out to look for Crazy Kieran. They think he's got somethin' to do with that priest's murder. Thought you should know."

"Understood. Cheers, mate." The UVF boss ended the call and frowned. Kieran was the last person he wanted talking to the PSNI. The kid was a hot head, and he knew too much. And what was that about him being linked to the priest's murder? Inglesby certainly would *not* be happy to hear about *that*. Peters decided it was time to cut ties with Kieran. He motioned to his second-in-command, who approached the table and leaned down to hear the boss' instructions. He nodded, signaled for a couple of the other crew members to join him, and slipped out the back of the pub.

THE ENCOUNTER

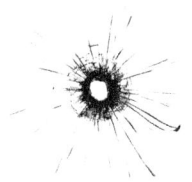

THE DAY AFTER PATRICK LINDEN'S APPEAL HEARING, Paula
Hall traded schedules with one of her assistants. Her new dog-
walking route would keep her near the Botanic Gardens all day,
close to QUB. The assortment of keys in her pocket would easily
allow her to duck in and out of homes as needed while following
Claire Davis.

Paula did her homework and discovered Claire's office was
on the seventh floor of a modern brick and glass building called
Main Site Tower. Her home address, provided by Mickey Shanahan, was conveniently nearby on College Green. The university
kindly posted Claire's photograph online, so Paula had everything she needed to establish a tail.

Paula planned to use the first few hours to learn the layout of
the neighborhood and scout good places to use as cover. Then
she hoped to catch Claire on the way to lunch. Otherwise, Paula
would wait for Claire at the end of the workday and follow her
home. Paula was still unsure how to split her time between the
law professor and the psychologist, but Claire seemed to be the
higher priority for Shanahan. In any event, she already watched
the psychologist for a few weeks without anything exciting to
report.

Paula exited the first flat on her list with an arthritic black lab who moved slowly. The pace suited her just fine. The next residence on the list belonged to a meticulously groomed poodle with a pink bow in her hair who seemed less inclined to go slow, but thankfully had tiny legs. Paula turned the corner at University Square on her way to stop number three and came face to face with her target.

Paula pretended not to recognize Claire Davis and tried to navigate around her unobtrusively, but the poodle had other ideas. She darted in front of, and then behind, the law professor, wrapping the leash around Claire's ankles and bringing the woman to a halt. Claire laughed and bent down to say hello to her new friend. Ordinarily, Paula avoided direct contact and remained unnoticed in the background, but this encounter was unavoidable.

Claire looked up at Paula and asked the dog's name. She spoke with a faint Belfast accent.

"Princess," Paula answered. The poodle yipped at the sound of her name.

"What a cutie. And who's this ol' fella?"

"That's Cornelius." The old lab looked sideways at her.

"Well, you have your hands full with these two," Claire said cheerily as she untangled herself from the poodle.

Paula untwisted the dogs' leashes and dropped her bundle of keys in the process.

Claire picked them up and handed the large keyring to Paula. "Have a wonderful day."

"Cheers. You too."

As Claire headed in the opposite direction, Paula cursed her bad luck. It was going to be difficult now to keep a close eye on Claire without being easily recognized. And if she was recognized more than a time or two, it could make Claire suspicious. Paula decided her best bet was to learn as much as she could today—even at the risk of another encounter—and then disappear from Claire's life for a long time.

———————

Paula watched across a wide expanse of lawn when Claire headed to lunch later that day. The law professor met two well-dressed men and a woman at a nearby Indian restaurant. Paula kept vigil from a flat across the street as the group talked animatedly at a table by the window, hunched over a stack of papers. Claire then returned alone to Main Site Tower.

This dog-walking route had more homes on it than Paula's usual one. Consequently, she had less free time to sit and wait for Claire. Still, she got to know the area well and found the best place from which to monitor the only two approaches to Claire's home at the end of the day. Around 15:00, Paula established discreet observation of Claire's residence through the upstairs curtain of a home at the end of the block. She had a good field of sight in several directions and already knew what Claire was wearing, so it would be easy to spot her.

After ninety minutes of waiting, Paula saw Claire walking alone along Botanic Avenue toward College Green. Paula watched as her target headed up the street and paused in front of the door to her flat. But instead of entering the home, Claire stood and waved at a male figure approaching from the other direction. Paula could see he was a tall, athletic chap, but it was not until he was nearly at the door that Paula recognized Aaron Thornton from the office on Ormeau Road. She began snapping photos of both faces, and of the couple's embrace when Thornton leaned down to kiss Claire. No surprise there—Shanahan said the two were linked online.

Paula continued her dog-walking routine throughout the neighborhood until about 19:30 but saw no further activity at Claire's residence. She called it a night and texted the photos to Shanahan as she headed home.

STAND DOWN

WHILE PAULA HALL KEPT AN EYE on Claire Davis, Mickey Shanahan refocused on the late Rebecca Tucker.

His contact at the central records bureau determined beyond a doubt that a legal secretary by that name died in a car crash thirty-four years ago. There were no current digital records for the name in Northern Ireland, yet someone clearly signed *Rebecca Tucker* on government documents in the past several months. Unfortunately, the dead woman's signature was not a perfect match for the one on the recent paperwork. So Shanahan needed a definitive answer. *Was there a second—living—Rebecca Tucker or not?*

If so, then the paperwork related to Thornton's new practice was likely legitimate, and the Provos could relax. If not, then the documents were forgeries and Thornton posed a threat.

Shanahan decided to attack the problem from a new angle. He brought two of his men to the home of the highest-ranking Catholic serving in the PSNI—Chief Superintendent Seamus O'Brien. Ordinarily, the Provos forced Catholics out of police service—one way or another—but they left O'Brien alone in hopes he might one day be useful to them. That day had come.

The team waited on motorbikes at the end of the block and watched as O'Brien's security escort pulled away and the chief superintendent entered his home alone. They stayed still a few more minutes to be sure all was quiet, then pulled up to the house. Shanahan dismounted and knocked on the front door while his comrades remained on their bikes out front, helmets in place to conceal their faces. The door opened.

"Good evenin', Mrs. O'Brien. May I please have a word with the chief superintendent?" It was a bold move, designed to catch the family off guard and instill fear.

O'Brien appeared behind his wife before she had a chance to respond. "It's alright, love. Go inside with the kids. I'll only be a minute." Mrs. O'Brien withdrew, and the chief superintendent stepped into the doorframe, surveying the scene outside. Shanahan suspected there was a revolver tucked in the small of his back, and perhaps a shotgun just inside the doorway.

"We're not here to hurt ya, Chief Superintendent, or ya'd already be bleedin'. We just need a wee favor is all. A colleague of ours will call ya at the office tomorrow and identify herself as yer daughter, Margaret. You'll interrupt whatever yer doin' and take that call. Then our colleague will give ya a name. You will run a Level 5 query on that name, print the results, seal them in an envelope, and bring the envelope home with ya. We'll be back to collect it from ya. Do exactly as I say, with no tricks, and yer family will be fine. Ya have me solemn word. Otherwise, we know where ya live and who yer children are. Do we have an agreement?"

O'Brien started to protest but caught himself. A Level 5 query would unlock all sealed records in each of the PSNI's databases. Depending on the name to be searched, the results of that query could be devastating in the wrong hands. But O'Brien, grim-faced, nodded.

"That's a good man. Yer Catholic brethren appreciate yer support, sir."

The two men withdrew from their conversation, and the Provos disappeared into the night.

———————

The next evening, Shanahan studied the results of the Level 5 query. It seemed there was a second Rebecca Tucker after all, whose records were sealed by court order to protect her from a stalker. It was the sort of stuff a clerk at the central records bureau would not have access to. Shanahan sighed in relief. He had other matters demanding his time and attention and was glad to cross this one off the list.

KINDRED SPIRITS

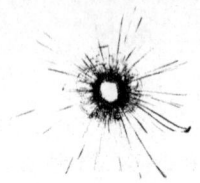

TOMMY MAGEE ARRIVED AT WORK the morning after his confrontation with Kieran at the flat. He was still shaken by the event and more determined than ever to move out. Tommy hung his coat in a locker in the break room and joined his colleagues in the garage.

The mechanics were already in the bays organizing parts for the day's repairs. Paul, the member of the group closest to Tommy in age, beckoned to him. "Gimme a hand with this, will ya?"

"No problem, mate." Tommy jumped into the pit under the raised car and helped remove the oil pan.

"Somethin' troublin' ya?" Paul had a knack for reading people.

Tommy gave an abbreviated version of the previous night's events, leaving out mention of the gun and the UVF. "So if ya know someone with a flat to rent, I'd be grateful for a heads up."

"Sure thing. I'll keep me ears open. Not sure how ya managed livin' this long with Crazy Kieran."

"He's not all bad, to be honest. But I need to make a change."

"I imagine so. Ya don't seem like ya'd have much in common with Kieran," Paul said with a laugh. He grew somber when he saw Tommy's expression change. "What is it, mate?"

"Aww, it's nothin'."

"C'mon, mate, I can see on yer face it's not *nothin'*. Did I offend ya?"

"No, no. It's not that," Tommy quickly reassured his co-worker. "It's just that Kieran and I *do* have somethin' in common. Kinda dark though. Don't want to ruin yer day with it."

"Out with it, mate."

"Don't know if he ever told ya, but Kieran's dad was in the RUC and shot dead by the IRA. His mum died of cancer not long after. The IRA killed me mum and dad too. That's how we ended up as foster brothers."

Paul let out a soft, slow whistle. "Fuckin' Fenian bastards. They ever catch who did it?"

"Naw. Neither one. Still bitter about that, to be honest."

"I don't blame ya, Tommy. I'd be mad as hell meself. Now it makes sense why you two stayed close. So is that why ya started workin' here?"

Tommy looked at Paul, puzzled.

"Don't worry, mate. We all have our reasons," Paul said with a wink.

"I don't know what ya mean, Paulie. I started workin' here cuz no one else would hire me." Tommy realized how that sounded and corrected himself. "I mean, I *want* to work here. But I'd given up on findin' a job until Gerry took me on. A friend of a friend sort of thing."

"Well, Gerry's a good sort of friend to have. How'd ya meet him?"

"I didn't actually know the bloke. But when I showed up on the first day, Dorene said somebody named Garth gave him my name."

"Garth *Peters?*" Paul was impressed.

"Yeah, that's it." Tommy recognized the name.

Paul whistled again. "Yer one well-connected fella."

Tommy was perplexed by Paul's reaction, but liked it.

The pair worked quietly on the car for a couple minutes before Paul broke the silence. "Tommy, do ya mind me askin' exactly how yer parents died?"

Tommy hesitated. "It was a bomb. We were at a furniture store on the Shankill Road when it went off. I was eight at the time and waitin' in the car while me mum and dad ran inside. They were only gonna be a minute. The last memory I have of 'em is walkin' through the door together. Then there was a bright white flash. After that, everythin' sounded strange. The blast tore both me eardrums." Tommy's voice faltered, and his hands balled into fists as he recalled the day.

"Jayzus, Tommy. I didn't realize ya saw the whole thing. I'm sorry, mate."

"No worries. It's easier to talk about it now. It's just the anger and the desire fer revenge that still get to me."

Paul nodded. "How old are ya, Tommy?"

"Thirty-three. Why?"

"So that means ya lost yer parents in '94, does it?"

"Yeah, that's right."

"Ya say it was a furniture store on the Shankill Road? Was it Sheehan's, by any chance?"

Tommy looked startled. "Yeah, but how'd ya know?"

"There's a few folks around who lost family or got injured in that explosion. And just like you, they want justice fer what happened to 'em. Ya ever talk to the Historian?"

"I don't even know who that *is*."

"He's a Loyalist fella who pieces together details about unsolved terror offenses in hopes of doin' what the police can't or won't do. He doesn't give a shite about the politics or people's sensitivities or amnesties. Only justice fer the victims."

Tommy listened intently. "What does he do with the information?"

"Well, every now and then he gathers enough clues to figure out who's responsible, either directly or indirectly. And when he does, he passes the details to the UVF. They take it from there."

Tommy pressed his lips together until they turned white. Then he looked at Paul and said, "I want to meet the Historian."

THE HET FILE

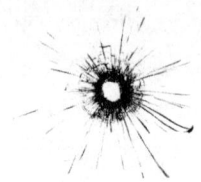

LIAM O'MALLEY'S DESCRIPTION OF THE CHILDREN at the scene of the explosion still haunted Thornton days later. He believed O'Malley's claim that things went terribly wrong. And he knew from his work at the prison in West Virginia that criminals sometimes grew remorseful as they aged.

Thornton's desire to help O'Malley find forgiveness therefore remained unchanged. But as time passed, Thornton grew apprehensive about O'Malley contacting the victims. It seemed unlikely they would react charitably, no matter how sincerely O'Malley wished to apologize. There was no telling how the survivors, or their families, might respond. For that matter, the authorities might intervene and send O'Malley back to prison. "Hypothetically speaking" only worked within the confines of therapy.

The more he thought about it, the less inclined Thornton was to facilitate a meeting. But he promised to help his client identify the boy or girl, and he would not break his word. It was important that O'Malley see him as a reliable and trustworthy ally. They could talk more about the potential pitfalls later, Thornton reasoned. It might prove impossible to locate the children anyway.

Regardless, it was O'Malley's decision to make, if and when the opportunity presented itself.

Thornton originally planned to leverage Robert Inglesby's connections to learn more about the victims of the explosion. It would be awkward to do so now, while Claire and her father were feuding. Instead, Thornton decided to enlist his wife's help. It secretly bothered him to be so dependent professionally on his family, but he knew no one else in Northern Ireland he could ask for favors. At the same time, O'Malley had stuck his neck out to help Thornton, and the American wanted to repay the personal favor *and* keep his professional promise. Besides, a mentor once told him it was important for psychologists to humble themselves from time to time and accept help from others. *I guess it's all part of being a good therapist. And I know just how to persuade Claire to agree.*

———————

Claire entered the flat that evening to the smell of her favorite dish—homemade lasagna using a recipe Thornton learned while a freshman in college. He made it for her on their first date, mostly because it was the only thing he knew how to cook.

Claire walked into the kitchen and found the table set with a white tablecloth, flowers, and candles. A bottle of her favorite red wine stood at the ready, and a loaf of Italian bread fresh from the bakery lay on the cutting board. Thornton had just finished making the salad.

"Surprise!" He grinned as she surveyed the scene.

"You know it's not my birthday, right? And it's not our anniversary either. What are you up to, Aaron Thornton?"

"Can't I do something nice for my wife just for the heck of it?" he asked plaintively.

"I know you too well, hon. You either did something that's really going to upset me, or you want something."

Thornton frowned exaggeratedly and placed a hand over his chest as if wounded. Then he laughed. "Don't worry. You won't be mad. Go ahead and sit down. Your timing is perfect."

Claire took a seat as Thornton brought the food to the table and joined her. They ate and joked and talked about their days for half an hour until Claire finally said, "Out with it, Aaron. I'm dying to know what this wonderful dinner is all about."

Thornton laughed and raised both hands in a show of surrender. "I need a favor…"

"I *knew* it," Claire said triumphantly. "You are *so* transparent."

Thornton continued, "I need to review some police files for work, about things that happened during The Troubles. But I don't want to ask for them through the usual channels, since it might draw unfair scrutiny of my clients. I thought maybe you could ask for them through CNICS?"

"Hmmm. We aren't representing any of your clients though. I'm not sure that's a good idea."

"I thought you might say that. But think about it. I already have the legal authority to request any files related to my clients' treatment and monitoring. It's just that sometimes my clients bring up things the authorities may not know about. It's never enough to warrant a call to the police, but it *does* leave me wanting more background to make sure I understand what I'm dealing with. The problem is, the police and the courts know who my clients are. If I ask for any files that seem unusual, the authorities might get suspicious and start asking questions. I don't want to accidentally get one of my clients in a jam."

"I'm not worried about you seeing the files—you already have a right to them. I just don't want to expose the university or CNICS to any unnecessary scrutiny or second-guessing. We already have enough opposition in some quarters."

Thornton persisted. "But CNICS basically has *carte blanche* to look at any Troubles-related files, doesn't it? You don't have to *represent* someone to review a folder, right? Isn't it fair game as long as it's in the best interests of Reconciliation?"

"Actually, that *is* true. They gave us access to all the files for two years. So you only need files pertaining *directly* to your current clients?"

"Absolutely. No one else."

"I guess there's no *legal* basis to object. I have unrestricted access through CNICS, and you have unrestricted access through your work. It just feels deceptive to request the files through CNICS and hand them to you."

"Except for the reasons I mentioned. I do *need* them to support my clients—which the courts and prison system hired me to do. But if *I* ask for them, it could result in unfair interference by the police. And CNICS is all about protecting people from that sort of unfair treatment. I mean, we can't sort out the past if we're constantly at risk of intervention from the authorities. If anyone ever questions it, I think we can justify it on those terms."

Claire mulled it over. "Alright. How many files are we talking about?"

"Right now, there's just one event I need to know more about from 25 years ago. So it's everything related to that. I'm just not sure how *many* files that is."

"Oh, *that* shouldn't be a big deal. I thought you were talking about a *lot* of files. I might even have a spare request form." Claire rummaged through her work bag on the floor by the table and produced an envelope with a blank form inside. "Here you go. Just fill out the requested information as best you can and pop it in the envelope. I'll give it to my assistant in the morning."

"You're the best, hon. I really appreciate it." He leaned across the table and gave her a kiss.

"I'm glad it helps. And how could I say no after such a grand meal?"

———

The next morning, Claire handed the envelope to her administrative assistant for processing without looking at the contents. Inside was a form seeking all records pertaining to an explosion that occurred on the afternoon of January 4, 1994, on the Shankill Road.

THE HISTORIAN

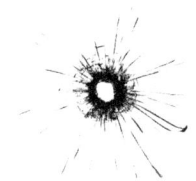

ROBERT INGLESBY INTENTIONALLY SAT ALONE at the bar in the Cocky Rooster. He made small talk with the barkeep while sipping on his third Old Peculier. Garth Peters and his crew were out, and their table in the corner under the telly remained empty. The guard sat in the courtyard outside smoking another cigar.

At half nine, a pensioner known as the Historian passed through the pub's private back entrance. He surveyed the room as he strode to the bar and sat next to Inglesby. "Evenin', Robert," the man said. He lit a pipe while the barkeep sauntered to the opposite end of the bar to give the pair privacy.

"Cheers, mate," Inglesby answered without turning his head. "I was surprised to get yer call."

"True, it's been a while." The Historian puffed on the tobacco. "But what I'm about to tell ya is best conveyed in person. And I think you'll agree it's worth the risk of bein' seen together."

Inglesby looked sideways at the Historian with eyebrows raised. "Don't keep me in suspense then."

"It's about the lad named Tommy Magee you sent to work at Gerry's garage."

Inglesby was momentarily at a loss. Thornton never named

the client who needed a job, but Inglesby connected the dots. "Go on."

"Robert, he was orphaned by the same bomb that killed yer Courtney."

Inglesby swung his head and locked eyes with the Historian. "Does he know who's responsible?"

"No, no. But he was in a car a short distance from the blast and remembers quite a few details. He was clearly traumatized by the explosion and still has nightmares in which the scene replays itself. Oddly enough, he insists he wasn't interviewed by the police. If ya can arrange it, I'd like to see the police file and test the accuracy of his recollection. Maybe he spoke to them without rememberin'. And if I prime him with a few details from other eyewitness accounts, I may be able to jog his memory and get more information. We're not likely to get other fresh leads at this point."

"I'll do ya one better, mate," Inglesby said. "Shortly after they began work in 2005, I asked the HET to make sure the police hadn't overlooked anythin' back in '94. The second investigation produced a few new tidbits, but nothin' actionable. I'll get ya *both* sets of files and a dissident photo book too. Maybe you and the lad can spot somethin' the rest of us missed. I have nothin' left to lose at this stage. Still, I need yer absolute discretion."

"Of course, Robert. I may be old, but I haven't forgotten how to cover me tracks. And yer hand in this shall remain, as always, unseen." The Historian rose from the stool and dropped a twenty-pound note on the bar. When he turned toward the back entrance, Inglesby grabbed his forearm.

"Thanks, mate. And look after the lad. He's probably our only hope of catchin' the killer."

MISSING

SEVERAL DAYS PASSED SINCE ROBERT INGLESBY met the Historian. Inglesby intended to pull the investigative files about the 1994 explosion sooner, but he was too busy to break away from the office. Because he wanted to retrieve the files unofficially and avoid leaving a paper trail, Inglesby needed to appear at the archive in person and exercise his authority as head of undercover operations.

It took just fifteen minutes to drive from Palace Barracks to PSNI Headquarters. Inglesby followed Hawthornden Way until it became Knock Road and then turned right into the fortified complex of red brick buildings. The sentry at the checkpoint recognized him and waved him through. Inglesby headed for the building that housed the restricted area where the archives and HET files were locked in storage cages. He parked behind the building and entered through a side door that never latched properly.

Inglesby rode the elevator two levels below ground and approached the service window. The constable on duty asked how he could help.

Inglesby presented a color-coded credential that identified him as a senior official with unrestricted access to files. Although his name and photo were genuine, the credential omitted his title and any reference to MI5.

The constable examined the credential briefly before asking again how he could help.

"I need to review the RUC and HET files for an explosion that occurred on January 4, 1994, on the Shankill Road."

"Do you know the street number, sir?"

"It's the only bombing that occurred on the Shankill Road that day," Inglesby answered impatiently.

"Of course, sir. Let me search the index using a wild card for the street number." The constable scrolled through the results and scanned the monitor for a minute. "Here it is. HET file number 06-077R."

"If I remember correctly, the R indicates that relevant RUC files have been consolidated into the HET record?"

"That's correct, sir, although I'm afraid they're not here."

"Were they placed in the RUC archive by mistake?"

"No, sir. I mean the file you're looking for has already been signed out."

Inglesby's surprise was apparent. "Signed out by whom?"

"I don't recognize the abbreviation, sir. It's C-N-I-C-S."

Inglesby did not immediately recognize it either. "There must be a person's name listed there as the responsible party."

"Checking now, sir. Here it is. The file was requested two days ago by 'M. Kehs obo C. Davis, QUB.' It was delivered by courier yesterday. There's a phone number here for Kehs if you'd like me to write it down for you."

"No need, thank you."

Inglesby turned and strode back to the elevator. His mind raced as he tried to deduce why someone at Queen's University requested the HET file—*that* HET file—on behalf of his daughter. *And what the bloody hell does CNICS have to do with it?*

FOLLOWED

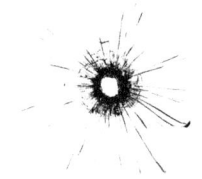

THE PSNI OFFICERS LED BY DI NICHOLS split into four teams of three constables each. Before leaving the station, the PSNI alerted MI5, who agreed to let the police handle the search for Kieran Oliver. The teams used a secure secondary police channel to coordinate a sweep of the Shankill Road area, starting at Oliver's last known address. The white panel van was nowhere in sight, and nobody answered the door or appeared to be home. The neighbors, of course, claimed to know nothing.

The police units fanned out in a coordinated, ever-widening grid from Oliver's flat. DI Nichols was aware of UVF sympathizers on the force and opted against an all-points lookout for Oliver and his van. The four armored undercover vehicles searched for Oliver on their own.

Unbeknownst to them, Garth Peters' three UVF men simultaneously roved the Shankill on motorbikes, coordinating their own movements with wireless microphones and earpieces built into their helmets. They enjoyed several advantages over their PSNI counterparts. The UVF bikes were faster and more agile, and the crew knew the UVF haunts most frequented by Oliver. Oliver presumably had no idea they were searching for him, so they also had the element of surprise. And like the PSNI, the search team worked alone—the UVF, too, suffered leaks.

The searchers—both PSNI and UVF—were stymied by unusually good weather that lured most of Belfast outdoors. The streets choked with traffic, and the sidewalks grew inscrutable with throngs of pedestrians.

But Brianna Donovan was already way ahead of the searchers. She had been waiting on a motorbike a block from Oliver's flat at sunrise when the wanted man jumped into his van and drove east to the city center. Brianna followed him and watched him ditch the van in an underground car park, where he switched to a high-end motorcycle. She wondered why he returned to surveil his own flat.

Throughout the morning, Brianna kept vigil as Oliver tailed his flatmate to a mechanic's shop several minutes away and waited discreetly across the street with his face obscured by a helmet. When the roommate left for lunch, Oliver kept a close watch. *Is he protecting him?*

Brianna stayed close as Oliver followed his flatmate to a sandwich shop. But instead of returning to work at the garage, the bloke took a bus from the sandwich shop to the city center. There he strolled past Hatfield House and entered a modest brick building on Ormeau Road.

A block away, Oliver parked in a row of motorcycles and scooters used by couriers and kept his helmet on. The constant ebb and flow of messengers provided a natural cover.

Brianna established her own observation post across the street, on the ground level of a covered car park where the shadows concealed her. She had an unobstructed line of sight, but the low light forced her to raise the tinted visor of her helmet.

Brianna found it strange that Oliver kept watch while his

roommate remained inside the modest brick building for nearly an hour. If he was there to provide protection, he was too far away to be effective. Brianna grew more curious when the roommate finally exited the building, departed the area, and Oliver remained in place. *So that's it! He wanted to see where the bloke went.*

She noted Oliver discreetly taking photos of the building and everyone who entered and exited. *Who's he gathering intelligence for—and why?* Brianna's thoughts were interrupted when Liam O'Malley opened the gate to the brick building's front walk and passed under the torn green awning. She was not certain, but she thought a man might be shadowing *him* too. *What the fuck is going on?!*

Brianna recognized O'Malley from press photos and assumed Oliver did as well. She quickly assessed the situation. The man accused of killing Devin Dingle and Billy Hoyt—the top two leaders of the New IRA—was now stalking a legendary Provo targeted for recruitment by the New IRA. It looked like the UVF was trying to dismantle and thwart Brianna's crew.

O'Malley was too valuable an asset to lose—he had a huge role to play in Brianna's larger plan. The *femme fatale* initially intended only a reconnaissance mission, but now she realized she had to act before Oliver got close to O'Malley. Brianna reached into her bag, removed the mobile, and dialed a number she had not called in a very long time.

THE MISTAKE

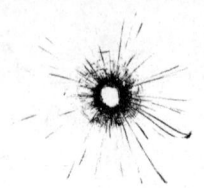

On the evening of January 3, 1994, Patrick Linden and Maxwell Mayhew met Liam O'Malley at a farmhouse about an hour from Belfast. In his makeshift underground workshop, O'Malley excitedly unveiled his latest invention—the first explosive device triggered by a mobile phone call. It allowed the bomb to detonate from a safe distance, at a flexibly precise time, and without interference from the Brits' sophisticated jamming techniques.

The mobile phone detonator worked flawlessly during trials in rural settings, but it had never been tested in an urban environment. O'Malley wanted Linden and Mayhew to join him for a field test in the Shankill ward the next day. Mobile phone service was still relatively new in Northern Ireland, and few people used the devices routinely. The Provos were not yet certain the cellular signal in Belfast would be sufficient to trigger detonation. O'Malley decided it made sense to test the device near its intended target—the UVF's headquarters in a local pub.

It was risky to send operatives to hostile territory, especially close to a sensitive site. So to draw less attention to themselves, the Provos chose a test location a few blocks away at Sheehan's furniture store. The plan was simple—place an inert device with a mobile attached to it in the back of a parked delivery van. The crew would call the device from a vacant office across the street and a couple blocks away. It was the same post—with an unobstructed view of the pub's entrance—from which they would launch the real attack using the same van parked much closer to the target.

Mayhew was mostly unknown around Belfast and would drive the test vehicle. O'Malley and Linden would place the call from the observation point. To avoid suspicion, Mayhew planned to wear a delivery uniform, exit the van, and visit a local shop before returning to the vehicle and driving away. If the phone left in the van registered a missed call, the team would know cellular service in the area was up to the task.

Linden suggested they simply have Mayhew place a call from the phone while walking past the pub. But O'Malley insisted the test mimic the intended field conditions—he wanted to be sure the cellular signal would penetrate the walls of the van and the large package within which the mobile (and eventually the bomb) would be concealed. A dummy device was already prepared for the test.

The next day, Mayhew drove the van to Sheehan's store at midday, when the lunchtime rush afforded more cover. He exited the vehicle and crossed the street to enter a local business as planned. Linden and O'Malley watched from a couple blocks away. A young red-haired girl stood at the window of a sweet shop; she reminded O'Malley of his sister, Deidre, and the strawberry-banana Toffos. Another little girl chased after a pensioner taking her puppy for a stroll; the child wore a pendant that flashed in the sunlight and caught O'Malley's eye. Other children walked with their parents farther up the street.

Linden let O'Malley do the honors and call the mobile phone in the back of the van. To O'Malley's dismay, the vehicle unleashed an explosion and fireball that obliterated Sheehan's store and nearly the entire block. They stared, mouths agape, at the devastation and chaos below. Neither one said a word for about ten seconds. Then Linden gave O'Malley a congratulatory slap on the back and exclaimed, "Well done, mate—it works!"

But O'Malley was horrified to see the ginger girl traumatized at the side of the road, clutching a Paddington Bear. The old lady, the puppy, and the other wee girl disappeared under the rubble. A small boy sat screaming in the back seat of a blown-out car, clasping both ears. None of them were the intended targets, and none of this was supposed to happen. They were all innocent. O'Malley headed for the stairs. "We have to help the wee 'uns."

Linden grabbed O'Malley's arm and pulled him back, much like he did all those years earlier when the Saracen crushed Deidre's head. "We have to leave, Liam. It's not safe. Let's find Max and get out of here before they cordon off the place."

Linden led O'Malley down the back stairs of the building. Mayhew waited for them outside, looking bewildered. Linden grabbed the mobile from O'Malley and called for an ASU to extract them from a meeting point three blocks west of the explosion. The heavily armed team, in three vehicles, was already there when the trio arrived on foot.

———

That night, O'Malley confronted Linden at the farmhouse after Mayhew left. "How did a live explosive end up in the back of that fuckin' van, Patrick?"

Linden shrugged. "I must have picked up the wrong one."

O'Malley was incensed. "The real bomb was in a separate room, Patrick. There's no fuckin' way you confused the packages—I placed the inert one on the table before we went to bed, next to the van keys. Did you switch them? Or did Max?"

"Easy, mate. What difference does it make now? We know the device works, and that was the whole point of the exercise."

"*Ya didn't answer me.*" *O'Malley breathed heavily, unable to calm himself.* "*Why, Patrick? Those were innocent people you killed.*"

Linden flashed O'Malley an angry look and said, "*Don't lecture me about fuckin' innocence! There's no such thing anymore. And I didn't kill anyone. You designed the bomb. You set it off. That's the job, Liam. And there's no escapin' it.*"

HINDSIGHT

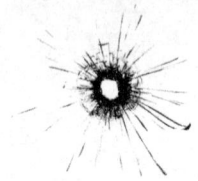

THORNTON SAT IN HIS OFFICE and opened the HET file he requested through CNICS. A courier delivered it to Claire's office that morning, but she was busy with lectures all day and suggested Thornton pick it up himself.

It was actually a collection of files, bundled in a large accordion-style folder with the HET logo on it. Most of the files bore the RUC emblem and were clearly older. The RUC records were a mix of handwritten notes and typed documents. Some pages looked as if they were printed by a teletype machine, with letters formed by a series of tiny dots. Each sheet had two holes punched at the top and was pinned to the file with two metal prongs. A single manila file folder—much thicker than the rest and emblazoned with the HET seal—contained purely computer-generated material.

A letter addressed to Claire accompanied the files. It explained that the PSNI archives serve as a repository for all records produced by the defunct RUC and the disbanded HET, as well as the PSNI itself. According to the correspondence, the collection contained all files in the archives' possession pertaining to "the specified incident of January 4, 1994." Thornton wondered if there might be other files *not* in the archives' possession.

He decided to tackle the material in chronological order. He went page by page and read every line. There were logs of the initial emergency calls after the explosion, descriptions of the scene filed by the first constables to arrive, and technical accounts written by subsequent investigators. Inventories of evidence found at the scene included gruesome photos of bodies and body parts and heart-wrenching lists of personal items. Lab reports identified the type of explosive used and the technical components of the bomb. One examiner noted what appeared to be the first ever use in Northern Ireland of a mobile phone to detonate an explosive device. A separate entry recorded the date and time at which the RUC notified MI5 of that development.

A list of persons killed preceded the individual autopsy reports. The oldest, Elizabeth Treadway, was 74 and a widow. Her daughter identified the partially burned remains. Courtney Davis was just 4 years old and the youngest victim, but Thornton found no mention of any relatives in the police statements or on the list of victims. He found that odd, but kept flipping through the pages.

Witness statements, forensic analyses, and CCTV footage all led nowhere. The van in which the bomb went off was stolen. The police found no fingerprints or viable DNA evidence on remnants of the vehicle or bomb. No one saw anything suspicious before the explosion or had any idea who was responsible for the bomb. Neither the RUC nor any news outlets received a warning before the blast.

Thornton compared details from Liam O'Malley's description to the police files and found them accurate. The location near Sheehan's furniture store was correct, and the reports described a heavily damaged Vauxhall Astra among several vehicles at the scene. A quilted handbag like the one O'Malley described appeared on the inventory of evidence. The elderly woman walking her dog, followed by a little girl, aligned with the list of persons killed.

However, there was no mention of the young girl with red hair who survived—the one who reminded O'Malley of his sister, Deidre. Nor was there any indication of a middle-aged male survivor with a limp who carried the ginger girl away to safety. Thornton kept flipping through the pages, looking for the identity of the little boy in the Vauxhall Astra. Some of the pages seemed to be out of order. He imagined the HET investigators might have pulled some of the documents to copy them and returned them in the wrong sequence. He made it to the end of the RUC file without spotting the boy's name.

Thornton grabbed the only remaining file in the pile—the one produced by the HET. In 2005, they reviewed all the original RUC files with the benefit of hindsight and new intelligence gathered in the eleven years since the blast occurred. Thornton scrutinized every word. The report mostly restated what he already knew, but there were a couple pages with new details. A confidential informer told HET investigators the blast was an accident—it was intended for a bigger target at a later time. However, the informer did not know who or what the original target was, nor could he or she explain why things went wrong.

There was also new surveillance footage not found in the RUC files. A grainy, still photograph extracted from the footage showed a man crossing the Shankill Road near the blast just seven minutes beforehand. He was alone and appeared to be wearing a trade uniform and cap of some sort. Constables did not find him there, alive or dead, after the explosion. The origin of the footage was unspecified, and there was no explanation for its absence from the RUC investigation. The photograph showed only a fraction of the man's face, and even that much was partly obscured by the cap. Facial recognition software developed in the years since the blast was unable to produce a match.

Thornton closed the last folder with a sigh. He had hoped to find the children's names in the records and at least give O'Malley the option of apologizing to them, if only via anonymous letters. *Maybe it's better this way.*

APPREHENSION

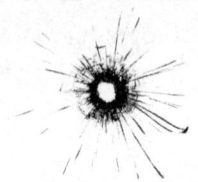

ROBERT INGLESBY ANGRILY EXITED THE GATE at PSNI headquarters and headed home. He wondered what on earth Claire and CNICS wanted with the HET file. *Was it somehow linked to Patrick Linden's appeal? Was Linden responsible for the bomb that killed Courtney? Is Claire keepin' secrets from me?*

Inglesby dismissed the idea. Claire was a stubborn idealist, but he felt certain she would never side with her sister's killer. *There must be another explanation.*

His focus shifted to the Historian and the orphan who witnessed the explosion. If the lad knew information that could solve the case, then surely the Historian could coax it from him with the aid of the HET file. Inglesby desperately wanted to get his hands on it.

He had to move quickly. Kieran Oliver was still at large and posed a threat. If the PSNI got to him before the New IRA, then Oliver would surely say anything to avoid prosecution for the priest's murder. Inglesby dialed James Dwyer's mobile again. Still no answer. He pounded a fist on the steering wheel and cursed.

Inglesby weighed his options as he battled Belfast traffic. He decided he had no choice but to call Claire. She surprised him by answering.

"Hallo, Daddy," she said coolly.

Inglesby knew from her tone to tread lightly, but he could not help himself. "Claire, love, what are ya doin' with the police file about Courtney's death?"

Claire, stunned by the question, said nothing at first. "So no apology then? Fine. And I have no idea what you're talking about."

Inglesby described his visit to the PSNI archive and the file's absence. "The clerk said it was signed out in yer name by someone named M. Kehs at CNICS? Who is that?"

"Michele isn't part of CNICS. She's my assistant at the university. Not that I owe you any explanation." Privately, Claire herself wondered why Michele requested the file—especially *that* file. Then she remembered her husband's request to look through the old police records. Her chest tightened. "Daddy, are you and I mentioned anywhere in those files?"

The apprehension in Claire's voice caught Inglesby off guard. "Claire, what is goin' on?! We've been over this before. It wasn't safe for either one of us to be named in those reports. I needed to keep the media at bay. There's absolutely no record of us bein' anywhere near the explosion."

"But Courtney's last name was listed as Davis."

"Yes, love—yer mother's name."

"*My* name, Daddy. *My* name."

"Love, do ya realize how many Davis families there are in the UK? There's no way to trace it. I sealed yer and Courtney's birth records anyway. There's no link to me. And why are ya suddenly so worried? *What is goin' on?*"

Claire debated how much to tell her father. Thornton said he needed the file for his work with an unspecified client, who was traumatized by The Troubles. Most of Northern Ireland fit that category. Claire never talked to her husband about Courtney or her own trauma, so he had no reason to be curious in that regard. If the files were sanitized, as her father claimed, there were no dots for Thornton to connect. Still, she was uneasy. "Daddy, I requested the file for Aaron. But I didn't realize which file he was asking for." She bit her lip.

"*Bloody hell*, Claire. Why did *Aaron* want to see it?!" His mind raced in a dozen directions.

Claire recounted the conversation she had with Thornton a few nights earlier. "He filled out the file request, and I left it with Michele at my office. I didn't even look at it, Daddy. I had no reason to think it was about the bombing." In hindsight, Claire realized it sounded foolish, even reckless. "The file isn't at my office, so Aaron must have picked it up already and taken it with him to work."

"See if ya can get him to return it quickly. I need that file to follow up on some new information. But I don't want him to know that I'm interested in it. Let me know when it's headed back to the archives."

"I don't suppose you're going to tell me why you need it so urgently?"

"Ya know I never talk about my work, love. It's safer that way."

THE BREAK-IN

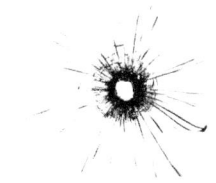

ROBERT INGLESBY DISCONNECTED THE CALL with his daughter, already convinced it was foolish to wait for the HET file's return. He switched to a secure phone and dialed a trusted undercover operative. He gave the MI5 agent explicit instructions and the address to the building on Ormeau Road.

That evening after dark, the operative deftly picked the lock to the rear door of the office building and ascended to Thornton's suite on the second floor. He deployed a jamming device, but there were no alarm systems or security cameras to disable.

At the outer office door, the operative again made quick work of the lock and stepped into the small anteroom. He took a series of photographs with his mobile, so he could ensure when he left that everything was in its proper place. Then he continued to the inner office.

The operative was accustomed to highly secure spaces with sophisticated locks and storage. The psychologist's office was child's play. Only one file cabinet was locked, and it gave the agent little resistance. He knew exactly what he was looking for and quickly identified the large accordion folder with the HET logo.

Clandestine photographs of paper files are the tradecraft of spies everywhere. With gloved hands, he expertly snapped and turned, snapped and turned, until every scrap of paper was digitized. Almost as soon as each image was taken, his mobile encrypted it and transmitted the file wirelessly to Inglesby's secure server. If the operative were caught in the act, a coded entry would wipe his phone, and the transmitted photos would already be safely squirreled away for MI5's examination. No one would ever be able to determine, let alone prove, what he was there for.

The operative finished the task and returned the folder to its precise original place. He checked to make sure everything in the office still looked as it had when he entered. Satisfied, the operative departed. No one would ever be the wiser.

THE NOTES

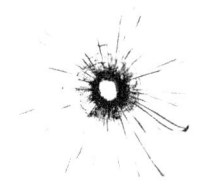

ACROSS TOWN, CLAIRE LAY NEXT TO HER HUSBAND in bed and gently asked how things were going at work. He assured her the judicial referrals kept him busy and feeling useful. "It's different than prison work, but not as different as you might imagine. People are people, and emotions are emotions."

"How's the poor man who witnessed that horrible scene with the children?"

"I haven't seen him yet this week, but he's making a lot of progress."

"Did everything go smoothly with the HET file?"

"Oh, I forgot to thank you for that. Yeah, I picked it up from Michele this morning." He kissed her on the forehead. "Thanks for doing that, hon."

Claire knew if she pressed any further, Thornton would recognize an unusual degree of curiosity about his client. She couldn't let him know of her interest in the file, so she stopped asking questions. Instead, she kissed him goodnight and waited for him to fall asleep.

When Thornton began to snore, Claire slinked out of the bedroom and down the hall to the study. Using only the light on her mobile phone, she looked through the contents of his bag to see if the HET file was there. It was not, and she surmised he stored it at the office. That left her with one much less palatable alternative. She would have to look at the clinical notes on his laptop. She felt awful, but she had to know why her husband was probing the explosion that claimed her sister's life and nearly killed Claire too.

Claire booted up the computer. She remembered the power-on password from the time she borrowed the laptop to give a presentation while traveling. Claire scanned the screen for the medical records software. She spotted it, double-clicked, and confronted a login screen. Thornton's username was auto-filled, but the password required a manual entry. She guessed incorrectly. Claire tried a second time, but again her entry was wrong. The software warned that only one incorrect guess remained before a 24-hour lockdown began.

Claire's husband was a methodical creature and followed a formula to create passwords he could remember. She had already tried the most obvious ones. Then it hit her—he set up this password when he was in grad school at Johns Hopkins. She bit her lip as she typed in the school's mascot. *B-l-u-e-j-a-y*. Then she hesitated. Thornton always added the # symbol and a two-digit number at the end of his passwords. She had one guess left and needed to choose between 89, her husband's year of birth, and 14, his year of graduation. Claire gambled on the latter and finished typing the characters. Then she held her breath and pressed *enter*.

Yes! The welcome screen greeted her, and she studied the menu trying to figure out where to look for the notes she needed. Claire took her time, clicking and scrolling until she found her husband's session notes. Thornton was still building his practice, and the government had referred a limited number of clients so far. There were only a couple dozen names to search through.

One by one, Claire intruded on the personal lives of her husband's clients until she reached the surnames beginning with "O." The name *O'Malley, Liam* stood out. *The famous Republican who just got out of jail.* She scanned the notes for any clues. Her husband used only keywords and phrases, sometimes in his own form of shorthand, to remind him what was discussed. At the end of each entry were prompts about where to continue during the next session.

Then Claire found the explanation she was looking for. "Nightmare. Window across the street. Shankill bombing 1994. Ginger girl with bear. Sister Deidre. Saved by man with limp. Wanted to rescue. Patrick restrained. Boy in Vauxhall Astra. Mother's handbag. Severed arm." *Patrick Linden?* Claire compulsively read the rest of Thornton's entries. Then she exited the app, shut down the laptop, and returned it to her husband's bag. She clasped both hands over her mouth in an effort to stop sobbing. Her whole body trembled.

That explains Daddy's interest—and silence.

Claire's loyalties to her father, sister, husband, client, and the law collided in her heart and mind. She thought she might vomit. *What am I going to do now?*

IDENTIFIED

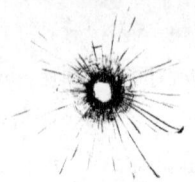

THE MORNING AFTER MI5'S BREAK-IN at Thornton's office, the Historian pored over the HET file about the 1994 Shankill bombing. The professorial old man was already familiar with the events of that day and the efforts to find the perpetrators. Yet the HET file introduced two enticing new clues—the presence of a previously undetected deliveryman shortly before the blast, and reports that the bomb was intended for another unknown target at a later time.

Satisfied with his review of the expanded file, the Historian called Gerry at the garage and asked him to send Tommy over for an extended lunch meeting. Gerry knew the Historian's prominent role in UVF circles and readily agreed.

Tommy appeared at the Cocky Rooster for lunch as instructed. The barkeep pointed him to a private back room where the Historian waited away from prying eyes and ears.

After breaking the ice and sharing a meal, the Historian asked Tommy to describe everything he remembered about the day his parents died. Slowly and expertly, the Historian probed Tommy's memory for more details until he was certain there was nothing more to retrieve. Then he shifted to descriptions of Tommy's nightmares, taking care to pause from time to time. Everything

Tommy described so far aligned with the police reports. Tommy's memory was entirely accurate—and he was correct, the police never interviewed him, for reasons the Historian neither understood nor cared to explore.

Next, the Historian produced the thick photo book of known dissidents. He directed Tommy to study, page by page, each photo in the "IRA yearbook" for any familiar faces. Tommy was halfway through the tome and growing weary of the exercise when he sat straight up, stabbed the page with his finger, and exclaimed, "He was there. *He* was there!"

The Historian glanced down at the man indicated by Tommy. "Are ya sure, lad? What do ya remember?"

"I'm *sure*! He's the deliveryman who parked a van in front of the furniture store. My parents walked right past it on their way to the showroom. I watched him get out of the van, cross the street, and disappear into one of the shops. I remember because I was hungry and he wore a uniform and hat that reminded me of an ice cream vendor. The bomb went off several minutes later, and I never saw him again."

The Historian beamed. He had deliberately withheld the HET's discovery of a deliveryman at the scene in hopes Tommy might corroborate it. "Well done, lad! You may have just cracked the case!"

Now Tommy was beaming too. At the Historian's insistence and with renewed energy, Tommy finished looking at the book. None of the other faces was familiar. "So who's the man I recognized?" The yearbook showed only faces and ID numbers—no names. The man identified by Tommy was nonetheless well known to the Historian.

"His name is Maxwell Mayhew, and he was a high-ranking member of the IRA in those days. He worked closely with just one man—the IRA's best bomb maker, Liam O'Malley. Mayhew was essentially an apprentice to O'Malley, but not nearly as clever. O'Malley was a genius with explosives, detonators, timers, and the like. Always inventin' new ways to kill people. A diabolical man. The bomb that killed yer parents was the first one ever detonated with a mobile phone. It was too advanced for the likes of Mayhew—but O'Malley had the skill to pull it off. The bomb was probably in that van ya saw Mayhew get out of."

Tommy's fists clenched while he listened to the Historian. The old man noticed and decided not to reveal that the bomb was likely experimental—that would explain why it went off prematurely and missed its intended target. The Historian also withheld his belief that UVF headquarters—and maybe Robert Inglesby himself—was the intended target. The Historian knew Inglesby ran an unsanctioned undercover Loyalist hit squad at the time, and he suspected the IRA knew it too. But it would not benefit Tommy to know any of those details.

The Historian reached out and placed a hand on Tommy's shoulder. "Don't ya worry, lad. We'll take care of it. Ya cracked the case for us and solved the murders of fourteen Protestants. Now we get justice for them and their families—for *you* and yer parents."

"*I* want to do it. Where do I find O'Malley?

"I understand, son, and I like yer enthusiasm. But O'Malley won't be an easy target. Leave it to the UVF boys. They have loads of experience in these matters."

Tommy broke eye contact with the Historian and nodded. He had no intention of backing down though.

RANSACKED

THERE WAS NO SIGN OF THE WHITE PANEL VAN when Tommy arrived home after his interview with the Historian. He entered the flat and immediately sensed something was off. Things looked out of place. Tommy called out for Kieran but got no response.

Tommy meandered about the flat. Here and there, a cabinet or drawer was left open. The cushions on the lounger were in the wrong position. A couple boxes in the bedroom closet were missing their lids. It looked as if Kieran had misplaced something and done a hasty search for it.

Probably looking for all me money. He was glad Thornton agreed to safeguard it for him. The doc insisted on sealing it an envelope, though, and having Tommy sign his name across the seal. He also gave Tommy a receipt for it. They jokingly dubbed it "the escape money"—a wad of cash that would allow Tommy to finally break free of Kieran and live independently.

Tommy put things back in order and sat on the lounger to watch some telly. He looked about the place and concluded it was definitely time to move on.

PURSUIT

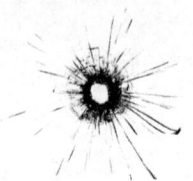

THE HISTORIAN WAITED UNTIL THE NEXT DAY to tell Garth Peters about Tommy's identification of Maxwell Mayhew in the photo book. He wanted to go over everything one last time in his head before sentencing two men to death.

The pair agreed to meet at the Cocky Rooster at 14:00. The Historian arrived a few minutes early via the private rear entrance. He joined Peters at the table under the telly. The barkeep delivered an Old Peculier for the newcomer and returned to the bar. A handful of patrons sat across the room.

Peters greeted the Historian solemnly. "Inglesby can't join us, so I'll brief him later."

The Historian nodded. "We know who's responsible for the bombing at Sheehan's."

Peters showed no emotion. "Tell me."

"Maxwell Mayhew placed the bomb, which means Liam O'Malley designed it. The lad recognized Mayhew from the IRA yearbook and saw him exit a van parked in front of the furniture store a few minutes before the blast. Mayhew and O'Malley worked almost exclusively together, to protect against informers. O'Malley was certainly capable of manufacturin' a mobile phone bomb at that time. A confidential informer says the blast went off early. I think UVF headquarters, and likely Inglesby, were the targets."

Peters remained stoic. The revelation was no surprise—he and Inglesby long suspected as much. Nonetheless, his pulse quickened. Focusing on the task at hand, Peters said, "O'Malley will be easy to find, but I haven't heard Mayhew's name in a long time. We'll need to track *him* down."

"I'm afraid I'm not much help there," the Historian admitted. "Just be careful. Once you make a move against either one of 'em, the Fenians *will* retaliate."

"Me best crew is trackin' someone else down as we speak. As soon as they're done, I'll send 'em after those IRA cunts." Peters glanced down at the vibrating phone on the table. "Speak of the devil." The UVF boss pressed the green button and jovially answered, "Kieran, mate. Where the hell are ya?"

A REPRIEVE

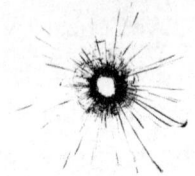

KIERAN OLIVER WAS UNCHARACTERISTICALLY BREATHLESS with excitement when Garth Peters, still sitting with the Historian at the Cocky Rooster, answered his call. Peters maintained the appearance that all was normal.

Kieran could not contain himself. "I just saw Liam O'Malley go into a building on Ormeau Road. I'm right outside."

Peters' eyes widened. "Are ya certain, mate?"

"Aye, it's him, I tell ya. There's no doubt about it. Here, I'll text ya his picture."

Peters peered at the photo on his phone in disbelief, then showed it to the Historian. Both men agreed it was O'Malley. Peters said to Oliver, "Good work, mate. Are ya armed?"

"Does a deer shite in the woods?"

Peters saw no sense wasting an easy opportunity to kill O'Malley. "Alright then. Have a look about and take into account anyone who may be with 'im. And remember the bloke is good with a gun. If ya have the chance, take him out, but for Chrissake do it quietly and *don't get caught.* We don't want a war with the Provos."

"Aye. I'm on it." Kieran ended the call.

Peters dialed the leader of the hit squad. "Change of plans. Leave Kieran be for now and come back to the pub. I have a new assignment for ya." With Kieran on O'Malley's tail, Peters planned to send the hit squad after Mayhew instead.

Mayhew, though, would be a fool's errand. Mickey Shanahan had already buried him in a bog near the Republic after shooting him between the eyes in the basement of Clonard Monastery.

THE PHOTOS

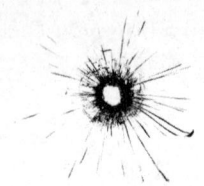

MICKEY SHANAHAN WAS SCROLLING THROUGH EMAILS and texts on his mobile when Paula Hall arrived home from her last round of dog walking. She set a bag of burgers and chips on the table, took a seat next to her lover, and leaned in to look at his mobile. On the screen was the photo she texted him of the law professor and the American psychologist standing outside their flat on College Green. "Such a cute couple," she said.

"She looks familiar," Shanahan mused. "Did you send me any other pics of her?"

"Nope. Just that one."

Shanahan scrolled through earlier texts and bolted upright when he reached the one of Claire Davis sitting with Robert Inglesby on the mezzanine at Fox restaurant. He received it from the watcher Paula enlisted to help monitor Claire. "Holy shit, love. Is it just me, or is that the same woman?"

Paula peered at the two photos. "It's definitely her in both pics. Look at the ears. Ya can always match the ears. But who's the bloke in the second photo?"

Shanahan looked pale. "That's Robert Inglesby, MI5's head of undercover operations."

"Jayzus, Mary, and Joseph."

"Aye, we're fucked. Patrick was right. It's a fuckin' set-up. The American psychologist—*the one who works with Liam O'Malley*—is shagging a woman with ties to MI5. Bloody hell. I need to warn Liam and Patrick."

Just then the phone buzzed and Brianna Donovan's name appeared onscreen. The couple exchanged puzzled glances before Shanahan cautiously answered the call. "I didn't expect to hear from *youse* anytime soon."

"And I didn't expect to be callin' ya, but I thought ya should know yer man Liam O'Malley has a UVF hitman named Kieran Oliver waitin' for him outside a building on Ormeau Road."

Shanahan instantly recognized the location and prayed the watcher was close to O'Malley. But he was also suspicious of his rival at the New IRA. "How do ya know this, Brianna? And why are ya tellin' me?"

"I *know* cuz I'm standin' 'ere looking at him. And I'm *tellin'* ya cuz I want ya to know who did ya the favor."

"What the fuck are ya talkin' about, Brianna? What favor?"

Brianna left the line open but said nothing. Instead, Shanahan heard a motorcycle accelerate and wind rushing past the microphone. Then the bike idled, and Shanahan heard Brianna say, "Excuse me." Next, two gunshots, a woman's scream in the background, and the motorcycle's loud acceleration. Brianna returned to the call. "You owe me, Shanahan." Then the line went dead.

"Jayzus." Shanahan hastily dialed O'Malley's watcher.

"Yeah, boss?"

"Is everything alright? Is O'Malley okay?"

"Sure, boss. All good. He's inside with the doc. Someone just shot a messenger on the corner, though, and took off on a Ducati. Two shots at point blank range. A real pro."

"Get inside and don't let O'Malley out of yer site. And keep him close. That dead messenger was a UVF hit man after O'Malley."

"Whoa, fuck *me*. Headed inside now, boss. Don't worry. Nobody's gettin' past me."

"I'm gonna hold ya to that."

———

Brianna gunned the Ducati toward West Belfast, where a New IRA crew would dispose of it. She hoped her goodwill gesture would ease tensions with the Provos. In reality, though, killing Kieran Oliver helped her achieve two goals. It guaranteed her selection as Devin Dingle's replacement to lead the New IRA, and it protected Liam O'Malley, her most valuable future asset— and the key to her long-term strategy.

Devin Dingle only *pretended* the New IRA had the SAMs, as part of a public relations stunt to boost his credibility. But Brianna actually *found* the missile systems. And she needed O'Malley to activate them.

EUREKA

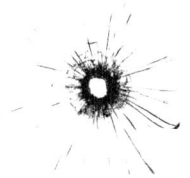

THE DAY AFTER HIS MEETING WITH THE HISTORIAN, Tommy Magee dropped into the comfortable chair in Thornton's office. "Wait till ya hear *this* week's news."

Thornton raised his eyebrows. Tommy's confidence and mood were much improved since he started therapy. "This must be good. I'm all ears!"

"So, the job is great, and I get on well with me mates there. Some of 'em are startin' to feel almost like family. But here's the *best* part. They introduced me to this fella they call the Historian, and he helped me figure out who killed me parents."

Thornton cocked his head. "Wow! Tell me more."

Tommy described the Historian's work with unsolved murders, their interview the day before, and the photos he looked at. "It took a while, but I finally recognized one of 'em. I remembered seein' 'im get out of a van right before the explosion. The Historian said he was a known terrorist, and I helped solve me parents' murders and the murders of twelve *more* people!"

A dozen questions floated through Thornton's mind, but above all he needed to support his client. "That must have felt great, Tommy. Congratulations! So what happens next?"

Tommy hesitated and stared at the floor. He bit his lower lip and squirmed.

Thornton waited.

Tommy finally looked up at the American. "I guess the Historian takes it from here." Thornton's expression reminded Tommy of the look his father used to give him when he knew Tommy was lying.

"Is there something you're not comfortable telling me, Tommy?"

Tommy squirmed some more. He liked the doc and felt guilty lying to him, but he did not want to say anything that might interfere with getting revenge. So he decided to convince Thornton that street justice was the right course of action. "I should probably tell ya what happened to me parents first.

"It was a Tuesday, after lunchtime, but we hadn't eaten yet and I was really hungry. School was still on a holiday break. My parents took me with them to Sheehan's to pay the balance due for some furniture they ordered. They said it would be a quick stop and then we'd get some food. I didn't want to go inside, so I waited in the back seat of our car.

"I'm an only child and used to play little games with meself. One of them was tryin' to guess what people's names were. It was just a stupid activity to pass the time when I was bored. So I watched all the people walkin' past the car and tried to guess their names. There was a couple holdin' hands, a businessman who looked like he was in a hurry, and a rubbish collector who talked to himself. I also saw a grandmother walkin' a dog with her granddaughter. The little girl carried a Paddington Bear like the one I had as a little kid. In the sideview mirror I saw another little girl lookin' at the sweets in a shop window, and that just made me hungrier.

"Being hungry is what made me remember the driver of that van I told the Historian about. He wore a uniform and hat that made him look like one of those ice cream vendors they used to have. I watched him cross the street and go into a store. A few minutes later there was a bright white flash, and then a huge fireball rose past the rooftops. Stuff flew in every direction, and then it got really quiet and looked like it was snowin'. I couldn't hear anythin' except a sort of buzzin', ringin' sound. My ears hurt really bad, and I felt something warm runnin' down both sides of my neck. It was blood, and I remember thinkin' I had to stop the bleedin', so I pressed my hands to my ears to keep it all from drainin' out of my body. Stupid kid, right?

"Anyway, everythin' seemed to sort of freeze in place for a while. Then it was like someone turned a switch and people started runnin' everywhere. The grandmother, her granddaughter, and little dog were gone. So were the van driver, the rubbish collector, the couple, and the businessman who had been lookin' at his watch. The girl from the sweet shop ran over and hugged a Paddington Bear lyin' on the sidewalk. I assume it was the same one the granddaughter was carryin'. Then a man in a suit ran up, grabbed the girl and the bear, and carried them across the street. I don't know if it was her father or just someone else tryin' to get her away from there.

"The windows in the car were shattered, and it was cold outside. I looked toward Sheehan's store for me parents, but the building was gone. Like it was never there. But there was a big pile of debris. There was no fire, but somehow it looked like it was givin' off smoke. I kept lookin' around for me mum and dad to come and get me, but they never did. My head hurt, I couldn't hear anythin', I was scared, and it was cold. And then I realized I was alone and nobody was comin' for me."

Tommy's voice cracked, and tears flowed.

"I looked straight ahead through the hole where the wind-screen had been and saw it. My mother's handbag. I knew it was hers cuz me dad and I picked it out as a birthday present fer her. It was really colorful and made of different pieces all stitched together like a quilt. I wanted to grab it and save it fer her, just in case she came back. The car door wouldn't open, so I crawled out the missin' back window. We had one of those Vauxhall Astras with a short boot that I could slide down. And then I ran over to get me mum's handbag.

"Her hand was still holdin' it. At first I thought she was buried under the mound and I could dig her out, but only her hand and part of her arm were there. I know this will sound stupid, but as a confused kid I thought maybe if I saved her arm they could reattach it when they found the rest of her. So I brought her arm and handbag back to the car with me and waited fer someone to come and find me. And that's all I remember. Fer years I've tried and tried to remember what happened next, and I just can't."

Thornton looked like he just witnessed the explosion himself. The color drained from his face, and he wore a stunned expression.

Tommy misinterpreted the look on Thornton's face. "I know that's some heavy shite, Doc. Sorry to hit ya with that. But I thought ya should know how bad it was, and why it's so import-ant to find justice fer me parents and all those other people."

Thornton swallowed hard and braced himself. "Who is the man you identified to the Historian?"

"He said his name is Maxwell Mayhew, an IRA man who worked with a guy named Liam O'Malley. The Historian said those are the two responsible fer the bomb. He told me to leave everythin' to him, and I said I would. But honestly, Doc, if I find them first…" Tommy remembered the limits of confidentiality. "Anyway, I have no idea where to find them, or even what they look like. Kieran probably does though…" Tommy instantly regretted mentioning Kieran's name again. "You okay, Doc?"

Thornton was having trouble maintaining eye contact. A bead of sweat appeared on his forehead. "Yes, yes. I'm just taking it all in. That sounds awful, Tommy. That's a lot to process at *any* age, but for someone so young…" Then Thornton broke a cardinal rule of therapy and looked at his watch. Five minutes remained in the session. "We need to talk more about everything you just shared, Tommy. Unfortunately, I cannot extend our session today. Is it okay if we pick this up again next week?"

"Sure thing, Doc. Between you and the Historian, I'm all talked out anyway. I've managed this stuff on me own all these years. One more week ain't gonna make a difference." Tommy thought Thornton looked relieved.

"Alright then, Tommy. Let's take this up next time."

Tommy wondered why Thornton walked him all the way downstairs to the street. *He's probably just makin' sure I'm okay.*

Tommy had no idea Liam O'Malley was due in fifteen minutes.

AFTERMATH

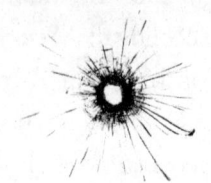

FOURTEEEN MINUTES LATER, MICKEY SHANAHAN'S MAN burst into Thornton's waiting room breathing heavily—at precisely the same moment the psychologist opened the inner office door.

O'Malley's head swiveled awkwardly between the two men.

The IRA watcher ignored Thornton and said, "Liam, mate, I need a word." His tone was serious.

Thornton saw O'Malley was surprised and apprehensive. "Is everything okay, Liam?"

O'Malley stood motionless and speechless. Both men stared at him. Finally, to prevent Thornton from confronting the watcher directly, O'Malley assured the psychologist everything was fine and excused himself. He beckoned for the watcher to follow him into the hallway.

"What the fuck are ya doin' 'ere, mate? Can't ya see I'm busy? This isn't the time or the place to be bringin' up business."

"Shanahan sent me. The UVF had a hit man waitin' for ya outside, but they took him out before he got to you. I'm not to leave your side until we get ya somewhere safe."

A thousand questions flowed through O'Malley's mind, but

he decided to let most of them wait until they had more privacy. "Well, I can't leave until I talk to the doc. I'm safe with him. Stay in the waitin' room until we finish."

The watcher fidgeted, unsure if Shanahan would approve the arrangement. Still, he found it hard to refuse a legend like O'Malley. And it would be a few more minutes until Shanahan and his team arrived to safely escort them from the building. The watcher decided they were as safe in the office as anywhere and nodded.

Before heading back to the anteroom, O'Malley asked, "How did they know I'd be here?"

"Don't know, mate. I was watchin' the building from across the road when I saw someone pull up on a Ducati and shoot a messenger at point blank range. Almost immediately Shanahan called to say there was a hit on you and to stay close."

O'Malley hesitated. "So who was on the Ducati? And who's the dead messenger?"

"Shanahan said the messenger was a UVF hitman. I assume Shanahan sent the Ducati, since he knew about the hit as soon as it happened. I didn't ask a lot of questions."

O'Malley grew uneasy. If Shanahan had so little time to warn the watcher, then the UVF hitman must have been a surprise. Events were unfolding quickly, and it sounded like his comrades were barely keeping up. "Alright. I'll keep things short with the doc. We don't want to make a scene in front of 'im. He's the key to my continued freedom, so be discreet."

The watcher nodded, and the two men entered the waiting room. Thornton was still there, apparently to be within earshot in case O'Malley needed help. O'Malley hoped he and the watcher kept their voices low enough in the hallway.

"Nothin' to worry about, Doc. Just a wee family emergency. I can't stay long, but I do want to check in with ya. Me mate's gonna wait here and then give me a ride home."

O'Malley thought the doc seemed uncomfortable as he followed him to the inner office. *Did he overhear the hallway conversation?*

THE CONUNDRUM

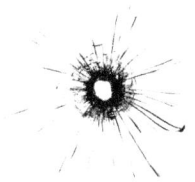

THORNTON SAT UNEASILY ACROSS FROM O'MALLEY. Twenty minutes passed since Tommy Magee left his office, and Thornton was still uncertain how to approach the situation with O'Malley. On the one hand, the psychologist had promised to help O'Malley identify the children from the scene of the bombing. But now Thornton knew Tommy was the boy in O'Malley's story—intent on revenge and finally aware of O'Malley's identity.

But Tommy was, for the moment, uncertain where to find O'Malley or even what he looked like. Thornton assumed that would all change soon. At a minimum, he needed to make sure Tommy and O'Malley never crossed paths at his office. But Thornton had a bigger problem.

The psychologist had a legal obligation to warn O'Malley if Tommy posed a "clear and imminent danger" to his well-being. Such a warning to a man like O'Malley could put *Tommy* in danger. And breaking confidentiality would undo all the trust and progress Thornton built with Tommy and likely keep him from seeking help—or trusting anyone—ever again. To make matters worse, O'Malley just arrived with obvious trouble brewing. *Had Tommy and O'Malley already crossed paths outside?*

O'Malley and Thornton sat awkwardly across from each other with worried, distracted looks on their faces.

"Sorry, Doc, but I need to leave in a minute. Did ya have any luck identifyin' the kids we talked about? Those nightmares won't give me any peace."

Thornton shifted in his seat. He needed time to clear his head and choose the best course of action. So he lied to a client for the first time in his career. "I'm afraid I don't have any news, but I'll keep working on it."

O'Malley studied Thornton's face but said nothing.

Thornton continued, "Before you go, is it okay to switch your appointments to the same time on Fridays starting next week?"

"Why's that, Doc?"

Thornton did not have an explanation prepared and blurted the first thing that came to mind. "I just need to free up time for some personal matters."

"Sure, Doc, no problem." O'Malley stood and went to join the watcher in the waiting room.

———

O'Malley knew a lie when he heard one. Years in the IRA, dealing with touts, peelers, and the security services, taught him to read a bluff with exceptional accuracy. *What's the doc hidin'? And why the strange behavior on the very same day a UVF hitman tried to kill me outside the office?*

A rattled O'Malley recalled Patrick Linden's suspicions and warnings about Thornton. He decided to tell Mickey Shanahan about the psychologist's odd behavior.

LINKED

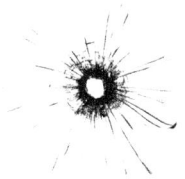

MICKEY SHANAHAN FIDGETED IN THE VISITING room at HM Prison Maghaberry. There was a lot of bad news to share, and this unscheduled meeting with Patrick Linden would surely put the boss in a tailspin. Shanahan's only comfort was the fact that, so far, his people had managed to contain the problem.

The electric lock clicked, and a guard escorted Linden inside. The IRA men waited until the screw left.

"What's wrong?" Linden asked.

"It's bad, boss. No two ways to look at it. You were right to be suspicious about that American fella."

The blood drained from Linden's face. "What the fuck happened?"

Shanahan explained in a hushed voice how watchers photographed Thornton's wife meeting with MI5's head of undercover operations. Then a known UVF hitman laid in wait for Liam O'Malley outside Thornton's office. For reasons still unknown, the New IRA's Brianna Donovan neutralized the hitman before he got to O'Malley. And when O'Malley appeared for his next appointment with the psychologist, the American acted strangely.

"Jayzus, Mary, and Joseph." Linden looked as if he might explode. "Show me the photo of the American's wife with MI5."

Mobiles were not permitted in the visiting area, but Shanahan came prepared. The boss liked to see things for himself when possible. Shanahan removed from his wallet a folded paper printout of the photo, smoothed it on the table, and slid it over to Linden.

"That *bitch*," Linden shouted as he recognized his CNICS attorney, Claire Davis. "I *knew* it was too good to be true."

The guard entered the room and threatened to take Linden back to his cell if there were any more outbursts.

Linden waved in acknowledgement and waited for the guard to exit. Further discussion could wait. He was in full damage control now. He gave the orders so quietly, Shanahan had to strain to hear him. "Break into the psychologist's office tonight and figure out how much he knows. Not just what Liam's told him, but everything anyone *else* told him. And tell the Nutting Squad to get the farmhouse ready. I'll give you the first target once we figure out what the psychologist knows."

Shanahan left the room. As the guard walked Linden back to his cell, the head Provo weighed whether to go after Inglesby, Thornton, or Davis.

THE NUTTING SQUAD

THE NUTTING SQUAD, officially known as the Internal Security Unit (ISU), was the IRA's counterintelligence and security section. In the United Kingdom, *nut* is slang for head. The unit got its nickname from the practice of shooting traitors in the back of the skull.

The squad reported directly to the IRA's Army Council and had authority over not just the entire IRA, but the larger Republican community too. Their resources and tactics were unlimited. So was everyone's fear of them. And cooperation with ISU investigations was mandatory.

The Nutting Squad had far-reaching responsibilities. They vetted new IRA recruits and interrogated Republicans detained by the security services to make sure they had not flipped while in custody. When an IRA operation failed, the Nutting Squad swooped in to find out why. They subjected anyone suspected or named as a tout to extreme forms of torture.

In 2003, UK media exposed a British agent who infiltrated the Nutting Squad and rose to the top of its ranks. Since then, the ISU had gone to extraordinary lengths to ensure no such security failure occurred ever again.

Patrick Linden intended to introduce Inglesby, Thornton, or Davis—maybe all of them—to this new and improved version of the ISU.

THE MONEY

MICKEY SHANAHAN PERSONALLY HANDLED THE BREAK-IN at Thornton's office. The stakes were high, and he needed to ensure the job was done right. That meant finding every scrap of useful information. Apart from Patrick Linden himself, Shanahan knew the most about the current state of IRA affairs in Belfast and was the best man outside prison to recognize relevant information.

Paula Hall served as a lookout. Shanahan could not afford to get caught and wanted no interruptions. He always joked there was no one better than Paula to be your backup during a bar fight, and he meant it. Shanahan trusted her with his life.

While Belfast's wiliest dog walker kept watch, Shanahan scoured every square inch of the psychologist's office. The MI5 operative who preceded him a few nights earlier knew exactly what he was looking for and quit searching once he found it. Shanahan had no idea what was there and had to examine everything.

Thornton's personal belongings were on and in the desk. A kitchenette adjacent to the WC had some snacks and a few bottled drinks. The psychologist kept a spare jacket and umbrella in the closet. But there were few paper records to peruse, either

351

because the doc really *was* new to Belfast or, more likely, he kept electronic records. Shanahan searched in vain for a computer and surmised the psychologist took a laptop home with him each day. He called his favorite hacker, explained the situation, and asked him to see if there were any laptops connected to the Wi-Fi at Thornton's residence.

While the hacker worked his magic, Shanahan continued searching the office. He struck gold in the bottom drawer of a locked file cabinet that was easily picked. There it was—a white envelope labeled *Escape Money*, with the name *Tommy Magee* scrawled across the back. Shanahan held it against the light on his mobile phone and confirmed it was thick with cash. He texted Magee's name to the best researcher on his payroll and promised twice the usual rate for any information she could produce by morning. Then he locked up the doc's office and joined Paula outside.

On their way home, the hacker called to report partial success. Thornton used the default password for his home Wi-Fi network, which allowed the hacker to access remotely all devices connected to it. There were two mobile phones, two laptop computers, a wireless printer, and a smart TV. As instructed, the hacker focused on the laptop used by Thornton and remotely copied its contents.

The computer whiz easily spotted the electronic medical records software on Thornton's laptop and launched a tool to crack the password. The time needed to unlock the data would depend on the password's complexity. Since Thornton had not even bothered to replace the default code on his Wi-Fi router, the hacker predicted a short wait. He promised to alert Shanahan as soon as he knew more.

Six hours later, the hacker's call awakened Shanahan from a light sleep. The computer whiz now had full access to the psychologist's notes and needed a list of keywords to search for. Shanahan groggily mentioned *Liam O'Malley, Tommy Magee, Patrick Linden,* and *IRA.* He would text any others he thought of later.

"I'm on it," the hacker said. "I'll email you any matches within the hour."

FATHER AND DAUGHTER

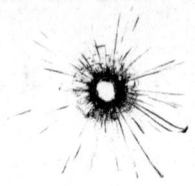

CHRISTINE MURRAY, THE CLERK at the Central Records Bureau who traced Rebecca Tucker for Mickey Shanahan, now researched Tommy Magee. She easily confirmed a link between Magee and Thornton from the diversion summons logged in the judicial database.

Murray pulled Magee's parents' names from his birth certificate and determined they died on the same day in 1994. She quickly established they perished in the Shankill bombing, after which their only son became a foster ward.

Next, Murray searched for more information about the bombing and learned the PSNI just days ago delivered all records about it to Claire Davis at QUB. Davis was a professor who worked for a group called CNICS. CNICS received a lot of attention from Belfast news media for its efforts to have Patrick Linden released from HM Prison Maghaberry.

Since the police file was a dead end, Murray checked employment records for Magee and learned he started work at a garage in the Shankill ward several weeks ago. The only mention of the garage in the news media suggested it had ties to the UVF. That bit of information, and the knowledge Magee's parents were killed by a presumably IRA bomb, prompted Murray to keep digging.

Murray was a keen researcher and an even better networker. She reached out to a Republican sympathizer who used to work at the PSNI archive and asked if there might be any other files to review apart from the HET portfolio already signed out.

"HET portfolio, is it? Then yer in luck. Before they started reviewin' the records, the HET digitized everythin' because the original police documents were old and fragile. They also wanted to use optical character recognition to perform electronic queries. The original plan was to work only from those digital copies, but somehow the government purchased—some said deliberately—only two licenses for the necessary software. Since there wasn't more fundin' to buy additional licenses, the HET ended up relyin' mostly on the paper files after all. The digitized ones are still available though."

"How do I get a digital copy of just one file?"

"I know one of the software developers who's sympathetic to the movement. I can ask him where the data's stored. Then ya just need to find someone with access to that particular server."

"Thanks, luv. Do it. But I need the info fast. Anyone who helps, includin' yerself, gets very well paid in cash as soon as I receive the data."

———

Two hours later, Murray's source called to report the software developer—who was on the line with him—had full access to the data through a backdoor built into the program. He could pull any record—he just needed the HET file number.

"I have it. It was on the sign-out log I saw." Murray scanned her records. "Here ya go. The HET file we need is 06-077R. If ya can email it to me securely, that'd be grand."

"Not a problem," the software developer said. "Did ya want just the official file, or the original as well?"

Murray perked up at the question. "I don't follow ya."

"Fer the time frame yer looking at, the RUC used all paper records. But sometimes files had to be 'sanitized' to protect sensitive information. Stuff like undercover operations, information obtained from informers, reports from the security services, and the like. But they couldn't just destroy all that information. So fer sensitive files, there were always two copies—the official *sanitized* one kept in the RUC file room, and the original, unfiltered one hidden in a RUC vault few people had access to."

Murray wondered if the Provos knew about that. "Tell me more about the vault."

"Officially, it didn't exist. But someone tipped off the HET, and since the HET had a mandate to look at everythin'—*especially* the secret stuff—they got access to the vault. So everythin' in the vault was digitized too. That's why some files have two versions. Ya can tell from the file number. They digitized the files with sanitized versions first. Everything starting with 06, the first full year of the HET, involves a sanitized file, so there will always be a second uncensored file to go with it."

"Yer a genius, love. Definitely send me both files. And fer yer efforts you'll be paid double."

"Happy to help me Republican brothers and sisters."

Ten minutes later, Murray had both RUC files open side-by-side on her computer. She painstakingly identified and summarized all the redactions. The significance immediately became apparent. The name of one young girl was removed from the final version of the report—Claire Davis. Murray assumed it must be the same Claire Davis who requested a copy of this very file from the PSNI archive. *But why was her name removed? Why was there no mention of her parents? Was she any relation to the victim, Courtney Davis?*

It cost her a princely sum, but Murray got access to the sealed birth certificates for both Davis girls and found the answers. Courtney and Claire Davis were the daughters of Robert Inglesby and Barbara Davis. The girls no doubt took their mother's surname because their father just happened to work for MI5. That probably explained Claire Davis' removal from the file and the absence of her parents' names. Murray wondered if Inglesby was the intended target of the bomb that killed his younger daughter. Claire Davis' interest in the HET file, and her willingness to represent Patrick Linden, must be part of a plot to avenge her dead sister.

Murray excitedly dialed Mickey Shanahan—partly because she knew he would be pleased with her work, but mostly because the bill for *this* job was a big one.

CONNECTED

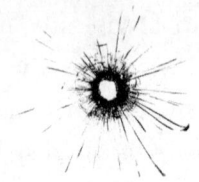

MICKEY SHANAHAN AND PAULA HALL made breakfast while waiting to hear from the hacker. Shanahan was just about to throw some bacon on the electric grill when his mobile rang. He clicked the green button. "Hallo."

"It's Christine at Central Records. Yer not gonna believe this. Claire Davis is the daughter of Robert Inglesby, head of MI5 undercover operations. And her sister was killed in a 1994 bombing at Sheehan's furniture store in the Shankill."

"Fuck *me*. Are you *sure*?"

"One hundred percent."

"Alright. Send me the bill." Shanahan ended the call and threw the phone at the lounger. "Bloody fuckin' *hell*." Before he could tell Paula the bad news, the mobile dinged to signal arrival of the hacker's email. Mickey studied the contents, and soon his hands trembled.

"Fuck," Paula said. "What is it?"

Shanahan summarized the bad news. The American psychologist met weekly with a Brit orphaned by the 1994 bombing of a furniture store in the Shankill. The Brit, named Magee, wanted to avenge his parents' deaths. Magee just learned O'Malley and a second IRA fella were responsible. Magee's roommate was the hitman who waited for O'Malley outside the American psychologist's office yesterday. The doc had "escape money" for Magee in his office. The shrink's wife—the attorney who claimed to be leading Patrick Linden's appeal for an early release from prison—lost her sister in the same blast that killed Magee's parents. "And the fucking icing on the cake? The attorney met last week with MI5's head of undercover operations, *who just happens to be her father.* The whole fucking lot of them are working together."

"Fuuuuuck, Mickey. The American and his wife set us up *good.*"

"That's not all. Liam's gone soft. He told the shrink he feels guilty about what he did and wants to distance himself from the movement. And get this, he even wants to apologize to his victims. Can ya *believe* this shite?!"

"Are ya sure, love? Not Liam. There's no way, I tell ya. He's as Republican as they come. I'd stake my life on it."

"*He described the fuckin' Shankill bombing to the Yank, Paula!* It's in his notes. And those Reconciliation meetings he's been goin' to have him second-guessin' everythin'. He doesn't come right out and say his *full* name, but he even mentions Patrick a couple times. Read it all fer yerself." Shanahan slid the laptop over to Paula.

"Jayzus, Mary, and Joseph." Shanahan rubbed one hand over his face. "We have some serious cleanin' up to do."

CHATTER

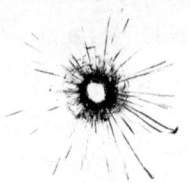

EVER SINCE FR. MATTHEW CLARK SIGNALED he was in danger, his MI5 handler, Mongoose, tried in vain to locate the source of Clark's betrayal. The murder of a valuable informer—minutes before his planned extraction to an MI5 safe house—was a major source of embarrassment to Mongoose and the entire organization. Even worse, no one had been charged with killing the priest.

The director was preoccupied with the possibility the IRA had infiltrated MI5. He authorized the deployment of additional undercover agents within the Republican community whose sole job was to find a possible Judas. Their instructions were clear—gather as much information as possible about dissident activities and report it to Mongoose.

Although no mole was identified, the effort was still a success. Immediately following the drive-by shooting of UVF thug Kieran Oliver on Ormeau Road, all three operatives reported an increase in Republican chatter about an upcoming operation. The surveillance wing at Palace Barracks noted a corresponding uptick in Republican activities throughout Northern Ireland. Something was up, and the director—determined to thwart another intelligence failure—authorized unlimited resources to monitor developments.

Mongoose worked with a team of analysts to assemble the fragmented reports. Mobile phone logs showed surprise communications between the Provos and the New IRA. Patrick Linden had an unscheduled visit at Maghaberry Prison from his right-hand man, and the guards observed unusually cautious communication among all dissident prisoners. Facial recognition software identified a suspected member of the Provos' Internal Security Unit arriving in Belfast by train. A couple weeks previous, a formerly well-placed IRA operative, Maxwell Mayhew, was recorded boarding a train from the Republic to Belfast. Liam O'Malley changed residences and suddenly had a very visible security detail.

Mongoose was troubled. Cooperation between two rival factions of the IRA signaled something big. So did the unscheduled consultation with Patrick Linden at Maghaberry and the possible summons of a Nutting Squad. At first glance, though, it seemed the IRA was rallying to protect itself—not to attack Loyalist interests. Mongoose was privy to all MI5 and PSNI anti-Republican operations—there was nothing major in the works. *So why was the IRA ramping up its defenses?*

Mongoose had no idea but could not take any chances. Consequently, an urgent alert went to all MI5 operatives in Northern Ireland, on the director's authority. "Intelligence reports suggest major IRA operation of unknown intent is imminent. Possible collaboration between Provo and New IRA factions noted. Exercise extreme caution in all activities. Report any unusual developments immediately through chain of command."

It was too little, too late.

UNIVERSITY AVENUE

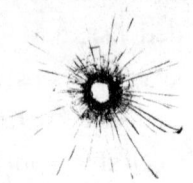

AARON THORNTON HOISTED HIMSELF from lane six of the pool at QUB and toweled off before heading to the locker room. The American glanced around for Siobhan Dooley, but she was nowhere in sight.

In the men's changing area, Thornton showered before donning his street clothes. He exited the sports complex, turned left, and cut across Botanic Gardens toward home.

Mickey Shanahan's crew knew the American's routine and waited for him near the junction of College Park and University Avenue. A spotter tailed the psychologist northward on foot and kept an eye out for any problems before giving the all-clear signal.

The stolen cargo van swept into position alongside the American. The side door slid open and two hooded men dressed in black coveralls jumped out and grabbed the shrink. Keeping his arms pinned to his sides, they shoved Thornton headlong into the van, where two of their hooded colleagues forced their victim face down onto the floor, zip tied his hands and feet, and threw a sack over his head. The American was too stunned initially to resist, but as he gathered his wits he tried to roll toward the street. In the same instant, the door slid shut and the van lurched back into traffic. The entire maneuver took six seconds.

When the van sped away, the spotter grabbed Thornton's discarded mobile from the street and tossed it onto the roof of a passing lorry headed in the opposite direction. *Trace that, ya British bastards.*

The driver of the getaway van steered west and then south. Once clear of the city, she pulled to the side of the road behind a second van of a different style and color. The crew transferred Thornton, now shouting and thrashing against the restraints, into the new vehicle before dousing the first one in petrol and setting it alight.

Just a few miles short of Northern Ireland's border with the Republic, the van veered deep into the countryside toward an isolated farmhouse with unobstructed views in every direction. An IRA observation post kept watch from a nearby hill. If the Brits attempted any type of rescue, the kidnappers would have ample warning.

That night, when the PSNI appealed to the public for witnesses to the kidnapping, they received several conflicting accounts. The handful of people who came forward agreed on just one thing—the whole incident ended quickly.

CCTV

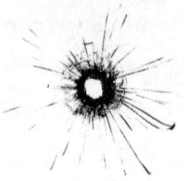

CLAIRE DAVIS GREW ANXIOUS when her husband failed to arrive home after his usual swim at QUB. The couple planned on takeaway that night, and Thornton was ninety minutes overdue. At first Claire assumed one of his sessions ran late, but it was odd he didn't text to let her know. Her calls to his mobile went unanswered, but that was normal when Thornton was with a client.

Claire switched on the news. A reporter was live on the air from just a few blocks away, where witnesses described seeing a man abducted off the street about an hour earlier. The PSNI were reviewing CCTV footage to establish the victim's identity and appealed to the public for information about him, the abductors, or the getaway van. The broadcast then shifted to a story about a pensioner who died waiting for an appointment with the Public Health Service. A flicker of dread crossed her mind, but Claire quickly dismissed it. *Why would anyone want to kidnap Aaron?*

She paced about the room, running one hand repeatedly through her hair. *Is someone opposed to Patrick Linden's release trying to get to me through Aaron?* Claire grabbed the phone and called her father.

"Stay calm, love. It's probably nothing. I'll ask the lads to ping his phone and see where he is. I'll get back with ya as soon as I can."

———

Sixty minutes elapsed, during which MI5 located Thornton's mobile moving north along the M2 near Ballymena. Inglesby asked the PSNI to intervene, and local constables tracked and stopped a lorry carrying produce. The surprised but cooperative driver had no idea who Thornton was. Technicians reconfirmed the pinged mobile was somewhere in the stopped lorry, so constables detained the driver while they searched the vehicle thoroughly. They finally found the mobile wedged between the cab and body of the truck.

When consulted by phone, Inglesby concurred with release of the lorry and the driver. Then he rang Section 6, two floors down from his office. "I'd like to review all footage of this afternoon's abduction near Queen's University. I'll be there in ten minutes."

The Section chief greeted him at the entrance to the control center and led him to Station 1. "Sir, the footage is already cued up."

Inglesby pushed the start button, and his heart sank. He watched stoically as a team of professionals plucked his son-in-law off the streets of Belfast. Turning to the Section chief, he said, "The victim's name is Aaron Thornton, and he's married to my daughter. Finding him is our top priority."

———

Mongoose whistled softly when an all-hands message advised personnel about the abduction of Inglesby's son-in-law. No one predicted *this* to be the major operation for which the IRA was preparing. Still, it made sense for them to strike personally at MI5's head of undercover operations. Then Mongoose shuddered involuntarily. The IRA had already summoned the Nutting Squad. Inglesby's son-in-law faced a *very* unpleasant future—and a very *short* one if MI5 did not act quickly.

THE VAN

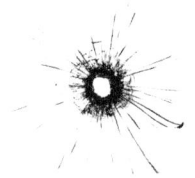

THORNTON LAY IMMOBILE, face down in the second getaway vehicle. He could scarcely believe what was happening. He struggled to gather his thoughts and recalled a distant memory. Years ago, as part of orientation to the maximum-security prison in West Virginia, he completed mandatory training on how to handle a kidnapping.

He knew his best chance of escape was at the moment of abduction, so he tried instead to learn more about his surroundings. He no longer had a phone with which to convey information though—one of the kidnappers knocked it from his hand on the sidewalk in Belfast.

Thornton suspected these were career criminals. The kidnapping was quick and well-executed. He knew, too, that they switched vehicles. The smell of gasoline as they hustled him into the second van suggested they burned the first one to destroy evidence. Thornton could not see through the hood, but knew the second vehicle was also a van from the sound of the side door sliding open and closed.

Thornton counted five kidnappers. From the sound of her voice, Thornton knew the driver was a woman. She had at least four male accomplices in the van, all of whom rode in the back with him. Two of them grabbed him on the street. The second pair immobilized him in the van. All wore black balaclavas. He saw only that they were Caucasian. The abductors rarely spoke to each other and did not use names.

The bare metal floor beneath Thornton was channeled and uncomfortable. The zip tie dug into his bare wrists, but the one around his crossed ankles was cushioned by socks. There were no distinctive smells to help him identify either the kidnappers or his location. Thornton abandoned efforts to memorize their route because the frequent use of roundabouts in Northern Ireland made it impossible to count lefts and rights or maintain a sense of direction.

Thornton imagined they were on the road for more than an hour. The van now travelled at constant speed, and the American surmised there were no traffic lights or other cars to contend with. Then he sensed the vehicle ascend and descend a steep hill before slowing to make a right turn. The road grew bumpy, and eventually he heard the crunch of gravel under the wheels. Then three or four dogs began to bark as the van came to a halt.

Thornton spit repeatedly into the hood, hoping some DNA evidence would seep onto the floor of the van. A moment later, two pairs of hands grabbed him under the shoulders and hoisted him roughly to his feet and out into the fresh, clean air. They must have traveled longer than he realized. There was no faint light visible through the hood now. Everything was pitch black.

CONFIRMED

ROBERT INGLESBY LEFT SECTION 6 and hurried to his office. He lifted the phone from its cradle and held it in midair. It pained him to deliver unpleasant news to his only surviving child. Inglesby debated whether to give it in person, but decided to remain at Palace Barracks and supervise the search.

"Daddy, what took so long? My stomach is in knots."

Inglesby shattered Claire's world with three words. "They took Aaron."

Claire dropped the phone and wailed at the ceiling. Then she doubled over, clenched her fists, and screamed at the floor.

Inglesby cleared his throat. "Claire, love. Pick up the phone."

Claire could not hear her father. She collapsed on the floor as the room began to spin. Her heart raced. It was difficult to breathe.

On the other end of the open phone line, Inglesby regretted his decision to remain at the office. But it was too late now. He pressed a button on his desk, and his assistant entered the room. "Please send a couple constables to my daughter's flat. Here's the address."

The assistant nodded, took the slip of paper, and left to make the request.

"Claire, love. Please pick up the phone. I need yer help to find Aaron." Inglesby waited apprehensively to hear his daughter's voice.

After several minutes, she returned to the call. Sniffling, she asked, "Why, Daddy? Why is this happening?"

Inglesby decided to tell his daughter nearly everything he knew. He needed her to be careful in case there was more to the plot. "We learned a few days ago the IRA was plannin' somethin' big. We now think it might have been Aaron's kidnapping. The team that abducted him clearly knew what they were doing."

"Can't you identify them from CCTV, or track his phone or something?"

"They wore balaclavas, love, and tossed his phone onto a movin' lorry so we couldn't track him. The PSNI stopped the truck near Ballymena, but Aaron wasn't there and the driver didn't know anythin'. An abandoned van was found burned— empty—outside the city. It's likely the getaway vehicle, and we don't know yet what type of car they've switched to. But don't ya worry, love. We've found people with far *less* to work with." He tried to sound reassuring despite his own doubts.

"This doesn't make any sense. What would the IRA want with Aaron? He's *American* and hasn't even lived here a year. He barely knows *anyone*."

"It's probably got somethin' to do with me, love." It hurt to admit it, but once again Inglesby's work seemed to have impacted his family. "Maybe ya should leave Belfast until we get this sorted."

"Absolutely not. I'm not leaving Aaron behind. They might try to contact me, or bring him home. I need to be here."

Inglesby ignored his daughter's naïveté. "Love, he's probably nowhere near Belfast now, and a ransom call is unlikely. That's not how the IRA works."

"Maybe it's not the IRA. Maybe you're wrong about the big plot—they could be planning something *else*. Maybe this is just a regular kidnapping. A coincidence."

"I suppose that's possible, love. Can ya think of anythin' unusual that's happened in the last week or two, either to you or Aaron? At work or at home? Any unusual calls or visitors?"

Claire bit her lip. "No, nothing comes to mind." She kept quiet about the therapy notes on Aaron's laptop and the client who identified her sister's murderer—it was yet another secret she had to keep to protect herself.

Inglesby knew the Loyalist community had nothing to do with Aaron's abduction, but he asked the question anyway. "Has anyone threatened ya about yer efforts to secure Patrick Linden's release?"

"No. There's only been the usual partisan bickering. Nothing serious, and nothing directed at me personally." Then Claire had an idea. "Daddy, could anyone *within* the IRA be opposed to Linden's release from prison? Maybe a rival or someone else whose interests are harmed if he gets out?"

It was a fair question, and Inglesby had not considered it. "Competition among dissident factions *is* tense at the moment. The abduction *could* be an attempt to gain leverage over you and sabotage Linden's release." Inglesby silently dismissed the notion though. Claire was just one of many attorneys working on the appeal. She alone could not stop the effort, and a case of such notoriety had a momentum all its own.

Claire asked, "Could this have something do with *Aaron's* work?"

A knock at the door interrupted their conversation. Claire rushed to the front of the flat and was disappointed to find two PSNI constables standing alone at the entrance.

Speaking into the phone, she said, "I assume I have you to thank for the policemen standing at my door?"

"Guilty. Until we figure this out, I think it's wise to be extra cautious. If ya think of anythin' that might be important, let me know. I'm goin' to get back to work and make sure every resource is devoted to findin' Aaron."

"Thank you, Daddy. I love you."

"I love ya too, sweetheart."

Inglesby wondered how long Claire would be willing to sit at home waiting for news. At least the constables were there to keep an eye on her.

DESPERATION

CLAIRE PACED BACK AND FORTH. The phone call from Inglesby did little to calm her. In fact, she grew more anxious as she weighed the unanswered questions. Claire decided it was pointless to wait at home and do nothing. Aaron needed help, and time was not on their side. She took stock of her options and realized there *was* something she could do. It was a long shot, but one worth taking. Claire picked up the phone and dialed her assistant. "Michele, I'm sorry to bother you so late, but I need your help."

Thirty minutes elapsed before Michele called back to confirm everything was arranged. Claire snuck out the rear of the flat and hailed a taxi to HM Prison Maghaberry, unseen by the constables. Her assistant scheduled an after-hours meeting for Claire and Patrick Linden. Such privileges, though rarely exercised, were granted to barristers engaged in ongoing litigation who needed to consult with their clients.

The prison guards inspected Claire's bag as she passed through a metal detector. An older officer led her to a private visiting room and signaled for Linden to be brought down.

Claire waited alone, pondering her strategy. She *had* to convince Linden to help her.

But when the door swung open, Linden lunged across the table at her. He nearly had his hands around Claire's throat when the guard yanked him back and threw him against the wall.

It was not the reaction Claire anticipated. Though frightened, she tried to appear unfazed.

Claire watched from the far side of the room while the officer held Linden against the wall until he stopped struggling. After several minutes, the officer sat Linden forcefully in a chair and hovered over him. Claire wanted to talk privately and asked the guard to wait outside. At first he refused, but Claire insisted. Finally, the officer shackled Linden's wrists to a metal loop under the table and left the room.

"You've got some nerve showin' yer face here, ya Loyalist cunt."

"Mr. Linden, I don't understand. Why are you so upset?"

"Don't play coy with *me*, ya deceitful bitch. I *know* who yer father is, and I know what yer husband's up to. I'm not a fool." Linden spat on the table.

Claire's heart skipped a beat at the mention of her father *and* husband. Words momentarily failed her. How could she possibly convince Linden to help the daughter of a senior MI5 official? She decided to be as transparent as possible. "My father and I see the world differently, Mr. Linden. To him, everything is black and white. He's stuck in the past and can't let go of old grievances. And he fervently opposes my efforts to have you released. We had quite a row over it. So it's a mistake to assume we're anything alike. In fact, I came here to make you a very generous offer."

"Ya lying *cunt*. And I suppose you'll try to convince me the American shrink isn't yer husband?"

Claire noted Linden's second reference to Aaron. She needed to know why Linden was angry with him. "I *am* married to an American psychologist. We met in Washington and went to school together. He came with me when I accepted a job in Belfast several months ago. But what does all *that* have to do with anything?"

"Ya play it cool, I'll give ya that. Probably how yer daddy trained ya. I bet ya thought it was clever to use an American fer yer dirty work. No one would suspect *him*, right? And to be extra clever, ya used a different name from yer daddy *and* yer husband. Ya must have thought we were a bunch of plonkers who wouldn't figure it out."

Claire's adrenaline surged again. Clearly the IRA suspected Aaron of "dirty work" against them. That meant his life was in grave danger. *But what exactly was Aaron mixed up in?* Claire struggled to remain rational as fear tightened its grip. It was now or never. "Mr. Linden, I'm going to tell you something I've never told *anyone*. The IRA killed my sister, Courtney. When she was just four years old. It was that bombing on the Shankill Road in January 1994. And I know now that you were partly responsible for it."

Linden scoffed at Claire, but the pulsing vein on his right temple betrayed his anxiety. "I don't know what yer talkin' 'bout."

"I don't need your confession, Mr. Linden. I have a witness. And his recollection will be enough to sink your appeal. But I'm willing—"

Linden tried to stand abruptly, but never made it past a crouching position. The shackles dug into his wrists, and he cried out in pain. He sat back down, fuming.

Claire persisted. "I'm willing to forget about the witness and continue with your appeal on one condition. You help me get my husband back safely."

"*Ya fucking British CUNT!*" Linden tried to stand again with the same result.

The guard peered through an observation window in the door, but Claire signaled everything was okay. She wanted no interruptions now. "It's a fair trade, Mr. Linden. Your freedom in exchange for my husband's. Both sides can claim victory, and neither one suffers any harm. We simply call a truce and carry on with our lives."

Linden glared at her. Through gritted teeth he said, "I don't know where yer fucking husband is. And I don't know anythin' about the bomb that killed yer sister. But I *will* tell ya this. You and yer family fucked with the wrong crew, and now there's a price to pay. There's nothin' anybody can do to fix it. Not yer daddy. Not you. And not yer fuckin' husband."

"I don't understand. What exactly do you think my family has done?"

Linden leaned forward. In a hushed voice he said, "I already knew youse figured out who killed yer sister. And youse tried to get revenge fer it. But Liam and the crew are safe, aren't they? And ya say yer *husband's* gone missin' now? How did *that* happen, luv? I guess ya can't be too careful these days." Linden leaned back with a smirk.

Claire stood without another word and picked up her purse. She moved slowly toward the door and was about to knock for the guard when Linden called out.

"Say hello to yer sister for me."

Claire froze. She turned her head and locked eyes with him. "I'll see you soon, Mr. Linden."

THE FARMHOUSE

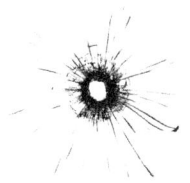

PAULA HALL EXITED THE DRIVER'S SEAT and followed Mickey Shanahan and the rest of the team as they led Thornton to the farmhouse. Shane McGinley, the Nutting Squad's lead interrogator, greeted them just inside the door. "Take him downstairs."

The kidnappers had freed Thornton's ankles but left the zip tie around his wrists and the hood in place. The men hustled the prisoner to a stone cellar. The air was cold and damp and smelled of metal. A solitary bulb shone from a wall sconce. Handcuffs attached to a chain hung from a hook in the ceiling. On one side of the room, two muscular men waited. Near the dangling chain, someone had placed a collapsible table with a digital recorder on it. A thin, balding man with glasses sat there with a prepared list of questions.

McGinley reached overhead for the handcuffs and signaled for the kidnappers to free Thornton's wrists. They kept a tight grip on his forearms when the tie was cut and quickly raised them above his head. McGinley swiftly handcuffed the American. One of his colleagues tightened the slack in the chain until Thornton's toes barely touched the floor. When Thornton started to protest, McGinley punched his face.

McGinley instructed the second muscular man to cut Thornton's clothes off. The psychologist protested again and took a punch to the gut. The naked American writhed and twisted.

McGinley ordered the kidnappers to wait upstairs. The ISU always conducted interrogations privately.

Thornton was alone in the basement with the Nutting Squad.

McGinley nodded to the balding man, who started the recorder. "Aaron Thornton, ya stand accused of conspirin' to murder a member of the Irish Republican Army."

RESPONSIBLE

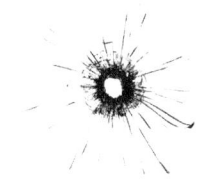

CLAIRE WALKED QUICKLY FROM THE PRISON to her car and called her father. "Daddy, Patrick Linden's crew took Aaron. He essentially admitted it."

"What the devil, Claire?! Where are ya?!"

"I'm at Maghaberry. I arranged to see Linden after hours. He tried to attack me, but the guard shackled him to the table. I'm fine. But Linden knows everything."

"Slow down, love. Start at the beginnin'."

Claire took a deep breath. "They know you're my father, and they know about Courtney. They think we're using Aaron to get to an IRA man named Liam." She still could not bring herself to reveal she knew Liam's surname.

"Aye, that would be Liam O'Malley, most likely. Aaron has been supervising him since O'Malley was released from prison. O'Malley and Linden are like brothers. But how would we use Aaron against the IRA, and why?" Inglesby, too, was playing dumb—he never told Claire the Historian named Mayhew and O'Malley as the bombers who killed Courtney.

Claire maintained the charade. "I don't know."

Inglesby mulled things over before asking, "Are the constables still with ya, love?"

Claire paused. "No, Daddy. I snuck out of the flat."

"Jayzus, love. It's not *safe*. Go back inside the prison and wait at the visitor desk until I get an armed escort to ya." Inglesby pushed the button on his desk, scribbled a note, and handed it to his assistant.

"Daddy. You need protection too. Linden is angry at *all* of us."

THE BAT

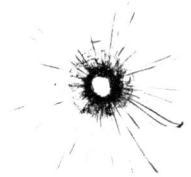

SHANE McGINLEY STOOD WITH A BAT in his right hand. He looked up at Thornton, who shivered in the cold.

The American tried to relieve the strain on his arms by supporting himself with his feet, but the ISU intentionally suspended him so he could barely touch the floor.

"Ya can make this easy on yerself by confessin' now."

"Confessing to what?! I haven't done anything!"

McGinley swung the bat upward at Thornton's testicles, and the American howled in pain. "It only gets worse from 'ere, Doc."

Thornton groaned in agony but refused to confess anything.

McGinley began the pre-planned series of questions. "Is Robert Inglesby yer father-in-law?"

Thornton hesitated but figured it might help to appear cooperative. Surely the IRA knew the answer already. He nodded.

"Out loud, please."

"Yes."

"Are ya married to his daughter, Claire Davis?"

"Yes." *God, please don't get Claire mixed up in this.*

"Did yer wife represent Patrick Linden during a recent appeal?"

Again, they must already know. "Yes."

"Is Liam O'Malley yer client?"

Thornton groaned. "You know I can't answer that. Therapists aren't allowed to name or talk about their clients."

McGinley swung hard and cracked Thornton's left rib cage with the bat. The American screamed in agony. The break was uneven, and the jagged edges of bone sent shockwaves through Thornton's torso with every twist and turn of his body. The psychologist gritted his teeth. His heavy breathing made it hot inside the hood, which became wet with sweat and made breathing even more difficult. The smell reminded him of a wet dog.

"I'll ask again." McGinley traced the other side of Thornton's rib cage gently with the end of the bat. "Is Liam O'Malley yer client?"

"Yes." Thornton loathed himself for breaking confidentiality so quickly.

"Good lad. Now that wasn't so hard, was it?" McGinley again touched the bat lightly to the right side of Thornton's rib cage. "Is Tommy Magee also yer client?"

Oh God no. Please don't go after Tommy. "I can't…"

The sound of more ribs cracking pierced the air. Thornton hissed as he swayed and jerked grotesquely. Through clenched teeth he snarled, *"You Goddamned motherf—"* Another blow to the testicles sent his body into spasms that triggered an explosion of pain in his rib cage. Thornton passed out.

McGinley leaned the bat against the wall. Nodding toward the stairs, he addressed his colleagues. "Let's eat."

TRACKED

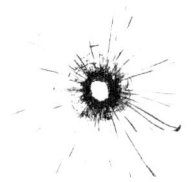

ROBERT INGLESBY PASSED THE DETAILS of Claire's conversation with Patrick Linden to MI5's analysis section. MI5 was already watching for a major IRA operation before Thornton's abduction. It therefore gathered more widespread intelligence than usual during the past week. The new information from Claire allowed them to concentrate on specific people of interest.

Patrick Linden was an obvious choice. Liam O'Malley and Mickey Shanahan, as Linden's most trusted associates, made the list as well. Paula Hall also earned a spot, as Shanahan's closest confidante and flatmate. All four individuals' movements and communications received intense scrutiny.

Technicians scoured Linden's visitor and mail logs at Maghaberry too. They assessed which guards spent the most time with him. The team also checked if any screws had disciplinary infractions, sick relatives, financial difficulties, or other potential vulnerabilities the IRA could have exploited. Analysts even reviewed who was on duty at the courthouse during Linden's recent appeal hearing.

Mobile data tracked O'Malley, Shanahan, and Hall to within three blocks of their precise locations at all times. Parties to— but not the contents of—every phone call, text message, and email were identified, along with the dates and times of contact.

Analysts also traced number plates and captured facial matches on CCTV. They consolidated credit card usage and other financial transactions. Even Wi-Fi connections were tracked—along with the serial numbers of all other devices connected to the same networks.

Aaron Thornton and Claire Davis' activities received the same level of attention. Thornton's client list was deemed highly relevant to the investigation, so MI5 requested and easily received a list of all offenders referred to him for monitoring.

But analysts first obtained authorization from MI5 headquarters in London before including Robert Inglesby—as a family member of the victim and a named target for IRA reprisal—in their analysis.

Analysts poured every scrap of information into a massive database for analysis by artificial intelligence, or AI. The prompt was straightforward—determine the most likely location of IRA kidnap victim Aaron Thornton.

The result was almost immediate. Analysis revealed increased contact between Linden and Shanahan in the days preceding the abduction. Shanahan and Hall were at the scene of the kidnapping and at the victim's office beforehand. Hall also was noted near the victim's residence and elsewhere in proximity to his wife. Shanahan communicated extensively with multiple burner phones immediately prior to the kidnapping.

Within minutes of the abduction, Shanahan and Hall headed southwest together and briefly stopped near the town of Moira. At that point, their cellular signals dropped, presumably when their mobiles were turned off or destroyed. The report concluded Thornton was likely being held in County Armagh, which traditionally gave strong support to the IRA. The organization was believed to have an active network there, including several safe houses. AI recommended aerial surveillance to identify areas of unusual activity.

Finally, the analysis revealed extensive contacts between Robert Inglesby and UVF boss Garth Peters. Peters had frequent cellular communications with Kieran Oliver, who shared an address with one of the victim's patients, Tommy Magee. Oliver—a suspect in the unsolved murder of Father Matthew Clark—was himself murdered outside Thornton's office just days previously.

An MI5 tactical team reviewed the report. It ruled out the immediate use of drones to conduct aerial surveillance because horses and dogs likely to be present in the targeted area would react, alert the kidnappers, and jeopardize any rescue attempt. Instead, the team requested and received approval for satellite support. It would take several hours to reposition the equipment and receive the first images.

THE SECRET

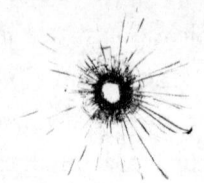

THORNTON REGAINED CONSCIOUSNESS and immediately wished to black out again. His arms seemed ready to rip from their sockets, and it was excruciatingly painful to breathe. His mouth was bone dry. He felt dizzy and nauseous. He needed to urinate.

Why the fuck is this happening?! What did the man in charge say? Something about trying to murder Liam?

Thornton realized it was absolutely quiet around him. He strained to pick up any sounds but heard nothing. He considered calling for help and decided against it.

The sound of a door opening in the distance struck fear into him. He heard heavy boots on the stairs and several men approaching. Thornton kept still and pretended to be unconscious.

A bucket of cold water splashed on Thornton's bare chest. He jerked involuntarily and cried out in anguish.

"Good, yer awake." Shane McGinley stood behind Thornton this time. "I asked ya a question. Is Tommy Magee yer client?"

"Yes."

"I didn't hear ya."

"*Yes!*" Thornton bellowed.

"Much better. Now, is it true Tommy Magee wanted to kill Liam O'Malley?"

"He wanted revenge for the murder of his parents, but he didn't know for sure who killed them."

McGinley moved in front of the American. "That's not quite true, is it? Do ya have any children, Doc?"

"No."

"Would ya like to?" McGinley extended a gloved hand and cupped Thornton's testicles.

"Why are you doing this? I didn't do anything. I'm a therapist. An American. I had no part in what happened here."

McGinley tightened his grip. "Did Tommy Magee think Liam O'Malley killed his parents?"

"Yes."

McGinley relaxed his grip. "See? It's always easier to answer the question. Now, ya say yer an American. How did ya get a license to practice so quickly?"

"My father-in-law helped me."

"Aye, Mr. Inglesby. Did he help ya get work from the prison and the police too?"

"Yes."

"And those jobs put ya in contact with Tommy Magee and Liam O'Malley?"

"Yes, but that's just coincidence."

"Did yer father-in-law also get Tommy Magee a job with the UVF quartermaster?"

"He used his connections to get Tommy a job, but I don't know what a quartermaster is."

"How did yer wife's sister die?"

"My wife doesn't have a sister."

"How long have you known yer wife?"

"Fourteen years."

"And in all that time she forgot to mention her dead sister? Doesn't that seem strange to ya? I mean, she saw it happen with her own two eyes. Or are ya lyin' to protect her?"

"I swear to you I know nothing about my wife's sister."

McGinley twisted Thornton's scrotum viciously. "Stop lyin'!"

Thornton vomited inside the hood. His body reflexively bent at the waist, and the pain again knocked him out.

SATELLITES

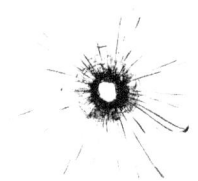

AS THORNTON SWAYED UNCONSCIOUS in the farmhouse cellar, brothers Benny and Jack Wilson sat at their controls four hundred miles away in the Telemetry and Command Station (TCS) at Royal Air Force Base Oakhanger, southwest of London. The brothers worked as private contractors in support of the Satellite Control Network, or SCN. The SCN, under supervision of the United States Space Force, controlled military satellites for the United States and its NATO allies using a series of command centers across the globe.

Routine satellite operations are relatively automated, and the evening shift at TCS started quietly. There were no labor-intensive launches or maintenance tasks scheduled for the next twelve hours, so Benny had just opened a takeaway box of prime rib and mashed potatoes. Jack was playing *Call of Duty* on a standalone computer. Then a counterterrorism alert flashed on their monitors and spurred them to action.

One of the Five Eyes requested the urgent reprogramming of sophisticated, high-resolution spy satellites to achieve saturation coverage of a roughly 500-square mile area in Northern Ireland. The Five Eyes—consisting of the United States, Canada, the United Kingdom, Australia, and New Zealand—had a long-standing agreement to collect, analyze, and share signals intelligence among them. Their joint capabilities, though highly classified, were astonishing to those who knew about them.

The desired coverage required the brothers to reprogram dozens of satellites in Low Earth Orbit (LEO). Each satellite—about the size of a Rubik's cube—orbited earth sixteen times a day, so none were in position over the target area for very long. The technicians had to enter an array of exhaustively precise coordinates and computer code to ensure that a series of successive LEO satellites had uninterrupted camera coverage over the desired area for the next twenty-four hours. It was no small feat.

Jack and Benny quietly got to work. As twins, they were highly attuned to each other and worked synchronously with minimal effort. They were the TCS' top team and finished the assignment in little more than a couple hours.

The secondary request—for imagery of the same area captured during routine passovers of the last forty-eight hours—took more time.

When they finished, Jack marked the task complete in the tracking system while Benny walked to the kitchenette to reheat his takeaway box. The brothers were oblivious to the drama unfolding in the cellar of a farmhouse four hundred miles away.

THE INTERROGATION

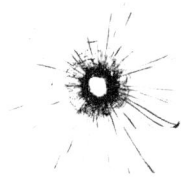

THE ENTIRE NUTTING SQUAD WAS PRESENT when Thornton regained consciousness the second time. He heard their movements and asked to be taken to the bathroom.

"Do what ya need to do right there," McGinley said.

"I just want to use the toilet. I'm in no condition to escape or fight you."

"Ya can pee or shit right there."

Thornton, too exhausted to plead any further, pissed himself.

McGinley resumed the interrogation. "Is it true yer wife wanted revenge fer the death of her sister?"

Weary and exasperated, Thornton replied, "I already told you. My wife doesn't have a sister." *Why hide something like that from me?*

McGinley motioned to one of his assistants, who produced an acetylene torch from beneath the stairs. The interrogator opened the valves on both cylinders and uncoiled the gas lines. Next he used a striker to light the end of a welding tip before depressing a lever to unleash a menacing whoosh of gas. He paused for effect and passed the flame across the back of Thornton's left thigh.

The American unleashed a string of expletives.

McGinley burned the prisoner again. The stench of burnt flesh filled the poorly ventilated space.

"What the fuck do you want me to say, you sick son of a bitch?!" Thornton had nothing to divulge, but he realized his torturer was not going to quit.

McGinley yelled back, "I want ya to admit yer wife wanted Liam O'Malley dead fer killin' her sister!"

"What are you *talking* about?!" *He thinks Liam O'Malley killed Claire's sister?! How? When? I'd know if that really happened…*

"Stop playin' games, Thornton. We know yer wife's sister died in the same attack that killed Tommy Magee's parents. She blamed Liam O'Malley fer her sister's death, and she and her MI5 father wanted O'Malley dead."

"No, no, no." *It can't be true. The ginger girl in Liam's description—the one who isn't mentioned anywhere in the police files? Claire? She would have been six in 1994. The youngest victim was a four-year-old girl…the one with no relatives named in the report. Her sister?! But she wouldn't hide that from me. No way. Oh my God—the man with the limp was Inglesby!*

McGinley wanted a recorded admission that Robert Inglesby, or at least Claire Davis, was involved in the plot against O'Malley. He burned Thornton a third time with the welding tip. The flesh sizzled and bubbled and released an awful smell. Thornton still did not implicate Claire or her father, so McGinley changed course. "How do ya know Kieran Oliver?"

Thornton could only mumble faintly. "I don't. Shares a flat with Tommy. Never met him."

"Did ya in any way help Kieran Oliver try to kill Liam O'Malley?"

Thornton rallied. "What?! No!! I tried to *protect* Liam!"

The interrogator paused. "Protect him from what?"

"From accidentally running into Tommy. Their appointments were back to back. Tommy figured out Liam was involved in killing his parents. I was afraid he'd bump into Liam and hurt him. So I changed Liam's appointments."

McGinley pondered the explanation. "Then explain the envelope in your office labeled *escape money*, with Magee's name on it."

Thornton's chest tightened. "That was Tommy's money. He asked me to hold it for him so Kieran wouldn't find it at their flat and take it. Tommy was saving for a place of his own. It had nothing to do with Liam, I swear."

McGinley wanted Thornton to admit a plot against O'Malley. Ideally, he would implicate Inglesby. But the American was stubborn. McGinley decided to increase the pressure. But first, he wanted to question someone else.

THE PROMOTION

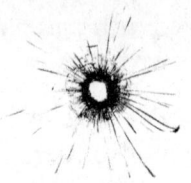

BRIANNA DONOVAN LAID LOW for several days after shooting Kieran Oliver. Once assured the coast was clear, she emerged from the safe house to pursue the rest of her plan.

At its next meeting, the crew chose Brianna to be their new leader—and the first female to helm a major faction of the IRA. Brianna, like a good social media influencer, recorded a video of her outstretched pistol firing two shots into Kieran Oliver's heart. Her jade ring momentarily—purposefully—flashed on camera. She played the video for the appreciative crew at their new headquarters in a makeshift bunker beneath a bookmaker's shop. She handily won the election.

The bunker was used originally to count and store money, so its reinforced door and walls offered better protection than Devin Dingle's room at the Chinese restaurant. Security cameras monitored all approaches to the site. There was even a concealed escape tunnel. The bookmaker's constant ebb and flow of customers upstairs provided easy cover for the crew's comings and goings.

Brianna installed Dwyer as her second-in-command, and together they ensured the crew's business operations returned to full strength. The resumption of a self-sustaining cash flow allowed Brianna to shift focus to the final phase of her takeover strategy—the recruitment of Liam O'Malley and the activation of the SAM systems.

There was just one problem. After learning—from Brianna, ironically—that Liam O'Malley was targeted for assassination, the Provos assumed a defensive posture. O'Malley abandoned his residence and changed locations every couple nights. Two rings of skilled bodyguards surrounded him at all times. O'Malley used a new disposable mobile each day to thwart tracking, and he never rode in the same car twice.

The extra security measures made it too difficult even for Brianna to reach O'Malley directly. She originally planned to show him the video of Kieran's assassination—she knew Mickey Shanahan would confirm she was the gunman. But now, after observing the heightened security around O'Malley, Brianna realized she would get just one chance to win him over. So she went all in to guarantee O'Malley's support—with the one thing he prized above all else.

THE HOOK

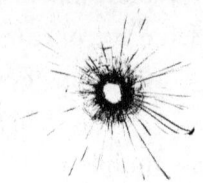

BRIANNA DONOVAN'S NETWORK GREW EVEN LARGER when she became head of the New IRA. People throughout the Republican community sought good relations with the new boss and her crew. Of course, most residents quietly did favors for the New IRA *and* the Provos, since it was never clear which rival faction had the upper hand at any given moment.

Brianna capitalized on the surge of goodwill and finally pieced together enough details to locate the rowhouse where Liam O'Malley was likely to spend the next night. She found a coffee shop a block away on the opposite side of the street and sat by the window. She sipped a latte and updated her Instagram account while waiting for O'Malley to arrive. Brianna happily noted 5,000 new followers and a corresponding bump in income from her paid promotions. *Just for posting pics of me tits and arse.*

After an hour, a car pulled up to the safe house. The driver and passenger remained in the front seat when the engine cut off. *O'Malley must be using a back entrance.* Brianna did not know it, but Mickey Shanahan's preferred crew were busy at a farmhouse an hour's drive away, so a backup team was in charge of O'Malley's security.

Brianna exited the coffee shop and strolled across the street. She purposely wore a tube top and yoga pants that highlighted her impressive physique. She kept her hands empty and visible as she approached the driver. When the window lowered, she said the code word a source gave her to put the watchers at ease. "I have a disposable mobile for Liam."

Neither man recognized Brianna, and both were instantly smitten. Protocol allowed anyone with the code word to approach the house, where a second team handled additional screening. The passenger in the car dialed someone inside and reported a blonde woman was approaching the door.

"Cheers, boys," Brianna called as she sexily approached the entrance. She felt them staring at her. *They're all the same.*

Brianna pressed the button. The door opened to a darkened main floor and two big men waiting in the foyer. She knew a third and likely fourth man watched from the shadows at the back of the house. Brianna flicked her hair with one hand and heaved her breasts. She repeated the code word and added, "I'm here to see Liam."

"He's not here," the taller of the two greeters said.

Brianna suspected a lie but came prepared. "Then it's your job to carry out Mickey's instructions." She pulled the disposable phone from her purse and said, "Give this to O'Malley. The passcode is his mother's birthday, using six digits."

The taller man inspected the phone casually. There was no reason to be suspicious of a messenger from Shanahan who knew the code word and the location of the safe house. "I'll be sure to give it to him if he shows up."

"Thank you, boys." Brianna turned, opened the door, and headed toward the street. Her jade ring flickered when she waved goodbye to the men in the car.

The man in the foyer went upstairs and handed the mobile phone to O'Malley. "Shanahan sent this over. Your mum's six-digit birthday is the passcode."

"Cheers, mate." O'Malley set the phone on the table beside the bed. "Any news?"

"Naw," the man said on his way out. "All's quiet."

Thirty minutes later, a soft ping announced receipt of an encrypted text message on the newly delivered phone. Liam unlocked the device and furrowed his brow at a video waiting to be played. He clicked on the image and watched an outstretched hand fire a pistol twice into the chest of a man on a motorcycle. A second text read, "I stopped the man who tried to kill you. I need a favor in return."

O'Malley recognized Kieran Oliver from the photographs in news reports aired after the killing. "I'm grateful, but who is this?" he texted back. Shanahan never told him who eliminated Oliver.

"A friend. I have another gift for you."

O'Malley was intrigued. Shanahan obviously did not send the phone. But whoever did was exceptionally resourceful.

"I assume it comes with a string attached."

"Only if you choose to repay me. Open the file in your downloads folder."

O'Malley swiped up to close the text window and look for the file. He spotted a document titled *Open Me*. It contained only a name— Ian Sweeney-Crestfield.

O'Malley texted back. "Should I know the bloke?"

Several seconds passed. Then three blinking dots appeared. "He's the driver who killed your sister."

HALO

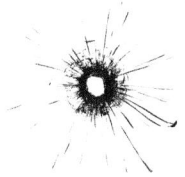

MILITARY OFFICIALS FROM THE UNITED KINGDOM'S elite Special Air Service, or SAS, pored over data obtained from the Satellite Control Network at their secret base in Herefordshire. The Wilson brothers' reconfiguration of the spy satellites produced spectacular results. It also presented the SAS' Hostage Rescue Team, or HRT, with some formidable challenges.

The imagery showed unusual activity in County Armagh around four farms dispersed across a valley five miles wide. The terrain was flat with unobstructed visibility. Only one road, from the west, crossed the surrounding grassy hills, and it appeared to be guarded at the summit by a stone building with 360-degree views. Thermal imaging showed two people inside the lookout post around the clock.

Intelligence analysts knew they were looking for at least ten people. CCTV in Belfast recorded five kidnappers seizing one hostage, and they would have met at least four terrorists from the Nutting Squad. Yet thermal imaging showed only two to five individuals in each farmhouse. They speculated about the possibility of underground bunkers and perhaps tunnels between the buildings.

In all, seven vehicles were spotted. Six dogs roamed freely.

A stealth approach by land was impossible, and helicopters offered no better chance of surprise. A HALO jump was the only viable alternative.

In this instance, a High-Altitude Low Opening jump meant one SAS troop of sixteen parachutists from Squadron D. The team was on standby around the clock for precisely this type of complex emergency. They would have to fly one hour on a military transport, deploy from an altitude of 35,000 feet, free-fall at a terminal speed of 126 miles per hour for two minutes, and then open their chutes at 3,000 feet above ground. There was little room for error, but the highly trained troops had done HALO jumps successfully dozens of times across the globe in support of the UK's national security interests.

Conditions for a HALO jump that night, though, were less than ideal. A nearly full moon and windy forecast made the drop especially risky. To maintain the element of surprise, the operators would have to land a mile from their objective and hike in. The dogs could easily be neutralized with suppressed gunfire from half a mile away, but the wind meant no use of disabling gas on the terrorists. The parachutists would have to engage the enemy at close quarters.

Highly advanced helicopters from the Joint Helicopter Command Flying Station Aldergrove—just twenty minutes away—were already on standby for exfiltration.

There was just one remaining problem—there simply were not enough resources to storm all four buildings at once. Leadership refused to attempt a rescue until analysts determined which farmhouse held the hostage.

Operation Swift Shadow was on hold.

THE SUMMONS

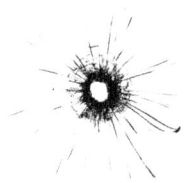

SHANE McGINLEY'S INTUITION AND EXPERIENCE told him Thornton might be telling the truth, so he paused the interrogation. McGinley left the basement to talk privately upstairs with Mickey Shanahan.

Shanahan was surprised to hear the American had not confessed yet. Most people caved much sooner.

"Show me the psychologist's notes again."

Shanahan accessed his email and opened the hacker's message with the keyword search of the psychologist's therapy notes. He turned the screen toward McGinley and let him read the contents.

After several minutes, McGinley observed, "Everything here is consistent with what he's been saying downstairs. But it would be one fucking hell of a coincidence if his wife's sister and Magee's parents were both killed by the same bomb. *Liam's* bomb. And what's the likelihood the wife never said anything about her sister?" Still, he thought Thornton might be telling the truth. "Something else bothers me though."

Shanahan looked at McGinley.

"Liam mentions 'Patrick' a couple times and puts him at the scene of the bombing. He also describes the bombing in detail.

And what's all this about feeling guilty and seeking forgiveness? Then there's the fucking Reconciliation meetings. We might have a *bigger* problem. Bring O'Malley here."

"For interrogation?" Shanahan asked uneasily.

"Naw, not without proof. But I *do* want to see how he interacts with the American."

Shanahan called the safe house and told the security team to bring O'Malley to the farmhouse.

THE ARRIVAL

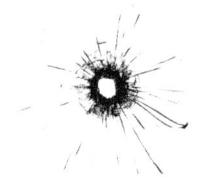

IT TOOK LIAM O'MALLEY THIRTY MINUTES to compose himself after learning the name of Deidre's killer. Outside, a storm was brewing. In the light of a distant streetlamp, O'Malley saw the wind whip first in one direction, then the opposite way. A few stray raindrops slid down the windowpane.

As a youth, O'Malley vowed to avenge Deidre's death. Now he saw the situation in shades of gray. True, the driver of the Saracen took an innocent life and escaped justice. But Deidre was gone, and nothing would bring her back. *And I sure as shite made the Brits suffer for what they did to us.* O'Malley thought of the boy from the Reconciliation meeting and the endless cycles of remembrance, hatred, and payback. *Haven't I done enough already? This can't go on forever.*

A knock at the bedroom door interrupted O'Malley's thoughts. The head of the security detail called through the door, "I'm supposed to bring ya to the farmhouse."

"At this hour of the fuckin' night? What the hell for?"

"Dunno. Just doin' what Shanahan tells me."

"For fuck's sake. Alright, gimme five minutes. I'll meet ya downstairs."

The security man retreated to the ground floor.

The wind howled and rattled the window. O'Malley went to the jacks, where he stared at the mobile for a minute. He pressed the first three numbers but stopped and set the phone on the sink. He studied himself in the mirror, ran one hand through his hair, and exhaled. Then he grabbed the phone and finished dialing. After a short conversation, he sent a text message which he promptly deleted from the sent folder. Then he scribbled on a piece of paper and shoved the scrap in an envelope that he folded into his pocket. With the phone still in hand, O'Malley exited the loo and headed for the stairs.

———————

Nearly two hours later, O'Malley and three men from the security detail stopped at a stone building atop a hill. The driver said something to the sentries before continuing with a follow car in tow. Minutes later, both vehicles pulled up to a remote farmhouse at the far end of a large, flat field.

Mickey Shanahan greeted the new arrivals at the door and waved them inside. He motioned to the security men to have a seat and pointed O'Malley toward a door at the far end of the room. "McGinley wants to talk with ya alone."

O'Malley descended into the cold, damp basement and stopped short when he saw a hooded, naked, severely beaten man hanging from a hook in the center of the ceiling. "What's all this then?"

Thornton recognized O'Malley's voice and called to him. "Liam! Is that you? You gotta help me!"

"Doc?!" O'Malley was incredulous. He fixed his eyes on McGinley. "What the fuck is goin' on here?!"

McGinley was unfazed. He told O'Malley everything about Thornton—about his links to MI5 and his wife's sister dying in the Shankill bombing. About a patient whose parents died in the same bombing, and the patient's desire for revenge. How the patient figured out Liam designed the Shankill bomb and sent his roommate to kill him. About the money stashed in the doc's office for the patient's escape. All confirmed by the watchers and in the psychologist's notes.

O'Malley was hurt. And confused. Then angry. "Doc, I *trusted* you!"

Thornton summoned the energy to plead his case. "Liam, no. It's all a misunderstanding. I tried to *protect* you. I didn't know about my wife's sister. *Please*, let me explain."

THE KEYCHAIN

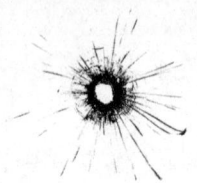

ROBERT INGLESBY SLAMMED THE PHONE into its cradle. The SAS commander refused to authorize a HALO jump without knowing at which of the four farms Thornton was held captive.

Inglesby knew time was running out. He frantically emailed each Section chief for updates, but there was no news. Then he left a voicemail for the Historian, hoping to glean one more detail from his conversation with the orphaned lad. Every passing minute led them closer to catastrophe. He wracked his brain for anything he might have missed, but already knew he was grasping at straws.

The intercom buzzed, and Inglesby's assistant announced Claire's arrival. He had summoned his daughter mostly to hear more about her conversation with Patrick Linden, but also to keep her safe.

She looked exhausted. "Is there any news, Daddy?"

"I'm afraid not, love. All of MI5 is workin' on it though. And I've been reviewin' everything we have to see if we missed anythin'," Inglesby said, waving his hand over dozens of intelligence reports strewn across his desk.

Claire dropped into a chair dejectedly.

"I'm glad yer here, luv. I want to know more about yer visit with Linden. I'll just run down the hall first."

Claire stood up and paced the room while her father went to the jacks. She stopped at one end of the desk and glanced at the photographs and reports arrayed there. One of them caught her eye. It was a surveillance photo taken years ago—but Claire still recognized the subject.

Inglesby returned to find his daughter holding the picture.

"Daddy, who's this?"

After a pause, he said, "She's datin' one of the men we suspect of takin' Aaron."

"I know her. Well, I've *talked* to her, at least. She was walking a couple dogs near campus and I got tangled up in their leashes. She's older now, but I'm sure it's her."

Inglesby picked up a notepad and pen. "The kidnappers must have watched ya, too, before they grabbed Aaron. Tell me everythin' you remember."

For the next twenty minutes, Claire described the encounter with Paula Hall to her father in excruciating detail. Finally, she said, "Daddy, I doubt we talked for even a minute. It was very brief."

"Just one more thing, luv. You said she dropped a bunch of keys that you picked up and handed back to her. Car keys? House keys? Industrial keys?"

"I dunno. They were *keys*, Daddy. Just normal, everyday keys. Nothing unusual about them. There were a lot of them, all attached to a big ring with a cow on it. I remember thinking she really liked animals."

"What sort of cow?"

"The black and white kind. It was a logo of some sort, with the cartoon head of a cow, tilted to one side. And the cow was smiling."

Inglesby picked up the phone and called the research section. "This is Inglesby. Run a search for business designs or logos featuring a black and white cartoon cow head, tilted to one side and smiling. It was seen on a key ring. Send me anything you find right away."

Father and daughter were both surprised when the research section called back minutes later to report two possible matches. Inglesby opened the images on his computer and showed them to Claire.

Claire pointed to the one on the left.

"Send me everything you have for image 98304A."

Moments later, a link to the electronic file arrived. Inglesby double-clicked and read the screen that opened. "That's it, luv. Well done! It's the logo of a dairy farm that shut down twenty years ago."

"And how does that help us?"

"It's in County Armagh, luv."

"But there must be dozens of dairies in Armagh."

"Aye, but this one's in a valley with three other farms."

OPERATION SWIFT SHADOW

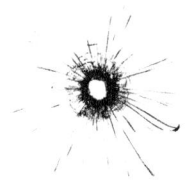

WITH UPDATED INTELLIGENCE about the defunct dairy farm in hand, the sixteen parachutists from SAS Squadron D deployed immediately. Conditions for the night drop remained suboptimal, with moderate winds and a full moon at the target site. But the squadron had overcome worse. In any event, the government was keen to avoid the public relations nightmare of an American murdered by the IRA on British soil.

The commandos first neutralized two IRA men in the lookout post at the top of the hill. Then they silenced the dogs. While four operators kept watch from the ridge, the rest of the squadron moved into an arc formation alongside the farmhouse.

Of the four farms in the valley, the target was closest to the lookout post. The moonlight nonetheless made it difficult to stay concealed in the flat, open terrain. The men relied on their camouflage, tactics, and marksmanship as they belly-crawled toward the stone farmhouse. Their comrades on the ridge provided cover.

The structure had two doorways. While four men remained prone, their colleagues rose to their feet and breached the entrances in twin diamond formations, using stun grenades to temporarily incapacitate the two occupants seen in thermal imaging on the ground floor. The rest were presumed to be in a cellar.

Inside they found only a startled elderly couple and an empty basement. The squadron commander called for the two Dauphin helicopters on standby to come and pick his men up.

MI5 later learned all the farms in the valley were once part of the same dairy consortium and shared the cow's head logo.

THE BASEMENT

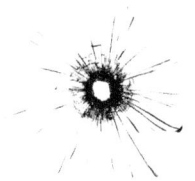

WHILE THE SAS RAIDED THE WRONG FARMHOUSE, Thornton
—still suspended from the ceiling—pleaded his case five miles
across the valley. "Liam, I know how bad things look, but I swear
to you I knew nothing about my wife's sister dying from a bomb
and had no idea her father works for MI5, if any of that's even
true. They never told me *any* of that."

O'Malley turned to the interrogator. "Can ya take the fucking hood off so I can hear 'im at least? And ya might as well take
him down. You've made yer point, and he's in no condition to
fight youse."

McGinley tossed his head slightly, and the two guards freed
Thornton, sat him in an empty chair, and removed the hood.

Thornton involuntarily tensed when his bare buttocks
touched the cold metal. He struggled to find a comfortable position. Stabbing pain accompanied every movement and made
him inhale sharply. Even the smell of his own urine assaulted
him. He blinked rapidly in the sudden light and rubbed his
chafed wrists. Once his pupils adjusted, Thornton recoiled at the
site of his bruised and burnt flesh. *Fucking animals.* Behind him,
the overweight guard wheezed as if he, too, were struggling to
catch his breath.

O'Malley and McGinley simply stared at the battered American.

Thornton knew O'Malley was his best hope for getting out of the situation. "Liam, it was just a coincidence. You were randomly assigned to me at Maghaberry, and when Tommy robbed the store, *he* was randomly assigned to me too. No one could have predicted or planned that. Tommy didn't even know who you were in the beginning."

"How'd ya get the job at the prison and the one workin' for the courts?"

"My father-in-law got them for me through his connections, but we never talked about my clients or my work. Ever. I don't even talk about my clients to my *wife*." *Christ, I hope they don't know how Tommy got his job at the garage.*

"Ya said this Tommy fella didn't know who I was in the beginnin'. How'd he find out?"

"His co-workers introduced him to someone who investigates unsolved murders. Somehow they figured it out. I don't know the details."

"Where's Tommy work?"

Goddammit. "He works at a mechanic's shop in the Shankill."

"Does he now?" O'Malley turned to the head of the Nutting Squad. "Wasn't the guy who tried to kill me from the UVF crew there?"

"Aye, he was," McGinley answered. "And this Tommy fella was his roommate. The doc was holdin' onto the escape money for 'im."

How do they know about the money? "Liam, Tommy didn't get along with his roommate. He was secretly saving up money to move out. I was just holding onto it so his roommate wouldn't steal it. We called it his escape money. It had nothing to do with any plot to kill you. I don't know anything about that. In fact, as soon as I realized Tommy knew your name, I tried to protect you."

McGinley interjected. "Ya almost have *me* convinced, Doc, I'll give ya that. But yer not as innocent as ya claim, are ya? Do ya remember that beautiful brunette with the blue eyes at the swimming pool? The one ya met for a pint at Maggie Mays?"

"The graduate student?"

"Is that what she called herself? Aye, she's a smart one. Ya told her ya had connections in the government, didn't ya? And something about being able to get people out of prison? Ya even told her ya could get her secret files from the HET. Now, Liam, does that sound like someone *who doesn't have a fuckin' clue what's going on?!*"

"That was just my ego talking. I was exaggerating to impress a beautiful woman. C'mon, we've all done it. And I wasn't talking about my father-in-law. My *wife* has access to the files for her work to get wrongfully convicted people out of prison. *That's* what I was talking about."

"I've heard enough of this shite." McGinley stood up.

"Liam, *listen.* If I was in on it, I could have killed you myself, or let the killer wait inside my office with less chance of being seen. Remember how I wanted to change the time of our weekly meeting? That's because Tommy's appointment was right before yours, and I was afraid he'd bump into you and recognize you. I was trying to protect you but *couldn't say why because of confidentiality!*"

Loud banging on the door at the top of the stairs interrupted them. Shanahan called down, "We just got word from an informer at the base that two Dauphins are headed this way."

Everyone except Thornton knew Dauphins were the security services' preferred means of transportation. Still, the American recognized a sudden urgency among his captors. And he knew an agitated killer is a volatile, dangerous one. His attempts at verbal persuasion had failed and now time was running out. A strong sense of foreboding overtook him. He had not felt such intense dread since the white supremacist attacked the rival gang leader and then turned on Officer Grace. But this time, there was no one to toss him a baton and no ERT. Only two options remained: fight or flight. Thornton's survival instinct kicked in, and he quickly surveyed the room.

McGinley ordered O'Malley and his men to the vehicles. "I'll finish down here."

Thornton's senses went into overdrive. Every movement, sound, and smell seemed exaggerated and threatening.

O'Malley was the last one to reach the steps. He turned to watch McGinley pull a pistol and aim it at the American's forehead. "Aaron Thornton, this tribunal finds ya guilty of conspiracy to murder Liam O'Malley and sentences ya to death."

"Wait!" O'Malley interjected. "Our DNA's all over this place, but without a body they can't prove murder. Bring him with us and finish it later where no one will find 'im." Then O'Malley turned and looked directly at Thornton. "We'll show him the IRA's *more* than just a pretty face on a mural."

Shanahan shouted again from upstairs. "*Now*, boys. We're outta time."

O'Malley bounded to the first floor, leaving Thornton alone with McGinley. The head of the Nutting Squad stood behind the American and pushed him roughly toward the stairs. "I don't give a shite what that old man says. I'll put a bullet it ya right 'ere if ya slow me down."

Thornton labored up the stairs surprisingly well. Seeing a gun at his face caused a surge of adrenaline that numbed his pain—and motivated him. Two steps shy of the top, Thornton launched himself backward into McGinley. The interrogator lost his footing, and the two men tumbled down nearly the entire flight of stairs. McGinley's right elbow cracked on the stone floor, and the gun slid into a darkened corner of the room. Thornton winced but rolled purposefully to one side.

The dazed Irishman struggled to his knees just in time to watch Thornton light the uncoiled welding torch. "Ya swore an oath, Doc. Do no harm."

"Fuck. You." Thornton bathed his tormentor in a blue-orange flame that washed over the top and down the sides of him. It was the last thing McGinley saw. The American let the flame burn until the gas ran out.

Shanahan was the only Provo still upstairs and heard the commotion. He started down the steps and saw the burned body below. "For fuck's sake, McGinley. Ya were supposed to bring 'im with us. They'll still be able to identify 'im from dental records."

Thornton dragged himself across the room and grabbed the gun. He had never fired one before and hoped a simple trigger pull would suffice. In the shadows, he sat on the floor with his back against the wall. He aimed at the stairs as Shanahan's lower legs came into view. The American's hands were shaking badly, so he raised his knees as best he could and braced the gun between them.

Shanahan descended two more steps and stopped. "McGinley?!"

Thornton closed his eyes and pulled the trigger twice in quick succession.

"Fuuuuuuck!" Shanahan fell hard and tumbled down the remaining steps. He clutched his right knee in agony. "You *fuckin'* pain in the *arse.*" The Provo drew his own pistol and aimed toward the sound of the shots.

This time, Thornton kept his eyes wide open and locked on the threat. He aimed at Shanahan and pulled the trigger repeatedly until the pistol was empty. Shanahan died, gun in hand, without firing a single shot.

Outside, O'Malley and the rest of the Provos sped toward the SAS Squadron.

THE TOLL

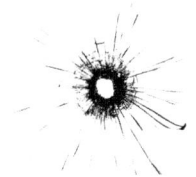

THE SAS LOOKOUTS ON THE HILL spotted the line of fast-moving, heavy-duty vehicles in plenty of time to alert their colleagues in the valley below. The men recognized two of the vehicles from satellite imagery shared during the mission brief. The squadron commander ordered his men to shoot out the tires. The entire band of dissidents was shot dead as they exited the stopped vehicles and fired automatic weapons at the soldiers. One commando took a bullet to his leg that was later determined to come from Paula Hall's weapon.

The two Dauphins landed moments later and evacuated the squadron once specialized units from the PSNI and MI5 were on-scene. The commandos took with them the severely injured American hostage—found unconscious alongside two deceased males in the basement of a nearby farmhouse. One of the helicopters touched down briefly on the roof of Musgrave Park Hospital in Belfast to discharge the injured commando and the American before returning to base.

Thornton's injuries caused internal bleeding that required emergency surgery. He spent nearly seven hours in the operating suite and recovery room. Claire Davis anxiously awaited her husband when hospital staff finally wheeled the groggy American into a private room. Claire held his hand, unsure how to talk about what happened. She felt relief when he drifted off to sleep.

Across town, Robert Inglesby perused initial reports about the kidnapping and rescue. He was pleased to see Liam O'Malley listed among those killed—there was finally some justice for Courtney and all the other victims of the Shankill bombing. Patrick Linden's right-hand man, Mickey Shanahan, also perished, along with ten more dissidents. A thirteenth body would have to be identified from dental records. It was a serious blow to the Provos and to Linden's inner circle. Inglesby—who still inwardly celebrated Kieran Oliver's demise—was happier than he had been in a long time.

CONFRONTED

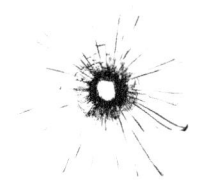

THORNTON GLANCED ABOUT THE HOSPITAL ROOM. The doctors stopped sedating him the previous night, and his mind was nearly clear. As the drugs wore off, memories of his ordeal surfaced, one after another in surprising detail. With them came waves of emotion. By the time Claire arrived after lunch to visit, Thornton was hopping mad.

"You're awake!" Claire rushed from the doorway to kiss her husband. Her perfume mixed with the smell of antiseptic.

Thornton turned away and gingerly raised one elbow to keep her at bay. The faint beeping of his heart monitor and the hum of the medicated IV drip provided white noise. In the distance, an anonymous voice paged hospital staff.

"Hon, what's wrong?"

Thornton stared at a whiteboard on the wall. The monitor beeped faster.

"Hon, I know you've been through a lot. Talk to me. I want to help."

Thornton refused to meet Claire's gaze. His thoughts flew in a dozen unpleasant directions. He had never been this angry.

"*Aaron. Stop it.* Tell me what's wrong."

Thornton's resolve crumbled, and his eyes darted at Claire. "What's *wrong*? Did you *seriously* just ask me *what's wrong*?! I nearly *died*, Claire. They hung me from a hook, beat me with a bat, broke my ribs, burned me with a blowtorch, and accused me of all kinds of bullshit. *Because of you and your father!*"

Claire stepped back and covered her mouth. The authorities had spoken to her only in general terms about what happened at the farmhouse. She began to cry. "Because of *me*? And Daddy?"

"Tell me the truth, dammit! Did you have a sister? Who died in an IRA bombing?"

The expression on Claire's face answered for her.

"How could you *keep* something like that from me?"

"Aaron…" Claire halted. "I…I am so sorry, love. I promised my father years ago I'd never speak about it to anyone. It wasn't *safe.*"

"But I'm your *husband*, Claire. And *I* didn't feel so safe in that fucking basement. They accused me of plotting with you and your father to get revenge for your sister's death. I don't even know her fucking name. Hell, you haven't told me anything about your mother either. And we've been together *fourteen years.*"

The blood drained from Claire's face. "My God. *Aaron.* I never meant for this to happen. We were just trying to protect you. I know it's hard for an American to understand."

"We're *married*, Claire. I uprooted my life to move here and support you. I don't remember you saying it might be a bad idea. That I wouldn't *fit in*. Hell, I figured we'd *stay* here. And you know what? That's *bullshit*. You're a grown woman and don't need your father's permission to tell your husband anything. Who *better* than me to confide in—I'm a fucking psychologist, for Chrissake. *How could you not trust me?*"

Snippets of past conversations with Claire bounced through Thornton's mind. Still in a raised voice, he said, "Is *this* why you didn't want kids? It actually makes sense *now*. Fuck, if you had just told me the truth I would have understood everything a whole lot better. But instead you forced me through *this* bullshit."

A nurse passing in the hallway peeked into the room but decided not to intervene.

"Aaron, what they did to you is horrible. Inexcusable. I can see how much it's...rattled you. I can't imagine—"

"No, no, no, Claire. You don't get to do that. Don't try to shift blame from you and your father. What the *fuck* kind of work does he do, anyway? Those men clearly didn't think too highly of him."

Claire lowered her voice. "He's in charge of undercover operations at MI5."

Thornton would have thrown something if he could have moved his arms. The heart monitor sounded an alarm. "Oh, that's just fucking fantastic, Claire. You kept *that* a secret too? If you were so damned worried about my safety, you might have mentioned *that* little tidbit." A second alarm sounded in the room and in the corridor. "They found the paperwork he filed for my license and practice and assumed I was working for him." Thornton's face darkened, and his eyes narrowed. "Did your father *know* it was O'Malley's bomb that killed your sister? *Did he fucking use me to set O'Malley up?*"

The suggestion horrified Claire, and she jumped to her father's defense. "No, *no*. I didn't tell him, Aaron, I *swear*." She caught herself too late.

"Wait, *you* knew about O'Malley and the bomb?"

Claire panicked. "No. *No*. Well, not at the *beginning*, Aaron, *no*."

"*Then. When. Claire? And how?*" The alarms still droned in the background.

Claire fumbled for a plausible explanation that would not make things worse. She failed. "I read it on your computer when—"

The alarms switched from a rhythmic beeping to a steady tone. "*My computer?!* You read my *notes* and violated my patients' *confidentiality*? Christ, Claire, who *are* you?!"

"Aaron, let me—"

"Get out."

Claire's eyes welled up. "Hon?"

"Get out." Then louder, "*Get out!*"

A nurse finally appeared to check on the alarms.

Thornton addressed the newcomer. "I don't want any more visitors. Including Ms. Davis."

The nurse glanced uncomfortably at Claire, who looked embarrassed and afraid.

Claire lowered her head and her voice. "I love you, Aaron." Then she retreated from the room.

The nurse silently fussed with the equipment until Thornton's heart rate and blood pressure returned to normal.

THE WRATH

THE THIRTY-DAY WAIT FOR Patrick Linden's final appeal hearing ended on a Thursday.

Claire Davis arrived at the courthouse with dark circles under puffy eyes. Her normally tidy red hair flew wildly in the wind. The black jacket she wore over a navy-blue blouse matched the severe expression on her face. Even the staccato clicking of her high heels sounded angry on the marble floors.

Her husband rarely spoke to her since the kidnapping. His decision to get a room at the Ibis hotel made clear he wanted nothing more to do with Claire and her father. Thornton already closed his Belfast office and was at their flat now packing for his return to the States. Claire doubted he would be there to say goodbye when she returned home. The only member of her family untouched by The Troubles—an innocent man and her one true love—was now traumatized by them. And Claire blamed Patrick Linden for all of it.

Linden's hearing convened at 10:00 under the same tight security protocols as before. Claire's colleagues at CNICS did all the preparation this time, so Claire could be with her husband. But she felt a sense of duty to the law and insisted on attending the hearing.

The barristers took their seats, and a pair of constables escorted Linden into the courtroom. The Lord Chief Justice moved swiftly and efficiently through the procedural steps. The Public Prosecution Service acknowledged they had no new charges to file against the prisoner and withdrew their objection to his release. The CNICS team had nothing new for the record. Linden sat with a smug expression on his face. The Lord Chief Justice was about to order the prisoner's release when Claire took a deep breath, stood, and asked to address the court.

The Lord Chief Justice raised his eyebrows but nodded. Claire's confused colleagues turned to one another. Patrick Linden's face clouded.

Claire stepped forward, smoothed her hands over the front of her black skirt, and registered an objection to Linden's release. The chief prosecutor eyed Claire keenly. The CNICS team called for a recess, which the Lord Chief Justice denied. "I want to hear what Ms. Davis has to say."

Claire noted her husband's recent kidnapping and torture, which generated headlines across the United Kingdom. "My Lord, Mr. Linden is responsible for my husband's abduction."

Patrick Linden maintained his composure in front of the Justices and prosecutors but glared at Claire.

The Lord Chief Justice remained inscrutable. "Go on, Ms. Davis."

"Thank you, My Lord." Claire told the courtroom about her husband's work with the late Liam O'Malley, and O'Malley's self-admitted involvement with the Shankill bombing of 1994 and his implication of Linden. She described Linden's belief that she, her husband, and her father conspired to kill O'Malley in revenge for the attack. Because of that belief, Linden ordered her husband's abduction and torture and threatened her and her father.

Claire halted but held one index finger in the air. The courtroom waited. In a strong, clear voice, Claire continued, "Mr. O'Malley, Mr. Linden, and their co-conspirators in the IRA murdered my four-year-old sister, Courtney Davis, in that attack. A building collapsed on her and other innocent victims. I saw it with my own eyes from farther up the street. And they deserve justice."

The Lord Chief Justice interlocked his fingers. "These are serious charges, Ms. Davis. I assume you have proof? And why are *you* introducing these allegations instead of the Public Prosecution Service?"

Claire walked to the end of the barristers' table where she left her bag. She placed it on the table and removed a file folder and a small digital recorder. "My Lord, this folder contains a printout of the clinical notes with Mr. O'Malley's description of the Shankill bombing during court-ordered therapy. Since the patient is deceased, he has no claim of confidentiality. And because the notes pertain to a terror offense, the law does not protect them. The Public Prosecution Service can obtain the original digital file from the successor to my husband's practice. As for Mr. Linden's knowledge of my husband's abduction and the threats toward me and my father…"

Claire pressed a button on the digital recorder, and Linden's words from the night of his meeting with Claire at Maghaberry echoed in the courtroom.

You and yer family fucked with the wrong crew, and now there's a price to pay. There's nothin' anybody can do to fix it. Not yer daddy. Not you. And not yer fuckin' husband.

I already knew youse figured out who killed yer sister. And youse tried to get revenge fer it. But Liam and the crew are safe, aren't they? And ya say yer husband's gone missin' now? How did that happen, luv? I guess ya can't be too careful these days.

Say hello to yer sister for me.

Excited chatter erupted throughout the courtroom. Linden banged his fists angrily on the defense table.

"Order!" The Lord Chief Justice had heard enough. "Remand the prisoner to Maghaberry pending the Public Prosecution Service's response to these new charges. The hearing is adjourned."

CAGED

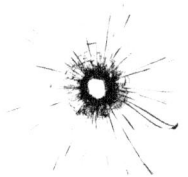

PATRICK LINDEN PACED the short length of his cell. The grief, the loneliness, the helplessness, the lack of hope, and especially the anger washed over him. Memories of Catholic homes burning, the beatings, the gunfights, and that fateful afternoon at Sheehan's furniture store swirled in his mind.

Patrick lost his best friend, Liam, and his right-hand man, Mickey. The Brits killed the entire Nutting Squad and decimated his crew too. He took stock of the situation and concluded the future looked grim—hardly worth living for. He silently recited the names of his dead comrades. *The lucky bastards.*

It was supposed to be different. Patrick and Liam were the movement's favored sons. They were accomplished, successful Provos with a loyal following and an impressive record of resistance. Patrick had been poised to walk out of prison and once again take up the noble fight on the streets of Belfast. But the future, like his comrades, was stolen from him. *The Brits and that bitch lawyer made sure of that.*

Patrick now faced a new trial on terror charges, and CNICS abandoned his appeal. To add insult to injury, Brianna Donovan seized on the Provos' setback to boost the New IRA's standing in the community. Just when Patrick thought he was already at his lowest, Officer Loftis and another screw arrived to toss his cell.

THE TROUBLESOME LIBYANS

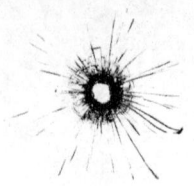

On his last night at the safe house, Liam O'Malley felt unsettled. The failed attempt to kill him and the summons to the farmhouse of course made him uneasy. And the whole business with the American psychologist and Patrick Linden's suspicions about him added to the anxiety.

Now came an anonymous savior who spared him from assassination and delivered the long-awaited name of Deidre's killer. It was a lot to process.

While the security detail waited downstairs, O'Malley stared at the bathroom mirror. He appreciated the savior's goodwill gestures but remained wary of strangers. Still, he sensed time was short. He might not get another chance.

O'Malley dialed the number that sent the texts to his new mobile. He was surprised when a woman answered.

"Hallo, Liam. I'm glad ya called."

"Do I know ya?"

"No, but we're on the same side. I think I've proved that now."

"What do ya want from me?"

"I need yer help with a couple troublesome Libyans." It was the Provos' old way of referring to the broken SAM systems.

"I'm a long way from all that, friend. I'm afraid I can't be much help to ya."

"*Think on it, love. Ya may be our last hope. The UVF won't stop trying to kill ya. And it's only a matter of time till the Brits pin something else on ya and send ya back to prison.*"

The last sentence in particular stung. The Brits did screw him the last time he was released. And it looked like they teamed up with the American to try again. "*I'll have a think and let ya know.*"

"*Do it for Deidre.*"

O'Malley ended the call. Competing desires clashed in his heart and mind. In their own way, each one made sense to him. O'Malley drafted a text to the mystery woman and stared at it for a minute. He heard heavy footsteps on the wooden stairs and knew the security detail was ready to leave.

O'Malley hit send, deleted the text from his phone, and met the bodyguard in the hall. He waved the phone in the air and said to the head of the security detail, "*We need to make a quick stop at Clonard on the way.*" The security man assumed the instructions came from Mickey Shanahan and nodded without protest.

JUSTICE DELAYED

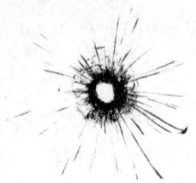

RUTH McGOWAN SAT INCONSOLABLE in the church office after Liam O'Malley's funeral. Clonard Monastery filled to capacity for the occasion, and the Republican community gave a proper send-off to its martyred son. The procession to Milltown Cemetery stretched for blocks.

O'Malley was McGowan's nephew. When his mum sank into depression and alcoholism after Deidre's death, Aunt Ruth—who had no children of her own—took O'Malley under her wing. For security reasons, they kept a low profile in public. But they were bound by blood and privately confided in each other.

McGowan thought about the last time she saw O'Malley, just a few nights earlier when he stopped by her apartment at the monastery on his way to the farmhouse. He spoke quickly when she answered the door. *Keep this envelope in a safe place. If something happens to me, there's a name inside. Check him out, and if he's the driver who ran Deidre over with the Saracen in '72...*

"Say no more, luv," she told him. "I'll take care of it."

———

Two weeks later in the English countryside, Army Lt Col (Retired) Ian Sweeney-Crestfield took his dog, Cromwell, for the usual evening stroll while his wife babysat their granddaughter. Shortly after the dog relieved himself and turned to lead his master home, a delivery truck accelerated up the street, plowed into Sweeney-Crestfield from behind at fifty miles per hour, and fled the scene.

Mrs. Sweeney-Crestfield found her husband's mangled, lifeless body in the street after Cromwell came home with blood on his paws. She never knew why a roll of strawberry-banana Toffos lay next to her husband's body.

RETRIBUTION

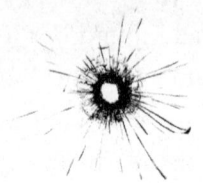

Little more than an hour before Fr. Clark's murder, MI5 security agent Robert Frye exited the surveillance van near the junction of Falls Road and Leeson Street to use the loo at a nearby fast-food restaurant. Inside the WC, he locked the door and placed a call to Kieran Oliver, with whom he previously collaborated—using the alias John Sandford—on several off-book UVF activities. Oliver looked up to the MI5 man, who showed him more respect than Inglesby and treated him as an equal.

"Sandford, how ya goin', mate?"

Frye was glad to hear Oliver was inebriated. The drink made him more impulsive and reckless. "There's somethin' I thought ya should know. But ya didn't hear it from me. An IRA informer's cover is blown, and MI5 is gonna extract him to a safe house from the Bobby Sands mural at half seven tonight. But the man's been runnin' guns for the IRA for more than twenty years and has a lot of Loyalist blood on his hands. Now that his cover's blown, he's useless to us. We shouldn't be protectin' the prick any longer. I figured ya might wanna settle the score before the bastard disappears. I'd do it myself but I'm on duty."

"Yer bloody fuckin' right I do. Half-seven at the Sands mural. I won't let ya down. Where's he comin' from and how will I know 'im?"

"He'll be on foot and comin' from Clonard Monastery, so I'm bettin' *he'll take Clonard Street to the Falls Road. Otherwise, Ross Mill Avenue. Either way, ya can't miss 'im. He's a fuckin' priest who looks like Father Christmas."*

SCHEMATICS

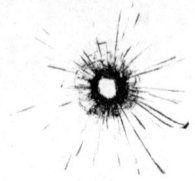

BRIANNA WAITED SEVERAL DAYS TO VISIT the storage locker identified in the text message Liam O'Malley sent on the night he died. She glanced down at her phone again and used the specified combination to unlock the compartment. It contained only a black three-ring binder. Brianna flipped through the contents, which at first resembled a mathematics notebook. She recognized Arabic text on some of the pages and broke into a grin. O'Malley posthumously delivered the schematics for the SAM systems, complete with his handwritten notes and instructions in the margins.

Brianna considered the irony. Long before she joined the crew, New IRA leadership provided the anonymous tips that sent Liam O'Malley and Patrick Linden to prison in the first place. It was a strategic move to undermine the Provos' dominance in the Republican community. When the amnesty unexpectedly prompted O'Malley's early release all those years ago, the New IRA ensured his quick return to prison with another tip about weapons and explosives in the safe house where he was temporarily staying.

Now Brianna had manipulated him into surrendering the one advantage that assured the New IRA's supremacy over the Provos.

FULL CIRCLE

THE SPECIAL FORCES' raid on the wrong farmhouse and the subsequent gun battle received a customary review. It concluded, despite the massive loss of life and media scrutiny, that MI5 and the SAS conducted themselves appropriately.

With that matter settled, MI5's director resumed the hunt for Fr. Clark's betrayer with added zeal. The anonymous call about Kieran Oliver's van in the vicinity of Clark's murder—and the discovery that Robert Inglesby redacted that information from an earlier intelligence report—put the head of undercover operations under intense scrutiny. Of added concern was the sudden unexplained disappearance of one of his undercover agents, James Dwyer. As more and more information came to light, top management quietly told Inglesby to retire.

Elsewhere in MI5, Mongoose faced a different kind of pressure. Field operatives reported widespread indications that the New IRA *did* possess two SAM systems *and* the recently acquired means to activate them. Mongoose was using every resource to locate and destroy the equipment.

Meanwhile, at QUB, Claire Davis continued to teach law, for the time being. Her decision to act against the interests of her client, Patrick Linden, prompted Claire's removal from CNICS and placed her under professional review, for which she had to remain in Belfast.

Her husband, however, returned to the States—driven in part by the trauma he suffered but also by his wife's duplicity. The couple diplomatically agreed to a trial separation but knew it would become permanent.

FULFILLMENT

WORD OF THORNTON'S DEPARTURE for the States initially hit
Tommy Magee hard. He was fond of the American and felt
indebted to the shrink for turning his life around. But the two
agreed Tommy was ready to move forward on his own. With
Thornton's endorsement and the testimonials of co-workers
and mates, the court released Tommy early from the diversion
program.

As time passed, Tommy received more responsibility—and
money—at the garage. The extra income allowed him to rent
a posh apartment with nice furniture and functional modern
appliances. He even bought a brand-new Victory motorcycle to
keep pace with his many work and social engagements.

Tommy's colleagues at the garage easily convinced him to
join the UVF. He quickly bonded with his Loyalist "brothers"
and became a popular member of Garth Peters' crew. At first,
he spent most evenings at the Cocky Rooster and other Unionist
hangouts. Before long, though, a young lass named Molly vied
for his time and attention.

Molly studied nursing at the Open University in Belfast. The
pair met during trivia night at a pub near Tommy's workplace
and dated for several months before moving in together. Now,

Molly busied herself in the kitchen waiting for Tommy to arrive from work. She heard his key in the door and rushed to greet him.

"How was work, luv?"

Tommy opened his arms wide to embrace her. "It was fantastic. But the best part of me day is comin' home to you."

"C'mon, I want to show ya somethin'." Molly grabbed Tommy's hand and pulled him toward the kitchen. She picked up a clasp envelope emblazoned with the National Health Service logo.

"Did ya get that nursing job ya put in for?"

"Even better, luv." Molly opened the envelope and removed a grainy black and white image. She grasped it with both hands and extended it toward him while jumping up and down.

Tommy looked at it, confused.

Molly laughed giddily. "Haven't ya seen an ultrasound before? Yer gonna be a daddy, Tommy!"

Tommy's jaw dropped. He snatched the image from Molly's hands and studied it closely. He traced the outline of the tiny human form with the tip of his finger. Then he tossed the photo onto the kitchen table, let out a high-pitched whoop, and embraced his girlfriend tightly. "I'm gonna be a fuckin' dad!"

The couple did a celebratory dance before dropping breathlessly into a couple chairs.

"When is he due?"

"Who said it's a he?! I'm only two months along, so it's too early to say."

"It doesn't fuckin' matter. We're gonna be parents, Molly!"

The pair talked excitedly for a couple hours about all the changes awaiting them. When hunger finally set in, Molly started dinner. While she stirred a pot of stew, Tommy taped the ultra-sound image on the stainless-steel refrigerator next to Thornton's handwritten goodbye note.

BETRAYAL

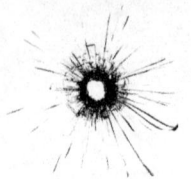

JAMES DWYER SMOKED A CIGAR on the balcony of a penthouse apartment overlooking the beach in Marbella. The glass door behind him slid open. Brianna Donovan stepped outside and handed Dwyer one of two beers she carried. Together they savored their drinks, the view of the Spanish coastline, and their takeover of the Republican movement. MI5 should not have trusted a professional hacker—especially one recruited under duress.

Dwyer despised being a tout, resented Robert Inglesby's control over him, and doubted the government would protect him if anything went wrong. So from the very beginning, he revealed MI5's ploy to Brianna and Devin Dingle. The trio agreed to turn the tables by feeding Inglesby harmless information about the crew's activities and staging failures to convince him Dwyer was disrupting the New IRA's plans.

At the same time, Dwyer provided valuable information to his new comrades. Of particular interest to Brianna was the revelation that Inglesby had a keen interest in the SAMs and coached Dwyer to listen for any mention of *two troublesome Libyans*—the Provos' coded reference to the missile systems.

As time went by and they plotted the New IRA's expansion, Dwyer and Brianna grew suspicious of Fr. Matthew Clark. The priest had been the leading Republican arms dealer for decades. Yet he seemed to operate with impunity, while nearly every faction of the IRA suffered occasional—and sometimes significant—setbacks.

The couple's shared concern prompted Dwyer to hack the priest's phone records. Dwyer spotted repeated calls to the same number he himself used to contact Robert Inglesby—innocently listed in the priest's contacts as *Church Secretary*. To erase any doubt about Clark's betrayal of the movement, Dwyer used a highly secretive hack to convert the priest's phone into a listening device. In short order, the New IRA had proof Clark was feeding MI5 information about the IRA's activities.

Unbeknownst to Dwyer, the priest's mobile carried malware detection software that eventually alerted him the phone was compromised. Clark signaled to Mongoose that he was exposed and set in motion plans for his extraction to a safe house. Neither Clark nor MI5 ever knew who hacked the phone.

QUANTICO

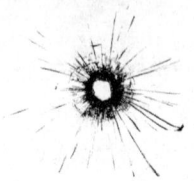

THORNTON DECIDED AGAINST A RETURN to West Virginia. Instead, he left Belfast for Washington, DC, where he hoped the network of Georgetown alumni would expand his social circle and help him find work. Upon arrival, he agreed to housesit for a classmate who was deployed overseas for six months. It seemed like just the right amount of time to recover, reacclimate, and plot his next move.

Initially, Thornton was content to sleep late, meet with friends a few times each week, and exercise as often as his still-healing body allowed. After the first month, though, he felt listless. Life was boring now. His favorite, action-packed movies and television shows—*Game of Thrones* included—seemed humdrum. Even the prospect of restarting his practice appeared tedious. But when it came time to complete fifteen hours of continuing education to renew his psychology license, Thornton found his spark.

Thornton enrolled in several advanced courses about the psychological dynamics of kidnapping, human trafficking, freed hostages, and crisis negotiation—for twice the number of credits he needed. The program required participants to take part in therapy throughout the course of study as a means to cope with the difficult subject matter. It was a boon for Thornton. By the time he graduated at the top of his cohort, Thornton was effectively managing his trauma and itching to put his new skills to use. No more sitting passively across from clients in an office—he wanted to be part of the action.

As soon as his studies ended, Thornton began looking for work. His unique background appealed to government recruiters, and soon he found himself before an FBI hiring panel. The screeners asked the usual questions but were especially curious about his time in Northern Ireland and his progress since the kidnapping. They also inquired about the state of his marriage and other relationships. Thornton laid everything on the table, including his pending divorce from Claire and his pursuit of therapy to recover from his ordeals in West Virginia and Northern Ireland.

The transparency worked in his favor. After passing a preliminary background check and with the endorsement of his therapist, Thornton received a conditional offer to join the Bureau's National Center for the Analysis of Violent Crime in Quantico, Virginia, as a Behavioral Analyst—the real-life version of television's *Criminal Minds* team. He completed orientation and several more training courses but could not begin case work until he was fully vetted.

It took eight months to complete the extensive background investigation needed for a Top Secret clearance. By then, supervisors concluded Thornton was better suited to join the Crisis Negotiator Program and work alongside special agents in the field. Quantico remained home base, but the Bureau sent Thornton where needed throughout the country.

Thornton's first year on the job proved management right—he negotiated the peaceful resolution of several high-risk and well-publicized hostage and domestic terror situations. The most recent incident involved a heavily armed bank robber who surrendered peacefully after Thornton persuaded him, over the course of several tense hours, to release eight hostages unharmed.

Thornton was back at Quantico wrapping up his report on the bank robbery when his supervisor called. He picked up the receiver, hoping the dinner plans with his cute neighbor were not in jeopardy. "Yeah, boss."

"Aaron, I just got off the phone with the legat in London," referring to the FBI's legal attaché. "They're looking for a crisis negotiator to consult for MI5."

"No problem. I'll give them a call in the morning, since it's already nighttime there."

"Actually, you'd be consulting in person. They want you to fly to London, join a team there, and then deploy elsewhere. Given your experience in Northern Ireland, I just wanted to be sure you're okay returning to the UK."

Thornton glanced at the framed photos on his desk. In one, Tommy Magee sat next to his girlfriend, Molly, on a leather sofa in a swank apartment. Tommy sent the photo as a thank-you for Thornton's help. Across the back he scrawled, *Thanks for believing in me, Doc.*

The second frame held a newspaper tribute to Liam O'Malley, published a month after his death. At the bottom, Thornton affixed a label that read, *More than a pretty face on a mural.*

"I'm good, boss. Sign me up. Just curious though—why me and not one of the more senior negotiators?"

"Because they asked for you specifically."

ACKNOWLEDGEMENTS

Getting your first book into print is a daunting task. I could not have done it without the love, support, and patience of my family. Thank you for putting up with me.

I will be forever indebted to Matt Henderson Ellis, whose expertise as an editor improved both my writing and the story—and whose encouragement kept me energized. Copy editor Sean Leonard polished the final draft for publication with a keen eye for the details. Iram Allam masterfully and creatively designed the interior layout, while the ad campaigns and eye-catching cover are the work of the extraordinarily talented Nick Castle. I am deeply grateful to all of them and look forward to our next collaboration.

Special thanks to the colleagues, neighbors, and other friends who contributed ideas, names, or a willing ear. And of course, thank you to everyone who read early drafts and provided essential feedback—I took it all to heart and appreciated your candor. You are too numerous to list here, but you know who you are. Know, too, I am sincerely grateful.

I also want to thank you, the reader, for taking a chance on my debut novel and on me as an author. It means more than you know.

Finally, may the people of Northern Ireland—all of them—find peace in this lifetime.

ABOUT THE AUTHOR

DAVID A. DUMMER is a traveler, writer, and author of the new novel, *Born of Bombs and Bullets*. He uses his background as a crime investigator and clinical therapist to masterfully weave complex characters and pulse-pounding plots into travel-inspired thrillers.

His travels have taken him to 46 countries across 5 continents, where Dave discovered hidden gems and intriguing stories that inspire his writing. He hosts a travel blog for fellow explorers at www.trexpose.com.

Dave holds degrees in International Affairs from Georgetown University and in Clinical Counseling from Johns Hopkins University. He lives on the east coast of the United States and always has a bag packed for the next adventure. Join his reader list at www.daviddummer.com for updates about his next novel.

Printed in Dunstable, United Kingdom

66421326R00258